The

Professor

Earl & Janet

Your friendship
and generous spirits
are blessings in my life

Love,
Carole

The

Professor

William Schutter

and

Carole J. Greene

Stone Bridge Press

Published by:
Stone Bridge Press
PO Box 110826
Naples, FL 34108-0114

In conjunction with:
Old Mountain Press, Inc.
2542 S. Edgewater Dr.
Fayetteville, NC 28303

www.oldmountainpress.com

ISBN: 0-9742853-0-7
Library of Congress Control Number: 2003094721

First Edition
Printed and bound in the United States of America by Morris Publishing •
www.morrispublishing.com • 800-650-7888
1 2 3 4 5 6 7 8 9 10

To the people who believed in me and trusted me...

To my adoring wife Pamela, whose support provided the inspiration and courage to complete this novel...

To Jessica Lynn, whose compassion and understanding have carried me...

To Nicholas, Angelina, Christina, Cole and Tyler; the loves of my life...

To Carole J. Greene, who appeared from the north with a sleigh full of talent, patience and kindness...

AND, to "Evie" who is now in God's loving hands. It was her constant motivation that provided the foundation for attempting this undertaking.

My journey to complete this book has been more than professorial. The experiences during this period have been fraught with pain and disappointment.

From the very beginning it appeared as if I was destined not to write *The Professor*. The personal suffering I endured during its incipient stages was difficult to accept.

I paced the beaches during the evenings looking for guidance and direction. Many times I felt betrayed and abandoned as the wind whipped tears across my face. It was only the sound of waves cascading against the sand that said, "struggle on my friend."

I have been both wise and foolish. I unwittingly hurt the ones who cast the barbs so deeply in me. For this I am sorry. I have forgiven them and pray each night for their understanding.

And to those of you who continue to drown in the squalor of darkness, may your companions treat you well. May you somehow find clear skies and safe harbor when you need them. May you find peace and tranquillity to heal your self inflicted wounds.

Someday our eyes shall meet again and I hope our hands will join in the bands of dignity and love. We must each, in our own way, seek the light of human compassion. Life is not about being right but rather about being kind.

To experience the epiphany of righteousness, we need courage, gratitude and patience. When we discover these values our lives will be encompassed in a peace we have only dreamed of.

WAS

The Professor

CHAPTER ONE

Evening light slanting through wooden shutters created a shadow of patterned bars on the plush carpet. Two women crouched behind a massive cherry desk. The older one, Erin, feverishly jabbed a key into the drawer lock. "Damn it. You'd think one of these keys we found in his desk drawer would work."

Danielle grabbed the ring. "Here, let me try." One by one, she wiggled all the keys into the lock. "No. Nothing works. He probably keeps the one for this file drawer in his pants pocket. Right next to the balls he'll lose if we uncover what I think we will."

Frustrated, Erin sat down on the plastic carpet protector between the desk and Wiggams' high back executive chair. "I can't believe you talked me into this. If we're caught, your internship is out the window and I can kiss my associate professorship good-bye. Christ, we could go to jail. This is B & E, you know. A felony."

Danielle shook her head. "We won't get caught, stop worrying. No one comes to the business office late on a Saturday afternoon. She put her finger to her chin. "Got an idea. Hand me a paper clip."

Erin reached up and plucked a clip from the desktop holder and handed it to Danielle, still crouched in front of the drawer. "Would he really keep secret files in a drawer that could be opened with a paper clip?" She plunked herself back onto the carpet protector to watch her friend.

"Yeah, he would. He thinks he's invincible, that no one has any idea he's pulling a scam." Danielle fashioned the clip into an L, inserted it deftly into the lock and turned it. "Voila."

"You amaze me. Where'd you learn to do that?"

Danielle, pulling herself up on her knees, opened the drawer, started thumbing through the files. "One of my jobs in high school. My father thought I should pay for my own cashmere sweaters, so I got a job after school at a locksmith's shop. I can cut keys, reset combination locks, open file drawers." She grinned. "Comes in handy at times like these."

Erin crept on hands and knees to help Dani remove the files. "All this stuff says *Tristar*, whatever the hell that is."

"Let me see. You're right. The big secret must be this Tristar Investment business. I think we've hit the mother lode." Her heart thumped in her chest. Palms sweating, she pulled out a folder marked *Corporate Filing*.

She scanned the first page. "Okay, this corporation was set up seven years ago as a brokerage firm in the state of Delaware. Incorporating papers filed by. . . HKS. . . let's see. . . that's probably Hoover, Kane & Simpson."

Adrenaline was pouring into both their bodies as Danielle yanked out another manila folder. "Maybe the *Corporate Minutes* file will tell us more. Here it is: President is C. Albert Kane; Vice President, Harmon H. Dawes and Secretary/Treasurer, our very own host, Mr. John F. Wiggams, comptroller of Madison University." She leapt to her feet, bumping her knee on the open file drawer. "Jesus, that hurt."

Danielle stifled a chuckle. "A battle scar. You sure are a spotlight grabber." She handed another stack of files to Erin. "You go through these and I'll take the others."

"Look at this," Erin said a moment later. "The university has invested large sums in this Tristar Investment Inc. The returns are not all that bad. But why all the secrecy? Why do we both get vibes that there's a huge scam going on?"

"Does it look like they're embezzling?"

"Don't think so, but too early to tell." Erin slapped a folder down on her lap. "I do know that somebody is making a hell of a lot of money and chances are it's not the university. We have to copy all these papers."

"Good God. Tonight?" Danielle glanced at the window. "It's almost dark. Do you think we should risk turning on lights?"

"No. We'll just have to come back tomorrow night."

"Break in again? Hey, you know me, I like adventure as much as the next gal, but isn't that pressing our luck?"

"I say we come back. I think we're onto something much bigger than we expected."

Danielle looked around the office. "Let's straighten up and get the hell out of here."

"Right. I'll restore everything to its original state. I doubt anyone will show up between now and Monday morning, but you never know. Are you sure your paper clip trick will work again?

"I'm positive. Should we copy anything tonight?"

Erin swept her hair off her face and gave Danielle a look from behind furled eyebrows. "Don't push it."

Erin replaced everything just as they'd found it. She set the useless keys to God-knows-what precisely where she'd found them in Wiggams' center drawer then rolled the supple leather chair up to the knee hole of the desk and shut the file drawer. Get a grip, she told herself, and don't do anything stupid.

"Okay. Let's get out of here." With the corporate folders replaced and the desktop looking as they had found it, Danielle pocketed her paper-clip key. She patted her pocket as the two let themselves out of Wiggams' office and locked the door.

Neither spoke until they were safely inside Erin's car. "I'm not sure what all this means," Erin started, "but by late tomorrow night, I will know."

Danielle wriggled in her seat. "Don't you just love the thrill of doing something naughty?"

"Naughty? Thrill? I was scared shitless in there. And here I am planning to go back tomorrow. Am I nuts or what?"

"Not nuts. Fascinated by the possibilities of discovering some really big scheme. And exposing some bastards for what they are. That's always a good feeling."

Erin stopped the car in front of Danielle's apartment. "Yeah, if we don't get caught first. Then it's a bad feeling"

Danielle hopped out. "Want to come in for a glass of wine? Might knock the edge off your jitters."

Erin shook her head. "Hardly. I'll be a basket case for the rest of the night. We still have to get through tomorrow night. Once that's over, we can celebrate."

On the drive home, Erin pondered what little she knew of Tristar Investment Inc., which at that time amounted to little more than the names of the three men in the corporate papers. How could her boss be involved? He seemed like a good guy. Professor Harmon Dawes just didn't fit the greed and power mold of Kane and Wiggams. This mystery was one she would look forward to unraveling.

HARMON DAWES RELISHED his Sundays. He loved the stares of admiration when he escorted his gorgeous Ginny to church. He reveled in the assumption that most of the men at First Baptist Church of Charlotte gazed on his wife with lust in their hearts. This ego boost propelled him far above his mundane role as a conservative college professor. He liked having something other men coveted.

Dawes knew that following the church service, he and Ginny would spend hours in bed. He smirked at the knowledge that while the preacher's sermon droned on, the open hymnal on his lap covered the true intensity of his thought.

Dawes kept no secrets from himself. He knew exactly what he had in Ginny. . . and what she had in him. Back in high school, he'd been the class genius. She went out with him, he knew, because of his brains. And the presumption that he would make something of himself and carry her along with him out of her dismal upbringing.

But it hadn't taken her long to discover he had something else she admired: This gangly, bespectacled intellectual was not only well endowed cerebrally but also physically.

He touched the tip of his member, which now grazed his mid-thigh. Could anyone see the trouser bulge edging out beyond the hymnal? He squirmed on the pew and shifted the book to hide what it could.

At the sermon's end, he rose to sing the closing hymn. Ginny entwined her fingers with his and moved their clasped hands to his inner thigh. When she felt what awaited her, a flirtatious smile flitted across her down-turned face, erasing any effort at piety.

How Harmon Dawes loved his wife's ability to transform in an instant from church parishioner to bedroom prostitute.

He had it all: the prestige and respect of his position as a full professor—and chair of the economics department—at one of the South's foremost universities, a beautiful and passionate wife, and enough wealth—thanks to Tristar Investment Inc.—to indulge her every whim.

Ginny, too, had it good. After humble beginnings on the wrong side of the tracks, she now lived in the affluence she used to dream about. She drove a Mercedes, a new one every two years. Her impeccably decorated and maintained home was the envy of her social-climbing acquaintances. She had only to leave her checkbook on the kitchen counter and her husband would deposit more thousands into it. Her status in society provided her entree to any club or philanthropic organization she desired. And, while her husband kept busy at the university, she discreetly bedded the most sought after bachelor in the city.

When Dawes opened their front door, Ginny sniffed the air. "Hmmm. Judging from that aroma, cook left us something scrumptious for lunch." She headed for the kitchen while her husband started up the winding staircase. "I'll be right up, Honey. Just want to check to see the oven's on low so lunch won't burn up while we play."

Ginny thought about undressing on the way up, presenting her nude beauty in the doorway of their bedroom. But she knew how much Harm liked to watch her disrobe in front of him, one agonizingly slow button at a time.

"Y'all ready, Harm Baby?" She rounded the corner at the top of the stairs. She could see his reflection in the hall mirror, the sheet tented above his body. "I guess you are."

Ginny stood at the foot of their king-sized bed. As her husband watched, eyes wide in anticipation, she rolled three golden bracelets off her wrists, backed up a couple steps and set them on the dresser. Then she kicked off her stiletto heels. Hiking up her skirt, she unclasped the garter belt first from her right stocking, then from her left. With a languid motion that she knew her husband enjoyed, she slowly rolled each stocking down and off, letting it fall on the dresser next to the gold bracelets. Her fingers grasped the side zipper on her slim skirt and tugged it gently downward. She stepped out of the skirt and let it puddle at her feet. She slipped off her silk panties, inch by luscious inch.

Next, she reached behind her neck and opened the safety clip on her diamond necklace. It joined the bracelets and nylons. She stood for a moment, clad only in blouse and garter belt. A smile played across her mouth. "How y'all like it so far?"

Dawes' voice was hoarse. "Like a fine wine, you get better with age, my love. Enough tantalizing. Get over here."

"But I'm not finished yet, Honey-child." With one hand, she held the front placket of her blouse while the other hand ever so slowly pushed each button through its hole. The blouse fell open to reveal that she wore no bra. Her breasts, not yet giving in to gravity—and, thanks to cosmetic enhancement, fully rounded—displayed brown nipples, already hardened with excitement. Clad only in the garter belt, its elastic strips swinging against her thighs, she approached the canopy bed.

Dawes held up the silk sheet. "Slide in here and let me get my hands on those gorgeous tits."

"They're all yours, Honey."

He nestled his face into her cleavage. "And I'm the luckiest man in the world."

You and my lover, Ginny thought, as she took her husband's head in her hands and pulled him upward. She had his full attention.

From years of their Sunday ritual, Ginny knew just what sounds her husband loved her to make and when, in their habitual foreplay, to make them. Twenty-five years before, when they were newlyweds, it had started out like a well rehearsed role, performed according to a script that would heighten their excitement. Now, the Sunday afternoon sex play afforded them both comfort—the serene pleasure that comes from long habit.

Harm was surprisingly giving in bed, not just in it for his own pleasure like some men she'd known. She guessed she loved him. She was certain he loved her.

He needed no urging. It was time for him to play his part in the ritual. He leaned down and whispered the words she loved to hear, as together their passion mounted then released in wave after wave of glorious sensation.

Lying side by side, an exhausted Professor and his wife slept with feelings of ecstasy.

WHEN ERIN PULLED up Sunday afternoon, Danielle was waiting on her porch. 4:45. Right on time. It was good to be punctual. Another quality Erin liked about her young friend.

After exchanging pleasantries, each lapsed into pensive silence on the drive to campus. The stakes were high this evening, and both knew it.

Retracing Saturday evening's route, they cruised through the university grounds and parked in the same spot as the night before. Erin jumped out and ran around to hold the door for Danielle, who held a large box on her lap. As Danielle climbed out, Erin looked around. In the vicinity of the business office, there was not a soul to be found.

So far, so good.

Once again, they entered the building and, as if by long habit, took the stairs to Wiggams' office. At a turn of the key, the door opened easily.

"You get your paper clip in action while I run down and unlock the copy room and turn on the Xerox. Here, I'll take that box of file folders with me and leave them for you in the copy room."

When Erin returned, Danielle had the file drawer open and had already pulled out six files labeled *Tristar Investment*. "Dani, you copy everything in these while I look around for some more. No telling what will be pertinent, so we may have to copy everything."

Danielle groaned. "Whatever you say, boss. I suppose we do want as much information as possible. If there really is something going on here, we want all the evidence we can get."

"Right. And I don't want to come back here again." Erin crossed her legs. "I already feel like I have to pee."

"Hold your water, as my father would say, till after we get what we need."

Erin settled herself into Wiggams' huge executive chair and opened a file marked *Caesar's Palace & MGM*. "Looks like our little baldheaded, middle-aged comptroller has a weakness for gambling," she said to the wall. She'd never known that a university comptroller could rate a $500,000 line of credit in Las Vegas. But there it was—Wiggams had a half million credit line at each casino.

Must be a heavyweight out there, she thought. As she read through the invoices, she laughed out loud at the image of Wiggams in "glitter city." Wait till Danielle heard this: He took direct flights approximately two times a month, flights booked in his own name as if he were above suspicion. He stayed most often at the MGM Grand and ordered room service. Ah, and by the looks of these bills, he did not dine alone. She clapped her hands together. "That bastard bought himself the company of some lovely young hookers!"

She reached for a second file, one marked *Computer Heaven*. She was certain this was the company that piqued Danielle's interest to get them started into this cloak and dagger activity. She set it aside to copy for discussion later with Danielle.

"What's this? What's this?" she said. "*Diskret Investigations*, it says. So, the s.o.b. hires P.I.'s. Hope their detective work is better than their spelling."

The file bulged. She opened it carefully, being sure not to let anything spill out. Was this circumspect little man doing background checks on all his employees? Or would she find something more sinister?

Moments later, she slapped her knee. My god, she thought, this guy has something on everyone. He's covering his ass with incriminating information on every partner in Tristar. Danielle will love this. Scam or no scam, this stuff's juicy!

"Finished." Danielle plopped into the leather chair in front of Wiggams' desk. "What a job." She handed half the folders to Erin, stacked the others on the floor. "Better put these originals back. You find anything interesting?"

"Did I. Wait till I tell you. This son of a bitch has his partners by the short hairs. Take a look at these pictures."

Danielle stared at each shot. "These were snapped by a pro." She continued to sort through the pictures, eyes wide, head shaking in dismay.

"Yeah and they're attached to reports from a private eye—really amazing shit."

"That little prick is a pervert."

"No, Dani, he's a businessman, and I'd say he's doing a good job of CYA. He trusts neither Dawes nor Kane and, because of his paranoia, has taken some very questionable steps to insure his future."

"Questionable? Negatory. This stuff is illegal. You can't invade privacy like this, then commit blackmail when it's convenient."

"Your father trained you well."

"You can say that again. Erin, we can't filch these photos. He'd notice they were gone."

"We won't take them. Just make the best copies that machine can produce. Now get to the copy room. Here, copy these files too—everything from the P.I., the one that proves his gambling addiction and, oh yes, the company that first aroused your suspicions."

Danielle stood at attention and gave a hearty salute. "Yes, chief."

Back in the drawer, Erin discovered *Contractor* and *Vendor* files. Without hesitation, she set them aside to be copied. Next, she stacked files marked *Kane* and *Dawes* on the growing pile to be copied. Looked as if they'd be here all night!

She began to replace some inconsequential files when a folder fell to the floor. "Must have been stuck to the back of another file," she muttered. Her heart stopped. *Baldwin Girl* leapt off the label. Could it be?

She leaned back against the chair, her head swirling. It appeared as if the bastard did a background check on Danielle. The Son of a bitch.

The report was comprehensive—from junior high to the present. Danielle had obviously been a very active girl. Private school. Cheerleader, drama club president, class treasurer. Valedictorian. Erin had plenty of opportunities to recognize she was smart, but head of the class? Now, that was a surprise.

More reports, this time on sexual activity. Well, ever since she'd met Danielle, she'd known she was. . . loose. But here it was, spelled out for her. With girls *and* boys. A wry smile played with her lips. Her new best friend was an equal opportunity roundheels!

"Wait a minute. What's this?" A full report on Dani's father, George Baldwin. "Very impressive." Dani had told her he was a powerful man in D.C., but just how powerful hadn't been apparent. Until now.

Degrees from Harvard in Law and Business Administration. She knew how tough the requirements were for both those academic degrees. This was followed by successful private practice, rising to senior partner in one of New York City's most prestigious law firms. Then, as a favor to the Secretary of State, George Baldwin was coerced into accepting a position in government.

And what a position. Jesus, he was the Deputy Director of the CIA!

The investigator had penned an opinion of his own: "not a man to be taken lightly."

She turned over the paper and her stomach plummeted to the floor. The next page was headlined "Summer Fling in Grand Cayman." She leafed through, her eyes narrow with rage. At this moment, she hated Wiggams with more emotion than she ever knew she possessed.

She and Danielle would have to go over this one at length. She would copy it herself—no point getting Dani riled up now. She rushed down to the copy room, arriving just as Dani pulled the last sheet out of the tray. "Don't shut it off." Erin held up her hand. "I want to copy this one while you return your originals to the drawer."

"Give it to me. I have this machine psyched. It doesn't even spit out extra paper."

Erin pulled the file to her chest. "No. Let me do it. I'll tell you why later."

Danielle cocked her head. "What's up?"

"Later." Erin's voice was firm.

The photocopying completed, the women checked other drawers, just in case they missed something. "Thank God for daylight savings," Erin said. "It's 8:30 and we still have some light." She rummaged through the top right-hand drawer. Well, look what I found." She held up several fresh packs of Trojans and hooted.

"What's so funny?"

"Our man Wiggams either has some fun right here in the office or goes to the nearest no-tell motel."

"You mean the old bastard is a sex maniac?"

Erin nodded. "Looks like it. And some copies of Playboy." She pulled one out, creased open to an article titled 'Those College Years.'"

"What you want to bet he jerks off to that one."

"Could be, but right now I don't give a damn if he's screwing the president of the university."

"No, Erin, I doubt it. Word is that she's a lesbian."

"Get out."

"I'm serious. A friend I graduated with is serving her internship as an aide to the president's administrative assistant. . ."

"And. . ."

"She told me her boss is always ordering flowers and buying mushy cards for the pres. to send out."

"Doesn't mean a thing. She is the president of the university and, I'm sure, has to kiss a lot of asses to stay on the good side of all the right people."

"Could be, but I think she's kissing something more than asses. Those flowers and cards always go to the same person."

"Pray tell how you know that?"

"My intern friend gets the scrub jobs, which include mailing letters and running errands for her boss. She noticed the colors of the envelopes the pres. sends."

"Go on."

"The red ones always go to the same place, to the same woman."

"Doesn't prove anything. Could be a good friend or a close relative."

"Not with the words the president writes in her own hand. They are definitely not the kind you would say to a relative or a friend. . . unless the friend is on the most intimate of terms."

"Well, I'll be damned," said Erin, "our pres might be a les."

"Yep. Now with that settled, lets get the hell out of here."

Danielle grabbed a bunch of files and headed for the door with Erin close behind.

CHAPTER TWO
Three Months Earlier

C. Albert Kane pressed the button to end one phone call and begin another. He punched "speaker" so he could move around his office while he talked. First stop, the door to his outer office, which he carefully closed and locked. He always made sure his secretary could not burst in when he talked to Wiggams.

Wiggams answered on the third ring. "Yes."

"John, you really need to develop a personality," Kane started in his slow, southern speech. "Most men in your lofty position would have the courtesy to say 'hello.'"

"I'll give it some thought. What's on your mind?"

Kane returned to his desk and slid into his chair. He ran his fingers through his shock of wavy brown hair. "Just hung up from an interesting phone call I thought you should know about." He paused, as he always did, waiting for the person on the other end to build up curiosity.

"Go ahead," Wiggams said.

"One of my Harvard classmates phoned. . .a George Baldwin. Ever hear of him?"

"Can't say I have. Unless he's related to that Baldwin girl who's sticking her nose where it doesn't belong."

"Her father, as it happens." Kane waited.

"Go on. Why'd he call?"

"Oh, he just wanted to make sure Madison University was doing right by his little girl. . . that she could count on the continuation of her internship." He let that sink in. "I told her she had nothing to worry about. See to it, John."

"Do you suppose she told him what she found?" Wiggams' voice sounded wary.

"Wouldn't be surprised. What, exactly, did she find, John?" His voice bore the sharp edge of steel.

"I had her doing some dog work, filing contracts, that kind of thing. She stumbled onto unauthorized payments for extras in the *Computer Heaven* file."

"You don't say. How did she find those files, John?"

"Her internship assignment involves the correlation of university payments against the actual contractual obligations. We do business with Computer Heaven. . ."

"I am well aware of that. How much did she see?"

"She reported to her supervisor that she'd found several instances of overpayment without change orders authorized by the comptroller. . . me."

Kane put his hands on the arms of his chair and hoisted his tall frame upward. Long legs carried him to his corner window, where he could just see in the distance the spires of Madison University sticking up higher than the buildings between it and his downtown law firm. "This is getting interesting. What happened next?"

"Nothing. . . for a couple weeks. Then the Baldwin girl attended an exit conference I chaired. The discussions among some senior staff got hot and she sided with me on an important issue. I must have smiled or something else encouraging, 'cause she lagged behind after the meeting to ask me if her boss had delivered to me the memo she'd written to advise of the overpayments."

"Mmmmm. Go on." Kane maintained his stance, staring out the window. He liked making Wiggams squirm.

"As I recall, I told her she was either very brave or quite insane to approach a department head with such information. I believe we parted with her thinking I appreciated her candor." Wiggams went silent. "But the next day I made sure she was bumped down to audit the expense vouchers turned in by all university employees. Routine grunt work where she won't run into anything . . . she shouldn't see."

Kane turned back toward the speaker phone on his desk. "And what happened to the Computer Heaven files?"

"I made sure to back-date change orders, in case her supervisor got nosy too."

"At least you had the good sense to do that. Now, if I may be so bold, where the hell are the Tristar files?"

"Safe in my private office, as always, under lock and key."

"They'd better be safe, you sonofabitch. They goddamn well better be."

No sound came through the speaker.

Kane wasn't finished. "I assured my friend George—who's powerful enough in Washington that he makes a better friend than an enemy, you understand—that his daughter would be reassigned to something more significant than dumbass expense vouchers. . . . Make sure that happens, John. Immediately." He poked a well-manicured finger against the disconnect button, noting that the two carat diamond in his pinky ring could use a good cleaning.

SHIT SHIT SHIT. Wiggams choked down the bile that had risen into his mouth while Kane was reaming him a new one. How he despised this partner. Yes, Kane had used his clout to get him hired as comptroller of Madison University, and made him a wealthy man through Tristar, but that didn't mean he had to like the man.

From the beginning seven years before, he'd known what he was dealing with: all honey and smiles to the public view, but behind the scenes, Kane would knife you in the back in a second. If it would get him what we wanted, Kane would exploit his own mother.

Deal with a snake and you're likely to get bit. Wiggams understood that. All the more reason to keep special files on Kane. And everyone else whose venom could harm him.

"Amanda," he said into his intercom, "I need you to take a memo."

A moment later Amanda poked her head around the corner. "Sure wish you'd learn to use the computer for something other than finances. Like sending an interoffice memo."

"That's why I keep you around." His eyes moving up and down his secretary's body proved another reason. "Memo to re-assign that Baldwin intern. . . Danielle, I think it is. . to checking university contract invoices."

Amanda's eyebrows lifted. "Didn't I just yesterday memo her to a low-grade job? I figured she was turning out to be incompetent."

Wiggams swiveled a bit in his oversized executive chair. "Not at all. In fact, if there's an even higher position than the one she had before, give her that one. A promotion."

Amanda's eyebrows lifted. Making a note on her steno pad, she gave her head a little shake. "Whatever you say. You want to offer any explanation for this yo-yo?"

"No. Just do it. Now get out of here, close the door and let me work."

Use the computer for memos? He worked on a computer as little as possible. Too easy to hack, even with firewalls, passwords and all that. The university's financial matters that he needed to supply to others on the executive staff, of course, he computerized. The secret stuff had to be kept out of the computer.

Wiggams wiggled a key out of the depths of his pants pocket and unlocked the left-hand file drawer. He pulled out a file marked *Computer Heaven*, opened it and ran his eyes down several pages. Yes, he had inserted back-dated change orders. No longer any red flags here.

He put back that folder and lifted out several others to examine. He picked up then slammed down the one marked Tristar Investment Inc. After replacing the folders, he tented his fingers and leaned his head back against the chair. Then he punched a phone number.

"Harm, we need to move some money. I've got to get away for a long weekend in Vegas."

He nodded as he listened to Harmon Dawes' reply. "Yeah, I suppose Ginny is due for a new Mercedes. If you and I are taking out some profits, Kane'll want some too. Let's decide what stocks to sell and how much. I could use a couple hundred thou. How about you?"

HARMON DAWES BOLTED upright, arms rigidly supporting his tense body. Sweat beaded on his forehead; he gasped for air.

Ginny lifted her head. "Honey-child, what in the world is wrong with you?"

"It's that dream again."

"I do wish you would tell me what it's all about. You always wake up shakin' and sweatin' like a hog."

"Go back to sleep, my sweet. I can work this out. I always do."

But he was becoming exhausted. John Wiggams' phone-call must have triggered this nightmare. He'd been thinking all afternoon about Wiggams and the problem he had become. For years, the comptroller had made no secret of his sexual addiction—he loved doing kinky things with Las Vegas prostitutes then tell Harm all about them. Thank God prostitution was legal in Nevada; at least, he wouldn't get picked up for illicit activity. That kind of publicity wouldn't do Madison University any good. And it certainly wouldn't help their little scheme. If the comptroller were arrested, people might take a magnifying glass to his life.

Lately, Wiggams' propensity for addiction had added a new wrinkle: gambling for high stakes. Well, Harm figured, a lonely, introverted bachelor like John didn't have much going for him. Taking risks at the Baccarat table in the special room for high rollers must be about the only thrill he ever got. He didn't have a Ginny in his life. Probably never would.

Then there was his other partner, Kane. Had he made a huge mistake in choosing Kane to develop Tristar? At the time, he'd done his homework—selected Kane for specific reasons. A young, up and coming criminal defense attorney, Kane had made a name for himself by winning several high profile cases. Obviously, he possessed the kind of creative legal mind that could maneuver around the law to gain acquittal for his surely guilty clients.

And he had something else Dawes could rely on—he loved money and the fine things it could buy. Not just enough to buy his way into a prestigious law firm. That he would soon earn through lawyering. No, Kane aspired to the lifestyle of an obscenely wealthy man.

He'd been right. Kane had worked the scheme to the immense financial benefit of all three Tristar partners. So far.

But recently, he'd heard rumors about Kane—his increasing immersion in politics. . . and subtle references to ties with the wrong kind of people. A deadly combination. If it was true. And he wouldn't be surprised if it was. Kane had always expressed a desire to enter politics "where the real power is," he'd said more than once. He had to admit, Kane was gifted with the kind of charisma that could propel him into public office, the higher the better. And the university's outside attorney was certainly the type of man who would cultivate a relationship with the devil himself if it would get him where he wanted to go.

Jesus Christ, what kind of men were these partners of his? If these vices and ambitions weren't brought under control, they could cause the collapse of their successful enterprise.

What had it been. . . seven years now. Seven years of escalating profits flowing into their pockets. Profits large enough to satisfy the hungers of a Wiggams and the ambitions of a Kane. Profits that kept Ginny in the only manner that would hold her as his wife.

Even though the spring semester was almost over and he could soon rest from his teaching and his departmental administration duties, Dawes felt stressed beyond exhaustion. In the past few months, he'd needed to spend far more time on Tristar Investments than on his university responsibilities. As chairman of the Economics Department, Dawes found that administrative accountability piled on top of a full teaching schedule left him worn out and stressed to the point of collapse. There were not enough hours in the day, and he was beginning to neglect his primary obligations.

Before his colleagues—fellow professors, administrators and the university executive staff—began to wonder what else could be taking up so much of his time, he would have to make some changes. Suspicions could lead to scrutiny, which could lead to. . . discovery, dismissal, prosecution.

He lay back down and closed his eyes. He had the answer. Tomorrow, he would elevate one of his instructors to associate professor. She would assume much of his teaching load for the fall semester, freeing up time for him to tend to the pressing obligations of Tristar Investment Inc.

ERIN GALLAGHER SAT on a straight-back chair outside Harmon Dawes' office, leafing through the department catalog, unsure why she'd been summoned. When the department chairman opened his door and motioned to her, she jumped up and followed him inside. The catalog clattered to the floor.

Dawes swept a stack of folders off a chair in front of his desk and waved his hand. "Sit, sit."

Erin sat. "One more week and it's all over."

Dawes looked up, eyes wide. "Oh, you mean the semester. Yes, yes." He settled back into his chair. "That's why I called you in."

Erin leaned forward. "Here I am."

"I'm quite busy these days, so I'll get right to it. Miss Gallagher, I think it's time that you added 'Associate Professor' in front of your name." He did not wait for a response. "It will mean more responsibilities, of course. And more money."

She hoped her face didn't give away the shock she felt. "Thank you. I. . . thank you."

He waved away her gratitude. "I will, of course, expect you to take on a full schedule of teaching, but you'll have a graduate assistant. During the summer, we can meet often until you feel comfortable with the course syllabus for each class."

"Professor Dawes, I am pleased with your confidence in me, but I must tell you I've planned a week's vacation in the Cayman Islands and have no intention of canceling it."

"Hmmm. It is imperative that you utilize the summer to prepare for these new duties."

Erin stood up, realizing she was almost as tall as Dawes. "With all due respect, Professor, ten days won't make any difference."

Dawes' head bobbed. "I would feel better if you would cancel your trip and concentrate on this promotion. Don't make me regret that I chose *you*."

Erin bristled at the way he emphasized *you*. She leaned over the desk so her face was inches from his. "I want you to get this straight. For the last four years, I have gone above and beyond what was expected of me, to elevate myself above your department's condescending attitude toward women faculty. If you didn't think I was the most qualified instructor to bail your overworked ass out of a jam, you wouldn't have offered me the promotion."

Surprised at her own outburst, Erin thought she must surely have blown her promotion. How could she speak to the department head that way? After that tirade, she'd be lucky to maintain her present position.

Dawes lowered his eyes to some suddenly important papers on his desk. When he looked up Erin, he was smiling. "Have a safe trip, Associate Professor Gallagher. Call me upon your return."

CHAPTER THREE

Erin lay on the rented *chaise lounge*; the Caribbean surf cascaded against the sand, shutting out all other sound. Even though her flight had landed only three hours before, already she felt the peace of being on vacation.

She closed her eyes and let the tension float away. Before long, she felt free of Madison University and its academic issues. For the next ten days, she would not have to hear any complaints from freshmen students in Economics 101. Ah, bliss.

What a year. She loved her job and came alive in the classroom. But the extra work—and all the ass-kissing—required of a young woman competing in a mostly male academic setting became a grind. It seemed that every man in the department took pleasure in reminding her of the male supremacy in the world of economics.

"So much for male supremacy," Erin said. "I was the one who got the promotion."

Ten feet away, a voice came from the next lounge. "What did you say? Were you speaking to me?"

Erin sat up and looked in the direction of the voice. "No. Sorry if I disturbed you. I have a habit of speaking my thoughts out loud. Some people find it distressing."

The young woman grabbed her towel and ran it over her glistening skin. "Not me. I sometimes do the same thing. Mind if I pull my lounge closer?" She didn't wait for an answer but dragged the aluminum chaise through the sand to a spot next to Erin. She held out her hand. "Danielle Baldwin."

"Erin Gallagher," she said with a firm handshake then released the younger woman's soft, slender fingers. "Where are you from?"

"Now or before college?"

"Well, start wherever you would like."

Danielle flipped open her sunscreen and slathered it on her slender legs. "Grew up in lots of places, but mostly New York. Then Washington."

"D.C. or the state?"

"District of Columbia. My dad's in government."

Erin nodded. "That sounds like a story."

"We just met. I'll wait until later to bore you silly with my family pedigree."

"Fair enough. Glad you're here. Otherwise, I'd be able to tan only one side of my body." Erin smiled and flipped over onto her tummy. She held out her bottle of sunscreen to Danielle. "Mind rubbing this on my back?"

"Sure thing." Danielle smoothed lotion onto Erin's shoulders, massaging down her spine and out to each side. "Mmmmm. Your very toned, nice shape."

Erin turned her head and looked at Danielle for a long time. "Thank you." Erin felt her face flush. Where was this embarrassment coming from? She lay quietly for several minutes, eyes closed, her ears tuned to the rhythmic flow of the surf. She heard Danielle adjusting her position and remembered they'd started a conversation. How rude she'd been, not to continue it. She cleared her throat. "And where from now?"

"Pardon?"

"You told me about before—New York, Washington—so tell me about now."

"Oh. Charlotte, North Carolina. I'm serving a post-graduate internship. Got my B.A. in accounting from Georgetown. Hope someday to work for Price Waterhouse Coopers. . . and meet my Prince Charming and have four kids, two girls and two boys."

Erin made no attempt to mask her feelings. "You earned a bachelor's from Georgetown, you aspire to PWC, you scored an intern position at one of the south's foremost universities and you still blather on about marriage and children? Forgive me for being blunt, but I'd have thought you'd aim higher than teething and diapers."

"Yeah, you're right. But that's way in the future. I have a lot more exploring to do." Danielle rolled onto her side and, with twitching eyebrows, did her best Groucho Marx impression. "Enough about me. . . for now. It's your turn."

Erin swung her legs onto the ground and sat up. "Say, I suddenly realized I'm famished. Breakfast on the plane was too awful to eat, and it's time to get out of the sun. Want to join me for lunch?"

Danielle fumbled around in her beach bag and pulled out her watch. "Jesus, you're right. If I don't get out of the sun this very minute, I'll be burned like the skin on a Thanksgiving turkey."

"First, I want to shower and change into something more appropriate for eating lunch than this sweat-drenched bikini."

Danielle let her eyes play up and down Erin's tall, lean body. "I wouldn't mind your wearing the bikini. It suits you."

"Thanks. I think." She felt herself redden. . . again. Why did this woman affect her that way? "Meet you in the Seawatch in. . . half an hour?" Erin gathered up her book, sunscreen and towel and rushed away before her new friend found another way to make her blush.

She could always blame it on a first-day-on-Grand-Cayman sunburn.

As SOON AS the waiter left with their lunch orders, Erin took a sip of her iced tea. "Guess it's my turn. I'm 29, which, as close as I can figure it, is about nine years older than you."

"Only eight. I just turned 21."

"I'm originally from New York and very Irish, as if you couldn't figure that one out. Green eyes, auburn hair, a decidedly Irish surname. And I come from a long line of cops. Dad. Grandfather. Even me."

"You're a cop?"

"Was. Dad was the stereotypical Irish cop—hard, demanding, slow to show affection, quick to whap you across the ear if you did something he didn't like. And I seemed to do that a lot. Guess I thought I'd finally win his approval if I became a cop. Didn't work."

"So you have father issues too?"

"You don't have enough time to hear them all. I have only a week of vacation."

The waiter set down their plates. Both ordered the same lunch: a mound of tuna salad nested inside a huge ripe tomato, crisp greens cradling slices of fresh mango, papaya and pineapple. No one spoke until he refilled their ice tea glasses and left.

"You said you were a cop. Past tense."

"Right. After college, graduating magna cum laude in economics and criminal justice—a double major—I joined the force. Worked my butt off as a patrolman. Took the detective's test. Passed it with flying colors. But never was allowed the badge. Then Dad got liver cancer and died. No more chances to earn his approval. And no promotions on the force. So I finally got enough of the 'good ole boys' club, resigned and went back to my first love and earned a master's in econ."

Danielle reached her hand across the table. "Sounds like you and I share the same feelings about men."

"Don't know about your feelings. Do know I'm not fond of men." Erin gently withdrew her hand from Danielle's and slid it into her lap. "All I've ever got from them is trouble. Hassles. All that 'male superiority' shit. Most are babies, emotionally infantile with demanding, impatient egos. They swagger around showing off their machismo and expect us women to swoon with desire. Bullshit." Erin erupted in a light, tinkling laugh. "Sorry. Got carried away. I'm usually not this bad. I'll blame it on the sun."

Patting the napkin against her lips, Danielle grinned. "Listen, I could match you word for word with my opinion of most men. In fact, just a couple weeks ago, I went a few rounds with the man who's head of the department where I'm interning." Danielle inched her chair closer to the table and leaned forward. "Erin, since you wanted to be a detective, maybe you could help me figure out a mystery."

She put down her fork. "What kind of mystery?"

"It could be nothing. Or it could be a tip of the proverbial iceberg. Maybe you can figure it out."

"You have my attention."

"Just before I left on this vacation, I was reprimanded, demoted, then for no apparent reason, reassigned to my original intern duties. . ."

"Which were?"

"To examine and file all contracts the university executed with private vendors. I found some discrepancies in the purchase of computers from a company called Computer Heaven. A lot of money flowed out to that vendor but I couldn't find any specs in the contracts to account for all those payments."

"Interesting. What did you do with the information?"

"I memoed my supervisor, who politely recognized it but, I think, didn't kick it upstairs to the boss man."

"Wouldn't the comptroller be the one to authorize payment? Maybe, he's part of the mystery."

"Yeah. That's what I think too." Danielle stopped talking while the waiter slid the check onto the table and poured more tea. "In fact, I approached him about it," she said as soon as they were alone again.

"Really. That's pretty ballsy of you."

"Oh, I do that sort of thing a lot. Speak my mind. Press my point."

Erin nodded. "I've picked up on that. So, how did he react?"

"He started out pleasant enough, but when I detailed the large amounts of unsanctioned payments, his eyes turned frosty. He issued what I interpreted as a veiled threat and took off for some meeting or other."

"Why do I get the impression he acted on that threat?"

"Because you're intuitive—and a former cop. The next day, my supervisor called me in and assigned me to make-work that should have been performed by a low-level aide, not an intern with a college degree. When I asked her why, she wouldn't say. But I knew."

"You said earlier that you were restored to your previous assignment. How did that happen?"

"I called in the big dog. My dad."

Erin laughed.

"Daddy knew the university's outside counsel, a Charlotte criminal defense attorney named Kane. They were classmates at Harvard. I suspect he called in a marker and Kane leaned on Wiggams, the comptroller. The day after I told my dad, I got my old position again."

Erin sat back. "I think you were right about the iceberg. Let me give some thought to how we can find out more." She pulled the check over and signed her name and room number. She got out of her chair and turned toward the door. "Now, what say we do some sight seeing. I don't want to catch any more rays today or I'll turn into a crispy critter."

"Good idea." Danielle stood and skipped a couple of steps to catch up with Erin. "I like to do my ray catching early in the morning. Where shall we go now?"

"I have all week, so I don't have to see all the tourist attractions in the first day." Erin reached the door then stopped and turned. "Oh, I'm sorry. I'm being presumptuous, aren't I?"

"About what?"

"That you want to join me to sun bathe, see the sights, eat all our meals. . ."

Danielle put her hand on Erin's arm. "Go ahead and presume. I was hoping to meet someone to pal around with. I'm really glad it turned out to be you. You're going to make my vacation really special. I just feel it."

Erin looked at Danielle's hand on her forearm. For some reason, it seemed to burn where she touched. "Yes. I feel it too."

Once outside, Erin pulled a sight-seeing brochure out of her carry-all. "Let's see. First we can visit the sea turtle farm. Then we can go to Hell."

Danielle laughed. "Excuse me? Did you say we're going to hell? We haven't even done anything yet."

It was Erin's turn to giggle. "Hell. It's this place where some kind of bizarre geologic formations look like someone's idea of a fire and brimstone image. Probably named by the first Bible thumpers to arrive on the island to Christianize the heathens."

"Wanna bet they sell t-shirts that say something like 'I've been to hell and came back to tell about it'?"

"No bet. It's a sure thing." Erin checked her wristwatch. "Tell you what. Since we lingered over lunch and it's already 3:30, let's go to Hell today and save the turtle farm for tomorrow."

"Sounds good. And the next day, I definitely want to swim with the sting rays."

"Me too. Definitely." Erin checked her brochure. "That sounds like a hoot."

Danielle put her arm around Erin's waist. "We're so much alike, I can't believe it."

"Yeah. And I'll bet before the week's over, we'll find even more in common." Erin let a secret little smile play with her lips.

THE NEXT DAY, after their early morning sun bathing followed by lunch, Erin and Danielle donned their "I've been to Hell" t-shirts and headed to the turtle farm. Once at the farm, they fell into place at the tail end of a tour group off one of the three cruise ships in port that day. They ambled their way along the cobbled paths around the 20 or so tanks filled with water and sea turtles of various species and sizes. "Come on," Danielle motioned to Erin. "Let's get closer to the guide so I can hear what he says."

"Jeez. Don't tell me you're one of those people who actually have to learn something on vacation to justify the expense."

"No, silly, I'm not. I happen to have a thing for sea turtles, ever since I snorkeled in Hawaii so close to half a dozen of the creatures that I could put my hand out and touch them. It was awesome. And the poor things are endangered."

Closing in on the guide, Erin playfully shoved Danielle right up to him. "My friend here wants to learn all about sea turtles." She gave the guide a thumbs up, then repeated the gesture to Danielle.

In a clipped British accent, the guide told the story of the farm—how few of certain species remained in the wild and how this farm collected and hatched eggs then protected the tiny hatchlings until they'd be big enough to have a good chance of survival in the open sea. "It's too soon to know if our farm will make a difference, but we have high hopes."

Inside a small hut at the edge of the turtle farm they sipped a Coke and shared some banana chips. "Ready to head back" Erin said

"Yup, I think I had enough of Big Jim Fowler for today"

On the walk back to their hotel, Danielle was exuberant. "That was even better than going to Hell. Thanks for pushing me near the guide. He was a hunk."

Erin felt a stab of emotion. "A hunk? Didn't notice. But I liked his accent. I'm a sucker for an Irish brogue or the crisp inflections of a Brit." She mimicked each of those dialects.

"Don't worry, he wasn't my type. Smelled too much like the turtle tanks." Danielle laughed. "How's your brain doing with our mystery?"

"It's far from solved, but I do have some more questions. Feel like discussing it as we walk?"

"Sure. Fire away."

"How much money was paid without authorization?"

"I had a chance to check only the Computer Heaven contracts in some depth. During one fiscal year, the university paid that company over $100,000 in payments that weren't authorized by the comptroller."

"That's not uncommon. Universities must order a lot of computers."

"I thought the same thing. But get this. For seven years running, this vendor got the contract. No competitive bidders that I could locate. Do you find that as odd as I did?"

"Absolutely. That's exactly the type of contract a university would be sure to pass around—give several local companies a chance to make some good money. Attracts more support for the school."

"My point exactly. I backtracked other vendor files and discovered that a good 75 percent of them had done business with the university for. . ."

"Let me guess: seven years."

Danielle lifted her hand for a high five. "Bingo. Know how long John P. Wiggams has been there as the comptroller?"

"How many guesses do I get?"

"Exactly one. I tried to get permission from my supervisor to acquire the actual canceled checks. I wanted to make sure the normal signature stamp had been used, find out where the checks were cashed and who endorsed them."

"Good idea. Your super must have been impressed."

"You kidding? She damn near cussed me out. I got a reprimand that went into my human resources file. Then I was reassigned ."

"No wonder your suspicions were so intense. If you were on the track of a possible embezzlement, the comptroller would be glad you uncovered it."

"Unless the comptroller was doing it. And that was my first thought, but now I'm not so sure."

"Why not, Danielle? Seems pretty clear to me."

"Clear something is going on. Not clear who's behind it. Wiggams did put me back into my old job and allowed me full access to the files. I checked before my vacation and they were in order."

"Okay. But did you check all the files?"

"No. I see where you're going: Perhaps he let me see only the files he wanted me to see."

Erin paused in front of her bungalow and extracted her key. "If secret files exist, we will just have to locate them."

"We?" Danielle's mouth dropped open.

Erin pretended not to notice. "I'm going to shower and lie down for a while. Meet you for dinner in two hours. Bye"

THE NEXT DAY, on the boat slapping the waves on its way to the sting ray encounter, Danielle could not control her curiosity. "Last night you dropped a bomb then refused to pick up the discussion.

Why did you say 'we' would look for secret files then stonewall me ?"

Erin looked into Danielle's eyes. "Your mystery piqued my cop's curiosity. The more you told me, the more intrigued I became. Then I realized. . . it was occupying too much of my time. It's vacation, for Chrissakes. I'll tell you my plans. . . when the time comes."

"Okay, okay. You don't have to get huffy with me."

"Just drop it. Please, Danielle. Let's get our gear on. We're almost there."

Erin spit into her mask, rubbed the moisture over the plastic lens and pulled the mask into place. She yanked it off to tighten the straps then returned it to her face. "Perfect," she said. "Let's go."

Together, Erin and Danielle plunged off the boat's dive platform, stuck their faces in the water and started to swim. All around them, coming from every direction, sting rays zoomed in as if responding to a dinner bell. The gently moving wing of one immense ray brushed Danielle's leg. She yelped, planted her feet into the sand and stood up.

Erin giggled. "Startled you, eh?"

"I wasn't scared. Really. It just felt. . . weird."

"I touched one with my fingers. It was so soft. I didn't expect that. Come on. Let's go get some squid to feed them."

Erin moved off to find a guide—during the orientation session on the boat ride out to the sandbar, he'd called himself a ray wrangler—with a bucket of squid. Just as the guide had showed them, each of the women made a fist with her thumb folded inside. Erin inserted a squid into the fist and held it out. Danielle copied her. Within seconds, one of the hundreds of rays swooped in and sucked the squid out of first Danielle's then Erin's outstretched fist.

Again, they baited their fists. And again sting rays appeared and vacuumed their lunch into the mouths on their undersides.

"Here," one of the ray wranglers motioned to the women. "Come hold this doozy of a ray and get your picture taken."

With Erin on one side of the guide and Danielle on the other, the boat operator snapped away with a digital camera. "You can check out your photo on board while we motor back to the pier. If you like it, for $15 it's yours."

BACK AT THE HOTEL, Erin plopped onto her bed. "Let me see that disk, Dani." She reached for it. "Okay with that nick name?"

"Sure. Most of my close friends call me that." She sat next to Erin. "What you plan to do with the disk?"

"Thought I'd check at the hotel and see if they can print out the picture. Two copies, one for each of us. To remember that totally amazing experience."

Danielle rested her hand on Erin's cheek. She slid one finger gently down to her chin, lifted it and leaned close. She brushed Erin's lips with her own.

Erin opened her mouth and pressed hard against Danielle's. They lay back on the bed and kissed again.

"Ever been with a woman?" Danielle murmured.

"Once. College, ten years ago. I'll tell you about it sometime."

ERIN RINSED HER mouth then sucked the bristles of her toothbrush before inserting it into the holder. She pulled on her bikini bottoms, gazing at her image in the mirror. Was she still the same person? She looked like the Erin Gallagher of a few days before. However, when she returned to Charlotte in one more day, she'd begin her duties as an associate professor. She'd help her new friend solve a mystery—perhaps uncover a scandal. Then there was the other element of her friendship with Danielle Baldwin.

The last three days of what Erin dubbed her "Cayman Caper" had passed in a blur of emotional turmoil and physical wonder. She couldn't get over her good fortune in meeting Danielle. The two of them acted like kids, as they alternated between friendly banter in public and sensual exploration in private. The sexual activity, though pleasurable, was foreign to Erin. Since college, she'd been too busy for dating, had never really had much in the way of sex. She wasn't sure how to feel. She'd have to work on it.

Danielle, on the other hand, seemed quite comfortable with her sexuality. What was all that crap about meeting a Prince Charming and mothering a litter of kids? Erin wondered. A smoke screen to hide her desire for another woman? Or was she truly bi-sexual? Another element of their relationship to explore. Sometime. Somewhere.

Danielle knocked at Erin's door. "Hey in there, it's 7:30. We're wasting good sun time on our last full day. Meet you on the beach. Got a surprise, so hurry."

"Wait for me, Dani. I'm almost ready." Erin tied her bikini top at the back of her neck, grabbed her beach carry-all and locked the door behind her. "So what's the surprise?"

"You'll see. Follow me."

Danielle took off down a path they'd never traveled. "Our beach is to the left, Dani."

"I know. That's why we're going to the right. It's a totally secluded beach where we can. . . well, like you said last night, college was a long time ago"

"So are you about to refresh my memory?"

"Today, my dear Erin, your college fantasy will pale to adult reality." Danielle reached for Erin's hand and pulled her into the water. They shuffled along at ankle depth, letting the sun warm their backs and the water cool their feet. After walking a couple of miles down the beach, Danielle stopped and looked around. "This is it. Fits the description the bell boy gave me. Spit of sand stretching into the water, sea oats swaying along the upper reaches of the sand. Truly romantic, don't you think?" She pulled Erin down and, together, they sat at the surf line, leaning backward on their elbows to let the warm Caribbean wash gently over their legs.

Danielle turned toward Erin. "I love the way the sun glints golden in your auburn hair."

Erin laughed. "You writing a poem, or what?"

"No, I mean it. You have everything I admire—from your gorgeous long hair to your long legs, to your taut tummy, to your nipped in waist, to your . . ."

Erin leaned over and brushed Danielle's lips with her fingertips. "Enough. I get the picture." She slipped her hand to her friend's back and unfastened her bikini top. "Do we really need this in such a secluded spot?"

She unfastened her own top and flung it behind her. She heard a swish in the sea oats. "What was that? Did you hear something?"

"No one's here, so don't worry. It was just your suit hitting the ground."

"Suppose so. Guess I'm just a little wary. Hand me your sunscreen."

Taking her time, Erin rubbed the warm liquid on her friend's body. She started at the ankles and slowly, slowly worked her way up. "Mmmm, are you enjoying this as much as I am?"

"No need to compare enjoyment levels. Takes too much brain power. Let's just enjoy. Period." Danielle breathed deeply, sat up and took the sunscreen out of Erin's hands. "Your turn."

As Erin rolled to her back, Danielle began slowly applying the sunscreen at her ankles. She meticulously worked her way over the shin and thigh area. As her fingers approached the golden triangle of erotica Dani's touch became much more sensuous. She could tell that Erin was excited and moved up to stroke Erin's breasts with the gentle touch of a long-time lover. She let her fingers glide lightly over Erin's now erect nipples.

"You know how much I love that." Erin pulled her friend's head over and kissed her hard.

Warm water rolled up the beach and lapped at the women's bodies. A light breeze rustled the sea oats. A rapid series of clicks blended with the sounds of crashing surf. The women were oblivious to anything but each other.

IN THE MORNING, Danielle waited outside the hotel for pickup by the airport shuttle driver. She sat on the larger of her two suitcases, swiveling her head back toward the lobby. Surely, she thought, Erin would come down to bid her farewell.

Just as the shuttle van screeched to a halt in the pedestrian lane, Erin left the check-out desk and waved. "Driver, I'm coming." She dragged her one large piece of luggage behind her. One of its rollers dropped off the curb before the other and the suitcase fell over. "Damn."

Danielle took charge. She told the driver to load Erin's bag then motioned to Erin to board the van. "Our flights must be scheduled about the same times. Why didn't you tell me at dinner last night when I told you my departure time?"

"What, and spoil my surprise?"

"Erin, after the emotional roller coaster this week has been for me—for both of us—I'm not sure I can handle another surprise." Danielle climbed into the airport van and flashed the driver a dazzling smile. He shifted the lever into drive and lurched away from the hotel. "So, out with it."

"We're on the same flight."

"You mean till we change planes in Miami."

"No, I mean all the way to Charlotte. I live there."

Danielle pushed her sunglasses down on her nose and stared at Erin over the rims. "What do you mean 'I live there'?"

"I teach at Madison, so I live in Charlotte."

Danielle wasn't sure whether to be thrilled or enraged. "You wait until now to tell me this, you little bitch?"

Erin grinned. "Yeah. Now you know what I meant when I said 'we' would work some more on solving your big mystery."

"Any other bombs you want to drop?"

"Maybe. I am Associate Professor Gallagher in the Economics Department."

Danielle smacked her hand down on her thigh. "You little shit. No. I take that back. You, Associate Professor Gallagher, are a big shit."

CHAPTER FOUR

As the plane banked sharply for its approach to Charlotte-Douglas International, Erin grasped Danielle's hand.

"You're not scared, are you, Erin?"

"Not at all. I just wanted to hold your hand while I tell you what's been going through my mind."

Danielle nodded. "You have been quiet for the *last thousand miles* or so."

"Now please don't misunderstand what I'm about to say." Erin looked intently into Danielle's bright green eyes. "I couldn't be happier about our. . . meeting and I want to. . . explore it more. But. . ."

"I knew there'd be a 'but.'"

"Let me finish. I promised Professor Dawes that as soon as I got back from this Cayman trip I'd throw myself into preparations for the fall semester's classes. That will take most of my time. And that's after teaching summer school. I'll have very little leisure. . ."

"So you won't have any time for me."

The plane touched down at the end of the runway and started to slow. Erin patted her friend's hand. "I won't have as much time for you as I'd like. Somehow, I'll fit you in. I have to eat, so maybe we can schedule dinners together. I don't know about. . . anything more. "

Danielle withdrew her hand.. "I see." She ran her fingers through her short blond hair. "What about solving our mystery?"

"It still pushes my buttons and I meant it when I promised we would dig some more. We will. We will. I was talking about. . . you know." Erin shifted uncomfortably in her seat.

The seatbelt sign flashed off as a bell dinged to signal their arrival at the gate. Danielle jumped up and yanked her carry-on out of the overhead compartment. She elbowed her way into the crowded aisle and barged toward the exit, leaving Erin still sitting.

"She took that well," Erin muttered.

After nearly 12 hours of sleep, Erin woke refreshed. She wolved down an Eggo waffle, all she could find in the freezer—she'd have to pick up groceries later. Then she showered and dressed casually in a light apricot colored cotton t-shirt and khaki walking shorts. As she drove to the campus, she rolled down her car window and breathed in the fragrances of early summer: gardens boasting glorious blooms, flowering trees and the sweet smell of just-mowed grass. She parked and walked briskly along the commons to her building, rehearsing how she would request what she needed.

Inside the Econ building, she found only a skeleton staff. She approached a secretary, who absently twirled her hair as she leafed through the latest issue of *People*.

"Excuse me, miss."

The young woman took her time to look up. "What is it?"

"I am Associate Professor Gallagher, here to pick up my summer school class schedule for Business Law 202."

"Where would I find your class schedule?"

"I assumed you would know, miss. . ."

Professor Dawes tapped her on the shoulder. "Professor Gallagher, how nice to see you. How was your trip to the Caymans?"

"It was just what I needed, except I wish it could have been longer"

"I think we all feel that way when returning from a vacation. What's going on here. Is there anything I can help you with."

Making no effort to hide her frustration with the summer help, Erin nodded. "As a matter of fact, I want to pick up my summer teaching schedule, but Miss People Magazine here is less than helpful."

"I'll be back in just a moment," and true to his word, he returned in short order holding a slip of paper. "Here you are—building, room number, scheduled meeting times for each of your classes. Any other assistance I might offer?"

Erin took the paper and flashed him a dazzling smile. "Thank you, no. To tell the truth, I'm quite impressed that the department chairman would bother doing what a summer secretary couldn't. Or wouldn't."

Dawes sat back on the secretary's desk with folded arms. "Perhaps I have helped to change your perception of faculty males as being something slightly less appealing than pond scum."

So that was his game. She wasn't about to let him off the hook. "Sorry, Professor. Although I appreciate your help, you have done nothing to relieve the department of its well earned reputation."

"I see. Is it your generalized dislike of all males or is it the department itself?"

"Both, if you must know. Until your department hires more women faculty and learns what 'equality' means, I am unlikely to change my opinion."

"I'd hoped your vacation in the Caribbean might have given you a chance to realize that some of us truly appreciate the quality of your work here. And even like you, personally."

"I am grateful for that, sir. It remains to be seen if your opinion of my academic accomplishments will be shared by others I've worked with these last four years." She skimmed through the information on the paper in her hand. "Thanks for this, Professor, but I have errands to run."

As Erin exited the office, Dawes admired her retreating shape. Her lithe body reminded him of a young Ginny, although Erin was much taller. As department chairman, he knew their paths would cross often. An intelligent, spirited woman, this Erin Gallagher. He liked her very much, as an instructor and as a person.

FOR THE REST of June and all of July, Erin poured herself into her duties as the newest associate professor in the Economics Department at Madison University. She managed a few dinners with Danielle and, now that summer school was winding down, a movie followed by a late drink.

Erin toyed with the straw in her Margarita. "This has been one busy summer, Dani."

"I know, and I'm trying to be understanding. But I miss you."

"You have no idea how often my mind sways off topic and back to our lovely times together. I look forward to more. When the time comes."

Danielle nodded. "And when might that be?"

"Soon. Summer school ends this week. I just have some grades to enter and I'm done." She looked around the pub to see if anyone might be listening. "Any ideas how we can start researching for information relating to the suspicious kickbacks?"

"Erin, before we get started I want you to know if you want out of your promise, that's okay with me. You just got promoted. Now's not the time to take risks—you stand to lose a lot."

"Dani, my instincts tell me there is much more to this than what you've uncovered. We have to pursue it."

"Why do you say that?"

"Kickbacks on contracts are not that uncommon. But they normally involve the purchasing agent, not the comptroller."

"But if Wiggams wasn't worried by what I might find, why did he reassign me?"

"That's just it. He was worried. The only reason he reinstated you was to please Kane, the guy your dad leaned on. That means he's afraid of Kane too."

Danielle didn't answer for some time. "You could be right. Why don't I sniff around the business office. It's pretty quiet now."

"You do that, but eventually, we'll have to snoop in Wiggams' private office."

"Omigod, Erin. I get a rush just thinking about it."

"You're going to have to do some leg work; I'm too well known. And don't use your own code if you have to copy something. Let me get you a different number from maintenance."

"I see where you're going. That way, no one will know who used the copier—safer for us."

The next morning, an eager Danielle Baldwin arrived in the business office before 9:00. Her supervisor, she knew, was vacationing in Colorado. The staff consisted entirely of under-grads fulfilling requirements for their work-study grants.

She fell into conversation with one named Chrissy. "Looks like your due date must be tomorrow."

Chrissy rubbed her swollen belly. "You have no idea how hard it is for me to do the filing. I can't possibly bend over to the bottom file cabinet drawers. And I have two more weeks to go."

"You know, Chrissy, I'm bored stiff with nothing to do right now, and I'd like to make it up to you for all the hassle I caused in the spring. Why don't I replace you for those two weeks."

"That'd be great, but I need to pay rent and buy groceries. My hubby's a post-graduate intern, like you, so you have a good idea of our income."

Danielle picked up some file folders and began to alphabetize. "I don't want your salary. Go home and put your feet up for two weeks while I do your work. Consider it a shower gift."

Chrissy hugged Danielle nearly hard enough to break her water. "Oh, wow, that's great. I'm outta here!" She detailed some typing assignments then fished her time card out of her purse. And a key to the building.

C. ALBERT KANE, Harmon Dawes and John P. Wiggams pow-wowed over lunch on the 15th of every month. The topic for their August meeting was change orders, putting Wiggams on the hot seat.

"You're quite certain that Baldwin woman won't make trouble, John?" Kane reminded him of last spring's fiasco. "I don't want any more calls from her father. And I don't want any more fuck-ups. Capice?"

Wiggams blinked several times and pushed his glasses up on the bridge of his nose. "Yes, Al, I get you. All she discovered was that someone neglected to authorize the extras. I rectified that and the files are now in perfect order."

"Can you be sure she didn't make copies?" Dawes asked.

"No record of it at the copy station. Even if she did, we could tell her the change orders were filed separately."

Dawes wasn't satisfied. "You swear she never saw any of the Tristar files?"

"Christ, Harm, you know I keep those files in my personal office. No one could ever get near them."

"I don't know, John. I might feel better if those files were not on campus at all. Maybe Albert should keep them in his safe."

Kane made a snuffing noise. "I already have the only other copies, Harmon. Besides, John's right—the safest place is right under their nose."

After lunch, Kane returned to his office and immediately intercomed his secretary. "I've had enough mendacity and corporate corruption for today. Do not forward any calls. Take messages or tell them to call back tomorrow."

On his way to the parking garage, he chuckled at his reference to corporate corruption. He defended rascals who thought they were smarter than the system and bilked the public of millions. Over the years, he'd learned all the tricks. Even came up with a few masterful maneuvers himself, to get his clients acquitted. He was good and he knew it.

That, of course, made him rich. Healthy retainers from well-heeled corporate clients constantly flowed into the coffers of Hoover, Kane and Simpson. His percentage of outrageous settlements piled up more money in his banking account. But it was Tristar Investment—the amazingly simple and deceptively profitable plan Professor Harmon Dawes had brought to him seven years ago—that put him over the top.

He was admitted to the bar in three states: Delaware, Virginia and North Carolina. He was building the kind of reputation that would propel him to the top in a political career that he intended to start very soon. He had worked hard to make himself smooth, polished, at home in various social circles, champion of the symphony, lover of opera. He occupied an enviable position as Charlotte's most sought-after bachelor. Handsome as Adonis, wealthy as Croesus, intelligent, suave, exuding a feeling of power—he had women groveling at his feet. Any woman he wanted.

One of those women should be at his mansion this minute, preparing for his arrival. Knowing what awaited him, he rubbed his swelling member as he dug into his pocket for the car's remote control.

It was just past 2:00 when he reached the front gates across his driveway. He activated the gate control, whizzed inside and past the illustrious fountain. At the top of the hill, his Georgian style home sat majestically, surrounded by lavish, well-manicured lawns and meticulously placed shrubs. The flower beds around the house were done by his own landscape architect and reflected vibrant southern color schemes. Their scent reached him easily as he drove up the Sycamore shaded drive.

He pressed the opener for bay one and let himself into the twelve-car garage. After parking next to his lovingly restored 1982 Corvette, he entered the house through the east wing. He punched the code to disarm the security system, noting in the log that a visitor's code appeared as an entry at 1:45 P.M.

He stopped at the great room bar to mix her favorite—a gin and tonic over shaved ice. She said she loved the warm glow it gave her. He made himself the usual Courvoisier on the rocks. As he carried the drinks up the massive spiral staircase to the mezzanine level and toward the master suite, his mind rapidly fantasized what they might do with each other this afternoon.

Kane slid open one of the carved mahogany double doors expecting to see her lying on his bed. It was empty, but turned down. He glanced around, never tiring of the luxury that surrounded him: The multi-media lounge area, his and hers bathrooms containing every possible comfort feature; closets the size of most people's living rooms; a window wall overlooking his indoor pool and exercise area. He strolled across plush carpet through a mirrored hallway and turned the Austrian crystal knob to the door of the Queen's Bath.

She was there, all right, lying in the deep Jacuzzi, nearly hidden by bubbles.

He handed her the gin and tonic, sat on the side of the tub and sipped his own drink. A thrill of pleasure tickled his spine.

"How did the meeting go with Harm and John?"

"Just fine, Honey, just fine."

"Thought I'd take a little bubble bath while I waited for you."

Kane swished the bubbles away from her body. "Adorable. You have the breasts of a twenty-year-old."

"Thank you, Darlin'; glad you like them."

Her round, full breasts floated in front of him, the nipples just breaking water level. As he leaned over to kiss her, he felt himself becoming increasingly aroused.

She returned his kiss with great passion, rising up so that she could press her torso against him.

After the long embrace, he breathed deeply. His excitement level became visible. "Honey, I want you now."

"Why Albert, I do declare that thing in your pants is about to explode."

He took her hand and pulled her up. "If we don't get going soon, that's exactly what will happen." He handed her a towel. This was far from their first time together, but he'd never seen her in the Jacuzzi. Trails of tiny bubbles cascaded over her breasts and clung to her torso. His mind raced.

With the towel wrapped around her, the woman led Al Kane to his bed. Slowly she removed his suit coat, undid the knot in his tie and slid it off, unbuttoned his neatly pressed white button-down oxford.. She slid her hand under the opened shirt front and rubbed her palm across his chest. Next, she pulled the shirt off, then his belt. She leaned into him with her pelvis, feeling the escalating pulsation's in his trousers.

Kane groaned. "Honey, enough tantalizing." He grabbed her and kissed her as if he wanted to devour her lips.

The woman let her hand glide to his groin. She felt him throbbing in her hand and knew the time was right. Unzipping his pants, she let them fall to the floor. She looked into his eyes, glassy with expectation, as he stared at his beautiful mistress. Stepping closer, she ran her hand from his neck downward across his rippled stomach and around to his firm buttocks.

Kane's lover dropped her towel and walked to the bed. She positioned herself on the satin sheets in a provocative pose. "Come on in, Darlin.' I want you now."

Kane, who had been ready since he first saw her in the Jacuzzi, tugged off his silk boxers and made his way to the bed. As he slipped his arm beneath his lover's shoulder and pulled her to him, he wondered what Harmon Dawes had ever done to be so damn lucky.

ERIN KNEW SHE had to carefully select the clothes she would wear when she made her request to Jake Gathers. She'd need to distract him, gain his favor. She knew just what to do. A pair of tight black slacks and a sheer white blouse should do the trick.

After she dressed, she left her apartment and headed for the university. Slowly, she drove the cobblestone campus roads looking for Jake's pickup, a white Dodge Ram bearing the school logo and the words "Madison University Maintenance Supervisor." She spotted the truck and, next to it, Jake himself stowing tools in the locker that ran the width of the pickup bed..

She rolled to a stop and leaned out her open window. "Hey, Jake, good afternoon."

He lifted his hand in a wave and sauntered over to Erin's car. "Professor Gallagher. Good ta see ya. What's up?"

"Nothing much. Just a small administration problem." She flashed her most seductive smile.

He leaned down and peered inside. "Lookin' good, Professor. How can I help ya?"

Erin knew the sun was shining at just the right angle to titillate him with a view of her sheer blouse—and the lacy bra beneath it. "I need to make copies of my doctoral thesis but the admin. staff insists it's not school business."

"Damn fools. Don't they know you gettin' a doctor's degree will only benefit them?"

She had him hooked. "Jake, sounds like you're a lot smarter than they are." She leaned back in her seat so his eyes could get their fill. "Tell me something, Jake. Why is it men like you have so much common sense while the males I work with can't figure out what time to eat lunch?"

"Can't answer that one, Professor. But I know one thing—you ain't goin' to Kinkos to make your copies."

"What you have in mind?"

"I got all the keys and codes for the reproduction room facilities. We can make copies any time you want."

"Jake, that's great. You're a true friend."

He shifted around so he could get a full frontal view of Erin's blouse. "Just one thing, Professor . . ."

"Yes?"

"Gotta do it after hours, say around seven some evening."

Her seduction was working, perhaps too well. He might push for more than she wanted to give. "Jake, you're too good to me. I hate to make you work so late. Why don't you just loan me a key and a code, just for one night. I can get everything done myself. How about it, Jake? I'd really appreciate it, and you could enjoy your well earned rest instead of staying on campus for unpaid hours."

He shuffled his work boots in the dirt at the curb. "Sure, Professor. Any time. Just call my office to make arrangements."

Erin put her hand out. He took it, acted as if he might plant a kiss on it. She wiggled her fingers and pulled her arm back inside the car. "You're super. Thanks for your help and. . . oh. . .let's keep this just between us."

He tipped his ball cap slightly. "You betcha. Just between us."

She drove through the elegant main entrance gates of the university and headed for Danielle's apartment to report her plan. Her friend answered after one ring and pointed her inside.

Erin's eyes took in her surroundings. Decorated in Country French tradition, the spacious apartment presented a quality of quiet elegance. "Nice. Really nice," Erin said.

"I'd hoped you'd be spending a lot of time here this summer," Danielle said. "What good is a beautiful home if you can't enjoy it with your friends?"

Danielle, dressed in shorts and a t-shirt, followed Erin into the living room. She waited for Erin to take a seat on the sofa before she sat next to her and crossed her legs. She surveyed Erin with appraising eyes. "What in hell are you dressed for?"

"This is my Jake Gathers outfit. . .guaranteed to get us keys and copier codes."

"Way to go! And I have a key to the building where Wiggams' office is located. And I didn't need to dress like a whore to get it."

Erin laughed. "Thanks a lot. I thought my outfit was great."

"Ohhhhh, it is, Erin, it is. You dress like that for me and I'd give you the keys to the university vault." She looked her up and down. "I hoped you wore it for me."

"Someday I might do just that."

"But not tonight, right?"

"No, Dani, not tonight." She filled her in on the rest of her plan.

"Impressive. You seemed to have considered everything"

"I hope so. I'll expect you to be under the window at 5:45 Friday night."

BRIGHT AND EARLY Friday morning, Erin phoned the maintenance office and asked for Jake. The detective part of her noticed that the person answering failed to get her name. How inept, but good for what she had in mind. No way to trace her call.

"Gathers here."

After making just enough small talk to keep him hoping, she got to the point. "I'm leaving town early Saturday to have a friend review my thesis. That means I need to make copies today. I was hoping I could pick up keys from you around five this evening."

For a moment, Jake remained silent. "Well, I s'pose that's okay, but one problem. I get off at 6:30 for the weekend and I can't let you keep the keys till Monday."

Erin pretended she hadn't already thought of that. "Gee, Jake, how could we arrange this so I don't put you out?"

"Tell ya what, Professor, you wear that blouse from last time I saw you and promise me you'll have the keys back before 6:30, and that problem will go away."

She laughed. "Not only will I have the keys back on time, but I will wear a blouse you might enjoy even more. I'll see you at your office at five o'clock tonight."

"I'll look forward to it. I truly will."

She hung up and spoke her thoughts out loud: "Fifteen minutes to show Jake some cleavage will put me at the business office at 5:15. Another half hour to go through all his keys to find the one that'll get me into the office. I told Dani 5:45. Perfect."

During her day—she had one final exam to give and office time to enter grades for the students in her two other classes—she found herself unable to concentrate. Her fingers drummed on the computer keys till she realized what she was doing and hit "delete" to erase the screen full of nonsense. Again and again, she went over her plans, making sure she'd thought of everything.

Finally, it was time to rush home and change. Jake loved to leer at the female students, so she'd dress like a coed.

The jeans she chose were so tight she had to roll on the bed to zip them. Then she tied the ends of her blouse to expose her midriff. A pair of sneakers, her auburn hair pulled into a ponytail, and she could pass for a 20-year-old. She opened three buttons of the blouse and practiced leaning forward, surveying the results in the mirror. She'd show Jake just so much and no more. Before she left the bedroom, she spritzed perfume onto her throat—a little heavier than usual. She took a deep breath and left her apartment on the outskirts of town.

Traffic was light as she motored through the city and turned her white Honda Civic into the rear campus entrance. Near the maintenance building, she found a parking spot between one of the university's vans and the pickup Jake drove during the day. Across the way, parked astraddle two spaces, stood Jake's well-known

Ford Explorer—shiny black, polished like an agate, with oversized tires and mag wheels.

As she passed a knot of maintenance men she knew, just getting off work, she waited for signs they recognized her. Leers didn't count as recognition, she figured. Relief flooded over her.

The outer office was silent and vacant. Jake's secretary must have left early too, she thought, inhaling deeply to calm her racing pulse. Peering around the door frame, she saw Jake, feet propped on his desk, eyes closed, catching a little snooze. She tip-toed across the floor and sat on the corner of the desk. Leaning forward just as she'd rehearsed, she whispered, "Hi, Jake. Got that key for me?"

"Go away. Come back Monday," he murmured without opening his eyes.

She leaned closer, till her lips nearly grazed his ear. "Jake, wake up. It's Erin Gallagher."

His eyes opened slowly and looked right down Erin's wide-open blouse. He made no effort to look upward but just continued to enjoy the view. Finally, Jake let his eyes lift to meet hers. "You were right, Professor. This blouse is even better." His eyes returned to their previous position.

"I came for the keys."

"Professor, y'all sure dressed yourself up like the cutest student on campus. If I didn't know better, I'd swear you're teasin' me."

"Now, Jake, you do say the nicest things. I just put on some old clothes. No point dressing up just to make copies, now is there?"

"You are welcome to visit me any time in this outfit. In fact, excuse me for not gettin' up, but that could be embarrassin' for both of us. They don't call me 'Big Jake' for nothin'."

Erin smiled playfully and stood to reveal her midriff. "Much as I'd love to pursue this topic, I do have a lot of copying to do. Would you please loan me your key ring for the business office building?"

"I thought all you wanted was the copy room key."

"That's right, but since you can't stand up right now, I figured it would be easier for you just to hand me the whole ring." Another playful smile.

Jake reached into his drawer and pulled out his key ring. "Here ya go, Professor. I believe I'll just sit here and watch your sweet cheeks as you leave."

Erin waved the key ring in thanks as she put a little more swing than usual into her walk. "I'll have these back before you take off for the weekend."

The drive to the business office was a short one. She parked in front and used the key Danielle had scored from Chrissy to open the main door. Easy. The opulent foyer was deserted, as she knew it would be at 5:20 on a Friday in late summer.

A glance at the lobby directory told her the copy room was #230 and the comptroller's office, #242. She bounded up the stairs, her sneaker-clad feet making little noise. Quickly, she located the copy room and used the key Jake had identified for her. In a second, it was open. She switched on the light and dropped her briefcase on the floor. Knowing it would take a few minutes for the copier to warm up, she pressed the button to start the process.

Seconds later, she was at the door marked #242. She knelt and began trying keys from Jake's ring, one at a time. Her hands were moist with perspiration, and jitters gnawed at her stomach. At 5:40, she still hadn't found a key that worked. In five minutes, Danielle would be under the window.

God, Jake had a lot of keys.

She started on the last half of the ring. Finally, a key slipped into the lock. Erin took a deep breath and turned it. Click. She rotated the knob and opened the door.

Wow. She hadn't expected this at all. Most of the campus offices were functional but spartan. This one looked more like an office in an upscale investment bank—tastefully decorated, with no expense spared.

Recovering from the initial shock of getting in, Erin quickly slipped Wiggams' office key off Jake's ring. She found a paper clip on the comptroller's desk and slid the key onto it. She quickly added to it the ones to the front door and copy room. She moved to the window and released the lock.

She prayed there was no alarm sentry on the window, raised it gently and leaned out. There was Dani, waiting below, just the way they'd planned. Erin dropped the keys to her and grinned when she caught them.

"Remember what to do when you get back from the locksmith?"

Danielle frowned. "Of course, tape the keys in an envelope and leave them in Chrissy's mail slot downstairs. You'll pocket the dupes, lock up everything here, replace the originals on Jake's ring, and have it back to him by 6:30. Did I get it right?"

Erin blew her a kiss. "Perfect. Now get out of here and let me copy my thesis, just in case."

As she watched Danielle take off for her car, just visible at the end of the block, Erin closed and locked the window. Taking a quick look around, she turned the button on the doorknob to the locked position and exited the comptroller's office. Then she headed down the hall toward the copy room. She could not help but hear the crescendo sound of loud mufflers from the front of the building, unmistakably Jake Gathers' SUV.

"Thank God I turned it on earlier," she said to the air as she began to copy her thesis. She leaned against the door and watched the pages spurt into the collator. Heavy footsteps pounded down the long hall.

"Hey, Professor, I was sittin' in my office thinkin' about. . . you. I cleaned that up a bit. Actually my thoughts were. . ."

"I get the picture, Jake. Tell you the truth, being the only one in this big old building was a little spooky. Glad you're here." She turned away from him to pull pages out of the collator. "Hand me that stapler, will you?" She needed to stall, to give Danielle plenty of time to get back from her mission.

"Glad to be of help. Anything else I can do for you?"

Erin glanced at her watch. 6:15. Danielle should be back. Sure hope she'll notice Jake's Explorer, she thought, and sneak in and out without coming up here.

"Can't think of anything. . . oh, wait, you could do something for me. How about carrying these copies down to my car."

"Sure thing. I parked right behind you. Is it unlocked?"

"Yes." How would she get the keys from Chrissys mailbox? Think, Erin, Think!

"I just thought of something else, Jake. When you come back from my car, stop in the mail room and bring me anything you find in the slot for Chrissy Jabers. She's in the hospital having a baby, and I promised to pick up her mail."

Jake saluted, scooped up all the thesis copies and disappeared.

In her mind, Erin went over everything: Wiggams' office was locked, so all she needed was the envelope and some time alone to replace Jake's keys on the ring. But how?

As Jake returned from the car and sauntered down the hall he bellowed, "you need to get yourself a sharper car, one that suits your personality." Jake leaned against the door, offered up a plain brown envelope. "This is all that was in her mail slot."

Erin hoped the relief she felt didn't show on her face. "Thanks. I agree that old Honda is not the real me, but a Jaguar convertible will have to wait till I make full professor." She pulled the envelope to her chest, feeling the hard metal items inside. She hit the switch on the Xerox. "I really appreciate this."

"Ready to go?" Jake asked. "Here, let me carry your briefcase." He turned the lock on the inside of the door knob and together they left the copy room.

"That's so sweet of you. Why don't you head on out to the car and I'll just make a quick pit stop and be out in a jiff."

Before he could protest, she disappeared into the restroom. Inside a stall, she carefully opened the envelope, pulled out the dupes and slipped them into her jeans pocket. Then she slid Jake's keys back on the ring, flushed, ran some water and made lots of noise yanking towels from the dispenser—in case Jake had waited around for her. She blotted the sweat from her face, flipped the light switch and headed for the stairs.

Outside, Erin scanned the perimeter to see if Danielle was around. As she approached Jake, leaning against her car, she jingled the key ring out in front of her. "I almost forgot to give you back your keys." She opened his hand and placed the key ring in his palm. "You can't imagine what a help you've been."

"Did you lock the building? I feel responsible, you know."

"Don't you worry, Jake. I took care of everything. Good night. See you soon."

As soon as the muffler noise faded, Danielle came out from behind the building. "God, that was close. I almost peed my pants!"

"It was a close call, but somehow we pulled it off. I think that's a good omen. We're going to find something big in that office."

"We're on for tomorrow then?"

"Tomorrow night it is."

CHAPTER FIVE
NOW

L oaded down with file folders, Erin and Danielle made their way to the car through fading light. Erin sat her pile on the ground for a moment while she lifted the trunk lid. Danielle let her stack slide from her arms into the trunk then turned to help her friend.

Erin slammed the lid down. "Think anyone saw us?"

"No, the whole place is deserted. Just a quiet summer Sunday evening on campus. You can relax now."

Erin took a deep breath, got in and started the car. "I don't mind telling you, I am not cut out for burglary. I'm used to being on the other side of the law. Christ, I was scared."

"Yeah. We were a whole lot braver while we were getting ready for this caper. But when we were pulling out every god damn file in the place, I kept expecting someone to walk through that door. Wiggams, maybe, or even Jake, your friendly maintenance man. "

Erin pounded her fist on the steering wheel. "I was so nervous the whole time, I thought my stomach would absolutely turn inside out." She laughed. "But now that we're out of there—and with the loot, I might add—I am downright famished."

"Me too. What say we scoot over to Angelo's for a pizza. They make the best crust in town." Danielle fished in her purse and extracted a cell phone. "I have the number in memory. What do you like on yours?"

"The spicier the better for me. Pepperoni and anything else you like."

"I go for mushrooms. I'll just order half and half." She gave the order and closed the lid on her phone. "Twenty minutes."

"We'll be there in ten, even if I hit all the lights on red." Erin reached over and patted Danielle's arm. "Thanks."

"For what? I should be thanking you. Taking this risk just to help me confirm my suspicions was chancy."

"Mmmm. I don't even want to think about that now."

"I must have been a real shithead to expect you to jeopardize a career AND become my steady after just one awesome week in the islands."

"No, you had a right to think that. I just had to get through the summer." She pulled into the parking lot behind Angelo's and felt for her purse on the floor.

Danielle opened the car door. "No, you stay here with the booty. I'll get the pizza."

"You're paying? Erin asked with a look of amazement. "Won't that break the accountant's oath or something?"

Danielle flashed her the finger and headed for the pizza parlor. She called back over her shoulder, "You know how I love to break tradition."

With the aroma of oregano, cumin, tomato sauce, pepperoni, mushrooms and mozzarella filling the car like helium in a balloon, Erin drove to her apartment building. "Let's run this upstairs and chow down. We can come back later for the files."

"Sure they'll be safe?"

Erin chuckled. "Who in their right mind would break into the trunk of a 15-year-old rattletrap Civic? What could I possibly have of value?"

"Good point. Let's go. I'm starving."

"On second thought, Dani, you take the pizza and I'll open the trunk and grab a few files to look over while we eat." Erin went to the trunk and opened it. She grabbed at random and slammed down the lid.

Danielle couldn't hold it in. "You're as curious as I am. You just can't wait."

Erin matched her grin for grin, unlocked her apartment door and pushed it open. "After you. The kitchen's all the way to the back."

"Cozy little place you have here. Very tasteful. Let me guess, your favorite color is. . ." she poked her head into the living room. . . "blue. With accents of buttercup yellow and white. Why, Erin, if I were writing this up for *Home Beautiful*, I'd say it reflects the ambiance of a New England seaside cottage."

"Let's eat." As soon as they reached the kitchen, Erin took two plates out of a cabinet, set them on the table. "Beer or soft drink?"

"What's pizza without beer?"

Erin bent to peer into the fridge. "Bud or Killian's Red?" She noted Danielle's expression. "I'm Irish, remember?"

"I'm not, so I'll have a Bud."

As they dove into the pizza, Erin opened the top folder in the pile she'd brought from the trunk. "Might as well start with this one," she said through a mouthful of pepperoni. She shut the folder and slid it aside. "You're right. Great crust."

"Why'd you change the subject?" Danielle reached for the folder but Erin pulled it away. "What's in that file you don't want me to see?"

"Finish your pizza. What's in here may make you lose your appetite."

"No more games, remember."

"Dani, before you read this, let me tell you what's in it." She realized she'd been holding her breath. "This is a background report—a comprehensive one, I might add—compiled by a private investigator. It details everything about you since you were in eighth grade, including. . . our time together in Grand Cayman."

Dani let out a whistle. "God damn! Did you have any idea we were being watched?"

"No. It never crossed my mind. And that's not all. There are. . .photos."

Danielle made a grab for the file. "I want to see." She sorted through several photos; some were close-ups made with telephoto lens. "These of us practically nude on the beach . . .are. . . good. Too bad we can't ask for enlargements."

"Glad you can laugh about it. You're taking this better than I did. You don't want to hear what went through my mind as a fit punishment for Wiggams when I found this."

Danielle put up her hand to silence her friend and pulled out a single page. "Let me read this to you. 'You will be particularly interested to learn that the woman companion of our subject is Erin Gallagher, recently promoted to associate professor in Madison University's Economics Department. However, I found no evidence to support the possibility that their meeting on Grand Cayman Island was anything other than coincidental. There's no evidence from my background checks of both that they knew each other before.' Son. . . of. . . a. . . bitch."

Danielle picked up the photos again. "Bet he shot a load while he was taking these."

"Here's the thing, Dani. The comptroller knows you had suspicions about him. Now he knows we have been lovers. He could use this information against us."

"You mean blackmail? Hell, everyone who knows me wouldn't be a bit surprised. They know I'm AC/DC, and more than a bit on the wild side. It's you I'm concerned about. He could make real trouble with your reputation."

"There's no law against homosexuality that I know of, even in the deep south."

"Maybe not, but . . .Jesus, Erin, I'm sorry I ever got you involved in this."

"But we did start and we're going to finish it. Now, let's get the rest of those files and see what we can uncover. If Wiggams thinks he has something on us, we'll just turn the tables."

Danielle flipped through the folder on her lap "Hold on there. Did you look at everything in this file?"

"What, the one with the report on us? No, after I saw that and the photos, I just put it aside to copy. You remember—it's the one I brought to the copy room myself. And I just ran everything through without looking. It was getting late and we had to get out of there."

"Yeah, I remember. So you didn't see these other photos?" Danielle picked up one, then another, turning them so Erin could see. "That bastard Wiggams has covered all the bases. Look at this one—it's a telephoto shot, but I'm pretty sure that's the illustrious C. Albert Kane handing over something or taking something from a sleazebag. His face is plastered on the evening news often enough," Danielle said, staring at the picture. "Yeah, that's him. What do you suppose, buying some coke? Taking a bribe? Paying off a blackmailer?"

"Who knows? Wiggams has something on him. That's what's important. What else?" She yanked another photo out of Danielle's fingers. "Do you recognize this woman, Dani? I'm pretty sure this is Kane's country estate we're looking at. . . everyone in town knows it. . .and some woman who visits him regularly for fun and games."

"See. . ." Danielle pointed at a page on her lap. . . "there's a written report detailing times and length of stay. And look. . . here's the same woman, shopping at high fashion stores and leaving the Uptown Club."

Danielle studied each photo before handing it to Erin. "Unless I'm blind, here's the same woman. . . making mad, passionate love to your boss."

"What? Professor Dawes? Give me those!"

"See for yourself." Danielle passed a stack of copied photos to here.

"That is definitely Harmon Dawes, and—either both Dawes and Kane use the same prostitute or. . ."

"This is Dawes' wife and she's having an affair with Kane."

Erin played with a corner of the pizza box. "Couple things don't add up. First, why would Dawes' wife bother with an affair, and why with Kane?"

"Who knows why people do things? Maybe she's bored and looking for excitement. It's easier to figure why Wiggams would pay the P.I. to get those photos."

"Sure, Dani. It's leverage. He can flash a couple of these shots in front of Mrs. Dawes and she'll do anything he asks, to keep him from exposing the affair to her husband."

"Yeah, and these pictures are so graphic, Wiggams probably uses them to beat off."

"Maybe, Dani, but I think he prefers younger blood. Remember the *Playboy* in his desk? He's more inclined toward someone like. . . you."

ONCE THEY RETRIEVED the rest of the copied files from the trunk, they spread them out on the living room floor. Erin set down two tiny calculators, one for each of them. "Why don't you start with the contractor and vendor files, Dani, since that's where the problem first came up."

"Right. Put my accounting degree to good use. For once."

Erin sorted through the files looking for anything with relevance to Tristar Investment, Inc. The incorporation files were the usual boilerplate. Nothing out of the ordinary there. She stacked those on the sofa and turned her investigation to spread sheets that detailed every dollar invested, the type of investment and the return. A good half hour passed in silence punctuated by the tapping of calculator keys.

"Will you look at this." Erin leaned toward Danielle and unfolded one of the spread sheets. "Tristar put money into stocks, futures, commodities, Real Estate Investment Trusts, all yielding above a 20% return on an annual basis. Here's one with a . . ." she made a quick calculation. . . "28% return. Wish my portfolio was this good."

"So this Tristar thing is making big profits for the university. Our les-pres must love that."

"Not so fast." Erin punched numbers into her calculator. She leaned back against the sofa. "So that's it."

"What did you find?"

"A very neat, very simple package. Look here. . .Tristar is a phony brokerage firm, which our friends Wiggams, Kane and Dawes. . .my god, my boss. . . use to make big profits, ostensibly for the university. But what they're doing is returning a small portion of those profits—looks like 8%, a pretty nice return—to the university. They keep the rest for themselves."

"Where does the money come from?"

Erin checked several files. "Wow. I can't believe it. It's really a fabulous idea. . . those three con artists are getting rich with money that belongs to the university."

"Come on, Erin, out with it. What the hell are they doing?"

"The average tuition is, what, $20,000, most paid in advance? And Madison University attracts how many students each year. . . 20,000? That comes to. . ."

"400 million. I can do that in my head."

"Add to that, room and board fees, private and corporate contributions and state endowments. All running through the general fund."

Danielle jumped up and twirled around. "Not all of it needed at once. It gets paid out week by week in salaries, supplies, utilities. . . ."

"Exactly. And all that time, it's earning money. . . the university thinks it's getting an 8% return from CD's, which isn't shabby, but really, these guys are raking in as much as three times that amount of interest!"

"Keeping 15% or so for themselves. Hot damn. But how does it work?"

Erin pulled a group of folders toward her. "Run through these. See what you think."

Danielle took a few minutes to study the information. "Dawes, Kane and Wiggams own this Tristar Investment, Inc.—a phony brokerage firm—that issues certificates of deposit to the university that yield. . ." she leafed through the pages. . ."some years six, some years seven, and even up to eight percent interest."

"The university board's happy with the comptroller's ingenuity and never questions the investments. Incredible."

Stunned by the magnitude of the scheme, the women remained silent for minutes. Finally, Erin shook her head. "Think what we've stumbled into. The university has more than half a billion dollars floating through its coffers each year. That's more capital than many major corporations have."

"And even some small countries."

"Kane's legal mind set up the brokerage firm, and Wiggams controls the university's monies, I can see that. What I can't figure out is where Dawes fits in. Unless. . ."

"Yes?"

"Unless he dreamed up the plan in the first place, persuaded Kane to come aboard. . ."

Danielle nodded. "And Kane, as university counsel, found Wiggams and finagled him into the comptroller's position. Seven years ago."

"And that's how long this whole thing has been going on. It all fits."

Erin grabbed her calculator, pencil and a pad of paper. As she leafed through files, she made notes, totaled figures. She let out a whistle. "They started out small, investing only half a mil the first year—probably to make sure the whole plan would work without detection. It did, so each subsequent year, they upped the amount they ran through Tristar. See here?'

Danielle looked at the figures on Erin's paper. "Yeah. By the third year, the comptroller increased the university's investment in Tristar to $5 million, and it yielded a return of $465,000. Rolled into the previous year's profits, looks like Tristar accumulated a tidy little nest egg of a million two. They upped the ante each time. . .for four more years. These guys have raked in millions." She punched some more numbers. "Looks like, for the most recent year, it's up to about three quarters of a million for each of them."

"You know the comptroller better than I do, Dani. Do you think Wiggams has the smarts to make all these clever investments, these puts and calls, for example?"

"No, Erin my friend, that sounds more like the work of your boss."

Erin shook her head. "I may have misjudged Harmon Dawes. I was actually starting to think he was an okay guy. Should have listened to my instincts. He's as much a criminal as the others. And a cuckold to boot."

"None of these bastards is an 'okay guy.' Look at this." Danielle opened one of the contractor files she'd been working with. "Computer Heaven isn't the only vendor with authorized 'extras.' Every year for the past seven, almost all the university's vendors and contractors were granted an additional 20% in authorized extras. All through change orders—obviously bogus—signed by. . ."

"John P. Wiggams. Okay, that's how money gets channeled out of the university. How do you suppose the vendors get it back to the terrific trio?"

"Haven't figured that out yet, Erin. But if I could examine the vendors' books. . ."

"If you're suggesting another break-in, you can just forget it, Dani. My nerves couldn't handle it. We'll just have to come up with another way."

"Here's a thought. The vendors could expense out these extras and convert them to cash. But I don't think so. More likely, they just purchase items they never receive. Like all those computers I stumbled on in the first place."

"You may have something there. Suppose they buy stock from Tristar, but the stock is worthless."

"I see where you're going. That's how the vendors funnel monies to Tristar, then write off the worthless stock as incurred loss."

Erin leaned forward to scribble another note. "Christ, Dani, nobody loses. Tristar 'borrows' university money, provides them a nice return and at the same time, feathers its own nest. Wiggams overpays on vendor contracts to make them happy. Then Tristar accepts a percentage of the overpayment back as bad investment. The vendors get a tax deduction for the loss, and both parties reap a gain."

"The university big wigs are happy with a tidy additional income from invested funds, the vendors have a guaranteed contract year after year, and the terrific trio sits back and gets rich."

Erin stood up and paced the small living room, tapping her pencil against her hand. "Now what, Dani?"

"Now what? We have all the evidence. Let's report it."

"Maybe not all. Some of it is conjecture. No proof that the vendors buy worthless stock as the conduit of monies to Tristar."

"Erin, even without that proof, we have enough to go to the authorities."

"You're right, but which ones? The FBI? State police? Local police?" She let the options sink in. "With all the connections C. Albert Kane has, he could be tight with the Charlotte police. Maybe even the feds."

"What are you suggesting?"

"I think we'd better just stash this stuff in a safe place and sleep on it. For awhile. Till we know some more."

"Okay. I'm in favor of the sleep part. . . I'm whacked."

"Yes, Dani, it's been quite a day. And I don't want to scare you, but we cannot say one word about this to anyone. Not one word till we know more."

"Are we in danger?"

"I have to think so. If Wiggams took the trouble to hire a P.I. to get the dirt on his partners—and he has the report and photos of us too, remember—he would stop at nothing to protect Tristar's little game."

THE NEXT DAY, Erin awoke and turned toward the alarm clock. 12:30? No wonder her stomach was gnawing her backbone. She padded to the kitchen and scoured through the pantry. Not much there. She really would have to start taking better care of herself, even if that meant keeping more food in the house. Finally, she poured some cereal, opened the milk and sniffed it. One whiff was all she needed. She poured the chunky white liquid into the sink, ran the disposal and sat down to eat her cereal dry.

A stack of mail drew her attention. An ornate envelope, hand addressed by a calligrapher, rested on top. She inserted the end of her spoon and ripped it open. "Ah, yes, the annual faculty/administration reception," she announced to the air. This year, she noted, the dinner dance would be held in the ballroom at the Hyatt Hotel. Saturday evening.

Erin tapped the invitation against the table top. Professor and Mrs. Dawes would surely attend. So would Wiggams. Considering their positions, it would be a command performance for both of them. Naturally, as university counsel, Kane would not only attend, he'd use it as an opportunity to glad-hand and make ambiguous offers of service in return for support in the political arena.

Well, Kane wouldn't be the only one to use the reception as an opportunity. She'd ask Dani to be her companion for the evening. Then the two of them could also use the event to their advantage. They would observe all the players in one room—at a time when they had no idea their every action was being analyzed.

Another idea flirted with the edges of Erin's mind. She'd persuade Dani to wear a low-cut, tight-fitting gown—one sure to get the attention of the coed-admiring comptroller.

Erin finished breakfast, cleaned up her mail and changed into her jogging clothes. She needed a good long run to clear her head.

After the jog, she headed for the shower. The hot water cascading over her body shut out all sound, allowing her to consider many of the ideas that had invaded her jog. Did the investment files found in Wiggams' office mean he was a key to this entire scam? Obviously, he had written a query letter about CD's on university letterhead to a phony investment firm. Did that mean his secretary was in on the scheme? Someone had to type the Tristar correspondence.

And what about the vendors and suppliers? Did they comprehend that Tristar was a sham? If they did, how did Wiggams or someone else set them up? Was anyone else from the university in on this? Did Tristar put its money in accounts with only one bank or several? How did Tristar purchase the investments? Through an authentic broker? Was he in on it too?

So many unanswered questions to investigate. She and Dani couldn't call in the authorities till they knew more.

She shivered, shut off the water and stepped out of her shower. As she toweled down, she looked in the mirror and admired her body. Her daily runs kept her in good shape. At 29, she had curves in all the right places. Full, tight breasts. Taut abs and a tiny waist. Her legs, which she always thought were the best part of her anatomy, were beautifully muscled, long and graceful.

The ringing of the doorbell jolted her out of her self-evaluation. She wrapped herself in a towel and walked over to the bedroom window. She parted the curtains to check on who stood on her porch..

She walked through the living room and opened the door. "Come on in, Dani."

"Ahhhh, do you always greet your visitors in a towel?"

"Sorry, I was just getting out of the shower when the bell rang. If it wasn't you, I would not have answered it." She closed the door and motioned Danielle into the living room.

"Here, sit and amuse yourself with these files while I dress. Help yourself to the refrigerator, as long as you don't expect much. Haven't been to the grocery for a while."

Danielle waved her hand in front of her face, in a vain effort to cool herself. The sight of Erin at the front door had activated her hormones, and they hadn't settled down yet. She glanced repeatedly from the files to the bedroom. When her hormones edged out common sense, she got up and walked quietly to the door. Standing very still, she peered into Erin's bedroom.

Erin, completely nude, was towel drying her hair. Danielle watched intently as her breasts displayed a shimmering grace. Her buttocks were well rounded and so firm they hardly jiggled as she vigorously toweled her auburn curls. Danielle felt herself becoming more and more aroused. She slowly pushed the door open and stood there in full view for Erin to see.

At the squeak of the hinge, Erin turned, walked toward Danielle and placed a finger to her lips. "Shhh. Don't talk. Just enjoy."

Erin's hand left Dani's lips and moved in a graceful way to her left breast. The other hand slowly glided across the small mound of her belly, moving downward until her fingers grazed the triangle of pubic hair.

"Mmmmm," Erin murmured, "you're absolutely on fire."

"I've never seen you act like this, not even on the island."

"Shhh. No talking." She reached for Danielle's hand, escorted her across the room and sat her on the bed, head tilted upward, staring at her friend. Erin stood directly in front of her, so close that their legs touched. She ran her fingers gently through Danielle's short blond hair. She cradled her head and slowly pulled it to her breasts.

For several moments, they embraced. Erin then pulled Danielle to her feet and began to remove her blouse. Not a word was spoken as she unfastened the white lacy bra to expose Danielle's milky breasts and soft pink nipples.

She stroked them gently then eased her hand down to the top of Danielle's shorts. She unbuttoned them and let them drop to the floor. Danielle stepped out of them and moved back slightly to lie on the bed. As Erin slipped her fingers under Danielle's white lace designer panties and tugged them down, down her legs, a long sigh escaped Danielle's lips.

At last, Erin moved up until their bodies melted to one another.

As they lay together afterward, Erin told Danielle about the upcoming event at the Hyatt. "I want you to come as my guest, but it's more than just a nice social occasion."

"Now what? After Grand Cayman I'm a little gun shy. Are you always full of surprises after sex?"

"No, you just titillate my thought processes."

"Ha, that's not all I titillate. Okay, what do you want me to do at the party?"

"I thought it would be a great time to show Wiggams your body?"

"What?"

"You could dress in something very revealing and sexy. Something that would raise more than his eyebrows."

"I have to tell you, Erin, the very idea of that little creep leering at me takes away all thoughts of being sexy."

"I have more in mind than just leering."

Danielle sat up and stared at Erin. "Please don't say what I think you're going to say." She waited, but Erin remained silent. "Ah, shit, ever since we found that *Playboy* magazine in Wiggams' office, I was afraid you'd come up with this idea. He likes college age girls, so you want me to tease him and hope he comes on to me. Then I bed him, we exchange pillow talk and I wheedle more information out of him."

Erin smiled. "I love the way you pick up on my brilliant ideas."

CHAPTER SIX

When would she have time to rest? Erin wondered as she dressed to meet her first class of the fall semester. Summer school had ended less than a week before. Then she and Dani had spent nearly two days preparing for and executing their file retrieval in Wiggams' office. And after what they'd found, she was jazzed. Oh, yes, exposing this could make her career.

Or cause her mysterious disappearance.

Would Wiggams have the balls to murder her—and Dani—if he found out what they knew?

They had to be careful, pile up a tight case before going to the cops. Dani agreed to take on Wiggams, the little prick, while she would concentrate on Dawes. Kane could wait.

Since she had a light schedule today, Thursday, she'd suggested this afternoon as the best opportunity to shop for dresses for Saturday's gala event. Danielle agreed to meet her for lunch and suggested The Palm, just around the corner from Southpark Mall, where they'd start their shopping.

Both arrived shortly after the lunch crowd and were served with drinks and salads in a matter of minutes.

"Let's try to limit our conversation about the. . .you know. . . ." Erin warned as soon as the waitress retreated.

"We have to come up with a code word, in case people might overhear us." Danielle thought for a moment. "How about 'TT' for 'terrific trio,' our sarcastic reference from Sunday night?"

"Super. That'll work. We have to talk about TT sometimes, but not today." She flashed a flirtatious smile. "So, what have you been doing this week, while I've been kicking off the fall semester?"

Danielle tore off a chunk of hot roll and buttered it. "Not much. Some intern stuff. Had a manicure and pedicure, got the Porsche detailed. Oh, yes, and a haircut and highlights."

"What a life," Erin said between mouthfuls of fresh spinach. "I definitely should have chosen more affluent parents."

They shared a good laugh. After more idle chatter, they dug into their lunch entrees, split the check and headed for the shops.

At Talbots, Danielle found nothing suitable. Erin tried on a sand-colored, sleeveless crepe column dress with a jewel neck and a waist-nipping fit. "God, you look good enough to eat," Danielle said, motioning for Erin to twirl around. "Simple, yet elegant. Like you."

"Simple? I always viewed myself as complex." Erin studied the tag "It's $158." She inhaled and let out a sigh. "I already own some accessories that will go with it, so I won't have to spend for those. Okay, if I eat hot dogs and peanut butter for a couple weeks, I can swing it.."

Danielle spun Erin around again, admired her friend from all angles. "Can't say I agree with your taste in food, but I definitely approve of the gown."

After Erin forked over the $158 plus tax, they headed for The White House with Danielle still in search of the "TT Dress." "People probably think I'm saying titty," Danielle said. They both roared as they crossed Morrison Boulevard to hit the Specialty Shops on the Park. For Erin, who had never stepped foot in these shops that catered to the city's rich and famous, it was a whole new experience.

Danielle found nothing to satisfy her in white—"too virginal"—so they ambled down the street to the Cache' Shoppe. "It carries exclusive designer evening wear, so I'll surely find something appropriate there," Danielle said.

After just ten minutes in the store, Erin pulled off the rack a black crepe sleeveless dress with a sheer georgette A-line overlay and held it up in front of Danielle. "Try this on. I think it was made for you.

In a few moments Danielle reappeared from the dressing room and Erin murmured appreciatively, "Oh, yes." From a low cut scoop neck, the black crepe fell to a point just above the knee. "Turn around and let me see the back." Dani twirled. "Oh, no back. Nice feature."

Danielle studied the three-way mirror. "I love it. It's definitely me."

"You'll set a new standard for seduction."

Danielle approached the hovering clerk. "It's a keeper. But I don't think I'll wear it out of the store. Just put it in a bag so I can match some accessories to it."

In another hour, the TT dress was completely accessorized—with a black silk evening bag and silk stiletto heels.

"Dani, pardon me for asking," Erin started as they walked toward the mall parking lot, "but how much did this little shopping spree set you back?"

"Let's see. The dress was $950, the bag was $130 and the shoes, $350."

"Are you crazy?"

"Why, what's the matter?"

"I'd have to work a month to buy the dress."

"Just doing what my daddy taught me. He said always to shop off the top shelf, because it's not that far from the bottom one."

"Don't get me wrong, I'm glad you can do these things, and maybe someday I'll be able to do the same."

"Believe me, if Dad weren't paying the tab, I wouldn't be spending this much."

"Your father treats you pretty well, doesn't he?"

"I must admit he does. I may be working on some bullshit issues with him, but he's still my knight in shining armor."

"Oh? Care to elaborate on those issues?"

"Not now. I'm having too good a time. Don't want to spoil it. But someday."

The women came to Erin's car first. "Shall we take my Civic Saturday night?"

"You gotta be kidding. You really want to pull up to the Hyatt in a car that's worth less than my dress? We'll make a much better impression in my Porsche. I'll let you drive, though, if you want."

"Not necessary. Pick me up at seven."

Saturday came quickly and at 7:00 p.m. Danielle was blowing the horn in front of Erin's apartment. Erin carefully descended the three steps off the porch and squeezed into the Porshe. Danielle whistled. "You know Erin, if I were a guy, I would love to make you tonight."

Erin giggled. "You've already done that and you're not a guy."

"No, I mean at the dance tonight, I'd expect any man in his right mind would be on the make with you."

"Whoa. Slap down that green-eyed monster. No guy's going to command my attention tonight. I intend to be doing other things. Don't forget, Dani, you too have a serious purpose for attending this affair."

"Oh Erin, lighten up. I already took my Pepto Bismol and I have Trojans in my purse. I'm all set for my mission." She made an exaggerated wriggle. "Yucky as that is."

At the Hyatt, Danielle took her place in the line heading for the valet service. Three cars ahead of them, a handsome woman stepped out of a black Mercedes sedan followed, from the driver's side, by a tall, well-built, distinguished looking gentleman with salt and pepper hair.

"Isn't that Gayle St. James, our university president?" Danielle asked.

"Sure is. And look at her escort—he's a real man. Are you sure the president is a lesbian?"

"I'm positive." Danielle couldn't take her eyes off the couple making their way inside. "Do you know how old she is?"

Erin nodded. "Looks great for a woman of 47, don't you think?"

"Hell, I wouldn't throw her out of bed."

"Danielle, with your sexual appetite, you wouldn't throw anyone out of bed."

They both smiled as two valet hunks approached the car. As they exited and ascended the steps to the hotel, Danielle whispered to Erin, "Did you see the buns on the one who opened my door?"

Erin threw back her head and roared. "See what I mean? You not only wouldn't throw a sexy person—male or female—out of bed, you'd squeeze them between your legs till they hollered uncle."

"Now Erin, if you want me to get up close and personal tonight with a short, baldheaded, mustachioed old fart, at least let me wet my fantasy before the suffering starts."

"As long as it's only your fantasy that gets wet."

Music from a piano and harp swelled around them as they entered the ballroom. No sooner had they picked up their table assignments than a waiter passing drinks stopped before them. Each selected a flute of champagne. "Nice," Danielle murmured. She turned to the corner and watched as the musicians filed in and took their places in the dance band. A moment later, the harpist and pianist wrapped up their song and a blast of trumpets announced that the evening's main event had started.

As they moved through the crowd to locate their table, a young man approached them. "You're Erin Gallagher, aren't you?"

"That's right. And you would be. . ."

"Robert Williams. I teach Advanced Macro. Just wanted to introduce myself."

Erin put out her hand. "Hello, then."

Williams tucked in his chin. "I've always admired you at our meetings, but seeing you. . .here. . .looking so. . .like this. . . was more than my shyness could withstand."

"I'm flattered, but I must admit I don't remember seeing you at department meetings."

"I've only been here a year. I've so much admired your teaching talents."

Erin glanced over at Danielle. She shrugged. "Really? And how, might I ask, have you done that?"

"Last year, when I first arrived on campus, I was assigned your class to observe and I have been observing you ever since."

Erin and Danielle exchanged glances. Danielle shrugged again.

"Thank you for your kind words, Mr. Williams. Perhaps we will see each other again, but please forgive me, Professor Dawes is beckoning me."

Danielle put her hand on Erin's shoulder. "Well, well, looks like Professor Gallagher has a secret admirer." She let her hand slide down Erin's spine.

Erin gave a little bun wiggle. "Jealousy will get you everywhere, Danielle. Come on. Professor Dawes is motioning to us."

Heads turned as they paraded across the dance floor to join Harmon Dawes and his wife. Erin returned Danielle's knowing smile. Yes, she thought, Mrs. Dawes looks every bit as beautiful with clothes on as she did in the secret photos they'd discovered.

And such clothes: a strapless red lace sheath that displayed her soft white shoulders and perfectly shaped narrow collarbones. An elegant, if aging, Southern Belle.

"Erin, I want you to meet my wife Virginia. Darling, this is Erin Gallagher, an associate professor in my department."

"Harmon has obviously been keeping you a secret. . . and I can see why."

Erin didn't answer that; instead she introduced Danielle. "She started here last spring as an intern, in the accounting department.."

"Miss Baldwin," Dawes extended his hand. Seconds later, his face blanched.

Erin ignored his embarrassment and asked whether he'd seen Wiggams yet this evening.

"Who? Oh the comptroller." Dawes' voice rose a good octave. "No, I haven't seen him."

Virginia Dawes was busy telling Danielle how absolutely gorgeous she was and repeatedly complimented her on the dress. "It's to die for. Harmon, how in the world could you have such young and beautiful instructors and not tell me about them? They are charming, my dear."

Dawes cleared his throat. "Erin is the instructor, Ginny. Danielle is an intern, one whom I have just met.'

"Didn't you work in Washington D.C. at one time?" Erin asked. "I thought your resume included George Washington University."

"Yes, I did, for about three years."

"Perhaps you knew Danielle's father, George Baldwin."

Dawes shook his head. "Don't believe so, should I have? Was he at the university too?"

Erin was enjoying this. "No, he is the Deputy Director of the CIA. I just thought you may have run into him at some time."

Erin noticed that Professor Dawes' hand, clutching his drink, began to tremble. Beads of perspiration dotted his forehead. In a second, he produced a handkerchief and patted his face dry.

Virginia Dawes shook her empty cocktail glass. "Harm, Darling, please refill my drink."

As Dawes rushed off, the three women jabbered about the beautiful dresses in the room, what they must have cost their wearers, and their favorite designers. A voice from behind interrupted them. "I must be the luckiest man alive. The three most beautiful women in the room and they are all mine."

"Why, John Wiggams, you old flirt you, what a nice thing to say. John, this is Erin Gallagher, a professor in Harmon's department and this is Danielle. . . I am sorry honey, but I am terrible with last names. . ."

"Baldwin, Danielle Baldwin. We've met." She offered her hand to Wiggams.

Wiggams took it, bowing. "Good evening, Danielle, nice to see my favorite intern again." Then he turned to Erin. "Miss Gallagher, a pleasure."

Erin bucked her chin at Danielle, urging her to get going on her mission. "It's nice to see you here, Mr. Wiggams."

His eyes assessed her. "Gorgeous gown. Please, Danielle, call me John. We're not at the office now."

"Isn't she just the most beautiful young thing you have ever laid eyes on, John?"

"She sure is, Virginia. I didn't even recognize her as I walked over here. As an intern, she mostly wears blue jeans or sweats. She sure does clean up well."

Danielle flashed Erin a sarcastic smile.

Wiggams moved toward Ginny, nuzzled her cheek, and hugged her in a way that allowed him a feel of her breasts.

Ah, Erin thought, that predatory little bastard will never be able to pass up Danielle tonight.

Dawes reappeared looking calmer now, his hand steady, his cheeks flushed. He'd obviously fortified himself with some liquid courage, Erin thought as he swaggered up with Ginny's drink.

"John, I see you have met the girls."

"I sure have, Harmon, I sure have." He made no effort to mask his leer.

"Did you know Danielle's father was the Deputy Director of the CIA?"

"Is that right. You must be very proud of him, Danielle."

What a lying s.o.b., Erin thought. He knows exactly who Danielle's father is. But he doesn't know that we know he's lying. That gives us the upper hand. So tonight, when Danielle snuggles up close and uses a few intelligence gathering tricks of her own, he won't know what hit him.

Erin swiveled her head to appraise the crowd. She recognized the university president and her escort making obligatory rounds. Gayle St. James was much more attractive than Erin had remembered. Up close, she looked even better than when she'd stepped out of her car. Her coral blue suit glimmered with pearl and gold buttons. Drop earrings of pearl encircled by gold and a sparkling gold and pearl necklace matched the buttons. Her brunette hair lightly streaked with blonde highlights made her appear more elegant than any university president Erin had ever known.

The president respectfully went directly to the department head. "Good evening, Professor Dawes, it's so nice to see you again."

Dawes gave a little bow to return the greeting.

"I would like all of you to meet my brother, David St. .James. He is visiting us from Boston and I thought it would be refreshing to have him meet some of the staff."

"Nice to have you join us, David." Dawes introduced the others.

"I finally have the honor to meet the infamous Erin Gallagher," the president said. "Professor Dawes refers to you so often, I feel as if I already know you."

Erin tilted her head. "Really?" She looked at Dawes for confirmation. He flashed her a respectful smile. "Thanks for the compliment. I don't know what to say."

"You are a beautiful young woman, Erin. I had expected a more. . .well, an older woman, perhaps my age."

"Forgive me, Dr. St. James, may I ask what Professor Dawes has said that would give you that impression?"

"Nothing directly. It's just that at some of the department head meetings, he uses you in examples of excellent teaching methodology and preparation. He always alludes to your integrity and intellect." She laughed. "And when the men flinch at this, he finishes with your opinions of self-centered males."

Erin made no effort to stop the smirk that came to her mouth. "Sounds as if Professor Dawes has it right, at least the part about males."

"From what I see and hear, Erin, he has everything right. Congratulations, by the way, on your recent appointment as an associate professor. I believe you have achieved this in shorter time than anyone else in the history of our university."

Was this woman flirting with her? Erin wondered. Unsure now, she kept a straight face. "Allow me to return the favor and mention how thrilled we all are to have you on board as our new president. We look forward to your leadership into the new millennium."

The band broke away from cocktail party music and launched into dance rhythm. Erin and Danielle made their way to table 12 and arrived to find that the Daweses and the lone Wiggams were also assigned there. This was either convenient or a disaster, Erin thought. By the end of the evening, she'd know which.

Another man and his companion were seated with their backs to Erin, their noses nearly touching as they talked. Professor Dawes arrived and took control of the seating. He motioned for Erin to sit to the left of the unknown gentleman, and Danielle next to her. Wiggams hurriedly scooted into the seat beside Danielle.

The man finally came up for air and looked around. He stood and offered his hand around the table. "Virginia, so good to see the sweetest southern belle in the room. Harmon, John. Glad we're all together—will make the evening a winner." He cast his eyes toward his guest. "May I introduce Catherine Petrini. Her father is one of our firm's best clients and a large benefactor of this university. I'm sure you all are familiar with the new Petrini Health Center just starting construction here on campus."

Dawes nodded gravely then forced a smile. "We certainly are. Miss Petrini, please pass along our gratitude to your father."

"Hi, Judge," Ginny said, a shy grin crinkling her lips. "It's good to see you. We don't see enough of you these days."

"Not yet, Ginny, but come November I will welcome the title. Now, who do we have here? Don't tell me these two gorgeous girls are faculty members. They are much too pretty and certainly not old enough."

Harmon did the honors. "Erin Gallagher and Danielle Baldwin, please meet C. Albert Kane, the university solicitor and the next Superior Court Judge of Mecklenburg County. And beyond that, he no doubt aspires to sit on our nation's highest court."

What was it Erin heard in Dawes' voice? A mixture of admiration and. . . what. . . contempt?

Kane never blinked at Danielle's name. Never so much as flinched with Ginny Dawes and her remark about not seeing enough of him. Erin had expected him to be smooth, but not this cool. The conniving criminal was an absolute iceberg. His steely cold eyes belied the warm smile and silvery voice. She could already see the two-edged sword of the politician—a man of little feeling and great desires.

It wouldn't take much effort to despise him, Erin thought. He was the very epitome of the self-centered, ego-maniacal male she loved to hate. If she thought he would be tough to get to before, she now worried they might never crack this man's facade.

"Hello, *University Solicitor* Kane, how nice to meet you. Speaking for both Danielle and myself, we thank you for your very complimentary words regarding our age and appearance."

"I speak only the truth, Professor. May I presume that you are a professor?"

"Associate Professor, but *Erin* will be just fine."

"Wonderful, and please forget my title for the night. *C. Albert* will be acceptable. I presume you teach English, from the way you so eloquently select and deliver words."

"You would be wrong. No, I am in Professor Dawes' Economics Department.'

Kane tugged at his bow tie. "My, my, who would ever think such an Epicurean woman with an intellect to match could indeed also balance a check book."

He roared with laughter, joined only by Wiggams and Ginny Dawes.

Erin took the bait. "C. Albert, I note by your demeanor as well as your reputation that you are a very astute man. However, I am certain those assembled here will not be surprised to learn that you will never know whether I am an Epicure. You must have me confused with someone else at this table."

Kane took a long drink from his water glass, assessing Erin over its rim. "Have I said something wrong?"

"Perhaps not. As I said, it may describe someone else at the table, but for you to know whether I am 'fond of sensuous pleasure'—the definition of Epicurean—is totally impossible."

Stunned silence enveloped the table. Ginny Dawes' face was now a bright crimson red, matching her dress, and Kane was nearly the same color as he struggled to keep his composure. Wiggams, Erin noticed, had everything he could do to restrain himself from laughing.

Kane waved his hand in the air. "I am truly sorry, Professor, but. . ."

"As I said, you may call me Erin."

"Oh yes, Erin, I'm sorry, perhaps I have misused the word. Forgive me, there certainly was no intent to characterize our relationship."

"Relationship? We just met tonight. We have no relationship."

"Miss Gallagher, I was simply trying to pay you a compliment."

"A compliment. I see." She forced a frown. "Mr. Kane, I will not have my sexual appetite or female intelligence made the butt of dinner table humor."

Erin looked around the table. Ginny emptied her table wine and her husband's too. Wiggams' face wore a wide grin; no doubt he was glad someone was finally taking on Kane. And take him on, she would.

Harmon intervened. "As I look at the appetizers on the way to our table, I truly do see an Epicurean delight that I could devour right now."

The mood was broken.

Erin laughed and selected some appetizers from the trays making the rounds. She'd accomplished her goal. From that point forward, Kane would not underestimate her.

She used dinner to make further assessments. First, Ginny Dawes. Confrontation was not her cup of tea. She'd downed two full glasses of wine in about a minute. She definitely could be pressured, and Wiggams knew it. She may be a great lay, but in an upright position, she was no mental giant.

Next came Dawes. His mannerisms were those of a gentleman who not only adored his wife but also respected her. He listened intently when she talked. He complimented her every chance he got. He was solicitous of her needs. Probably, Erin decided, he had come up with the Tristar scheme to give Ginny things he could never afford on his academic salary. She wondered what he'd do if he ever learned she was being unfaithful.

The plan to make Wiggams—the little bastard—come on to Danielle was definitely working. He couldn't take his eyes off her cleavage. The TT dress had actually turned into a titty dress. Erin suppressed a laugh. She'd tell Danielle later.

Kane remained an enigma Erin wasn't ready to tackle right now. She would stick to her plan and concentrate on Dawes.

As they waited for dessert, Erin turned to Ginny. "Tonight's dinner was superb, don't you think?"

"Excellent. I had no idea the Hyatt could match the cuisine at the Uptown Club, which I personally feel offers the best food in town."

"Do you eat there much, Mrs. Dawes?"

"Quite often, as a matter of fact. Have you ever been there, Erin?"

"Nooooo. A club membership is too rich for my associate professor's salary. You do have to be a member to eat there, don't you?"

Ginny nodded. "Quite right. It's very private, but I would love it if you would be my guest for lunch."

"I'd like that; however, my schedule gets pretty full now that the semester is starting.. Almost no chance for lunches away from my office."

"My husband probably loaded you down with classes he didn't want to teach," Ginny said, glancing over at Dawes. "But surely you can squeeze one afternoon out of your schedule." She shot her husband a smile. "Harm won't get upset, I'm sure. How about next week then? Friday?"

Erin received a barely perceptible nod from Dawes. "That's my lightest teaching day, so. . .sure. . .I will look forward to it."

"Suppose we meet there at noon; I will have accommodations made for you."

The band, back from their break, started to tune up when Danielle asked Erin to go to the ladies room. They bent to peer under the stalls, making sure they were alone. As soon as they locked the doors to their adjoining stalls, Danielle started. "Well, Prof, you sure reamed Kane a new anus."

"Danielle, you sure have a way with words"

"You were great. That maniac kept stepping on his over-used tongue. It probably bears tread marks now!"

"If he didn't know before, he now knows who we are."

"You, maybe, but I don't think he's aware I even exist."

"In that dress? Get real."

"Speaking of which, that lecherous bastard John P. has done nothing but try to bed me since our cheeks hit the chairs."

Erin flushed, opened the stall door, moved to the sink. She washed her hands and reapplied her lipstick "I told you the dress was perfect for your mission. I've been watching him. He can't take his eyes off you."

"Too true," said Danielle, joining Erin at the sinks. " I've been watching Kane, and I've got news for you. . . he can't get you out of his mind. Mark my words, Erin dearest, he has his sights set on you."

"I hope so; that was the plan."

"Wait a minute, I thought you were to concentrate on Professor Dawes."

"I am, but who knows, maybe I'll get the both of them."

"Oh sure, you get Dawes and Kane and I get the dregs of campus. Wiggams."

As the hallway door opened, Erin put a finger to her lips. "Careful. Names." She waited for the woman to enter a stall. "Think of the fun you're going to have."

Danielle rolled her eyes. "Yeah, right. Remember me, Erin? He is definitely not my type. He gives me the willies. Balling that old fart is far from my idea of fun."

Erin leaned close to whisper. "We're talking about securing information to convict the TT, not screwing the guy to death."

Danielle waited for the other woman to finish and leave the restroom. "Then why am I going to bed with the pervert tonight?"

"Oh, so you have made some progress already?"

"Are you kidding? He had me in bed before the entree came."

"Has he let anything slip at all about. . .TT?"

"Not a word. Everything's been about my dress, my body, my boobs and his exquisite apartment. He would like to show it to me after this reception."

Erin looked up. "Really? Have you accepted?"

"No, I told him I was a lesbian."

"You what?"

"Only kidding. Of course I accepted,. That was the plan, right?"

"Yes, but I do have misgivings. Be careful with him. He could be unpredictable."

"I will. If he gets out of hand, I might become the next Lorena Bobbit."

As soon as they returned, Wiggams jumped to his feet. "Danielle, will you honor me with this dance?"

She cast a grimace to Erin that Wiggams couldn't see. "I'd be delighted," she said, placing her hand in his and allowing him to lead her to the dance floor.

Harmon and Ginny also departed for the dance floor, as did Kane and Catherine. Erin sat alone, keeping an eye on Wiggams and Danielle. My poor friend, she thought, is in for a long night.

When the song ended, they all stayed for the next dance. Except Kane. He escorted his guest to her seat then leaned over Erin's shoulder. "Catherine and I were talking as we danced and agreed it was not very nice to leave you alone at the table. She practically insisted that I ask you to dance, Miss Gallagher."

Erin's eyes flashed. "Is this the request of a social worker?"

"No, my dear, it's a sincere offer from a man with a growing admiration for a spirited young woman."

She rose. "In that case, I would love to. What about Catherine?"

He led her to the raised parquet floor. "Don't worry about her. She needs to powder her nose."

To the rhythmic strains of "Till the End of Time," they gracefully glided across the floor. Erin expected him to embrace her too closely, and she was right. Kane's hand inched downward, toward the slight rise of her buttocks. Erin grasped his hand and returned it to the small of her back.

"I'm sorry, Miss Gallagher. . . Erin. . . for our earlier misunderstanding and trust it will not mar your opinion of me." He waited for a reply but got none. "I do respect your defense of women's rights. It took fortitude for you to verbally slap me in the face. But I did have it coming."

At the moment, she had the upper hand. Remain silent, she told herself, and let him do all the talking. . . make him trip over what Dani had called his "over-used tongue."

Kane twirled and dipped, an accomplished dancer. When the music halted, he squeezed her hand and stepped out of the embrace. "I thank you, Erin. You felt quite good in my arms. I was wondering. . . do you have a steady beau?"

"A beau? What a southern word. No, I have little time for that. My last four years here at the university, I've concentrated on my career. Not much social life." Let him think you're lonely, she told herself. Reel him in.

.He made no movement toward the table, but waited for the band's next piece. "I suppose you know I am a bachelor."

She nodded. Here it comes, she thought. Stay cool. "Seems to me I have heard you live alone in a big house on a hill."

"It's in the Lake Norman area. Around Charlotte, my home is generally referred to as The Mansion."

"I can almost hear the capital T, capital M. Must be a sight to behold."

"The estate is quite beautiful, if I do say so myself. Indoor swimming pool, racquetball court, projection room, game room and many other fine features."

"You must be very proud."

"I'd love to show it to you some time."

Don't say anything for a moment, girl. Let him think you are totally surprised by this invitation, that you haven't been leading him up to this.

"I might like that. When I can squeeze out some time. Do you have security on the grounds?"

"Of course. Cameras all over. We can watch what's going on everywhere within the estate and within the building."

"Interesting. Sounds quite elaborate. Are there cameras in every room?""

"Yes. If you are concerned about your safety, you needn't be. I have no need to prey on beautiful women. . . unless, of course, she would share my desires. I can promise, young lady, you will be quite secure."

That bastard, Erin thought. He probably taped his trysts with Ginny Dawes, has amassed quite a video library of his bedroom escapades. It's a fair guess that poor Ginny doesn't even know. Like Wiggams, Kane's covering his ass with stuff he can use against Dawes. Wonder what he has on Wiggams.

I see Catherine's back, could we return to the table?"

Back at the table, Ginny grinned up at them as they passed. "How nice to see you two making up."

Erin recognized it for what it was—a dig at Kane. He seemed not to notice.

Danielle wiped perspiration from her cheeks. "How did you make out with Kane? I saw you two dancing."

"Pretty good, I think. I'm invited to The Mansion for a tour."

"Christ, after a couple of twirls around the floor? Two more dances and you'll be replacing Ginny Dawes."

"On tape too. I found out he has an elaborate camera system."

"What the hell. Is everyone in Tristar paranoid?"

Danielle reached over to Erin's lap and dropped the keys for the Porshe. "John P. wants me to leave with him."

Erin handed back the keys. "Oh no, you're not getting stuck there. You take your car. I'll get a ride or call a cab, but you are definitely taking your car."

"As usual, you're right. I would feel better with the car there." Danielle stood up and winced convincingly. "Please excuse me, everyone. I have a dreadful headache. . . all this champagne and carousing. . . just too much for me."

Moments later, Wiggams said his goodnights and rushed off. "Have to be up early. . . for an 8:00 tee time," he called over his shoulder.

By midnight, the crowd had thinned considerably. Erin caught herself in a wide yawn. The world of academia was not a late night crowd, she reminded herself. She needed to cadge a ride.

"Did your friend's headache leave you without a way to get home?" Ginny Dawes to the rescue. "Come on, Harm, Darlin', let's take her with us."

Valet service brought Professor Dawes' Lincoln Town Car around and Erin slid into the back seat. "What a beautiful car," she said to Ginny.

"Thank you. My Harm likes to own nothing but luxury cars. He just bought me a new Mercedes. Didn't you, Darlin'." She squeezed her husband's thigh.

Not on a professor's salary, Erin thought. All luxuries are courtesy of Tristar, Mrs. Dawes, whether you know it or not. Out loud, she gave Professor Dawes directions to her home.

Ginny continued to stroke her husband's leg, giggling and cooing.

Dawes pushed her hand off. "Ginny, behave yourself. I know how you get after a few drinks. And you've had more than a few. Please remember, we have someone else with us."

Erin looked out the window, pretending she didn't hear anything being said in the front seat.

"Right. We have someone with us," Ginny said as if just realizing it. "Erin, you sweet thing, you most assuredly have a boyfriend, don't you?"

"I haven't had the time to even consider that."

"How long did you say you have been here at the university?"

"Four years now."

"And no boyfriend yet? My gracious, how does a young woman like you satisfy your desires?"

"Ginny!" Dawes almost screamed. "That's none of you business."

Erin merely chuckled. "The usual way for a single. Masturbation. . . and a few good female friends."

The car swerved, nearly hitting a tree along the roadway. Erin watched Professor Dawes swallow hard as he tried to keep control of both himself and the car. Nothing like a little shock therapy to provoke conversation, and with Ginny's tipsy condition, she couldn't wait to get started.

"You mean you're a lesbian?"

Dawes was flummoxed. "Ginny. That's enough."

"I don't mind, Professor Dawes. I'm out of the closet." She turned toward Ginny. "Actually, I am bi-sexual. How about you?"

Ginny slapped her thigh and let out a whoop. "I'm just sexual. Right, Harmie?"

Defeated, Dawes muttered, "Yes, Ginny, you certainly are."

"Erin, tell me, do you have sex with men and women?"

"That's right. But not at the same time."

"Was that beautiful girl with you tonight bi-sexual too?"

"Uhuh," Erin said, stripping her reply of emotion. She sat up. "Turn left here."

Dawes turned. "Ginny, for God's sake, no more questions."

"Now Harm, I want to learn something. Erin, have you two been with each other?"

Erin was having a ball. "You mean have we sexually aroused one another to orgasm?"

"I guess that's my question."

Dawes screeched to a halt. "Ginny, I mean it now. That's enough."

"I told you, Professor, it's okay. Yes, Ginny, we have. Sexual experimentation has its rewards. If you're single, that is. I assume you have only been with Professor Dawes."

Ginny's expression didn't change. "Of course. No one could give me what he does."

"Doesn't it get boring? Don't you ever think of being with someone else?"

"I have had fantasies," Ginny admitted, glancing at her husband out of the corner of her eye.

"Ever think of carrying them out? You are a very beautiful, desirable woman."

Dawes remained silent. Perhaps, Erin thought, he'd like to hear the answers to these questions, too.

"You mean with another woman?"

"Either."

"Never another man. Harmon keeps me well satisfied. He has quite a large. . ."

Dawes lunged across the seat and put his hand over Ginny's mouth. "You have said quite enough, my dear." His eyes pierced his wife's until she closed them in subjection. He dropped his hand. "Erin, isn't this your apartment building?"

"Oh, right." Dawes released the door locks so she could get out. "Thanks for the ride, I appreciate it very much."

"Goodnight Erin, my dear," Ginny called after Erin's retreating shape. "Don't you forget we have a date."

Erin reached her door, turned and waved. "How could I forget? I'll look forward to seeing you at the club at noon on Friday."

Once inside, Erin rushed to the bedroom window where she could see the Dawes' car. Just as she'd hoped, the two were engaged in a shouting match . Hot damn, she thought. The seeds I planted are taking root. The old "divide and conquer" principle was already working. Both of them would now be easy to approach.

CHAPTER SEVEN

For the first time in their marriage, Harmon and Ginny Dawes spent the night in separate bedrooms. In the morning, Ginny dressed for church in an outfit more revealing than usual. Surely, she thought, this will get Harmon to speak to me.

But it did not work.

At church, Dawes continued his silence, opening his mouth only to sing desultory hymns and utter prayers without conviction. Once back home, he marched immediately to his study and shut the door.

Ginny followed him upstairs, determined to make amends. She knocked on the door and burst in without an invitation. "Harm, this has gone far enough, don't you think? Please speak to me."

Dawes sat in a chair, stared out the window and said nothing.

"Harm, please believe me, I am sorry about last night. Please make up with me." She lowered her voice to a near-whisper. "It is Sunday afternoon, you know."

He did not look at her but only waved her away. "Why don't you just go to bed by yourself and enjoy the fantasy you told Erin about last night."

She strode toward him. "Harm, Darlin' I was only kidding with her."

"That's pure bullshit, Ginny. The alcohol you swilled down loosened your tongue so your true feelings came out. Tell me, who is it you fantasize about?"

She stood behind him and put her hands on his shoulders. "Harm, I fantasize only about you. You're man enough for any woman."

He leaned away from her caress, turned and bored into her eyes with his own. "Your actions do not match your words. I think it's only fair to inform you that I know all about your visits to Al Kane's home."

Ginny stumbled backwards. "What?"

"You heard me. I can give you exact dates, the time you arrived and when you left."

All the color in Ginny's body drained away. She stared at the floor, trying to compose herself. "Harm, I. . ."

Dawes pushed himself out of the chair. "I am not stupid, you know. Did you think you could pull this off forever, Ginny?" He headed for the door.

"Wait! Harm, I am so sorry. Please. . . believe me. I never wanted to hurt you."

Dawes halted at the door and turned to face her. "Again, your words and your actions don't match." He opened the door.

"Honey, Albert Kane means nothing to me. It was just. . . something to occupy my time. You're never home. Between teaching, running the department, seminars and Tristar, I never see you."

"What was every Sunday, 'throw Harmon a crumb' day?"

"No, no. I love our Sundays. They're wonderful. I beg you, Harm, let's make up. I'll do anything you ask. Anything."

Dawes whirled. "Forget it, Ginny. Save it for Kane. Or take Erin's advice and find another woman." In a second, he was gone. His feet pounded on the stairs. The garage door groaned up and, moments later, his car sped away.

Ginny slumped into Harm's chair and wailed. "Oh, God, what have I done?"

She leaned her head against the high back of Harm's chair. She could smell his after shave. She reached across the desk and jerked a tissue from the polished black dispenser. She had to figure a way to get him back, Ginny thought as she blotted the streaked mascara from her cheeks. Maybe she'd phone a friend and get some advice.

For the first time since she'd moved to Charlotte, Ginny realized how few friends she had. All her efforts to become accepted by the high and mighty society of Charlotte had left her bereft of intimate relationships. Money, jewels, designer clothing, social status . . . yes, but not a single confidante.

She had to phone someone. But who? And who had told Harm about her affair? Had he been suspicious, hired a detective? Or had Kane somehow let it slip?

In an instant, her curiosity transformed to anger. What the hell, she had nothing to lose. She grabbed the phone and punched a number. If he wasn't home, she'd leave a message. She hastily composed an idea while the phone rang. But he was home. "Albert, it's Ginny."

"What's the matter? Where are you?"

"At home. Why?"

"Are you crazy, calling from there? Your husband could pick up an extension."

"Wait, don't hang up. He's not here. He. . . he knows. . . about us."

"That's impossible. You didn't admit to it, did you?"

"I did. He knew all about it. . . dates, times, everything."

"Jesus Christ, Ginny, you panicked. He was probably only guessing."

"No, no. He wasn't bluffing." Ginny started to sob. "I know my Harm. I tried to tell him how sorry I was but he just left. Oh, Albert, what shall I do?"

"How the hell should I know? What I do know is that it's over between us. Fun while it lasted, to be sure, but I'm through. So don't get excited about it."

"Don't get excited? What the hell does that mean? It may have been just a fling for you, but my marriage is at stake. I need your help."

"Help? What can I do? As of this moment, I'm out of your life. Stop your whining and deal with it. When he comes home, jump his bones. Harmon'll come around."

"Albert, my god, don't you have any sympathy for me?"

"Sympathy? Don't know the meaning of the word. It's your problem, not mine."

Ginny slumped into the chair. "You are a bastard, Albert Kane."

"Okay, I can live with that. I have a great future ahead of me, and you, my dear Ginny Dawes, are not going to mess it up for me." He paused. "Do you get me, Ginny? You'd better not make trouble, if you know what's good for you."

The line went dead.

Ginny sat for long moments, her head in her hands. The ringing telephone jolted her. Maybe it was Harm, calling to tell her he'd cooled off and things would be okay again. She put a smile into her voice when she answered. "Virginia Dawes."

"You sound chipper, Ginny. Erin Gallagher here."

Ginny's mood plummeted. "Oh. I was hoping. . ."

"Sorry to bother you on a Sunday afternoon, but I got to thinking about last night.. I'm sorry about our conversation in the car. Things got out of hand. Under the circumstances, I have no intention of holding you to the luncheon date on Friday. It was a lovely gesture, and I appreciate. . ."

"Wait, Erin. . . I. . . it's so considerate of you to beg off, but. . ."

"What's the matter, Ginny? I can tell from your voice. . . something's wrong."

She had to spill everything to someone. Maybe Erin would be the friend she needed right now. "Harm and I had a big fight. . . over what I said to you last night and. . . other things. He walked out."

Erin sucked in her breath. "Ginny, that's terrible. I feel responsible. What can I do?"

"I have no idea. Everything happened so fast, I'm in a state of shock right now."

"Tell you what, let's meet for a late lunch and have some girl talk. What do you say?"

Ginny brightened. "I'd love that. I really would. Where?"

"You know Charlotte better than I do, Ginny. I don't get out much. You name it."

Ginny didn't hesitate. "Meet me in an hour at Mert's. It's in uptown Charlotte, on North College. They have a great Sunday brunch. . . good old southern cooking. And it's my treat."

Ginny hung up and took in a deep breath. Maybe she did have a friend after all.

Erin clicked off the phone and smiled to herself. Her divide-and-conquer plan had worked! She'd wanted an opportunity to get close to one of them—she didn't care which—but now it appeared Ginny would be the one.

Already dressed in black slacks and a white cotton sweater, Erin went to the bathroom, brushed out her long hair and pulled it back in a giant claw clip. She applied a little blush and a light lipstick, then headed for the car. It was early, but she wanted to get there ahead of Ginny, be already seated in the power position when she arrived.

When Ginny walked in, Erin waved her toward the table. She drank from her beer then placed it carefully on the place mat. "By the look on your face, this must be serious."

Ginny pulled out one of the chairs and slid into it. She unrolled the napkin and placed it on her lap. Finally, she looked at Erin and tears filled her eyes. "Oh, Erin, I don't know what to do."

Erin got the waiter's eye and shook her head. She wanted privacy. "I'll help if I can."

"You have no idea how much I need a friend right now." Ginny reached across the table and took Erin's hand.

Erin patted her wrist. "Tell me."

"I might as well just launch into it. To put it bluntly, after many years of being totally faithful to Harmon, I began an affair with a man in town. Harmon found out and today, after church, he blew up and left."

"I can't believe it. You seemed to have it all."

Ginny nodded. "Oh, I do. I mean, did. Now I've ruined everything. I don't know why I got involved with. . . someone else. Well, yes I do. Harm was always so busy. . . with school and his

other business. . . . I got lonely and when this man came on to me.
. ."

"I understand, Ginny. Do you think your husband was ever
unfaithful?"

"Not to my knowledge. Why?"

"Just curious. If he was, you could point out that he can't be
angry with you for doing something he also did."

"Oh, right. But no, I'm pretty sure he wouldn't do anything
like that. I never thought I would either."

"Then this man you had an affair with must be really
something. . . handsome, powerful. . .available when your husband
wasn't. . . to give you the attention you needed."

"You got it. He is all that. In fact, you know that yourself."

"Oh? How?"

"You had words with him last night."

"You can't mean Kane. . . C. Albert Kane?"

Ginny dipped her head.

Erin, playing out the drama, never so much as blinked. "I can
understand the attraction. He can be charming, I suppose."

"The worst part of it is that Kane's one of Harm's business
partners."

Erin's head shot up. "Oh? Professor Dawes has a business?"

"Yes, he, Kane and John Wiggams."

"The university comptroller. Yes. What kind of business?"

"It's an investment firm. They operate as brokers for foreign
dignitaries who want to invest large sums of money. Or so Harm
tells me. I really don't get involved in it." Ginny made a strangled
sound, a sardonic laugh. "I just spend the money."

Erin leaned forward. "I can't imagine what Professor Dawes
would be doing in this type of business. He has so little time for
anything but his university responsibilities."

"That's exactly what caused the problem. At first, when the
business was new—that was about seven years ago—what he did
took very little time. But in the last two years, it seems to be all
consuming. Harm is never available. That's why Albert and I got
involved."

"Kane's a busy man too. I don't get it. What in the world would take so much of your husband's time that he would neglect you?"

"Albert relies on others in his law firm to do some of his work for this brokerage business, but Harm has to personally select all the investments and complete all the research and development. He's the key man in the success of the entire operation."

"How does John Wiggams figure into all this? I thought he was full-time at the university."

"Harmon calls him the 'bean counter,' so I guess he does all the accounting work." Ginny motioned for Erin to move closer. She looked around to see if anyone was able to hear. "The business brings in a lot of money. I mean a lot."

"I guess that explains your beautiful wardrobe, the Town Car. . . things not usually affordable on a professor's salary."

"It's my fault, Erin. I grew up so poor I wore nothing but hand-me-downs. I didn't have my own pair of shoes till I graduated high school. I had to wear my older sister's clothes, shoes, everything. My poppa was the town drunk and my mama took in laundry. I was constantly hungry. . . ."

"You don't have to dredge up those bitter memories. I understand."

"When I married Harmon, he promised I could have anything I wanted. But on his salary. . . . I'm the one who wanted more. Harmon came up with a way to fulfill my every dream." Tears started down her cheeks. "What have I done? I have the best of everything, including—until today—a loving husband. When Harm left, I phoned Albert and. . ."

"What happened?" Erin put on her most sympathetic face.

"The bastard dumped me faster than a rocket breaking the sound barrier. Said he wasn't going to let me mess up his promising political future." Ginny rummaged in her purse for a handkerchief. She dabbed the tears from her cheeks. "I may have lost everything."

"Maybe. Maybe not. Things usually aren't as bad as they seem."

"What can I do? Erin, I need your help."

"Sure, Ginny, any way I can. Let me ask. . . are you and Kane finished?"

"I'll never let that s.o.b. near me again!"

"That's what I wanted to hear. There's more to this than meets the eye. . . I don't suppose you'd be interested in a little revenge?"

"Oh, my god, yes. I wish I knew how"

Erin knew she had Ginny where she wanted her. "You've trusted me. Now I'm going to confide something to you that you absolutely cannot reveal to anyone. Not anyone, including your husband, or all our lives would be in danger."

"What kind of danger? I had an affair. I didn't murder anyone."

Erin sat back and took a long drink from her beer. "Maybe I'd better not. You're in no condition to. . ."

"Please. . . I want to know, whatever it is."

"I'm pretty sure you can get your husband back, but you have to trust me and not ask any questions." She waited for Ginny's nod. "Okay, now listen carefully. Do you know where your husband keeps records relating to this investment business?"

"Yes. In his study at home. On the computer."

"I suspect he's also created back-up disks for safety. I need for you to locate all the information, make copies and bring them to me."

"Copies. I don't understand. How will this help me settle the score with that bastard?"

Erin let her impatience show. "I told you, no questions. It's important. That's all you need to know."

"Okay, okay, if it'll get Albert in trouble I'll get the information for you."

"When your husband comes home—and he will, Ginny, he will—get him to tell you how he found out about your involvement with Kane. I suspect it was through Wiggams, not Kane."

"Wiggams? What the hell. . ."

"No questions, Ginny."

"Right."

"Now, I have to ask one last thing. Ginny, if it meant saving your husband's life, would you sleep with Wiggams?"

Ginny shoved her chair backward. "Christ Erin. I'm up to my armpits in alligators now because I slept with one of Harm's partners, and you're asking me to sleep with the other one? That's crazy." Her eyes darted around the restaurant to see who may have heard her. Looking abashed, she sat down.

"It's not crazy. I told you there's more to this than you know. I doubt you'll ever have to go that far, but I had to ask. Please, Ginny, trust me and do what I say. Don't ever tell a soul, and you and Professor Dawes may just survive this whole thing. And if you don't do as I ask. . ."

"If I don't?"

"Your whole world will come to an end, making this affair with Kane seem tiny in comparison."

"This is really that serious?"

Erin bent forward and lowered her voice, confiding in Ginny as promised. When she was finished, she rested her back against the chair and watched Virginia Dawes process this revelation. "Remember, you don't dare tell a soul. Go home and do your best to make up with your husband. Stay low key. We'll meet as scheduled Friday, and you'll give me the copies of everything you find about the business." Erin motioned to the waiter. "Now, let's eat. All this has made me very hungry."

"I think even I could eat now. Oh, Erin, I hope you're right—that Harm will come back to me. I don't know what I'd do if. . ."

"Don't say it. Here, if you need to talk to me anytime, call me at home" She passed her a slip of paper containing her phone number and watched Ginny put it into her purse. "Now let's put this out of our minds and enjoy the brunch."

JOHN WIGGAMS LAY back in his leather recliner, his hand resting on the remote control. When the phone at his elbow rang, he waited until the fourth ring, muted the TV and clicked the button.

"John, get your ass over to my house this instant." Kane made no attempt to be civil.

"Is that you Kane? It's Sunday. I'm watching the U.S. Open. . . men's finals."

Kane roared into the phone. "You get here now or your balls are going to be swatted back and forth over the net."

"All right, all right. Give me an hour."

Kane had never before invited him to The Mansion. Things between them seemed fine at the party the night before. Something important must have happened.

As he drove, Wiggams scrolled through his mind, trying to think of anything that might have set Kane off. Could it have been his night with Danielle Baldwin? They hadn't left together. How would Kane even know the two had met later? No, it must be something else. Could it be a problem with Tristar?

At the ornate steel gate, Wiggams announced himself and watched it slowly swing open. He drove the winding lane up to the house on the hill, trying hard to stay on the pavement as his eyes took in the splendor of Kane's estate. He rolled to a stop on the brick-paved circular drive, and a uniformed man came out to meet him. A butler? Security guard? Perhaps both. The man greeted him deferentially and ushered him into the library, where Kane sat turning his Manhattan glass this way and that, to catch in the crystal prisms the sunlight streaming through the clerestory windows.

"Sit there, John. What'll you have?"

Wiggams sat. "A silver bullet, if you don't mind."

The servant handed Wiggams his drink and disappeared into the entry hall, shutting the double doors behind him.

"Why the summons, Al? This better be good."

"Don't get your back up; we're in this together." Kane sipped his drink. "We have some problems to resolve."

"Problems? Anything serious?"

"Not sure. Could be. Tell me, John, do you know of any reason for Harmon to be upset these days? Anything at all?"

Wiggams considered carefully before he answered. "No, can't think of a thing. Why?"

"You're sure? Has he been acting at all strange? Any signs of stress? You know how he gets sometime."

"As I said, can't think of any problem. What's going on?"

Kane stood up and went to the bar, made himself another drink. "You wouldn't have any knowledge of this, but I have been screwing Ginny Dawes. . . about two years now. She phoned me earlier today. . . . Harmon found out somehow and confronted her." He resumed his seat and twirled the ice cubes with his finger. "Ginny was spastic, but I couldn't give a shit about that. I am, of course, concerned about Harmon. . . we can't have him running around in a snit."

Wiggams downed his drink in a single gulp. "You're right. My god, Harmon could be a loose cannon. . . the way he gets so nervous at times."

"Exactly. I don't know how he found out, but I damn well am going to know soon. We have to get him settled down. That's where you come in."

"Me? Why? You're the one who was fucking his wife."

Kane let that slide. "I know you like to cover your ass. Might you have any information on our partner that we could use to get him back in line?"

Sweat popped out on Wiggams' face. "Mind if I have another drink?" He didn't wait for an answer but bounded out of his chair and over to the bar. A double martini this time. He took his time stirring the vodka in the ice-filled pitcher. Had to have a minute to think.

His mind raced to his last meeting with Harmon, a couple weeks ago. With the heavy debts he'd amassed in Vegas, he had to do something. He pressured Harmon to accelerate the investments, take more chances, return bigger profits. When Harmon refused, he panicked and told him about his wife and Kane, showed him the reports identifying the dates of their trysts along with her arrival and departure times. Flashed pictures of her getting out of the car in the front driveway but saved the really juicy stuff for future security. "Find a way to increase our take," he'd threatened, "or your academic career will be ruined. I'll see to that."

Kane's voice broke into his thoughts. "You seem to be pondering something. What is it? It must be good to have caused this outpouring of sweat."

"Nothing really. Only wondering how much pressure Dawes can take before he cracks."

"Don't give me that bullshit. I'm a damn good criminal defense attorney, John. I can tell when someone isn't leveling with me. Out with it."

Wiggams gulped his martini while he strode to the window, keeping his back turned to Kane. "About six months ago, when Harmon was getting nervous over our increasing the level of funds from the university, I hired a P.I. to follow him. He brought me some pictures of him and Ginny in some explicit sexual positions. Five quite amazing photos."

"My, my, John, you astonish me. No wonder you're sweating. Tell me, did the P.I.'s report include the fact that I was screwing his wife? You don't have to answer. Of course it did. I trust you had the good sense not to relay that fact to Harmon."

Wiggams kept his face averted. "Albert, you have to believe me. Yes, I knew of that but I never told Harmon."

Kane stood and moved to Wiggams' side at the window. He grabbed his arm and swung him around. "Christ, John, you're not kidding me. That's what set him off. But why were you blackmailing him? What did you want from him?"

Wiggams could not bring himself to look Kane in the eyes. He stared past him, his eyes blinking fast. "You know me, I love sex. The more the better. I simply wanted to screw his wife. I was jealous of you and Ginny. I have always wanted her, so finally I just asked him. I told him if he didn't set it up, I would destroy him at the university."

"John, my boy, you are full of shit all the way up to your eyeballs. Your love for money far exceeds the desire to hump Ginny. Now for the last time, why?"

Wiggams knew when he was beaten. "All right, I'll tell you. I got in too heavy with the Vegas crowd. I asked Harmon to increase the returns, to take more chances. I even told him I would get him more money from the university. He balked and in a panic I told him about you and Ginny. That's it, that's the whole truth."

"Finally." Kane squinted at Wiggams. "John, why didn't you come to me instead? You know I have connections out there."

"I thought I could solve it myself."

"When is the money due?"

"Next week. I have a trip planned out there. . .to meet our Boston banker."

"How much do you owe?"

Wiggams hung his head. "$500,000."

"That's a helluva lot of money. Jesus, what were you doing out there?"

"Mostly craps. Some blackjack, a little Baccarat, but mostly craps."

"How much do you have for them?"

"A little more than half—$300,000."

"Where is it going?"

"MGM Grand."

"Okay, you deliver that next week. Not a penny less. I'll take care of the rest with them. But heed me well, my friend. Make this your last trip there. If I find out you're in Vegas again, I will replace you the same way I did the last comptroller at the university. And they still haven't found him."

"No more trips to Vegas." Wiggams shook his head so fast, the drops of sweat from his brow splattered against the window. "I get the message. This will be my last gambling trip." He rubbed the wet spots off the window with his shirt sleeve.

"For your sake, it better be. Now get your sorry ass out of my sight. I need to decide what to do with Harmon."

As Wiggams exited the library, Kane checked his Palm Pilot and immediately jabbed into it a phone number in Las Vegas. Someone answered and, after a pause, Gino Barletta, the senior staff attorney for MGM Grand, came on the line. Kane explained his request.

"I'll do it, Mr. Kane, but when you reach that high political office I suspect you're aiming for, you can expect me to call in this marker."

"I'll consider it an honor, Mr. Barletta. Any way I can help you, any time, just give me a call."

Kane slipped his Pilot back into the center desk drawer and returned to his easy chair. The sun, now lower in the sky, hurt his eyes. Two long strides carried him to the window, where he yanked the burgundy damask drapes across the wide expanse of glass. He returned to his leather chair and sat quietly in the dim light.

ERIN DROVE SLOWLY around the last corner before her apartment. Things were working out better than she thought. She could hardly wait to tell Danielle about her meeting with Ginny.

She wouldn't have long to wait; Danielle was sitting on her front porch.

"How long have you been here?" Erin asked as she unfolded her long legs from the car.

"Not long. I didn't exactly wake up early."

"Oh? Late night?"

Danielle stifled a yawn. "Late, yes. Productive? Not very."

Erin unlocked the door and held it open for her friend. "What happened? Spill it."

"First, would you happen to have some coffee?"

"If instant will do."

"Fine." Danielle headed for the kitchen with Erin right behind her. "I'm a bit hung-over."

Erin flicked on the gas under her teakettle, spooned some freeze-dried into a mug. "Sweetener? Milk?"

"Black." Danielle held out her hand for the steaming mug. "Okay, what do you want to know?"

"Damn it, Dani, everything!"

Danielle carefully sipped the hot liquid. "Wiggams came on to me hot and heavy, just as we predicted. But I played it cool, let him have a feel here and there but held him off."

"Why? I thought we agreed. . ."

"Erin, you know I enjoy sex and don't much care whether my partner is male or female, but that little pervert gives me the creeps. I'll sleep with him if I have to. . . in the time-honored fashion of spies everywhere. . . but last night wasn't the time to start."

"Why not, if I may ask?"

"He refused to say much about Tristar. Every time I tried to pump him for info, he backed away. I wasn't about to reward him with sex when I wasn't getting what I wanted."

"He told you nothing?"

Danielle looked at Erin over the rim of her coffee mug. "The most significant tidbit I learned was that Harmon Dawes makes all the investment moves. Wiggams refers to him as 'The Wall Street Cherry Picker'."

"Did you at least leave him wanting more of you?"

"Oh, yeah. He's asked me to go to Vegas with him. . . next weekend."

"And you accepted."

"Yes, Erin, I did. Never been there. Could be fun. J.P. said he has to meet a banker from Boston. This could be where Tristar hides their funds."

"Good going. It might be the break we need. Maybe it's the disbursement arm that transmits monies back to Tristar."

"You're right. It could also be the issuing authority for the university CDs."

Erin held up her hand for a high five. Danielle slapped it with vigor.

"Dani, maybe you're not just a sex kitten after all. You've shown me a strong side of your personality that I have to say I admire. But now let me fill you in about my car ride home last night with the Dawes and today's lunch with Ginny," Erin related her stories, answering Danielle's questions as they popped up.

"She's on our team now. By the end of the week, we should have copies of everything in Professor Dawes' Tristar files."

"And when I get back from Vegas, we may have enough to call in the authorities."

"Things are really moving now, Dani. But we can't be too careful. The terrific trio could get nasty if they find out what we're doing."

THE SIGNAL FROM the front gate audio system made Kane jump. "Jesus, what now?" He switched on a light in the now dark room and pressed the intercom.

"Kane, it's Harmon Dawes. I need to see you."

"Now? Harmon, I've had a rough day, couldn't you. . ."

Dawes' voice was shrill. "Kane, let me in. It's important."

"All right. Come on up." He pushed the button to open the electric gate. He then pressed the intercom. Almost instantly, the butler opened the library door.

"Sir?"

"Escort Mr. Dawes to me here. I won't need you any further after that."

Minutes later, the butler bowed the visitor into the library. "I shall be leaving now, Mr. Kane." He backed out through the double doors, for the second time in one day closing them on Kane and a guest.

"Harmon, let me get you a drink. You look like death warmed over."

Dawes waved him off. "No drink. This is not a social call."

"Then why are you here? I thought you always reserved Sundays for your wife."

"You know damn well why I'm here."

"I can see you are upset, quite agitated about something. I can only assume you came to a friend for assistance. What's the problem, Harm?"

"Believe me, I've thought for hours before coming here. Hours just driving around.

Then sitting in my office, going over and over things in my mind. How could I be so stupid?"

"Stupid? You are anything but. . . ."

Dawes lunged toward Kane. "Damn it, you bastard, quit patronizing me. I know you have been sleeping with my wife."

Kane sidestepped the charging figure, let a light chuckle escape. "Oh, that. We have had a time or two together. . . certainly nothing of substance. She truly loves *you* very much." His eyes were like ice, daring Dawes to dispute him.

"Nothing of substance, my ass!! You have been seeing my wife for some time now. John Wiggams showed me all the dates and times she has been here. He did me a favor. He's a better friend than you'll ever be." Dawes flailed his arms in the air. "Why, Albert, why? Don't you have enough? You live in a mansion, you own half the real estate in town and you're sure to be elected a judge soon. Women throw themselves at you. Why did you need to have my Ginny?"

"Actually, Harmon, it was not my idea. Ginny was bored with you working almost 24/7 and simply wanted to fill some time. When she was with me, she always talked about you."

"I do not believe you for a moment. You are the coolest liar I've ever known. That's why you make such a good lawyer. . . and would have made an excellent judge."

Kane's head bucked. "What do you mean, 'would have'?"

"On the way over here, I was thinking. . . how would the voters feel if they knew about your sleeping with my wife? How would they vote if they knew about the skimming of funds from their university? It seems to me that I may have your future in my hands. Your greed, your ambition, your overweening ego are going to destroy you."

"Now hold on there, Professor, you are just as much a part of Tristar as I am. And as for your sexy and needy wife, I believe the public will understand that I was *her* victim, not the other way round."

"You're an egotistical maniac if you think you can tarnish both our reputations and still be elected judge. The community will never buy it."

"I see." Kane's eyes darted from his visitor to the draped window and back again. He leveled his gaze and carefully chose his words. "Maybe I was wrong, Harmon. What can I do to appease you? What is it you want from me?"

"First, I want you to apologize to Ginny in my presence. Second, remove all of those photos from John Wiggams' office and give them to me. And third, and most important, I want you to withdraw your name from the ballot this November."

"Whoa, Harmon, I slept with your wife, not your mother. The first two I will be glad to do, but I simply cannot withdraw from the race. That is out of the question."

"Your call, Albert. If you don't do them all, I will reveal everything. I have nothing to lose now."

Kane shook his head. "Harmon, I'll give you 10% of my 33% share in Tristar. You will have the controlling interest."

"No, no! You don't get it, do you, Albert. It's not the money. I gave you my terms. I want the answer now. I cannot go home tonight without knowing."

Kane tapped his fingers against his thighs. Finally, "Okay, Harmon, you win. I will apologize to Ginny at a time of your choosing. I will secure the documents from Wiggams' office for you and I will withdraw from the election before the October first deadline. Are you satisfied now?"

"For now, yes." Dawes got up, stalked out of the library and down the long hall. He let himself out. In a moment, the big Town Car growled to life and headed down the lane toward the gate.

Kane wagged his head back and forth. "Harmon, you give me no choice." Before Dawes had reached the road, Albert Kane was already in motion. He clicked his Palm Pilot and scrolled till he found the number for Johnny Portofino. He, unlike his Tristar partners, had always delivered for him.

When Johnny answered, Kane got right to the point. "Can you catch a flight out of Baton Rouge tomorrow?"

"Where to?"

"Here, Charlotte. Some things need your immediate attention."

"I'll phone you after I know my flight. With the time difference, I should be there by late afternoon. The usual place?"

"Right. Use my private number and say nothing more than the time you'll be at the meeting place."

Kane slammed the Pilot back into the drawer. What a day. Damn!

Johnny Portofino couldn't get here soon enough.

CHAPTER EIGHT

Six o'clock. Just those three syllables and nothing more, but Kane recognized the voice.

Now, he paced the meeting spot, a grassy dike guarding the Charlotte River, known as the River Commons. It was a remote area, never developed because of ordinances prohibiting building on a flood plain. He'd used this location before to meet people he would rather not be seen with. At 6:00 on a September evening, the fifty-year-old oaks and maples cast heavy shadows along the dike—heavy enough that Kane felt safe, incognito.

At 6:04 p.m. Kane could make out an imposing figure approaching from the south. He chuckled to himself. Portofino didn't dress like what he was. Every time they'd met, Johnny appeared in an Armani suit, cut carefully to show off his well muscled body. At 6'4", he was only slightly taller than Kane, but at 240 lbs., outweighed him by 50. His attache case couldn't be any thinner and still carry anything more than a couple sheets of paper. Or a couple hundred thousand in cash. Johnny Portofino appeared to be nothing more than a successful business man. In one respect, Kane supposed that was an apt description.

The distant figure strutted confidently toward one of several enclosed benches placed, a football field apart, for people to sit and observe the river. From the back and sides it was completely closed to anyone's view.

As the other man got closer, Kane observed that today's Armani was a gray pinstripe, double breasted. The black alligator loafers and dark silk shirt were equally impressive. Kane had to hand it to him; he wore his trademarks well.

Portofino lit a cigarette, flashing a heavy gold rope bracelet on his right wrist and a diamond bezel Rolex on his left. When he turned his shaved head toward him, Kane could see he still sported an enormous diamond stud earring in his left lobe.

Kane reached the bench first and, as he waited for Portofino to join him, felt a surge of adrenaline assault his stomach. "Right on time. I like that." He did not extend his hand.

Portofino's deep baritone rumbled in his chest. "We are both busy men." He dragged on his cigarette, flipped it toward the water. "What do you need?"

Kane sat and moved all the way to the back of the bench. He motioned for Portofino to do the same. "A man. . . Wiggams, by name. . . is involved with me in an investment operation. He's the comptroller at Madison University and point man for releasing funds to our investment firm."

Portofino focused his gaze on the river as he memorized those facts. "You're skimming or embezzling funds from the university?"

"Borrowing. Johnny, just borrowing."

"Is that the terminology these days?"

"Look, call it what you want. The important thing is that he has some files full of reports and photos that need to be removed from his possession."

"A little blackmail or extortion among friends, eh?"

"Let's just say I don't want him to have leverage on me."

Portofino lit another cigarette. "I understand. Where are the files?"

"In his office at the university, but he may have back-ups at home. He likes to cover his ass, so I wouldn't doubt it."

"And you want me to lift everything from both locations?"

"Yes. I don't care how you accomplish the university snatch; however, his apartment is to appear like a break in. To make it look like a burglary, take some valuables along with the documents. It will steer his thoughts far from me."

"Consider it done, counselor. What about the timing?"

"He's leaving town around noon Friday on a Vegas trip. He won't be back until Sunday evening. Anytime in between will be fine."

"Understood. But this is something you could have done with your other contacts. Why did you really call me?"

"Some problems with another partner as well."

Portofino snorted. "Sounds like a real dogs' breakfast here."

"I know. They are academic types, full of all that ivory tower bullshit. Christ, I slept with the wife of a professor who now demands that I drop out of the judgeship race so his wounds can be healed. The jerk rakes in $750,000 a year from this scam and he wants to throw it away to prove his wife is not a whore."

The out-of-towner exhaled smoke in perfectly formed rings. "This job sounds a little more complicated."

"That's why you're here, Johnny. I wanted the best. . . no trace, no trail."

"I take pride in my work, counselor."

"That I know, John, that I know."

"What do we do with the professor?"

"We need to lift everything possible from his house. He makes all the investment moves from there. Make sure you get everything. He is a very thorough man, so I suspect he'll have hard and soft copies."

"Will he be out of town also?"

Kane shook his head. "No, but I want it done over the weekend."

"Yeah, why not. I'm here. When will his house be empty?"

"It won't be."

"I see. Now I know why I'm here. We get rid of the files. . . and the professor too, right?"

Kane clasped his hands between his knees and stared at the swiftly flowing current. "I've made arrangements for his wife to meet with a friend of mine on Saturday afternoon for lunch.. . the chairperson of the Alfred Petrini Health Foundation."

"Alfred Petrini from the New York waste management family?"

"The same. We are building the Petrini Health Center here on campus right now. I twisted Alfred's arm to make some major donations; ergo the naming of the center. His daughter is in town to meet with architects, as she does from time to time."

"What time is lunch for the girls??

"1:00 p.m., but I'll make sure it lasts till 3:00. That should give you plenty of time."

"No problem. Have you identified a depository yet?"

Kane described the place.

Portofino murmured his approval. "Very good, counselor. Sure you don't want to change professions?"

"The professor and his wife had a major argument over my fucking her. I want this to look like he left her. Remove all his personal items, even his clothes."

"I get the picture."

"No mess. It needs to appear that he left on his own accord. Take his golf clubs and lose the car. Make it clean, no trail, no nothing."

"That's why they pay me the big bucks, C. Albert, speaking of which, we have not yet priced this project."

"You get what you pay for, I always say, and I always go with top quality. Name your price."

"The standard 100K per person fee still applies. However, because of the car disposal, I'll need to bring in an associate. The professor plus two break-ins and a car disposal will cost you $250,000."

Now Kane offered his hand. "Deal."

Portofino took it, crushing Kane's pinky finger against his diamond ring. "Clean cash."

The men headed in opposite directions. Once Portofino delivered him all the documents, Kane figured, his exposure would be eliminated. Until the election was over, he would let Tristar Investment Inc. stand in place.

ERIN SAT HUNCHED over her kitchen table marking papers to return to her Friday students. When would she ever learn, she wondered, to schedule her time better, so she wouldn't have to play catch up every Thursday night?

The ringing phone made her jump. Only Danielle ever called her when she was in the middle of something. "Yes, I know, you got three new outfits and are ready to travel."

"Actually I haven't been out of the house, but it sounds like someone has."

"I'm sorry, I was expecting somebody else."

"Quite all right. It's Ginny."

"My goodness, I didn't recognize your voice on the phone. I'm sorry again."

"Don't be silly. I just wanted to tell you that I think I have everything for tomorrow. Thanks to Harmon's propensity for organization, all the Tristar material was relatively easy to locate and copy. Most of the records were on disks, which I copied, while others were in files and ledgers. I copied those too."

"That's great, Ginny, good job!"

"Thanks. The only problem is that the pile is quite large and I wasn't sure if you wanted me to walk into the club with everything."

"No, I don't. Leave it in the trunk of your car. If you get there early, I can try to park next to you. We can do the transfer after lunch."

"I'm glad I called. I knew you would know how to handle this."

"Were you able to accumulate everything without Professor Dawes becoming suspicious?"

"Yes. It was rather easy. He has been very busy at the university and has not been getting home until around eight every night."

"Have you had any discussion with him regarding the Kane issue?"

"I have not brought it up and neither has he."

Erin put on her most sympathetic voice. "Must be able to cut the air with a spoon over there."

"It hasn't been much fun, but I'm doing what you said and playing everything very low key. It's only. . ."

"Only what, Ginny?"

"All the time I was going through his things, I couldn't stop crying. I feel guilty enough for my affair with Albert, and now I feel even worse about . . . spying on my Harmon."

"No, Ginny, it's not spying. You're not gathering information to expose him but to get him back. And get even with Kane, don't forget."

"I know that's what you said, but, Erin, I don't understand how. . ."

"Ginny, calm down. I'll tell you my plan . . . when the time is right." Erin decided maybe a change of subject would get her to stop thinking she'd betrayed her husband. "Are you sleeping together again?"

"No, we're still in separate rooms. And I hate it."

"Perhaps we can talk about it more tomorrow at lunch."

"I would like that, Erin. I feel so helpless."

"You are anything but, Ginny. And I'll prove it to you. . . just be patient."

Erin finished entering into the computer grades on this week's student papers and emailed them to the department head. Dawes. Poor Ginny was so desperate to win back her husband that she'd jump at any chance. Erin had counted on that. . . and won. She would have to keep stringing Ginny along till she somehow did come up with the plan she'd promised.

The phone rang again. This time it had to be Danielle.

"Erin, guess what?"

"You bought some clothes."

"Yeah, how did you know?"

"Women's intuition. Danielle, you're always buying clothes and with the trip to Vegas tomorrow I didn't have to be Einstein to figure it out."

"Am I that predictable?"

"Sometimes, but not very often, my dear."

"Now I feel better. Are you still going to have lunch with Ginny Dawes at the club tomorrow?"

"Yes, in fact I spoke with her right before you called."

"Wow, you're really getting chummy with Mrs. Dawes, eh?"

"Offering a shoulder to cry on, that's all. I told you about it last Sunday."

"I guess she is pretty broken up. Still, the way you are able to manipulate situations to your advantage amazes me."

"It's called seizing the opportunity, Dani, that's all. When you grow up poor, it's something you learn very early in life."

"So how's she going to help us?"

"Tomorrow, when we have lunch, she'll deliver to me all her husband's private files on Tristar. She has been copying disks and ledgers all week."

"Wow! Nice going, Erin. You're so calm about it. This is great!"

"The only missing part may be the banking connection, and I'm hopeful you'll be able to close that loop with information you get in Vegas."

"You sure know how to motivate people. If I don't get it, I'm going to feel like a failure."

"You'll do just fine. I know you'll come through for us."

"I am really jazzed now. No matter what I have to do to get the missing pieces, I'm up for it. Even if I have to bang Wiggams *and* the banker. It wouldn't be the first time a woman exchanged sex for information." Danielle laughed. "Pardon my sarcasm. I assure you, Erin, I will come home with the goods. Tired, bowlegged and sore, but with the goods."

"As I have always said, you certainly have a way with words. What time do you leave?"

"11:45 a.m."

"Have a great trip, Dani, and be careful. I'll see you Monday."

DANIELLE SLEPT WELL and, after breakfast, readied herself and left for the airport. Wiggams had offered to pick her up, but she didn't have a clue how this trip would go and wanted her own car waiting at the airport when they got back.

She arrived on time and headed for the U.S. Airways departure terminal. Wiggams was waiting for her. They checked their luggage and headed for the gate to await boarding.

"You're a bundle of gloom this morning," Danielle said.

"Sorry. Not a morning person."

The gate agent called the flight. Without another word, they joined the queue and inched their way toward the jetway, then onto the aircraft and down the narrow aisle, Wiggams leading the way.

"You know, John," Danielle said to his back, "it's okay if you have second thoughts about taking me on this trip. If that's what's bothering you."

His head snapped around. "Nothing's bothering me. Why?"

"Something else must be on your mind, because you have said not one word about my outfit. And I worked hard to make sure you'd like it."

"Is that all? Well hell, let me get a good look at you." He squeezed into his seat then turned to ogle her, not missing a thing. "Okay, honey, let's get this weekend off to a good start." Ignoring the glares from others waiting behind Danielle, Wiggams moved back into the aisle, pulled her to him and kissed her passionately.

"Welcome aboard, Sweetheart; I hope you enjoy your weekend."

"Now I feel better. For a while there I was thinking you may be human."

During the remainder of the flight, they passed the time pleasantly. They discussed restaurants to try, what show to see. Cirque de Soleil was Danielle's first choice; Wiggams voted for Wayne Newton. In the window seat, Wiggams watched the ground pass beneath them, occasionally pointing to sights he'd come to recognize on his numerous trips.

Danielle read, dozed, from time to time leaned over to see whatever her companion wanted her to admire. She casually allowed her breasts to graze his arm. She accepted a few kisses and when he ran his hand up her thigh, she didn't object. Keep him off balance, sexually stimulated, she reminded herself. When the blood's down there, it wasn't feeding his brain.

"You sure you're okay, John?"

"Yeah, why?"

"You seem preoccupied, as if something's on your mind."

Wiggams waved his hand. "Oh, it's nothing. Just got some information before we left that could cause some problems for me."

"Anything I can do to help?"

"Yeah," Wiggams squeezed her hand, "next time, leave your bra home."

"Can't you ever be serious? I was being genuine with you."

"I know, but I don't think you can help on this one."

She laid on the leer again. "You might be surprised what I can do."

"Hmph. I haven't met anyone yet who can control Albert Kane. Except your friend Erin. . . that night of the party. . . she was great."

"I have to agree. She put that arrogant ass in his place, didn't she?"

"I thought I would piss my pants watching her work him over. No one does that to Kane, no one. He is probably plotting to get even with her as we speak."

"He's the reason for your anxiety?"

"He had me squeezed on something. He pressed me until I gave him what he wanted. That's how Kane is."

"What did he want?"

"Oh, Harmon Dawes was all upset when he found out that Kane was screwing his wife. Kane called me in and wanted to know how he found out. I had to tell him it was through me. He got real mad."

"Really. How did you know about their affair?"

"Let's just say I have friends who keep me informed of things."

"Why was it necessary to tell Professor Dawes about his wife's affair? I don't understand that."

"It's a long story and we're not going into it now. Besides I've already told you too much."

"What can Kane do? You are the comptroller, tell him to go to hell."

"Danielle, believe me, you don't just tell Albert Kane to do that."

"Why not? Because he has money?"

"No, because he is connected."

"I don't get you. Connected to what?"

"To everything, everybody, everywhere. In fact, tell your friend to be careful. She really took him on the other night and Kane won't forget it."

That hit her like a blow to the belly, but she didn't show it. "Do you mean she's in danger?"

"Look, Danielle, let's just say it would be wise for Erin Gallagher to avoid future confrontations with C. Albert Kane."

"But she's my friend, I . . ."

"Enough. I don't want to talk about it. Let's just have some fun in Vegas." Wiggams winked and squeezed her thigh again.

The plane touched down on time. They collected their baggage and caught a cab to the MGM Grand.

The famed hotel-casino was immense, "grand" indeed. Danielle had to will herself to keep her mouth shut; it kept dropping open at every turn. They walked through the huge casino with its flashing lights, the clang of coins cascading into payoff trays, the occasional whoop of a winner at the craps table. She was stunned to see live lions sleeping in the sun within a glass enclosure. "Which one is the MGM logo lion?" she asked Wiggams. He merely shook his head and pulled her closer as they strolled.

"I booked us into adjoining suites. Just in case the university ever wants to be sure we were in separate rooms."

"The university? Why would they want to know?"

Wiggams shrugged. "You know how auditors can be."

"Don't tell me you wrote this up as a university expense?"

"Why not? An intern in my department and I are attending a conference on 'How to Reduce College Administrative Costs'."

"You have to be kidding."

"No, it really is being held here. I thought we could register and pick up a brochure or two. CYA. That way, the university will pay."

"Erin's right. You bastards are all cheap."

"What?"

"Nothing."

They completed registration and headed upstairs. In the elevator Wiggams played more grab-ass games but quit if someone else boarded. As they walked down the corridor to their respective suites, they agreed on a time to meet for dinner. But first, Danielle needed a shower and a chance to phone Erin.

She unlocked her door and her mouth dropped open. Her suite beat anything she'd ever seen in a movie. Its size and opulent decor nearly overwhelmed her. She was equally amazed by the sight of the famous "strip" rolling to the horizon from her 15th floor window. Wiggams must have gone all out with the university funds, she thought.

She walked about to revel in the beauty of her surroundings. The suite was done in hues of burgundy, cream and green. The focal point of the massive bedroom was an oversized canopy bed. The other room of the suite featured a sitting area, bar set ups, entertainment center, computer and a fireplace. It was 98 degrees outside and she had a fireplace? That wasn't all. She opened a door to discover a closet big enough to call a room.

The lavish bath was even more impressive with a giant, heart-shaped Jacuzzi tub, bidet, walk-in shower, triple bowl sinks, a television and two telephones—one next to the tub, the other reachable from the commode. Why all the phones? she wondered. To place bets? Call room service? Summon paramedics when a guest realized how much money he'd dropped?

A knock on the door disturbed her inventory. As she crossed the living room to answer, she noticed the sound had come from what apparently was the adjoining suite. She stopped and opened her side. There he was in all his splendor, stark naked, a red ribbon tied around his proud erection and a bottle of champagne in his hand. She could not help but burst out laughing. In his own way, Wiggams was sometimes very funny.

"What's the matter, you don't like Dom Perignon?"

She waggled her head. "No John, I love it, it's the red ribbon. . ."

"I thought you'd like that most of all. I had the maid tie it so nice for you."

"I'm just wondering which cork you're going to pop first."

"Truthfully, I thought you would be just coming out of the shower. You haven't even been there, have you?"

"No. I've been taking in this showcase of a suite."

"Do you like it?"

"You better believe I do. It's gorgeous. I could definitely get used to living like this."

"I thought you might want to take a shower together."

"You never stop, do you?"

"Not with you, baby."

Danielle wasn't ready yet. Think of something to stall him, she told herself. "You lie there on the bed and get started, I'll freshen up and be right in."

"I'll be waiting."

Danielle closed the adjoining door and went into the bathroom. A glance at her watch told her it was 5:00 back home. She wondered if Ginny had delivered the professor's files to Erin as planned. She undressed and ran the water so Wiggams couldn't hear her making a call.

As soon as Erin answered, Danielle launched into conversation. "I am sitting stark naked on a commode in the most luxurious suite you have ever seen. And that pervert is waiting on the bed and. . . get this. . . with a bottle of Dom Perignon in one hand and a red ribbon tied around his pecker, which about now, is in the other hand."

"How in the world did you get in this predicament already? You must have arrived just a few minutes ago."

"It's Wiggams. Need I say more?"

"No, so what's the urgency? Need a pep talk so you won't chicken out?"

"Not really. I know what I have to do. But I have a couple of things on my mind. First, I wanted to know how you made out with Ginny at lunch today."

"She did a great job. We have all of Professor Dawes' files and ledgers, including some disks she copied for us."

"Fantastic work, Erin. Have you looked at anything yet?"

"I haven't been home very long, but I can tell you he was very well organized so I shouldn't have too much trouble finding the evidence we need. Ginny and I had a long talk. I'll fill you in when you get back. What was the other thing on your mind?"

"Something that came up in our conversation on the plane. He cautioned me about Albert Kane, said he was connected to 'everything, everybody, everywhere.' Said for you to stay away from him, especially after the way you embarrassed him at the party. He said he is probably plotting to get even right now. I got a little worried and just wanted to tell you."

"Thanks, Danielle, but I had him pegged from the beginning as the real heavy in this, and after what Ginny told me at lunch, I certainly have no doubt."

"Be careful, Erin. I have to go now."

"You too. Don't forget the banker; he is key. No one seems to have a lead on him at all."

Danielle hurried to the shower, quickly washed everything but her hair, sprayed herself amply with the hotel's finest perfume and walked into Wiggams' bedroom wrapped in a towel. There he was, lying on the bed, prepared to the hilt.

"Now before we start, John, I need to ask you for a favor."

"A favor? What the hell you mean, a favor?"

"You remember telling me about the banker you have a meeting with?"

"Yeah, it's tomorrow morning. What about it?"

"You know how you had this thing about doing the Deputy Director's daughter?"

"I remember telling you that, Miss Deputy Director's Daughter. What of it?"

"I have my own fantasy. I've always had a desire to boff a blue-blooded, stuffed shirt, holier-than-thou banker."

Wiggams pulled off his glasses and set them on the bedside table. "Come here, honey. Let's talk turkey." He patted the bed. "You can't boff my banker. I'll find you another one, but this banker is off limits. However, when it comes to boffing, I am definitely RWA. . . ready, willing and able."

Danielle backed away from the bed. "Yeah, I can see that. But. . ."

"What do you mean 'but'?"

"Remember the favor I asked for?"

"Yes, but I can't give you that, Danielle."

"Why not, John? He's just a banker."

Wiggams put his glasses back on. He peered at Danielle before he answered. "Why are you bustin' my balls on this? I can't. Kane would kill me."

She sat down in a plush chair across the room from the bed and crossed her legs, letting the towel open just enough. "What does he have to do with it? I thought the banker had something to do with the university."

"He does."

"Aren't we here on university business?"

"Yes, but he acts in other capacities for Kane and me."

She stood up and let the towel slip to the floor. "Just forget it, John. We'll simply have a platonic weekend."

She turned her back to him and bent over to pick up the towel. With her legs spread slightly and her head bent towards the floor, she peeked back through them with a smile that she knew even Kane's influence could not control.

"Oooooh my, you win."

"Thank you, John, I thought you would see it my way."

"Please come over here now. The ribbon just broke."

AT THEIR FRIDAY luncheon, Erin and Ginny had tried hard to talk about other matters, but the subject kept returning to Ginny's predicament with her husband. "He refuses to accept my apology, Erin, and God knows I've never been more sorry about anything in my life."

"I wish I could somehow make you not worry. I really do believe he still loves you."

"I think so too, but he's so hurt. He even confronted Albert to defend my honor."

Erin's eyes widened. "He did what?"

"Yes, he told me he visited Kane last Sunday and took care of the situation. But I know Harm could never *take care of* Kane. My husband, as you know, is a gentle, loving, kind soul. Nothing like Albert, who is cold and calculating. He can be ruthless."

"I couldn't agree more, Ginny. If anyone is going to take care of anyone else, my money's on C. Albert Kane as the bad guy."

"That's what worries me so much. All Harmon would say is that Kane would presently offer me an apology. That doesn't sound like him at all. I think he just told Harm that to placate him and he has no such intention."

Erin found herself holding Ginny's hand. "Kane is a snake. How in the world did you ever get mixed. . . Ginny, forgive me. That's water under the bridge, and I know you will never do such a thing again."

"I sure learned my lesson. I've hurt my husband, who has never done anything to deserve such treatment. If Albert hurts him any further, I'll. . . I'll. . ."

"Don't say any more. We're not going to let Kane destroy your marriage. You let me analyze the information waiting for me in your car, and we'll make things right."

"Oh, Erin, I surely do hope so. But I'm so scared."

Me too, thought Erin, but she only nodded and continued to pat Ginny's trembling hand.

ONCE BACK AT her apartment, Erin spread all Dawes' investment files across the living room floor. *He's so organized, so detail* oriented, Erin thought, that it would be a piece of cake to follow the trail. She moved her laptop computer to the living room and slipped in the disks Ginny had copied. Amazing. Everything was there. Soon she had discovered lists of stocks, futures, puts, calls and money markets, each transaction recorded and filed by date.

Examination of all the hard copy stock transactions divulged each one was marked "confirmed by dsj." At least, that's what it looked like. But could it be DLJ Direct, the large New York brokerage firm? Was Dawes' "s" really an "L"? She doodled those initials several times on a blank paper to see if this were possible. It was, she decided, but it wasn't likely. She'd just have to figure out what that meant. Perhaps this mystery would be solved once she located a confirmation file showing account numbers, tax IDs, trade dates, quantity and price.

She shuffled through the well organized piles but couldn't find what she knew Dawes would compile. Maybe she'd locate it on one of the disks.

She was only just starting her digging when Danielle called from Vegas and warned her about Kane's connections. When she hung up the phone and returned to the files, her stomach churned with foreboding.

JOHNNY PORTOFINO, CLAD now in polo shirt and khakis—the Armani was stashed in the closet in case he had to meet Kane again—met his associate at the airport late Friday morning. He drove his rental car to the motel where he was staying, the La Quinta on South Tyron.

"Why here, Johnny? I figured you'd stay closer to the airport."

"This one suits me fine. It has a pool and exercise room so I can work out every day. Good breakfast every morning." He pulled into a parking spot and stopped the car. "It's low key, catering mostly to tourists, guys here for the races. We can blend in. I booked us two rooms, side by side. We can each watch whatever TV we like."

"Yeah, that's why I came all the way from Chicago—to watch television."

Johnny let out a snicker. "Benny, don't knock it. I get some of my best ideas from those crime shows on TV. Now grab your duffel bag and let's get upstairs. We have work to do."

Once inside his room, Benny flicked on the TV and settled into the sofa to channel surf. In the adjoining room, Portofino sat at the desk and scanned the Yellow Pages. He ripped out the listings he needed. He pounded on Benny's door. "Let's go."

Benny groaned and shuffled to the door. "Aw, I was just getting interested in this show."

"What I'm interested in right now is our project for tomorrow." He held the door open. "You coming?" he said, his deep rumble full of sarcasm.

The two men drove the town, checking out addresses on the yellow page. At the fifth one, Portofino slapped his hand on the steering wheel. "This is it. Karpet Kleen. No entry gate, their trucks are parked behind the building. And we got really lucky, 'cause there's a dry cleaners next door."

Benny looked puzzled but grinned agreement after Portofino explained.

To pick up other necessities on Portofino's list, they made a few more stops: a drug store, Office Depot, then, nearby, Home Depot. At 4:50, Benny walked into the dry cleaners and punched the bell to summon a clerk from the rear. "I gotta have them Karpet Kleen uniforms," he yelled toward the back.

A skinny teenager with unfortunate skin came through swinging half-doors. "Now? They usually don't get picked up till Monday. I'm not sure they're done."

Benny shuffled his feet. "Boss's making half the guys work tomorrow—big office building—so we gotta have clean uniforms. Make a good impression, ya know."

The girl hustled to the rear and returned bearing three uniforms. "This is all we have right now. "

"I'll take 'em. Try to finish up first thing in the morning, will ya? I'll tell the boss to send someone else in for the others." He signed the charge ticket and slung the uniforms over his arm.

Back at Portofino's car, Benny carefully laid the uniforms on the back seat before sliding into the front. "Worked just like you said."

"Of course. I leave nothing to chance. We will now look very professional when we show up tomorrow to clean carpets at the home of Professor Harmon Dawes.

CHAPTER NINE

I t was cook's day off, so Ginny put on a happy face as she made Harmon's favorite Saturday breakfast. Hot cakes, country sausage, scrambled eggs with a touch of sharp cheddar and her secret ingredient: Tabasco. She moved from counter to stove to fridge, cutting through the silence that stuffed the room like the sausage sizzling in the pan. It had been close to a week since Harmon had flung more than two words in her direction. She had to break through that awful barrier.

"Harm, you remember me telling you I'm having lunch today at the Uptown Club?"

"No." His head remained behind the newspaper.

"I've been asked to chair a fund-raising committee."

"More of Kane's gratitude?" he grumbled. He turned the page.

Ah, four words. Progress. "No, Catherine Petrini herself asked me."

Harm snickered into his coffee mug. "Who do you think pulls her strings?"

"Now, Harm, don't you go getting jealous because I'm finally getting some recognition at the university."

"It's not jealousy, believe me. It's reality. I know how the real world works."

She leaned over her husband's shoulder to set his breakfast plate on the place mat. "I'm having lunch with Catherine at one o'clock. I'll just ask her about how I was selected." She let her breast brush his ear.

Dawes ignored Ginny's effort to titillate him and forked egg into his mouth, then spoke around it. "You do that."

SATURDAY MORNING CAME too quickly for Danielle. With one eye open, she looked at the clock 9:43. What time had she got to sleep? It must have been after 2:30. But she had to force herself to rise and shine. That was a laugh. Oh, how she wished she had enough time to enjoy a long soak in the Jacuzzi. She'd have to settle for a quick shower.

She felt like an Arkansas hog.

As she hurriedly dried herself, she reached for the phone on the bathroom mirror and dialed the adjoining suite. The voice on the other end merely grunted.

"Get up, you sleepyhead. Do you know what time it is?"

He mumbled something unintelligible.

"It's 10:20, John, so you better move that ass like you did last night."

"Oh shit, I gotta go."

She smiled and hung up the phone. The horny little pervert sounded worn out.

She finished her make up, slid into a pair of beige slacks with pleated front, a slightly sheer white blouse and a navy blue blazer—appropriate attire for meeting the banker. She figured she could take off the blazer if it became necessary to display more of her figure.

Thirty-five minutes later, Wiggams rushed through the adjoining door. "Are you ready?"

"Yep, let's do it."

Wiggams opened the door to the hall and flipped the "Do Not Disturb" knob hanger to the "Please Make Up Room" side. Once in the elevator, he took Danielle's hand. "Now when we're with the banker, I don't want you to say much."

"About what?"

"Anything."

As they entered the restaurant, Wiggams panned the dining area. A hand waved from a table near the rear. He returned the wave and pointed the hostess in that direction.

Danielle, leading the way with Wiggams' hand in the small of her back, appraised the man already seated. She felt a strong jolt of recognition but couldn't place how or where she'd met the banker. His cold stare nailed Wiggams. Obviously, she thought, he's not thrilled about someone else joining them for brunch.

Wiggams stared down the banker until he blinked and turned his gaze toward Danielle.

He held her chair, scooted it in. "Glad to see you, David. Let me introduce Danielle Baldwin. She's an accounting intern at Madison, attending a conference out here with me."

The banker rose slightly, regained his stuffed-shirt demeanor and held out his hand. "Miss Baldwin, how very nice to meet you. John didn't tell me there would be three, so please forgive my casual appearance."

His salt-and-pepper hair and tall athletic build made him seem like he belonged in a business suit rather than the flowered shirt and khaki shorts he wore. Danielle knew she'd seen this distinguished looking man somewhere. But where? Although Wiggams had used her last name during the introduction he had avoided using David's. "That's quite all right;" Danielle said, "my presence is kind of like a roulette wheel. . . .. John didn't know until the ball stopped rolling."

"I see. I think."

The waitress greeted them as if they were long-lost cousins and asked what they wanted to drink. Wiggams ordered a Bloody Mary, David a Presbyterian, and Danielle a Mimosa.

"Are you staying here at the MGM Grand?" Danielle leaned toward David, waited for an answer.

"It's quite a place, isn't it? I'm in 1534, just down the hall from John's room. What do you think of Vegas?"

Danielle glanced at Wiggams before answering. "I haven't seen much of it yet, but so far what I've seen is pretty awesome."

"You're here for a seminar? When is it?"

"Later today, at one o'clock."

The waitress appeared with their lunch orders. Danielle buttered a slice of toast and looked from Wiggams to David and back again.

David looked over at Wiggams then back to her. "Perhaps when you're finished, I could show you around if you'd like."

"You mean after lunch?"

"No, I meant the seminar. I had in mind that we could get better acquainted later this afternoon."

Wiggams almost came off his seat. "David, don't forget you and I need some time together."

"Yes, John, we do. What time are you leaving on Sunday?"

"Our flight is at 3:30."

"Maybe Miss Baldwin can arrange a spa treatment in the morning while you and I take care of our business. We should be able to get everything done by 1:30, giving you plenty of time to get to the airport. That leaves this afternoon open, after the seminar, I mean."

"Does Miss Baldwin have any say in this?" Danielle asked. "I'd rather play the tables today, David, instead of taking in the sights of Vegas." She shrugged out of her blazer, Wiggams reaching over to help her. "Mr. Wiggams has volunteered to show me how to play craps, blackjack and roulette. It sounds too exciting to pass up." As she hung the blazer over the chair back, she made sure David got a good look at her shapely torso.

"I understand the attraction this place offers a young woman," David said to Danielle's breasts.

The discussion had taken them through lunch and as Danielle was finishing the last of her tuna salad, Wiggams plunked his napkin on the table and stood up. "Danielle, it's time for us to venture over to the conference."

"Already? I was just getting comfortable." Danielle smiled at David then twisted around to grab her blazer. She made sure David got an eye full.

It was quite obvious that they were leaving because Wiggams was uncomfortable with her being around David.

"You two go ahead, brunch is on me," he said.

Outside the restaurant, Danielle punched Wiggams' arm with her fist. "Why'd you hurry us out of there? I no sooner took my jacket off than you made me put it back on and leave."

Wiggams hurried on, silent.

"Was it something I said?"

The man turned and stopped so fast that Danielle nearly ran him over. "I told you not to say anything and you just babbled on about learning to gamble, attending the seminar and God only knows what else."

"So I was making small talk. Big deal. What's wrong with that?"

"I didn't bring you here to flirt with my banker. Oh, . . . just leave it alone." He motioned away from the elevators toward the stairs. "It's only one floor up. Let's walk."

As she followed Wiggams up the stairs to a row of conference rooms on the hotel's mezzanine level, Danielle gave herself a symbolic pat on the back. She'd got him going, she realized. This was going to be fun.

After registering and retrieving a few brochures, Wiggams jerked his thumb toward the staircase. "Okay, we've done the conference. Let's go."

"Where? We just got here. We didn't even go in. What the hell's wrong with you?"

"I have some matters to take care of. I guess my mind is on that."

Wiggams leaned against the wall and whisked off his glasses. He yanked out a handkerchief and briskly rubbed them spotless. He needed time to pay his $300,000 debt, praying that Kane was able to deal off the other 200 grand. He wanted very much to gamble while he was here but knew he couldn't. He'd be watched, it would be reported to Kane and his ass would be in a sling in two minutes. Better not take the chance.

He replaced his glasses and lifted one lip in a smirk. "Think you can manage on your own for a while?"

So much for promising to teach me to gamble, Danielle thought. He's such a weasel. "You bet. In this town, it shouldn't be hard to find a couple hundred things to do."

"I'll call you around seven; maybe we can get a bite to eat."

"Right. I'll try to be back in my room by then." She'd be damned if she'd let him see disappointment. "See ya."

She headed up to her suite to decide how to spend the afternoon. As she got off at the 15th floor and walked the corridor, she passed 1534. Only three suites down, just as David had said.

David. David who? Where had she seen him? She was certain she had met him somewhere but continued to be puzzled by the banker's familiarity. Maybe he was an actor she saw in a movie. Or doing a commercial. Familiar but unknown. Eventually it would come to her.

Tuckered out from the night before, she entered her suite, kicked off her shoes and sprawled on the bed. That damn Wiggams had the sexual appetite of a twenty-year-old. He wouldn't let her quit until they'd tried every position she'd ever known. She really was exhausted.

The ringing phone jolted her out of sleep. At first, it seemed a part of her dream; then she realized the sound was real and quickly reached over to answer. The clock's digital readout flipped to 5:00.

"Am I disturbing you, Miss Baldwin?"

"Is that you, David? I must have dozed off. I came back from the conference and lay down for a minute. And the minute became three hours."

"You should be well rested then. By the way, don't think it's strange to sleep during the day here in Vegas. Day and night mean nothing here. Have you noticed there are no clocks in the casinos? That's by design, and gambling goes on 24 hours a day."

"Is that what you called to tell me?"

A warm laugh. "My stomach knows when it's time to eat, even if there are no clocks around. I thought you might like to have dinner with me. I am quite aware of how much John likes to gamble, so figured he'd leave you on your own for several hours."

Danielle sat up, her interest renewed. "Dinner would be nice. Why don't you stop here for a cocktail first. What's the dress code where we're going?"

"Jackets required for men, if that'll help you decide. Can you be ready by six?"

"Sure. See you then."

She recradled the phone and jumped up. Ha! The blouse at brunch had worked. She had learned from Erin about men and their egos. This could be her only opportunity to extract information from the banker. Had to make the most of it.

For the next hour she primped and dressed for what she hoped would be an adventurous evening. And educational. She was determined to get the goods on Tristar. And the terrific trio.

When the knock came, she opened the door to admit the tall, distinguished man with salt-and-pepper hair. Her mind raced backward to the Hyatt hotel's valet parking. . . she and Erin discussing the cars in front of them when Gayle St. James got out of the black Mercedes, accompanied by. . . . She almost staggered backward with the memory. The man at her door was David St. James. Tristar's banker from Boston was the brother of Madison University's president.

SATURDAY MORNING HAD started well for Johnny Portofino and his colleague Benny. One of the three Karpet Kleen uniforms fit Benny perfectly. Portofino's bulging muscles created a bit of a problem, but he managed to squeeze into one of the zippered blue coveralls, the second one he tried on. "Sure glad you picked up three, Benny. Stroke of good luck, that."

In the pre-dawn gloom, the two drove across town toward Karpet Kleen. Portofino parked in a vacant lot a block down the street from the warehouse, unfolded his huge body from the rental car and headed for the trunk. "Don't know why rentals never have trunk latch releases," he muttered as he inserted and twisted the key. "Get a truck and drive it here."

Benny headed straight for one of the cleaning company's large vans. Operating like a surgeon, he slipped a narrow blade into the door lock and wiggled it until the lock tripped. He stepped up into the cab, dug around under the dash and hot-wired the engine. It roared to life. He shoved the gear shift into reverse, let out the clutch and backed out the drive and down the street to the vacant lot. Johnny was ready and transferred the items they'd need later.

In five minutes, they were out of there and headed toward the comptroller's empty apartment.

By the time they crossed town to Wiggams' building, the sun had come up. Benny switched off the headlights as he pulled into a parking space at the rear of the impressive complex, near the service entrance. Seconds later, they rolled up the rear truck door and Benny hopped up into the van and handed two large boxes down to Portofino. He eased an equipment dolly onto the ground, jumped and pulled the door down with him.

A flutter of breeze carried the sound of a dog barking. Benny jumped. "Christ, what was that?"

"Why are you so jumpy? You've pulled capers much more serious than this one. Someone's out walking a dog. . . at least a block away. Now get busy on opening that service door. . . before someone sees us. Here. . . put these on." Portofino handed Benny a pair of latex gloves, pulled another pair onto his own hands.

Moments later, they entered the elevator that whisked them to the penthouse floor. They arrived at Wiggams' door without being seen. Probably too early for the kind of people living in this building to be up and about, reasoned Johnny. Benny with his trusty lock picks was hard at work and they were in in no time.

Benny flipped the light switch and let out a long whistle. "Would you look at this fuckin' place."

Johnny Portofino ran his hand along the polished smoothness of an 18th century hardwood armoire. "Exquisite. This fucker's got good taste." He moved to a table and clicked on a lamp. "Ah, lovely, lovely."

"Jesus, don't get into your poetic mode, Johnny. You know I aint got no use for that. Let's just do what we came here for."

Portofino strode down the hall, calling back, "Here's the study. Come on in."

In thirty minutes, the two had filled one of the cardboard boxes with investment files. Certain they'd found everything stored in the den, they headed toward the bedroom to look for more. They found a few additional folders piled on the bedside table and stuffed them into the box.

"Johnny, are you getting a load of this place?" Benny's voice sounded awestruck.

Portofino whirled around so he could take in the entire room. "It's a fucking work of art. I really think he's a porno film producer."

Above the king size poster bed, a mirrored tray ceiling reflected the room's decor. Wall speakers, cleverly disguised as matted and framed artwork, marched across the wall behind the headboard. More speakers were strategically positioned in the other three walls.

Johnny leaned over to examine gold medallions embossed on the headboard. "What the hell are these?" He pressed one gold button, expecting to hear music throbbing with wanton rhythms. Instead, the bed began to vibrate. "I'll be damned." He punched another button, and out of the night stand swung a bar stocked with nothing but top shelf liquors and crystal cocktail glasses.

"Where's the god damn music?" Benny wanted to know. "It's gotta be here somewhere."

Portofino knuckled another button. Strains of Vivaldi filled the room. "Found it. But I'd choose something with a faster beat."

"Maybe he's older and fuckin' to a fast beat would kill him." Benny roared at his own joke.

"What's this? What's this?" Johnny hauled stuff out of the night stand. . . vibrators, dildos in graduated sizes, lubricants flavored and unflavored, blindfolds, handcuffs.

Benny sniffed a jar of lubricant, flicked some onto his finger, put it to his lips. "Strawberry. Your right the guy's runnin' a god damn porno shop."

Portofino looked around. "Let's search for cameras. He has everything else, I suspect he tapes his bedroom escapades." Buttons to activate cameras would be hidden within arm's reach of the bed. Of that, Johnny was sure. He lay on the bed and stretched his arms straight back, then to the sides, pressing anything his fingers touched. Two gold leaf clusters on the headboard. Pushing did nothing. . . but maybe if he turned. . . . Two cherry panels across from the bed rolled aside to reveal a giant screen. A twist of the other cluster caused the portrait over the headboard to slide open and a shelf to advance. On it stood a VCR projector, a remote control and a stack of video tapes.

"Hot damn!" Benny whooped. "This guy's unbelievable!" He clutched his crotch. "Wish we could hang around and watch some of these."

"No time for that. We have a schedule to keep. With the money you're earning on this project, you can buy all the triple-xers you want. Now let's get back to work. You start wrecking the place while I grab valuables. . . make it look like a burglary."

Portofino lifted artwork from the walls and cabinets and stacked them on the appliance dolly, shoved a Waterford crystal vase and some sterling flatware into a box. He jerked open drawers, located some expensive wristwatches, a checkbook and a couple of credit cards and threw those in too. They rushed through each room, yanked cushions off the sofa, overturned chairs and lamps, ripped a drape off its rod, pulled drawers open, dropped some onto the floor.

"Ever find the safe, boss?"

"No, Benny, but we'll try one more place. It has to be there." He headed for Wiggams' walk-in closet off the x-rated bedroom. He slid hangers one way and another till he found it, built into the wall about four feet off the floor. He'd cut his teeth on these. In a few seconds, it was open.

Inside, right in front, a 9mm handgun. "The jerk should keep this under his pillow or beside the bed," Portofino said. "Guess his brain can't think of more than one gun at a time."

"That's a good one, Johnny. Any dough?"

Portofino was already counting it. "About twenty grand. Several bonds, some loose diamonds and more files. My client was right: this guy had back-ups all over the place." He picked up a recipe box filled with 3x5 cards, each with a list of numbers. "Don't know what the hell this is, but could be important." He added it to the box on the dolly.

"That's enough. Let's take our loot down to the truck." After locking the door behind them, they headed for the elevator.

Portofino ripped off the hand protectors and handed them to his colleague. "Lose the gloves, Benny. . . the trash chute's over there."

Benny eased open the service entrance and stuck his head out. "Coast is clear." They trundled the cart to the truck, stashed everything in the back and got in the front. "I'll have this thing hot-wired in a sec," he said. "Is it lunch time?"

Johnny checked his watch. "11:28. Seems like days since breakfast. Plenty of time for a nice meal before our next assignment."

GINNY STOOD UP and stepped out of the bath tub. Toweling off in front of the mirror, she appraised her figure. Not as tight as it once was, but more than passable for a woman closing in on 50. This was what got her into trouble, she thought; maybe she could use it to get herself out of it. Wrapping up in a towel, she tiptoed to her husband's study and eased up behind him. She dropped the towel, covered his eyes with her hands and rubbed her breasts against the back of his neck. She felt him stiffen.

"I have a surprise for you, Darlin'."

"I think I've had quite enough surprises from you lately."

"Harmie, please, I thought you might like some make-up sex."

"I would. With whom would you suggest I have it?"

"Me, of course."

He continued to stare straight ahead. "Really? I thought you might want me to even the score by screwing one of your friends."

"Why would I want that?"

He rubbed his hand across his temple. "So you could feel as bad as I do. So you could know the pain, the hurt I've been living with this past week."

Ginny walked around the desk so she could look into her husband's eyes. "Harm, is that what you want? If that will heal your wounds, I'll find someone for you."

He shoved back his chair and leapt up, pounding his fist on the desk. "No! It is not what I want. I simply want to see Kane grovel, see him apologize."

"He is not about to do that. You know how massive his ego is."

"Oh, he is going to do it, all right. I can assure you of that."

"What makes you so certain?"

"If he doesn't apologize, that's the end of the investment business."

"You threatened to end it?"

"Yes, yes I did, Ginny. You see, I really do have balls after all."

"Oh my god, Harmon! He must be furious. Please, please be careful. Albert Kane is not a nice man."

The grandfather clock in the hall chimed the half hour. "Harmon, I have to run now. I'm so glad we've broken the ice. We'll talk more when I get back. . . about three o'clock." She kissed him on the forehead. "I made you some egg salad for lunch. Don't be an absent-minded professor and leave it out. . . it has mayonnaise in it."

After quickly dressing and brushing out her hair, Ginny applied her make-up and dashed toward the door. "I'm late, Harm. You take care of yourself while I'm away. I love you, Darlin'."

She heard nothing from his study. Shrugging, Ginny rushed through the kitchen and into the garage. She punched the door opener, fired up the Mercedes and headed for the Uptown Club and her appointment with Catherine Petrini.

"DANIELLE, YOU LOOK as if you're about to pass out. Are you okay?"

She backed away from the door, sank into the nearest chair. "Yeah, I think so, David." She felt clammy, lightheaded. "I'm fine, really. Let me get you a drink." She stood up, cautiously tried to walk. The dizziness was gone. "Come. Sit."

The visitor followed her toward the living room. "You sure you're all right? Perhaps we should forget dinner. Is that why you were lying down? Didn't you feel well then? You should have told me."

"I'm okay. Really."

"Here, you sit while I get the drinks. What would you like?"

She sat. "Some sherry sounds good. If there's Bristol Creme, I'll take that."

David went to the service bar, poured her requested drink and made himself a martini straight up. He brought the drinks to the couch and sat next to her.

Danielle's mind was traveling at warp speed trying to piece this together. As David St. James touched his cheek to her forehead to see if she had a fever, Danielle detected the scent of stale alcohol. Perhaps booze, not sex, was his Achilles heel. She might not have to bang him to get what she needed. A few martinis might loosen his tongue.

Danielle shook her head. "David, quit worrying about me and sit down. Let's enjoy our drinks and get some dinner later." She clinked her glass against his and watched him gulp what looked like pure gin.

"John tells me that you do quite a bit of work for him, David."

"Umm. John and I have worked together for years."

"Did you know him before he came to Charlotte?"

"I guess we have known each other for about ten years now."

"What did he do before coming to work at the university, if I may ask?"

"He was the comptroller of a major corporation."

"Interesting." His drink was gone. That was quick. "Here, let me get you a refill; after all you did the hostess job for the first one."

He handed her his empty. "Straight up, no ice please."

"Certainly, David."

As she made his drink, she watched him scan the room, taking in everything he could. The banker, true to his profession, was completing an inventory on her.

"Danielle, in all the confusion, I neglected to tell you how absolutely devastating you look."

"Why thank you, David. Coming from a man of impeccable taste, I take that as an extreme compliment. You, I might add, look pretty devastating yourself." That's it, massage his ego.

The banker dipped his chin. "I appreciate your compliment, too. Say, if you don't feel up to going out for dinner, we can order in. Please be honest with me."

"To tell you the truth, room service sounds great. It's been a whirlwind two days and I need some time to catch my breath."

Besides, it would give him a chance to drink in private. If she was wrong about which vice was his weakness, he could also use the privacy to make sexual advances.

It didn't take long to get her answer. "Danielle, I would love to stay in. I would appreciate having an intimate dinner with a beautiful woman in these luxurious surroundings. Much nicer than a noisy restaurant."

"It's a deal. Let's kick back and enjoy the evening." She handed him the gin. "Would you mind if I slipped into something more comfortable?" She didn't wait for his answer but headed for the bedroom while he attacked the second martini.. . . she'd made it a triple. She changed into a pair of shorts and a clinging sweater that left nothing to the imagination.

By the time she reentered the room, David had removed his jacket and loosened his tie. He grinned up at her. "My, aren't you the young coed." He stared at her legs, from her ankles to her crotch. "Nice. . .uh. . .shorts."

Danielle sat next to him and tucked her legs up beneath her. "Why don't you tell me more of what you do for J.P. and Kane."

"Kane? How do you know about Albert Kane?"

"From John, of course. He told me you do work for both him and Kane."

"I just act as an investment banker for them. That's all."

"As individuals?"

He nodded, took another swallow. "Yes, why?"

"John indicated they were in some kind of business together."

"I suppose you might say they are."

"What do they do?"

"Make investments with my bank"

"What bank do you work for?"

David put down his drink and turned to face her. "Why is this important to you?"

She didn't want to lose him now, just when his speech was becoming a little slow and slurred. She leaned back on the couch pillows and stretched her long legs out across his lap. "Oh, that feels so much better. Does this bother you?"

"No, actually it feels quite good."

The back of her calf felt pulsation from his crotch. He began to run his hand from her thighs to her ankles then reversed direction. She had him back.

"Gee, one's a lawyer and the other's an accountant, what kind of business could they be in? Reason I ask is, I just received my accounting degree and will be looking for work soon."

"They're in the brokerage business. They invest large sums of money in stocks, bonds and mutual funds. . . with me."

"You mean they invest *their* money with you or other people's money."

"Both."

"I didn't think universities paid so well."

"You are correct. Most of the money comes from another source."

"Where do they get the time to do all this?"

"They don't. I do all the investing for them."

"Are you saying the money just passes through them?"

"Exactly."

"Why can't the other 'sources' just deal directly with you? Why would they need Kane and Wiggams?"

"Because they don't want the source identified."

"This is intriguing. Sounds like a job I'd enjoy."

"If you only knew."

"Oh David, I would love to. Please tell me. This is exciting."

"Let's just say three men on your campus figured out a way to beat the system."

"Who's the third?"

"Harmon Dawes, the Department of Economics chairman."

Danielle shifted her legs, rubbed one of them against David's. "I have met him. They say he's a genius."

"He must be. He picks stocks as well as anyone I have ever known."

"So the three of them actually operate a bogus investment firm?"

David continued to caress her leg, his fingers climbing higher with each stroke. "Yep, John comes up with the money, Harmon picks the winners and I do the investing for them."

"What do you mean John comes up with the money?"

"Danielle, I've told you too much already."

"You can't stop now, this is too fascinating." She began caressing his chest. "Please go on."

"I really can't, Danielle."

She unwound her legs from his roaming hands. "Here, let me get you another drink."

He grabbed her hand and held it. "I've had enough already. What I need now is not in a bottle."

"What, David? Just tell me, I'll get it for you."

"Let's put it this way, my name might not be Clinton, but I sure can understand his desire for a young intern to . . ."

Danielle let a soft chuckle leak out of her pursed lips. "Say no more, I get the picture." She helped him unbuckle his pants and pulled them down to his ankles. When she slipped his silk boxers down along the same path, she realized he was no J.P. Wiggams, but he'd do.

Danielle abruptly stopped and sat down, leaving him there naked from the waist down.

"I'm listening, David."

"God, Danielle, not now."

"It's now or never."

"Jesus. You leave me between a rock and a hard place. No pun intended. All right. Wiggams uses university funds. He starts the scam by investing those funds with a bogus firm called Tristar. He buys CD's from them, which of course they can't issue. That's where I come in."

"So you issue the CD's to the university? But why can't Wiggams just go straight to you?"

"Because the revenue amounts are not the same. Auditors would pick it up immediately."

"I don't understand."

"Let's say Wiggams cuts a check from the university for $500,000. If he came to us, we would pay 8% per annum and have to record the CD. It would return $40,000 to the university, but tie up the principal, right?"

"Yes, I'm with you so far."

"Danielle, can't I tell you the rest after? I'm very hot right now. All this talk about money and playing with your legs are just too much."

"I can see that. I'll take my sweater off; perhaps that will hurry you along."

She stood up and removed her sweater and bra. David was Play Doh in her hands. "Please hurry and tell me everything, David; you're making me hot too."

Drops of sweat traveled from David's forehead to his chin. "Okay, okay, Tristar takes the $500,000 and invests it with my bank. With Dawes picking winners the way he does, they achieve a return of 20% or $100,000. I then create a paper trail which can't be followed and send a check for $40,000 to the university as if it's their yield on the CD. The remainder, or $60,000 in this case, would go to Tristar."

She slapped a fist into her other palm. "I get it. And Tristar still has use of the $500,000 principal it really is holding in its investments."

"Correct."

"Jesus, usable funds could really multiply."

"Indeed they have."

"And you, I presume, are paid a handsome fee for your services."

"It's a sweet deal all around, Danielle."

A noise and a voice. "You ready for dinner?" Danielle and David swiveled their heads toward the speaker. Wiggams stood in the opened door between the two suites. "My, my, what have we here?"

David crouched down, hands over genitals. "It's not what you think."

"Sure, Mr. President, I believe you. You did not have sexual relations with that woman."

Danielle bent forward so her breasts would fall into the bra she was latching at her back. "Damn it, I forgot to lock the door. Sorry, David."

Wiggams charged across the space between them. "I told you we would eat around seven, remember? Obviously, you just started without me."

Danielle collapsed in laughter. "Look at this!" She pointed toward David, frantically tugging at his shorts and trousers, which had become entangled. When he finally pulled them up, he damn near decapitated himself with the zipper. At the same time, Wiggams was unbuckling his belt and tugging his pants down Danielle nearly rolled on the sofa in hysterics. "One's putting them on, the other's taking them off."

She hooted at Wiggams. "John, don't you even think about it unless you want to finish the job I was just starting!" she said. She made hand motions to indicate what Wiggams would have to do to David.

"Ha. You gotta be kidding." Wiggams pulled his pants up faster than a roadrunner skating on KY jelly.

She could just imagine what Erin would say when she related this tale.

AFTER PAYING FOR lunch, Johnny Portofino poked his change into his pants pocket, stuck a toothpick in his mouth and wiggled it around with his tongue. "Back to the truck, Benny. We just have time for a side trip before our next assignment." As they approached the truck, Portofino headed to the driver's side. "You hot wire. I'm going to drive this time, since I know where to go."

He gunned out of the parking lot and turned left. In a few miles, he darted onto highway 160, headed north. "Got it so far?"

"North on 160," Benny said.

"Now watch for the turn off. It's the first left past an old gas station at a flashing light intersection."

"I better write this all down." Benny dug around in the Karpet Kleen truck till he came up with a scrap of paper. He set his feet and lifted his fanny off the seat so he could fish a stubby pencil out of his pants pocket, inside the unzipped coverall. He tapped the pencil lead against his tongue, reviewed the directions, wrote them down.

Portofino made another turn, right this time. "Put down 'right turn two miles down.' Your landmark is that giant oak tree over there."

Benny wrote.

They drove another four miles, Portofino advising Benny of mileage and landmarks. Then it was dead ahead about a quarter mile away: an old quarry sign. He turned in and they jolted and bumped down a dirt road that wound around discarded tires and abandoned appliances. As they entered a small clearing, tree limbs scraped the truck's sides. Portofino parked the truck, left it running, and together the men walked to the rim of a very deep quarry now filled with water.

"Lose the car here. Make sure it gets to the bottom of the lake so it won't be spotted from the air." Benny nodded, jotted a note. "Cut a tree branch and dust the tire tracks with it as you walk back to the main road. Stay out of sight. Call me on the cell. I'll be along to pick you up."

Benny jotted and nodded. "Give me your cell number again."

"Jesus, Benny, you haven't memorized it by now?"

"Just give me the damn number."

Portofino called out the numbers. "Now let's get out of here. I want to be at our next assignment no later than 1:15. . . and it's a good half hour drive."

This time, Portofino walked to the truck's passenger side. "If you drive the route, you'll be more familiar with it," he said, motioning for Benny to take the driver's seat. "No screw ups, you hear?"

The truck rolled into Harmon Dawes' driveway at precisely 1:15. The massive brick two-story Georgian colonial looked like something from the north, out of place with all the southern antebellum pretender architecture in Charlotte. Portofino reached behind him for the plastic bag from the office supply store. He got out of the truck, taking with him the clip board holding the stack of work orders he'd prepared in advance.

After the third ring of the bell, Harmon Dawes opened the door. "What is it?"

"We're the carpet cleaners, sir. Got a work order says to be here this afternoon." Portofino turned the clip board to allow Dawes a brief glimpse.

"Work order? To do what?"

"Clean your carpets, sir. This is the Dawes residence, isn't it?"

"Yes, but I didn't schedule. . ."

Portofino jabbed his finger at the work order. "Says here a 'Virginia Dawes' made the appointment. Says 'Saturday afternoon.' See for yourself." He offered the clip board to Dawes.

"She didn't say anything to me but we haven't talked. . . oh, well. . . guess you should come on in." He backed up and let them into the foyer.

"Benny," Portofino turned to his colleague, "we'll leave the equipment in the truck till we see exactly what we need."

"Right."

To Dawes: "We normally start on the second floor and work our way down and out. That okay with you?"

"Fine, fine." Dawes led them up the staircase and identified the three bedrooms, then his study. "I'll be here, working. Would you please leave it till last? Just do the bedrooms first."

"Sure, no problem." Portofino stopped at each bedroom, pretended to gauge the square footage. "Got a lot of furniture needs moving, Benny."

"Yeah, I see that. Big stuff, too."

Dawes registered surprise. "I'd have moved some of it if I'd known, you understand. Wouldn't expect you to do it all yourself."

"Good of you to offer. Getting furnishings out of our way comes with the territory. Most of the time, we have to do it. Benny, we'll definitely need the big dolly."

Benny shoved his fists into his overall pockets and rocked back on his heels. "Yep."

"Well then, I'll be in my study. If you need anything, just ask." Dawes turned and walked away.

"Thank you, sir. We'll do our best not to put you out."

"What a nice man," Benny said when Dawes was gone.

"I can't think of him that way."

"Right. I guess not."

Portofino and Benny retraced their steps downstairs then out to the garage. Portofino smiled. The Town Car was there.

"I'll go back up and do the job. I saw the car keys hanging on a hook just inside the kitchen. Open the trunk and look for golf clubs and other personal items. Remember, this has to look as if he's left his wife for good."

"And he will, boss, he will." Benny grinned and stifled a laugh. "Need any help up there?"

Portofino shook his head. "Just give me a few minutes. Then bring in that rug I got at Home Depot. Didn't figure him for quite this tall, but I think it'll do all right."

Benny started opening doors, on the lookout for personal items he should load into the Town Car. Portofino headed up the stairs.

He jammed his hand into his inside pocket, pulled out the garrote. This was his favorite tool. . . so simple. . .two pieces of wood connected by a wire. . . quick, quiet, no blood.

At his desk, Dawes, his back to the door, pored over the course syllabuses for the fall semester. He wrote furiously yet legibly, noting the texts his instructors were using, the additional reading they would require. He couldn't remember whether he'd told all his professors they would be responsible for putting the supplemental texts on reserve at the libr. . .

Like a pit viper, Portofino struck, plunging the garrote over Dawes' head and down to his throat. He crossed the wires behind his victim's head, using his typical left-over-right maneuver. He extended his crossed arms, tightening the wire.

Dawes scratched at the wire with his fingers, but Portofino was too fast for him, too strong. He gasped for air, clutching his hands at the tightening wire. His feet, now yanked up off the floor by Portofino's strength, viciously kicked at the desk. A coffee mug overturned, spilling brown liquid across white paper.

His back was now arched nearly horizontal as he flailed away, trying to grab something that would release his attacker's grip. A final effort. . . with every ounce of strength remaining, he set his feet against the desk and shoved. His head slammed into Portofino's chest. For an instant, the wire loosened. Dawes clawed his fingers between the wire and his throat.

The assassin regained his balance, yanked on the garrote, harder than before. Dawes went limp. Johnny let his body slump to the floor.

CHAPTER TEN

enny darted through the door and let go of the rolled rug. "You okay, boss?"

"Gotta catch my breath." Portofino leaned against the wall, his chest heaving. "This guy had a wiry strength I didn't count on."

"Them tall and lanky guys usually do have more than we give 'em credit for." With a pocket knife, Benny sawed at the twine around the rug. He shook it out full length in the middle of the room and dragged Dawes' body over to it. He rolled the professor up in the rug and hoisted it. "Heavy. Can you give me a hand getting this to the truck?"

"Yeah" Portofino groaned. They carried the rug down the stairs and out to driveway, the men stopped. A lawnmower sprang to life. . . in the yard next door. Benny swiveled his head in the direction of the noise. "What we gonna do now, boss? Someone could see us."

"Just keep going. What could be more natural than a carpet cleaning company loading a dirty rug into their truck?"

"That's real smart, Johnny."

"Being smart's what I get paid for," he said. "Raise the back door of the truck. Let's get this dude in here. . . he's heavier than I thought."

Benny did as instructed. Once the rug was safely locked inside the van, the men returned to the house. Benny went back to his job of rounding up personal items. He'd already discovered Dawes' golf bag and shoes in the Town Car's trunk. That saved him the trouble of searching for them. He grabbed a garbage bag from under the sink and tossed inside a pair of sunglasses and checkbook he found on the kitchen counter; next the living room, where he found some photos of Harmon and Ginny. Would Dawes take snapshots of happier times if he was leaving his wife? he wondered. He figured this guy was the kind who would. Benny stuffed them into a garbage bag.

Upstairs, in the master suite's closet, Portofino discovered three matching pieces of luggage. He threw them onto the bed, unzipped them and started packing up Dawes' clothing from the dresser. This man had some wardrobe, he thought; not much in the way of jewelry but really nice rags and lots of them. He realized the luggage wouldn't begin to hold everything.

"Benny," he yelled down, "bring up some garbage bags and give me a hand with his clothing. Get a move on; we're running late."

The associate scurried up the stairs as ordered and set to work. From deep inside the cavernous closet, Benny called, "Should I take all these shoes, Johnny?"

"Of course. Use your head. Who the hell would leave his wife without taking his shoes? Especially someone who obviously loved clothes. Seems to be the only thing he lavished money on."

"What about these goofy ties?"

"Benny, why the hell you bothering me with this? I told you, take everything. Empty the goddamn closet."

Portofino zipped up the suitcases and placed them in the hall. Back to the study to collect everything there. Kane had said the guy would have files on computer, maybe elsewhere. He'd just dismantle the whole room—take it all. He unplugged the computer, printer, scanner, shoved them into several garbage bags. Disks, files, desk drawer contents in another bag, which he tied up. No time to be careful. Besides, it wasn't as if someone would have to use the fucking stuff again. All he had to do was turn the files and disks over to Kane, who would surely dispose of them.

Could be back-ups stored somewhere. A safe. Where would that be? He checked the obvious places in the study. No safe. He darted back to the bedroom closet. No safe there either. Shit. The wife's closet. That must be it.

He opened the door and there it was—just sitting on the floor for anyone to see. He hunkered down in front of the safe. It took him about three seconds to open the combination lock and swing back the door. "Jesus Christ."

Benny rounded the corner from the other closet. "What'd you find?"

"More goddamn jewelry than any one woman ought to have. I've heisted a lot of rich bitches in my life, but I've never seen anything like this."

Benny held out a fresh bag. "We're gonna take it, ain't we?"

Portofino stood up, his hand pulling at his chin. "Don't know whether the hubby would do that."

"Shit, Johnny, if my wife pissed me off enough to leave, I sure as hell would take all her stuff. It'd serve her right."

"Yeah, I get your point. Okay, load 'er up."

Benny's eyes sparkled. "This'll turn into quite a bonus when we fence it."

"We'll have to sit on it for a while, and my client can never know." Portofino kept searching. "Benny, there has to be another safe somewhere. Found anything that looks like a hidden safe?"

Busy admiring the wife's jewelry as he swept it into the bag, Benny merely shrugged.

Portofino checked every picture in the room. Finally, a hinged frame over the bed swung open to reveal a wall vault. He hadn't yet found a safe that his skills couldn't plunder. It took him a moment, but when it opened he discovered that what the wife had in jewels, the husband possessed in greenbacks. Stacks of banded C-notes neatly piled. He wondered whether Kane knew anything about this stash, decided it would be okay to lift it. "Benny, add this to our personal bag, the one with the jewelry."

Benny was eager. "Hot damn. How much you suppose is in there?"

"At least a quarter million."

"Shit, man, I told my old lady this job could be big."

Portofino whirled toward Benny. "You told your wife about this job?"

"Had to. You know how she is."

"And who you were working with?"

"Yeah. Was that supposed to be a secret? She knows you use me for special cases."

"Did you tell her where you were going?"

"Ah, no, Johnny, I wouldn't tell her that." Benny thought he saw something in Johnny's eyes. "Is that a problem?"

"Huh? Oh, no, not at all."

"That's a relief. For a moment there, you had me going. Hope you're not mad."

"At you? Never. We've been friends for too long. Now, hand me one of his ties. I want to mark this bag so we can distinguish it from all the others." Benny fished in one of the garbage bags and retrieved a silk tie. Portofino wrapped it round and round the bag holding close to a million bucks worth of jewelry and cash. "We don't want this at the bottom of the lake."

The men hauled all the bags downstairs and tucked them into the appropriate vehicle—being careful that the computer and business stuff plus the bag of loot went into the truck. A quick once-over in the bedroom, study, living room and kitchen confirmed they'd removed what a furious husband would take when he split.

In the garage Benny opened the car door. "Guess I don't need these gloves any more. No problem leaving fingerprints on a car that'll rust away on the bottom of a lake." Benny tugged off his surgical gloves and threw them into the car. He patted his pockets, found the keys. He got behind the wheel. "See you at the quarry," he said as Portofino punched the garage door opener.

As Benny started to back out, Johnny pounded on the car. "Wait. Hold up."

Benny fingered the button to roll down his window. "What?"

"Almost forgot. You have to start the truck for me. That's one little skill I never learned."

Grinning, Benny stopped the Town Car and got out. With Portofino in the truck, he climbed into the passenger side and stretched over to the wires dangling below the dash. "There ya go, boss. Don't forget to turn your cell phone on so I can call you when I'm done."

Portofino gave Benny a two-fingered salute and drove the Karpet Kleen truck out of Dawes' driveway, followed by Benny in the Lincoln. It was 2:45; fifteen minutes to spare.

OVER LUNCH AT the luxurious Uptown Club, Virginia Dawes ingratiated herself to Catherine Petrini. "I'm just a little ole Southern Belle. . . never even been to New York. Here you are, such a sophisticated big-city woman. I am honored that you think I am capable to run your fund-raising campaign."

Miss Petrini lifted her champagne flute in a salute. "You were my first—and only—choice for this position, Virginia. I asked around and your name kept coming up. It appeared on everyone's list of local women with poise and status."

"That's what it takes to raise money, a strong network. Harmon sometimes made fun of what he called my social climbing, but I knew I was making the kind of important contacts that would pay off some day."

"That day has come. My daddy's money was enough to get the health center going, but now comes the big push. You are going to be my right hand."

Ginny pushed spinach around on her salad plate, trying to squelch her nervousness. "Five million dollars is no small amount to raise. But with your background and my local contacts, we should be able to reach that goal in. . . what do you think. . . six months?"

"Mmm, that's an ambitious goal. I won't be upset if it takes longer." She flashed a toothy smile. "Construction just started. It'll be a year before we need to install equipment. Of course, orders will require deposits, so it wouldn't hurt to have a couple mil in the bank early on."

"That won't be a problem. Ten phone calls and I'll have a million. That'll get the ball rolling." She took a bite, swallowed. "I need to ask you something." Her heart pounded in her ears. "Did C. Albert Kane tell you to offer me this position?"

"Albert? No, no." Catherine gazed to Ginny's right, staring at the potted plants hanging in the windows. She noticed how healthy the golden pothos looked. "He was one of the people I consulted, of course, but as I said, everyone mentioned you."

"That's a relief. I don't mind telling you, Miss Petrini. . ."

"Let me stop you right there. Ginny, by all means call me Catherine. We're going to work closely together, so enough of this 'Miss Petrini' stuff."

"Thanks, Catherine. My husband nearly convinced me that Albert forced me on you, because he. . . well, just because." That question answered, Ginny and Catherine settled into enjoyment of their luncheon.

When the check came, Ginny reached for it, "I'm the member here, this one's on me."

"I'm not accustomed to this. Usually I sign for everything."

"This time, you're my guest."

Cathy stood up. "Thank you Ginny. Now, let's go out to the construction site. Why don't we both drive, if you don't mind. I have an appointment, so I'll just leave from there."

At the site, Ginny's Mercedes followed Catherine Petrini's car, bouncing through the construction entrance, maneuvering around a bulldozer and past the contractor's trailer. Once out of her car, Ginny stumbled on stiletto heels as she walked through the rutted, hardened mud to join Cathy. "I sure wore the wrong shoes," she said, rubbing the ankle she had turned.

Cathy pointed at her flats. "Guess I'm used to it. Should have warned you. Sorry. Tomorrow, when you come for the kick-off of the fundraising campaign, you'll know better." She unrolled the architectural drawings on the hood of her Cadillac, pointing out where various elements of the health center would be located. "The more you can explain about the buildings and what all the center has to offer, the easier it'll be to raise the money."

"I couldn't agree more," Ginny said, peering over Cathy's shoulder.

After a few minutes of detailing the layout of the center as shown on the artist's rendering, Catherine Petrini brushed back her jacket sleeve to expose a diamond wristwatch. "Oh, wow, it's 3:45. My how time flies. . ."

". . . when you're having fun," Ginny finished for her. "I suppose you have to get out of here for your appointment."

"Ginny, I've enjoyed our time together more than I can say. We're going to do good things for this university, the city."

"I really think so, Catherine. And now I can hardly wait to get home and tell Harmon all this."

"You do that, Ginny. See you tomorrow at the kick-off." She backed her way out of the hard hat area, past the sign announcing what would soon rise on this land. She activated her cell phone, scrolled through the memory till she arrived at Kane's private number. "It's close to four o'clock, Albert, and Ginny Dawes is just now leaving the construction site. I've done as you asked, even kept her nearly an hour longer. You owe me one."

Ginny was so eager to get home, she had trouble staying under the speed limit. She was a punctual woman, and under normal circumstances, Harmon would have been worried about her being an hour late. But maybe, since they were barely speaking. . .

She recalled her attempt to break the ice before she met Catherine for lunch. Perhaps, if he did worry that she was late, he'd realize how much they loved each other. Hadn't she been sure to tell him "I love you" as she left the house? She did love him. Oh, how much she loved him. She couldn't bear the thought of losing him.

She entered the driveway and clicked the opener. As the door rolled up, Ginny was surprised not to see Harmon's Lincoln parked in its spot. Maybe he slipped over to the university; she thought; that's where he normally was when not at home. Or, just maybe, since it was a gorgeous day, he might have decided to play golf. She let herself into the kitchen, laid her purse on the counter and stopped. No dishes in the sink. Had he eaten at home? She tugged on the refrigerator door. . . the egg salad sat on the top shelf, untouched. That meant he must have gone to the club for lunch and golf. She was glad; it had been too long since he'd gotten in a round.

She made her way through the hall, into the living room, the silence of an empty house closing in on her. Perfect time for a nap; put aside the day's activities for a couple of hours. She'd start fresh with Harmon when he came home.

With her now muddy shoes in her hand she scaled the stairs and headed immediately for her bedroom. She shrugged out of her clothes, laid them on her husband's side of the bed, snuggled in between the soft sheets. When she awoke, the darkness startled her. How long had she slept? The clock read 8:40. Harm should have been home by now. Wouldn't she have heard him come in?

"Harm? Darlin', are you home?" Silence.

Sitting on the side of her bed in bra and panties, she called the number for his university office. No answer. She slipped on a robe, went downstairs. The garage still held only her Mercedes. This was so unlike him. Even though they'd hardly spoken during the past week, he would still have left her a note if he was going to be unusually late. No note in the bedroom, no note in the kitchen.

THE TWO DRIVERS stayed well within the speed limit. This was no time to be careless, when both the truck and the Lincoln held cargo not easily explained to a cop. As they neared the Karpet Kleen warehouse, Benny was surprised when Johnny did not turn in. This was an unexpected variance. Johnny always kept to his well-ordered plan unless something went drastically wrong. What could it be?

Benny's stomach turned over.

Portofino made his way out of town and down country lanes toward the deserted quarry, checking his rear view mirror often. Benny in the Town Car dutifully followed. As the truck lumbered down the dirt road, Portofino retrieved his back holstered SigSauer 380, checked that the silencer was properly attached, and placed it deep in his coverall pocket. He braked the truck twenty feet from the edge of the hundred foot quarry and left it running.

Portofino slowly walked to the edge and stared into the depths of the water. "Benny, come over here and tell me what you think."

Blinking fast, Benny approached the water, halting several yards away. "Think about what, boss?" He stuck his hands in his pockets, balled up his fists, pulled them out again. Something was wrong and he knew it. He glued his eyes to Portofino's every move.

"Where do you think is the best spot to put the car over? Don't want it getting hung up."

Benny pointed. "I was thinking maybe right there." His eyelids fluttered. "Johnny, why'd you change the plan? I thought you were going to make the exchange at the Karpet Kleen warehouse, then come and get me when I finished here and called your cell phone."

"Yeah, yeah, but I got to thinking you might need help here." Portofino slapped his hands on his thighs. "Shouldn't have worried. You've got it covered. Come on back to the car."

Benny followed him to the Town Car.

Portofino stopped at the trunk. "Open 'er up, Benny, I want to check something."

"What?" He inched toward the back of the car.

"You know me, can't stop worrying. It's the curse of a perfectionist. Want to make sure none of the bags got mixed up. I don't need my client's files at the bottom of a 200-foot deep lake. Just humor me and open it."

Benny fingered the remote and the trunk lid clicked open.

Johnny lifted it all the way up and sorted through the bags. "What's in this one, Benny?"

Benny sidled up beside Portofino. "Which one?" He bent over to open the bag Johnny pointed to.

With the back of his head to Portofino, Benny never saw it coming. Johnny rammed the barrel of the 380 in the base of his skull and squeezed off one shot.

"You should never have told her, Benny. You knew the rules."

Benny's upper body slumped over the bags in a pool of dark red blood. Portofino reholstered his 380, lifted the dead man's legs into the trunk. He picked up the keys Benny had dropped to the ground then slammed down the lid. "So long, my friend."

He got in, started it up and eased the car to the spot Benny had picked at the lake's edge. He shifted to park, left the motor running and jerked the hand brake up. He walked to the truck, grabbed the lengths of rope and concrete blocks he'd bought at Home Depot, carried them over to the car. The first rope he wound around the brake release under the dash; the second, he tied around the shift lever. Then he propped a concrete block against the accelerator, wedging it into place with another block. The powerful engine revved like an explosion.

Satisfied, he backed up with ropes in hand, yanked and waited. The brake release tripped. The lever dropped into drive. The car surged forward, disappeared over the edge and into the spring-fed lake. In moments, all that remained were a few bubbles. After a few more moments, even those were gone.

Ginny Dawes, now quite upset about her husbands whereabouts, ran up the staircase and into his study. Surely she'd find a note there, she thought. But there was no note. She looked around. And no computer. No printer, no scanner. "That's impossible," she muttered, yanking open the desk drawers. Empty. All of them.

As she bounded down the hall to their bedroom, her weakened ankle twisted under her. "Oowwww, damn," she cried out, halting for a moment to test her weight on that foot. Gingerly, she made it to the bedroom, flinging open the double doors to her husband's massive closet. "Oh, God, no! This can't be happening."

Ginny staggered into the bathroom. Shaving articles? Gone. Toothbrush, paste, everything. Missing.

Back in the bedroom, she pulled open all Harmon's dresser drawers, finding every one empty.

Color drained from her face. Her eyes rolled back in their sockets. She sank to the floor.

When she regained consciousness, she crawled to the bedside stand, pulled down the cordless phone, punched in Erin's number. "Thank God you're home," she said when Erin answered. "I need you."

"Ginny? Is that you?"

"Yes, it is. Can you get over here right now? Harmon's gone."

"Gone? What do you mean?"

"I mean he's left me. Gone. Gone for good."

"You can't be serious."

"Oh, Erin, help me. Please."

"Give me the address. I'll be right there."

When Erin arrived, Ginny met her at the front door, unaware she still held the phone in her hand. Limping, she showed Erin around the house, opening doors, drawers, cabinets. "See, he took all his belongings. Clothes, toilet articles, computer and files. Everything."

Erin reached for Ginny's hand. "I thought things were getting better."

"They were. This morning, before I left for my luncheon with Catherine Petrini, he seemed a little less angry. I told him I loved him. . . thought we'd pick up from there when I got home. But he wasn't here. He hadn't eaten the food I left for him. At first, I thought he just went to the club for some golf. I took a nap, but when I woke up—it was close to nine—he still wasn't home. I called his office. Not there. Then I started looking for a note. That's when I found. . . . Oh, Erin, what am I going to do?"

Erin led her to the bed, made her sit down. "I didn't expect this. I'm so sorry." She wasn't being very helpful, she realized. "Let me think a minute." Then, "Have you checked everything? Did he keep cash in the house? Is it gone too?"

"I don't know. I haven't looked in the wall safe. It's here, behind the picture over the headboard." She got up on her knees, tossed aside the pillows, threw back the framed art and twirled the combination. "Oh no! The money is gone too."

"How much was in there?"

"I have no idea, but it was substantial."

Erin leapt off the bed and over to Harmon's closet. "Ginny, there's not one shred left. Not one."

Ginny sobbed. "I know. He took everything."

"That's just it. Wouldn't a man have some suits, shirts or ties he doesn't like? Why weren't they left behind?"

"Never thought of that. Yes. Harm had lots of ties he despised. Wrong style—too wide, too narrow. He took even those? He must have wanted no shred of himself left in this house." Ginny's breaths came in giant gulps. "He really fooled me. I had no idea he was this angry."

"Sit down and take deep breaths before you pass out."

She sat, took air into her lungs as if it traveled up from her toenails. "I already did faint. . . before you got here."

"Ginny, look at me. I don't think your husband left you."

Hope leapt in Ginny's heart. "He didn't? What makes you think that?"

"Tell me something. Was Professor Dawes the sort that would take all the money and not leave you anything at all?"

"No, I don't think so. He has always been very generous with me."

"I assumed as much. What else did he keep here of value: checkbooks, jewelry, things like that?"

"I have a safe full of jewelry in my closet and there are checkbooks in his desk and in the kitchen. Why all these questions?"

"Do you feel well enough to open your safe?"

"Yes, but why? Harmon would never take my jewelry. He's just not that kind of man."

"Come on, let's look."

As she steadied Ginny, they walked across the room to her closet. If Erin's gut could be trusted, they'd discover that the safe was empty. She watched Ginny rotate the combination lock and open the door. Ginny fell backward against Erin.

"My god Erin, everything is gone. What's going on here? Harmon would *never* take my jewelry."

"That's what I thought." Erin backed out of the closet, sat on the bed. Should she tell Ginny what she was thinking? Was she strong enough to take it? She patted the bedspread beside her. "You'd better come and sit on the bed a minute."

Ginny stumbled toward her. "What's happening, Erin? What's gone on here?"

"Frankly, Ginny, I think someone has kidnapped Professor Dawes and tried to make it look as if he left you."

"Oh, dear God."

"Easy now, take a breath. Don't want you to pass out again."

"This is crazy."

"Is it? Think of who else knew about your fight with him."

"Nobody, just you."

"Think again."

"Erin, you are the only one I told."

Erin shook her head. "Didn't you tell me you called Kane? Didn't you tell him?"

Ginny's eyes widened. "That's right, I did." Wonder quickly turned to fear. "I know Albert is not a nice man, but would he. . . ?"

"If Harmon threatened Kane, he'd certainly have motive. . ."

Ginny looked steadily into Erin's eyes. "If he's hurt Harmon, I'll kill him."

"Ginny, if I'm right—and I hope I'm not—your husband is probably in grave danger. I think we'd better call the police and report Professor Dawes missing. For the time being, just tell them it was a domestic squabble. Let's not divulge the Kane involvement yet. We certainly have no proof at the moment."

Ginny nodded. "The police. Yes. But why don't we just explain everything and let them arrest Kane?"

"Remember, I told you last week that there was more going on here than you think. You just have to trust me."

Ginny jumped off the bed and whirled to face Erin. "I have put my trust in you and look where it's got me! My husband is missing or . . . worse."

"Yes, and I warned you, because of the bastard we're dealing with, this could very well happen, but I don't think anything we did caused it."

"Then, where the hell is my husband?"

"I don't know, Ginny, but I have the same strong intuition you have—that Albert Kane does."

"Ever since Harmon went to see him, I've been afraid something would happen."

Erin sat on the edge of the bed, deep in thought. Kane was too smart to be personally involved in this. He wasn't the kind to dirty his own hands. Hadn't Danielle told her he was connected? To a professional killer, maybe? That's it. Someone else had snatched Harmon.

"Did you notice if Professor Dawes' files were missing?"

"Nothing was left in the study. Computer, printer, scanner—all gone. Desk drawers empty. Rolodex, file drawers. Nothing."

"How about the disks, the ones you copied for me?"

"They're gone too."

"So all of the records of Tristar are missing?"

"Yes, all the material I copied from is gone."

"Back-ups?"

"Nope, his disks were back-up to his journals."

"Did anyone else have copies of this material?"

"He always made monthly copies for Kane and Wiggams."

Erin looked off into space. "I think we should change our plan a bit."

"What do you mean?"

"Let's not call the police in on this yet."

"Why not? They need to get started looking for him. I don't understand."

"Aren't you supposed to be at the Petrini Health Center campaign kick-off tomorrow?"

"Yes, but I can't go now."

"Ginny, yes you can. It's vital that you carry on as usual. If my suspicions are correct, Kane may make a move on Wiggams next."

Sobs shook Ginny's shoulders. "First Harmon, then Wiggams? Both his business partners? Erin, I'm so scared. I'll never be able to give my speech. I can just barely talk to you."

Erin shoved a bunch of tissues into Ginny's balled up fist. "You have to be strong. I'll go with you, sit in the front row and support you."

Ginny dabbed at her eyes. "But why? What good will it do?"

"Well, I'm guessing, but I would think the president will be, there along with Catherine Petrini and Kane."

"Yeah, so what?"

"I would like you to say hello to Kane and tell him you're sorry about getting angry at him. Tell him everything is all right and you and Harmon are back on good terms." She let Ginny process that idea. "If I'm right, that will shake him up good. If he's rattled, he might make some mistakes that would help us find your husband."

Ginny nodded. "Yes. I see. Okay, I'll do my best."

Erin stood up. "Come on. Pack a bag. You're going to sleep at my house tonight. Tomorrow, we spring our trap."

AFTER LEAVING THE quarry, Portofino drove the van back to the highway and headed toward the Karpet Kleen warehouse. Thoughts bounced around in his brain like dice on a craps table. He would return the van, transfer its cargo to his rental car and wait until it was time to deposit Dawes' body in the place Kane told him about. He'd cased the site earlier in the week and knew it wasn't patrolled.

At 5:30 he eased the van into the vacant lot next to where they had left the rental car. He carefully backed the truck up to the trunk of the car so the van was nosing out to the street. It blocked any line of sight from there. His luck held. Still no one around. He jumped out and unlocked the trunk lid. He pulled himself up on the van's wide bumper, unlatched and lifted the roll-up door. There was the rug, right where he and Benny had laid it. He grabbed the end of it and hauled it over to the edge of the van floor. Poking his head out, he looked around. Still lucky. He leapt down, grabbed the rug and tugged it over to his trunk, letting it fall into the large cavity. He bent it to fit and returned to the van for the computer equipment, files and disks he'd deliver to Kane. And the loot bag he'd keep for himself.

The trunk was filling up fast. He wished he had known, he would have rented a SUV. He placed as much as he could from Wiggams apartment in the trunk. The rest would have to go in the back seat of the car.

He re-entered the van and drove it a block south to the Karpet Kleen parking lot. As planned, no one was around. He slowly maneuvered the van into the vacant slot they had removed it from ten hours earlier. Looking around and now satisfied that all was as it should be, he exited the parking area and walked back to the rental car with out seeing a soul. Good. No cars, no people around. Only the sounds of traffic on a busy thoroughfare some blocks away. As he approached his rental car he fished inside the coveralls and found his car keys. He shrugged out of the coveralls and tossed them into the car. What was the expression these days? Piece of cake.

At the La Quinta motel where he'd been staying since Tuesday, his car was familiar. No one would question why it was back. He took the stairs to the second floor and strode down the hall. He unlocked his door, headed for the john. He hadn't pissed since after lunch.

Time to check out. At the front desk, the clerk who'd checked him in had been replaced by a black woman with as much personality as Benny currently exhibited. "I'm checking out room 234 and room 232."

"And you are?"

"I'm 232."

She stuck a fresh chunk of bubble gum in her mouth and mashed down vigorously. "Wanna put this on a credit card?"

"No, I'll just pay cash." He shot her a few bills. "That should cover the tab for both of us. I'll nap for a while but will be out of here by four in the morning."

"Whatever." A large pink balloon expanded from between her lips. She popped it with her pen and sucked the gum back into her mouth. "Here's your bill." She counted out the change on the counter then looked up at Portofino.

"Keep the change. Buy some more bubble gum."

Never give your real name. Always pay cash. Don't dress in a way to call attention to yourself.

No trace, no trail.

Once back inside room 232, Johnny Portofino sat on the bed and set his watch alarm for 2:00. When the buzz roused him, he rubbed his eyes, turned on the light. He got up, used the john, packed his duffel, retrieved his garment bag containing his favorite Armani plus accessories. He set everything by the door, including the extra bag of special items he'd need later, at the university. He reached for the phone. Better to call Kane on a land line than to use the cell.

Kane answered on the third ring. "You'd better have a goddamn good reason for calling me at this hour."

"I do," Johnny said, knowing his distinctive voice would identify him.

"Everything go okay?"

"Need you ask?"

"You have all the files?"

"From the two homes. I'm on my way to the university office now to pick up the rest."

"Any problems with Mr. D.?"

"None at all. He's in the car now, waiting to be deposited for safe keeping, just as you instructed. Cleaned out the house so his wife will think he left her."

"Good work. But that's what I pay for."

"Speaking of. . ."

"When you turn in your car at the airport, ask for Danny. He'll give you an envelope containing a key for an airport locker. Your money's in there. Clean bills."

"You will find all the files in the self-storage shed I rented for you, just where you told me. I'll mail you the key."

"Whose name did you use?"

"Yours, of course."

"Jesus Christ, are you fucking crazy?"

Portofino chuckled, his deep baritone rolling through the phone like distant thunder. "Got you going, didn't I. You'll find it under

Benny Caputto." He heard Kane let out a breath. "Got a couple matters to take care of before my flight, counselor. Au revoir."

He snapped off the light and opened the door to the corridor. Draping the garment bag over his shoulder, he lifted the other two bags and headed for the exit. "Slowest damn elevator in the world, bar none," he muttered to himself as he took the stairs.

Twenty minutes later, he drove his rental through the construction entrance of the new Petrini Health Center at Madison University. Just as Kane had described, he discovered a series of footer excavations for placing steel support columns for the building. He killed his lights and rolled to a stop next to one of the holes. He got out of the car, pulled on the coveralls again. The full moon afforded just enough light for his task.

The hole he selected, he guessed, would measure 4' x 4' x 4'—plenty large enough. He stretched his arms out to each side of the excavation and eased his way carefully down into the hole. A single vigorous tug was enough to remove the wire mesh already in place. Next, he peeled back the Visqueen, shining like a black pearl in the moonlight.

Climbing back out, he unlocked the trunk. Now the tricky part. . . getting the professor's body into the bottom of the excavation. He turned in a complete circle, making sure there was no one around who could see him. The long tube of carpet slung across his shoulders, Johnny strode quickly to the hole, bent forward and let go. The heavy burden tumbled into place four feet below.

The assassin leapt into the excavation and tugged and heaved until the carpet formed a semi-circle within the perimeter of the hole. Minutes later, he replaced the Visqueen over the body, shoveled about a foot of gravel over the black plastic then stomped on it to tamp it down. After he lowered the wire mesh into place, the hole looked exactly like all the other excavations. He was confident that when four feet of concrete would be poured, no one would ever know that here, Professor Harmon Dawes would occupy his final resting place.

Exiting the construction site, he headed his car toward the business office and parked alongside the building. He grabbed the extra bag he'd brought from the La Quinta and stole toward the front entrance. A quick pick of the lock and he was inside. The dim light from the Exit sign was enough for him to make out Wiggams' name and office number on the directory. He took the stairs two at a time and moments later, with the fingers of a veteran locksmith, picked his way into the comptroller's office.

No need to be neat, he told himself, since when he was finished, nothing would be left to worry about. He rifled through the four door metal file cabinet. Nothing there but university data. The right hand drawer of the comptroller's desk held only junk, sex magazines and condoms. The center drawer revealed the usual trivial garbage, including a bunch of keys. The left side drawer was. . . locked. This must be where he'd find the files he needed.

He figured it would take longer to try all the keys in the lock than it would to pick it. In seconds, he had the drawer pulled open. Pay dirt. He grabbed everything, removed the contents of the extra bag and placed them on the desktop, stuffing the now empty satchel full of Tristar files.

He shoved Wiggams' massive executive chair around the room, stopping several times to stand on it, stretch up to the ceiling and remove the heat sensor units from sprinkler heads.

Portofino's strong fingers twisted the cap off the economy size can of lighter fluid he'd brought in the extra duffel. He walked around the room in a uniform manner, squirting the fluid onto the carpet in a pattern he knew from experience would do the trick. He was particularly careful to pool the fluid just inside the door. Satisfied, he put down the lighter fluid and picked up a can of hair spray. He shook the first can and emptied it over the desk and credenza. The second can ran out of spray after he fogged the remaining office furniture and window blinds in vapor. He wrinkled his nose. The place was starting to smell like a French whore house.

He unzipped and wriggled out of the coveralls, tossing them onto the chair. They'd done their job; he wouldn't need them any more. He slung the bag of files over his shoulder and darted to the door before the noxious fumes in the room got to him. Once in the corridor, with the door safely shut to block any back draft, he squatted down and flicked a butane firelog lighter. He stuck the flame in the crack at the bottom of the door. As he sprinted down the hall, the whoosh of flames enveloping the office reached his ears. He hit the stairs running and was quickly outside.

As Johnny Portofino drove his rental through the rear campus exit, the flames within the business office were already visible. Soon the pressure would blow the windows and fire would light the early morning sky.

One more stop—to leave the files he'd collected from Dawes and Wiggams at the U-Store-It—and his work in Charlotte was done.

CHAPTER ELEVEN

At 3:45 a.m. six trucks from the Charlotte Fire department raced through town with sirens blasting. In the sky above the university buildings, layers of bright orange danced against the dark of night. It was as if the sun were trying to rise earlier than scheduled.

Campus security called Jake Gathers at home. He was already on site when the first fire trucks arrived. Mystified, he stuck his hands in his back pockets and rocked back on his heels. The north end of the building burned out of control while the south side appeared totally free of flames. He didn't even hear the fire chief's SUV as it wheeled up.

"Hey Jake, how long you been here?"

"About five minutes, Chief. Just before your guys started pouring the water to it. Damn, I never saw anything like this. It's as if our sprinkling system is only working on half the building."

"Yeah. Has it been inspected lately?"

"Come on, Chief, you know I keep this campus in good safety compliance."

"Yeah, I do, Jake. Asked out of habit. Sorry."

"What's the game plan?"

"Reports came in from my section chiefs while I was on my way here. From what they said, we may be able to save half the building, but don't count on it. Got to go, Jake, check with you later."

Jake leaned back against his Explorer and watched the blaze devour a good part of one of the university's most important buildings. Damn, he thought, this would surely earn him a tongue lashing from President St. James. He could even lose his job.

ERIN WASN'T USED to sleeping on her living room couch, but she'd figured Ginny needed the bed more than she did. Now, with dawn still an hour or more away, she couldn't find a comfortable position. Might as well catch the news, she thought, and flicked on the TV, keeping the volume low so it wouldn't wake Ginny. As she scrolled through channels searching for CNN, she stopped on the local station. A reporter she recognized stood in the bright light of the station's remote feed van, microphone clutched in her fist. Behind her, the sky billowed with smoke and flame.

". . . I'm standing in front of the administration building at Madison University, where a fire rages out of control. Spokesman for the fire fighters on the scene tell me they think the fire started about half an hour ago in the second-floor corner office occupied by the university's comptroller, John P. Wiggams. Mr. Wiggams is reportedly out of town. . ."

Erin knelt on the floor, inches away from the TV, mesmerized by the sight of immense orange tongues of flame soaring skyward through the roof of what had been Wiggams' office. Son-of-a-bitch, she thought. This had to be more of Kane's doing.

She sensed someone in back of her and turned her head. Ginny stood behind the sofa, her eyes wide as Frisbees. She held one arm out in front of her, like a sleepwalker. The other arm was bent at the elbow, her hand covering her mouth. Erupting through her fingers, like lava from a volcano's crater, vomit spewed onto the carpet. When the retching subsided, Ginny looked at Erin with panic in her eyes. "Erin, help me. I feel like I'm going to faint."

Erin leapt to her feet. "My god, Ginny, sit down. Here, put your head between your legs." She then headed for the bathroom and a wet cloth. When she got back, she found Ginny's shoulders shaking with uncontrollable sobs.

"I'm so sorry about your carpet. It's probably ruined."

Erin wiped Ginny's face with the cloth. "Don't worry about that. It's old. Besides, it'll clean up fine. I'm more concerned about you." She bathed the older woman's face with the cool cloth. "I guess you know Wiggams' office is on fire. But from the looks of it, the whole building is burning."

Ginny nodded, almost imperceptibly. "First, my Harmon's kidnapped, and now this. It's more than I can take. I can't stop shaking. I feel cold and clammy and my heart is going to jump out of my chest."

"Take a deep breath."

"I can't, I think I need an ambulance. I'm . . . going. . . to . . . faint." Her eyes fluttered and her body sagged.

Erin held her firmly. "Ginny, listen. You'll be okay. You're having a panic attack."

"What's that?" she mumbled.

"Your body starts releasing large amounts of adrenaline. You get very nervous and feel as if something real bad is going to happen."

"Something real bad IS happening!"

"No, no, it's not happening to you. When you're having a panic attack, you feel your own life is threatened."

Ginny's mind had been diverted. "How do you know this?"

"Because I've had them . . . when I was a student. They're very frightening. Just start breathing slowly through your nose and stomach. It's called diaphragmatic breathing. I don't want you to hyperventilate."

It was Harmon Dawes she was really worried about, not his wife. She had thought of Danielle's call from Las Vegas warning her to be careful. How Wiggams had said that the wily lawyer was probably plotting to get even right now. She suspected, as Ginny did, that Kane not only had something to do with Dawes' disappearance, but probably orchestrated it. The question now was how far had he gone and for what reasons. Was Harmon's disappearance a retaliatory measure to his threat to expose Kane? Did the fire at the business office building have something to do with the potential extortion files they had found in Wiggams' office?

"Ginny, Kane—or somebody—removed your husband's Tristar files. I suspect the fire took care of Wiggams' copies."

"Probably so. Why?"

"Well, with what I know, it seems that Kane is removing anything or anybody who can tie him to Tristar."

"Erin, what the hell are you saying? Do you really believe he has done something to Harmon?"

Erin paced the floor, swinging the wet cloth against her leg. "Right now, I don't know. Wiggams is alive and well in Las Vegas with Danielle, so maybe your husband is okay too."

"When are they due back?"

"Early this evening."

Ginny stared at the television, her eyes unfocused. She ran her hand through her hair, now wet from Erin's attempts to keep her conscious. "Erin, what are we going to do?"

"Nothing right now. We'll wait till Danielle gets back. She was with Wiggams all weekend; perhaps she can shed some light on this."

"Shouldn't we call the police now?"

"No, not just yet." Erin knelt on the carpet and cleaned up Ginny's vomit with the rag she'd used to calm her guest.

Ginny stared at the TV, unseeing. "I can't take any more of this. I surely can't stay alone."

"You can stay here for another night, but if we're going to trick Kane into thinking your husband is safe at home and you're back on good terms, you'll have to go home soon." She sat next to Ginny and picked up her hand. "You have to be an Oscar-caliber actress and carry on as usual."

Erin stood up and pulled Ginny to her feet. "Take a shower and get dressed. I'll make some breakfast."

With Ginny out of the room, Erin phoned Danielle. It was only six o'clock in Vegas. She prayed Danielle was not at breakfast. . . or still not back to her hotel room from the night before.

She answered on the fourth ring.

"Whew, I'm so glad I got you."

"Erin?"

"No, it's the tooth fairy. Did all that screwing affect your hearing?"

"Aren't you the comedian this morning? What's up?"

"Sit down and hold on. Professor Dawes is missing or worse and the business office at the university is burning down as we speak."

"Holy shit. I can't leave for one weekend without everything going to hell. What's going on, anyway?"

"I don't know yet, Danielle. I'll fill you in on more when you get here. What time are you scheduled to land?"

"Six-thirty, give or take. Why?"

"I need you to do something right now."

"Shoot."

"Can you call your father and get a wire tap on Kane's phone ASAP?"

"Oh sure, no problem. It's Sunday morning in D.C. and you want him to find the Attorney General to grant a tap on a friend's phone for an investigation that doesn't exist. Are you delirious?"

"I'm deadly serious. I know this is a stretch, but this afternoon, Ginny and I will try provoking Kane to do something stupid. Something that might expose him."

"Erin, my father is not going to buy that. Christ, at least give me something to use."

"I strongly suspect Kane has had Dawes either kidnapped or murdered. I also suspect he is somehow connected to the university fire. It appears as if he is moving against those who can or have threatened him in this Tristar fraud."

"Jesus, Erin, this is nuts. What about Wiggams? Is he safe?"

"I don't know, but be very careful until you get home. I would suggest you keep your distance from him."

"My father is going to shit when I lay this on him. You know that, don't you? He'll have a thousand questions."

"Yeah, I suppose he will."

"He's also going to jump in with both feet."

"No, Dani, he can't do that. It's too early. He'll blow the cover. We're his best pipeline right now."

"He won't buy it, Erin, I'm telling you. I know him very well."

Erin leaned against the kitchen sink and thought for a moment. "Can you at least get him down here tonight to speak with us?"

"I'll try. It's been a while since he's seen me. He may make the trip for that reason."

"Does he fly private?"

"Of course."

"Perhaps you can get him to come in somewhere near your arrival time. I can meet you at your place about 7:30 tonight."

"It's worth a try. I'll get back to you as soon as I can."

After she hung up, Danielle sat on the bed, her arms embracing her knees pulled up to her chin. Harmon Dawes was missing or dead? Wiggams' office burned to the ground? Was Albert Kane really crazy enough to do all this, or was Erin getting carried away?

She lay back and thought about how she would present this to her father. He was an extremely intelligent man who would never accept anything but the entire story from her, something she wasn't up to explaining at the moment. He would be furious about the situation getting this far without her informing him of her involvement. But Erin said to do it, so somehow, she'd manage.

As she dialed the number, she hoped he was in church.

But he wasn't.

"Daddy, it's Danielle."

He launched into the usual pleasantries, but she wanted to get right to it.

"This is important. I'm in Las Vegas right now but I'll be back in Charlotte at six tonight. Can you fly in and meet me? It's really important."

"You're in Vegas? What's going on?"

"It's a long story and I promise to fill you in later."

"I can live with that, but why the call this early on a Sunday? Do you need money?"

"That's not it. Not this time. Actually, I haven't even gambled. I'm here for a conference on university accounting practices."

"I'm impressed. That's wonderful, Danielle. Madison must think a lot of you to send an intern to something like that. Are you there alone?"

"I'm with the university comptroller."

"Traveling with your boss must be quite an experience for you."

Danielle cringed. "I hate to cut you short, Dad, but I need your help. There are some major criminal wrong doings going on at the university."

"Is this why you called?"

"Yes."

"I see. Are you involved?"

"My friend Erin Gallagher and I have been investigating fraud for several months now."

"Who is she?"

"I don't have time for all that now. Later. I promise. Daddy, I'm going to be blunt."

"What else is new?"

"I need you to either get a court order for a wire tap right now or fly into Charlotte tonight for a 7:30 meeting with Erin and me."

"It's that serious?"

"Yes, it is."

The line went silent for several moments. Finally, "All right, here's the deal. No to the wiretap, but yes to coming to Charlotte. Should be there about 6:30. It'll be good to see you."

"Hope you still think that after you hear our story, Daddy. I'm due in at 6:15. With airport security the way it is these days, you can't come to my gate, so I'll meet you at American Airlines baggage claim."

"Got it. I'll welcome seeing you, but this emergency trip had better be justified. I trust you know where to draw the line."

"I do, Dad. I'll see you later. I love you."

Danielle realized she was perspiring. What Erin had related to her was just beginning to sink in. Good thing no one knew she and Erin had copies of the Tristar files. If Erin was right about Kane, their ass would be grass if anyone ever found out.

Would it even be safe to be around Wiggams and David? she wondered. Should she take a separate flight home? Or would that raise too many questions?

Feeling antsy, she needed to do something, stay occupied, divert her mind from the danger she could be in now. She started hauling her clothing out of the closet, tossing it on the bed. After tugging open a dresser drawer, she remembered she'd brought her Pilates video. That's what she needed now. . . exercise. She flicked on the TV and shoved the cassette into the built-in VCR. Lying on the floor, she got into the positions identified by the soothing voice on the tape. Half an hour later, she felt relaxed, serene.

They were scheduled to check out at 12:30, have lunch with David and head to the airport by two o'clock. She had plenty of time to shower, pack and dress before Wiggams showed up to attempt a quickie before leaving Las Vegas. She climbed back onto the bed next to the open suitcase, lay down and closed her eyes.

At noon, a knock at the door startled her awake. In her bra and panties, suitcase open and clothes all over the bed, she couldn't help but laugh. Christ, she was right, the little weasel did show up early. She strode to the door. "Come on in, you pervert. You can look but don't touch." She flung the door open to a grinning David St. James.

"Oooooh, David, I'm sorry, I thought. . ."

"You thought it was Wiggams, right?"

'Yes, I did."

"I'm not a pervert but I probably have the same thoughts." As he moved across the room toward her, his eyes took in every square inch of her body. "God, you are beautiful."

He may be ripe for the plucking, she thought. After all, he had just spent the entire morning with Wiggams and may have new information.

He moved closer and embraced her, capturing her lips with a passionate kiss that she returned in full. She took his hand and led him to the bed. "Are you suggesting we pick up from yesterday before we were interrupted?"

"Mmmm, but this time, I would like to share all of you."

"I don't know if we have time. I'm sure there will be other opportunities in Charlotte."

"Perhaps you're right. I don't want to rush this either. I want to enjoy you without any time constraints."

"That would be best." Danielle ran her hand along his thigh. "I want you to have me totally, in any way. In every way."

"For a young woman, you have wisdom far beyond your years."

"Don't know if I'd call it wisdom, but I do know about timing. If you'd like, we can play Monica and Bill before he gets here."

"I would love to depart Vegas with that experience imbedded in my mind."

"You're on. Just one thing first. Will you give me something on Wiggams?"

"Christ, Danielle, why do you always press for information at a time like this?"

"I find it's the perfect time to negotiate." She laughed.

"It's blackmail."

"Yup, only in this kind, both parties win."

"All right, all right. What is it you need to know?"

"I've been to his apartment. Where does he get all the money from?"

"I told you, he does very well with Tristar."

"Let me be quite frank, David. He is a creep and I really need to get something on him."

"Why?"

"Because he's threatened to tell the university that I have been sleeping with him to secure a position in the business office."

"Have you?"

"No. I have plenty of opportunities for good jobs. I don't have to sleep my way in."

"Why don't I just tell my sister? She will protect you."

"Now, David, you know damn well she couldn't fire a comptroller on the word of an intern."

"I suppose you're right. Well, this should help you. When Al Kane found Wiggams, he was being held for statutory rape in Virginia. Kane had been called in to represent him and seized the opportunity to get his man at the university. He paid the victim's family a handsome settlement and they dropped the charges. The judge was furious, but no one could prove a thing."

"Hot damn. I knew he was a pervert."

"Sex is an obsession with him. He makes Hugh Hefner look like a Tibetan monk."

"So, then, Kane literally has him by the balls?"

"Speaking of which, our time is running out here."

Danielle looked at the clock. "Right. Your reward for information will be euphoric, now lie back and enjoy."

AT THE PETRINI Health Center construction site, two tiers of bleachers rose out of the scarred lot, just in front of footer excavations that outlined the building. A hundred feet away, sandwiched between a row of earth movers and the contractor's trailer, a platform sported a dozen folding chairs, a microphone and a speaker's lectern. In front of it, a thin carpet of Astro-turf made a desperate effort to cover the hardened mud. On top of the swath of green, ten long rows of folding chairs were quickly filling up with Charlotte's most important people. Ushers directed the rest of the audience to the hard bleachers in the back.

Over it all hung a pall of smoke. Ash fluttered like snowflakes in the gentle September breeze.

Erin couldn't get over the number of dignitaries gathered to launch the fund-raising campaign today. She recognized most of Charlotte's movers and shakers on the dais with the university president. Among them, the mayor, the chamber of commerce director, Catherine Petrini, C. Albert Kane.

She held Ginny's hand and helped her up the steps to the platform. "Go on. You'll be fine. I'll be sitting right down in front. Just look at me for moral support."

Ginny stopped on the steps and turned. "Erin, I. . ."

"Let me remind you, Virginia Dawes, you are the chairperson of the foundation. You have authority, power. Act like it."

And she did. She delivered her speech as if it were the crowning glory of her career. As if her husband were in the audience, beaming with pride.

After the ceremonies, Erin shouldered her way through the crowd to help Ginny put their plan into action. She found Ginny way ahead of her.

"Madam President, considering all that commotion with the fire this morning, I'm amazed you were able to be here, let alone officiate so superbly."

"The health center will be such a major addition to our university, I felt it was more important than talking with insurance adjusters. They can wait till tomorrow. You, my dear, were amazing. I saw a side of you today that I didn't know existed."

"I guess I have come a long way. I'm glad Harmon convinced me to assume such an important role in the community."

"Where is Professor Dawes? I expected he'd be here to cheer you on."

"He would have loved to, but he's at home recovering from a bad ankle sprain he incurred on the golf course yesterday."

Erin watched Kane for reactions. He swiveled his head from Catherine Petrini, at his side, to pierce Ginny with his stare. His brow furrowed.

Ginny was doing well with the act.

"I see you brought Professor Gallagher along in his absence," the president said. "Thanks for coming, Erin."

"My pleasure, indeed, Dr. St. James." President St. James turned to talk with someone else, then moved away. Erin looked past the president to Kane and Catherine Petrini, fast closing on their position.

Ginny glittered a smile in Kane's direction. "Hello, Albert, how nice to see you again."

He dipped his chin. "And you also, Ginny."

"Cathy, I think we are off to a good start. Just as we talked about yesterday, I already have several handsome pledges."

"I'm not surprised. And after that impassioned speech of yours, the money is sure to start rolling in." She looked over at Kane then back to Ginny and held out her hand. "I want to extend my thanks to you, again."

Ginny grasped her hand. "I won't let you down. I'm honored to be selected. In fact, with Harmon so busy these days at the university, this project will provide me with a wonderful outlet."

Kane inched closer. "Did I understand you to say Harmon hurt his ankle playing golf on Saturday?"

"Why yes, Albert, he twisted it getting out of a golf cart."

Kane flipped a handkerchief from his inner jacket pocket and swabbed the sweat from his forehead. "Give him my regards, please. Now, if you'll excuse me ladies, I must be on my way."

Erin and Ginny exchanged looks. "He can't get out of here fast enough," Erin whispered. "You really spooked him."

"Where do you suppose he's going?"

"To check on your husband, maybe? I'm going to follow him."

Ginny nodded. "Be careful. If you're right. . ."

"Yeah, you don't have to remind me. I'll see you later at my place. Just use the key I gave you and make yourself at home."

Erin kept several car lengths behind Kane. When he stopped at a public phone booth near the outskirts of town, she pulled into a parking lot across the street and slid down in her seat. Peering over the dashboard, she watched him wait for the party to answer. He anxiously tapped the window but mouthed nothing. He hung up, dialed again, waited, pounded his fist against the side of the booth.

He jumped into his car and laid rubber as he headed south toward highway 51. She eased her dirty white Honda into the traffic and followed, glad her old clunker was unobtrusive. After about ten minutes, he turned into the fenced yard surrounding several one-story buildings. He stopped next to the office of the self-storage facility. Erin parked across the street in front of a convenience store.

Kane sat in his car, creating a story that would get him into the storage unit. Portofino had said he'd mail the U-Stor-It key, but he didn't have time to wait. He needed to check things now, verify what Portofino had told him.

He opened his briefcase, unzipped a compartment and removed a badge. He'd done enough favors for the police chief. This official badge had often come in handy to gain him access to places he wanted to go. He yanked out a sheaf of papers, rifled through them. He found one that would work. He figured most people had never seen a real search warrant and wouldn't know what it was supposed to look like. Besides, no one ever looked very closely at such things.

Inside the office, he approached the solitary man watching a football game on TV. "You the manager?"

"Who wants to know?"

Kane flashed the badge. "Got a warrant to search one of your units. Rented to a Benny Caputto." He held out the piece of paper for the man to glimpse, then folded it up and put it back in his pocket. "Check your rental register. Should have been leased in the last few days."

The man shuffled over to the counter, opened a book. "That'd be unit 18. First row on the east side."

"Good. Now, the key?"

"Oh, yeah." He leaned over to the wall, lifted a key from a hook. "Do I gotta go with ya?"

"No, no. I can check it out on my own."

The man was already back in front of the TV. "You do that."

What an asshole, Kane thought as he returned to his car. He could always count on man's stupidity to allow his schemes to work.

He drove to the first row and halted in front of number 18. He unlocked the overhead door and shoved it up. There were the boxes and bags Portofino had told him he'd find. He opened a few and satisfied himself they contained what they were supposed to. If Harmon's files and computer equipment were here, then surely Portofino had done everything else as instructed. Johnny was the consummate professional. He would never have botched this job and left town. He would be aware of the consequences for that.

So, then, what was Ginny's game? If Portofino had done the job, she was lying through her skull to Gayle St. James. How could Harmon be at home with a twisted ankle? He was dead. And buried.

He was certain Johnny would confirm that when he finally reached him. Time enough to figure out what the hell Ginny was up to.

In moments, he was back at the office to drop off the key.

Erin saw it all, her heart pounding with excitement. She wrote down the number 18 then left the convenience store lot and headed back toward town before Kane came out of the office.

ON THE RETURN US Airways flight, Wiggams sat with his head against the cool glass of the window. Danielle couldn't let it go. "What's the matter? You upset with me or something? I thought we had a nice time together." She was getting good at lying to the pervert.

He stared at her as if he'd never seen her before. "What? Oh, no. Just. . . well, you'll find it out soon enough, so I might as well tell you."

"Tell me what?"

"My office burned down this morning. Kane called with the news."

"My god, John, that's terrible. Was anyone hurt?"

"Not that I know of."

"What about all your files and personal things?"

"All lost."

"What in the world will you do?"

"About what?"

"All the business files for the university?"

"No problem with those; they're backed up on disks and kept in a fireproof walk-in vault off premises. I'm surprised you didn't know that."

"And your personal stuff?"

"Gone."

"I'm so sorry. I'm sure, if your office was anything like your apartment, you had some beautiful things there. And probably some personal files. Taxes, things like that."

"Not to worry. I have back-ups of those at home."

"You do? Of your personal stuff?"

"Yep, everything except *Playboys* and condoms." He smiled.

"Good. I got you to smile."

Soon the plane landed in Charlotte. While they waited at the US Airways luggage carousel, Wiggams offered her a ride home. "No need. Don't you remember? I drove. My car is in the long-term lot."

He dug into his pocket and pulled out a roll. He peeled off a 50. "This trip was on me. That ought to cover your parking tab."

"Careful. You'll spoil your reputation. But thanks."

"When you see me at Madison during business hours, I'll expect you to forget this weekend ever happened."

"You don't have to worry, J.P. I'll remember my place. Lowly intern, totally subservient to the mighty comptroller."

"Too bad you didn't keep that in mind in Vegas."

"We both know I didn't go on that trip as an intern but as a playmate. You got your money's worth, J.P. " And, she thought, in return I got some very important information.

Danielle picked her bag off the conveyer belt, twinkled an eye at him and headed for the door. She'd pretend to wait for the shuttle to the long-term lot then, after Wiggams was safely out of sight, she'd make her way to the American Airlines baggage area to meet her father.

Moments later, Wiggams joined her at the shuttle stop. "I'm in long-term parking too," he said as he patted her on the rear.

Shit, Danielle thought. Now I'll have to walk up and down the rows pretending to look for my car until he finds his and drives off.

Fifteen minutes later, with Wiggams safely on his way, Danielle stowed her bag in the trunk of her Porsche, locked it and hiked back to the terminal to meet her father. She found him pacing impatiently near the deserted baggage carousel. When she saw him, she sprinted up with arms held out. "Daddy, it's great to see you."

He held her in a tight embrace. "Where the hell have you been? I've been worried. There was no American Airlines flight from Las Vegas."

"I know, Dad. I came in on US Airways." She stopped his protest. "I had a good reason. I'll explain later."

"The mystery deepens. Is that it?"

"Something like that. Let's get out of here and meet my friend Erin."

"Hungry?"

"Famished. After nothing more than pretzels and a Coke on the flight, I could eat a horse. But we don't have much time. Erin will be at my house at 7:30."

"Then we'll grab something light. It's your ball game."

As they walked to her car, she filled him in on what was going on. By the time they had picked up burgers and fries, he was showing signs of agitation. When he chewed his bottom lip and wrinkled his brow, she knew, the pot was starting to simmer.

WIGGAMS EXITED THE elevator at the penthouse level. No matter how good a time he had in glitter city, he was always glad to be home. This time even more than usual. The sex, the tension of paying off his debt and not being able to gamble—plus the news about his office fire—had put quite a strain on his 53-year-old body. Trudging through the doorway, he dropped his luggage in the foyer, plopped onto his sofa and closed his eyes. The supple leather cradled his tired little body like a nest holds a baby robin. Soon, as daylight turned to dusk, he reached to turn on the table lamp.

Stretching his arms over his head, Wiggams let his gaze move from object to object around the room he had so carefully furnished. He always felt a keen sense of satisfaction in his expensive possessions. His *objets d'art*, his prized Waterford vase, his state-of-the-art home entertainment equipment.

But where were his vase, his Picasso and Dali lithographs?

Galvanized, he leapt off the couch and rushed to the custom-built cabinet. He slid back the doors and gasped. It was empty. The 60-inch TV, combination VCR-DVD player, and all his stereo components were gone.

"What the hell is going on here?" he yelled.

He almost ran from the living room to the study. He entered the room and stopped. "God damn it!" File and desk drawers stood open. And empty. His 24k gold desk accessories were gone. Ditto artwork from the walls. He spun on his heels and charged toward the master bedroom. All he could think of was the safe.

He twisted the reostat to turn on the lights and in seconds realized this room had also been hit. He rushed to the closet and flung aside the clothes. The open safe revealed. . . nothing. Only an empty cavity. "Damn it to fucking hell! The bastards cleaned me out!"

Slumping to the bed, he bent forward, head in hands. His office destroyed. His apartment burglarized. Jesus Christ, it was almost more than he could bear.

He grabbed the phone and punched Kane's number. "Al, it's John. I just got home and. . ."

"Did you pay the boys?" Kane interrupted.

"Yes. Sure. That's not why I called. My apartment's been robbed."

"What?"

"The bastards took money, art, all my Waterford crystal, televisions, stereo stuff. Hell, they even took my files."

"What files, John?"

"All my copies of. . ." He stopped in mid-sentence, realizing Kane didn't know he kept duplicate files on all Tristar transactions.

"Copies of what, John?"

"Ah. . . tax returns and. . . stuff."

"John, I know you're lying. If it were just tax returns, you would have said so in the beginning. You had copies of Tristar, didn't you?"

"Don't you ever stop being a lawyer?"

"No, I don't. And thanks to your paranoia about blackmail, someone now has copies of our scheme at the university."

Wiggams stood up, turned around, as if searching for some way to escape this gaping hole he was ready to fall into. "What are we going to do?"

"Have you called the police yet?"

"No. You're the first call I made. Next I'll call the cops and my insurance agent."

"Don't report the burglary right away. Added to the fire at the university, it may raise suspicions."

"About what?"

"The comptroller's office burning down and his home robbed on the same weekend? Use your head, John."

"I thought you said more than half the building burned. It wasn't just my office, was it?"

"That's right, it wasn't, but we don't want to focus attention on you. Especially since we now have Tristar files floating around somewhere. You need to keep a low profile, let attention be directed toward the university, not you."

"Why would anyone do that?"

"All day long, there's been speculation that the fire was arson. If the cops learn your apartment was robbed, they may tie the two together and start investigating you."

"Christ, Al, I've been in Las Vegas. I have witnesses and alibis galore."

"Listen to me, John. For the time being, you are not to report it. Got it?" He waited. "Do you understand, or need I be more explicit?"

Wiggams sighed. "Yeah, I got it."

"Smart decision, John. Just sit tight. I'll be in touch."

Wiggams hung up and lay back on his bed. Christ, what a mess. Something didn't seem quite right, but he was too exhausted, physically and emotionally, to worry about it now. He had hardly slept since Thursday night. He knew tomorrow at the university would be hectic. . . trying to piece together a new office, prepare an inventory of what was destroyed, face the wrath of Gayle St. James. Too tired now. Had to get some rest.

DANIELLE HELD OPEN the door. "Come on in, Erin, and meet my dad. I've been filling him in. After all I've told him, he's dying to meet you."

Erin gave Danielle a funny look. "Yeah, I bet."

"No, not that. He just knows about our Tristar investigation and the terrific trio."

In the kitchen, George Baldwin stood and reached his hand across the remnants of their fast food banquet. "At last. It's a pleasure to meet the person my daughter admires so much."

Erin shook his hand and grinned at Danielle. "Thank you, Mr. Baldwin. The feeling is mutual. . . between us." She dropped his hand and sat down. "Please, sit, sit."

"I'm sure it is, but I want you to know that my daughter doesn't confer admiration easily. In fact, besides her mother and me, you may be the only recipient."

"Well, then, I am in excellent company."

"Very good. Danielle said you were intelligent."

"Okay, enough of the 'make a good first impression' garbage," Danielle said. "Let's get down to business." She turned to Erin. "I've brought Dad up to but not including the Vegas trip."

"No details about the fire or Dawes' disappearance?"

"Go ahead. You tell him."

Erin turned toward the Deputy Director of the CIA. "The short version is that the university business office burned down last night—J.P. Wiggams' office—and Professor Harmon Dawes, another Tristar partner, is missing. I suspect the two are connected."

"Why?"

"Just too coincidental. I don't have to tell you, in police investigations, that's a red flag."

Baldwin nodded. "Go on."

"It appears to me that C. Albert Kane—your old Harvard pal—is attempting to get rid of anything or anybody that can connect him to Tristar."

"Wow, slow down there. That's quite an accusation to level against a man who is of counsel to Madison University. Have any evidence?"

"Yes. And no. That's why I asked Danielle to request your help. With a wire tap?"

"You actually believe physical harm has come to Dawes?"

"I do. Absolutely. I've been with Mrs. Dawes since late last night. Whoever grabbed him worked hard to make it look like the departure of an angry husband who found out his wife's been unfaithful. I don't believe it for a minute."

Baldwin shook his head. "Evidence, Erin. I need more than your belief to get a tap."

"Daddy, Erin is an extremely intuitive person. I trust her gut feelings."

"Intuition is a wonderful tool, dear daughter, but you asked me here for professional help, not to admire crystal balls."

Erin laughed. "Dani, thanks for the vote of confidence, but your father's right. The strongest evidence we have right now is circumstantial. He didn't leave his wife a note. He suposedly took with him things that Ginny said he would have left, like her jewelry and his old clothing."

"Old clothing?" Danielle asked.

"If you were leaving for good, you'd take your golf clubs, some library books maybe, but wouldn't you leave behind some worn out ties or clothes or shoes that were out of style or worn out?"

"Sure."

"So would he. Anyone would. But his clothes closets were clean as a whistle, nothing left. And Ginny is one hundred percent sure he would have left her the jewelry he's given her over the years. But that was gone too."

Baldwin extracted a pen and notebook from his pocket and jotted something. "Does sound a bit strange to me too. But that kind of suposition is not enough to support your presumptions."

"I agree. Will you help us?"

Baldwin picked up a cold fry, brought it to his mouth, tossed it back. "Something criminal is almost certainly going on with Tristar, perhaps also with the fire and Dawes' disappearance. But this is not within the jurisdiction of the CIA. Any help I give would be unofficial."

Danielle wrapped the cold fries in the burger paper and took them to her trash can. Over her shoulder: "What can you do, then?"

"To begin with, report Professor Dawes as a missing person. Bring in the local authorities on that issue."

Erin shook her head. "Not a good idea."

"Why?"

"Because Kane has them in his pocket. He'd hear about it in two seconds; that would blow our story."

"If he's that connected, we're talking about a situation that puts the two of you in grave danger."

Danielle clapped her hands together. "That's what I have been trying to tell you!"

"Dani, Mr. Baldwin, I haven't had a chance to tell you what happened this afternoon, something that confirmed my fears." Erin explained how spooked Kane acted when Ginny told him Dawes was at home nursing a sprained ankle. How she'd followed him, watched him make a phone call, seen him open a self storage unit and check on what it contained. "Something is there that we should know about, I'd bet on it."

"You say Kane made a phone call? From a cell phone or a public booth?"

"It was a booth."

"Can you get me an address of a nearby building?"

"Sure. I remember exactly where it was. There were buildings across the street."

"Good. With that, I can have the call traced."

"Wow," Danielle said. "You can do that?"

"If it was long distance, yes. Now, Erin, since my daughter tells me you're a former cop, I'm certain you know the address of the self storage place. . . and the bin number." She gave them to him. He wrote them down.

"I've been thinking about something else you can help with, Mr. Baldwin. A sprained ankle wouldn't keep Professor Dawes away from his university duties. When he doesn't show up for his classes tomorrow, there are bound to be questions."

"Here's what you do. Have Mrs. Dawes report him as sick. Pneumonia maybe. Or mono. . . something that will require considerable recovery time."

"Okay."

"She should follow her regular routine. You too. She's taking care of her sick husband. You just adhere to your teaching schedule."

"She's staying with me for a couple of nights. She's too upset to be home alone."

"No, no. She has to go home. If her husband is ill, that's where she'd be. Kane will be sure to call her at home, check out her story. Let's keep him guessing."

"Your right. He will check."

Danielle smiled at her friend. "I told you my father would help."

Baldwin made more notes. "There's something else. If you're right about Kane, he'll stop at nothing. That means, if he learns you have the goods on him with Tristar, he'll get rid of you too." He looked at the young women, letting that sink in. "I want you to hide those files in a safe place."

"Where, Daddy?"

"Rent a locker at the closest major airport. Greensboro's probably the best. Use an assumed name, of course. In the mean time, I will try to find a local authority we can trust."

"Daddy, can you run a background check on John P. Wiggams? See if you can confirm what I was told?"

"Sure. And while I'm at it, I'll run Kane, Dawes and St. James." He jotted in his notebook again. "Listen, have Mrs. Dawes call her family physician and get a prescription for a strong antibiotic. When anyone asks—the university or Kane—she can tell them what medication he's on. That'll make it more convincing."

"My father thinks of everything, doesn't he, Erin?"

Her father pushed back his chair and stood. "Interesting as this conversation may be, I told my pilot we'd depart at ten o'clock. Have to leave now so he won't need to file a new flight plan." He hugged Danielle tight and, when she stepped out of his arms, reached for Erin. "You're almost family, my dear." He patted her back and released her. "I'll be in touch."

As soon as the plane leveled off, George Baldwin pulled out his notebook and flipped to tonight's jottings. Something about Erin's strong intuition plus the circumstantial evidence she'd related made him ready to take a risk. He checked his brief case, looked up the home number of the regional director in the Raleigh office. Moments later, the wire tap on C. Albert Kane's home phone was ordered.

CHAPTER TWELVE

Gayle St. James' administrative skills were being tested this September Monday. The university was in a crisis and she knew the Board of Trustees would be watching her closely. After all, she was not only a newly appointed president but also the first woman to hold this position in the history of North Carolina.

At 8:00 a.m. she already had John Wiggams sitting across from her. She studied the paper he'd handed her. "Desk, swivel chair, file cabinet, computer equipment etc. Yes, yes, we have spares of all these things in storage. They won't be as grand as what you lost, but they'll get you back in business. I'll check with Jake Gathers as soon as you leave, get you set up in a temporary office."

"You said we could install our accounting personnel in Chase Hall. I thought it was scheduled for demolition."

"It was, John, but we'll use it until we can rebuild the business office building. It's old and won't afford you the luxury you're accustomed to, but in a pinch. . . ."

"Of course, of course." Wiggams wriggled in the chair on the other side of the president's desk. "I was wondering. . ."

The president looked up. "What?"

"Was anything saved from my office? Anything at all?" He hoped her answer would be no. He hoped his blackmail photos and all the Tristar files were reduced to ashes.

Dr. St. James shook her head slowly. "Sorry, John. I know you had some beautiful things there—I've told everyone on campus they should visit your office sometime to see what exquisite taste you have. Everything's gone. The fire investigators are certain the blaze started in your office, so it burned longer there than anywhere else."

Wiggams stared at the woman. Was she implying something sinister or merely stating a fact? He didn't have long to wait.

"If it turns out to be arson, the investigators will need to interview you."

"Why? I was out of town when it happened. I have no idea. . ."

"John, there just routine questions, I'm sure."

He relaxed. "Your idea was a stroke of genius, Madam President." He caught her look of surprise. "You know. . . to keep daily back-up disks of all university business in a fireproof vault in another building. As you know, at first I thought it was unnecessary extra work, but now, it seems, you were prophetic."

"Hmmm. Careful, John, you'll have arson investigators questioning me." She grinned. "Now, if you'll excuse me, I have a great number of people to see today."

Wiggams thanked the president for her prompt action on his behalf and left the office just as the intercom buzzed. He couldn't help overhearing the president's administrative assistant inform her that Professor Dawes' wife had just called indicating he was suffering from pneumonia and could be out for several weeks.

Well, Wiggams thought, now that all his files were toast and Dawes wouldn't be around to pick stocks for a while, and Kane was making all kinds of threats he wouldn't hesitate to carry out, maybe it was time for Tristar to fade into history.

From the president's office Wiggams walked directly to Chase Hall. He shoved open the ancient front door and nearly gagged at the smell of mildew that hit him in the face. Jesus, how could he work in such a place?

Hearing the sound of an electric saw, he followed the noise through the corridors, lifting his feet over spots in the terrazzo floor where big chunks were missing. He turned the corner and nearly bumped into Jake Gathers coming out of a classroom.

"Hey, there, Mr. Wiggams, let me show you to your new office."

"I hope it's in better shape than what I've seen of this building so far."

"I'm whippin' it into shape for you. Come and see."

Gathers led him down the stark corridor with its ceiling tiles hanging to expose long fluorescent tubes, most of them not working. "You gotta remember this joint hasn't had any maintenance. It was supposed to be a tear-down till the fire changed all that. My men will have it lookin' and smellin' good in a coupla days." He turned another corner and pushed open a door. Its opaque glass pane in the upper half was so grimy it looked like the bottom, rusted steel, half. "See here? A nice corner office. Southern exposure. Good light."

Wiggams wrinkled his nose. "Disgusting. What is that awful smell?" It reminded him of jail cells he'd lived in years ago.

"Just a little urine. Rat crap too, prob'ly." With an oily rag, Gathers swiped at a rat's nest on the floor in the corner. "I'll pour the bleach to it and you'll be surprised at how nice this room'll clean up. I've checked the warehouse and we'll get you the nicest furniture we can find. Don't you worry. I'll take care of you."

"Yeah, yeah." He pinched his nose with his thumb and forefinger. "Don't call me until this place is fit for something better than rats. Jesus, I have to get out of here." He dashed for the hall. "Don't forget, I'll need nine private offices for my accounting staff. Furniture, equipment, computers, the works. President St. James has my list."

"I'll get it from her. Give me a few days. You won't know this place."

Wiggams nearly ran to the exit. Once outside in the warm September sunshine, he gulped great breaths of air. What a disaster this was turning out to be. His office destroyed, his home burglarized, Kane making not-so-veiled threats. What else could go wrong?

Until his makeshift office was habitable, he had plenty of time to kill. Might as well while it away in pleasant surroundings. He thought back to the news he'd overheard as he left the president's office. Maybe he'd pay a sick call on his good friend, Professor Dawes.

In his car headed for the Dawes' home on the south side of Charlotte, Wiggams mulled over this latest bit of news. Something just didn't fit. Kane had told him Ginny reported a week ago, right after the dinner dance, they'd had a huge fight and then Saturday night, she'd come home and found her husband had packed up and left her. Then she called the university two days later to say he has pneumonia? How could this be? Who was lying? Ginny? Or Kane?

His mind toyed with other thoughts. What had nagged him since he returned from Vegas last night? He'd been too tired to think about it then, but now. . . . Hadn't Kane phoned him in Vegas and reported that his office was on fire? Or had he said the building where his office was located? When he called Kane with news of the break-in at his apartment, Kane had insisted the cops would connect him to his burned office, if he reported the burglary. Was his office the target of an arsonist? His office or Tristar files? Kane had sounded so elusive. So threatening.

Ginny answered the door in jeans and a blouse. "Why, John, what brings you here?"

Wiggams stood on the front step trying to peer behind her into the house. "I heard that Harmon was sick and thought I'd come over to cheer him up."

She stepped outside and eased the door to behind her. "That is just so nice of you, and if Harm were awake, I'm sure he'd be delighted that you came all the way out here to see him."

"Oh. He's asleep."

"Yes. He had a terrible night, but the doctor prescribed some strong medication—Cipro for the pneumonia and something else to help him sleep. Halcion. He's really out, poor dear."

"Please give him my regards. I'll call later to check on him." He appraised Ginny. "You don't look so great yourself, if you'll pardon my being frank."

"Oh, John, I'm just so worried about my dear Harm. He's all I have. I. . ." She patted Wiggams' arm. "Thanks for coming. Especially since you have your own problems, with the fire in your office and all. I. . . really appreciate your dropping by" She stepped backwards, into the foyer, and closed the door.

As he strolled to the end of the brick pavers, Wiggams noticed the small access door to the garage had glass panes. He crept over and peered inside. Only one car there. Ginny's. If Harmon was upstairs sick, where the hell was his Lincoln?

Wiggams returned to his car and, on the way to his apartment, tried to focus on his suspicions. It seemed that every time he reached out to someone connected to Tristar, he came up empty. Even Ginny had said "the fire in your office."

Office files turned to ash, back-ups stolen from his home, Dawes sick and unavailable, and Kane. . . making sure he did not report the burglary. Why? What the hell was going on?

Only one man could provide the answers. He would have to confront him.

PRESIDENT ST. JAMES digested the information about Dawes and buzzed her A.A. "Set up a conference call for me with Professors Hanson and Klein."

"Will do. Mr. Kane is holding on line three."

"Tell him to hold or call back; I want the conference call first."

Moments later, the intercom sounded again. "I have Hanson and Klein on two."

President St. James hitched her chair up closer to her desk and pressed the speaker button. "Gentlemen, good morning. We have a minor crisis facing us. Harmon Dawes will be out sick for two weeks or more. I need to know if either of you has room in your schedule to fill in temporarily as department chair."

Hanson immediately responded that he couldn't even begin to consider it. Klein, however, volunteered to cover Dawes' administrative duties but couldn't help with his teaching schedule. "Very good. I appreciate your willingness to help out, Professor Klein. My A.A. will fax you a schedule of department meetings and my routine conferences scheduled with department heads."

She punched the interoffice button and learned that Kane was still holding. "Get me Professor Erin Gallagher. I'll talk to her after I finish with Kane. Oh, and bring me Professor Dawes' teaching schedule and run a computer check on who has gaps in their teaching schedule in the economics department." Without missing a beat, she turned her attention to the university counsel. "Albert, sorry for the delay, but we're a little busy right now. What can I do for you?"

"Quite understandable. I thought you might need some help, and I wanted to be sure you were clear regarding the fire investigation and our responsibilities."

"I could use some advice on several matters. I'm calling an emergency meeting of the executive committee for tonight at seven. Could you meet me about an hour before for a briefing?"

"Certainly. Where do you want me?"

"My office, and don't eat. I'm having sandwiches sent in."

"Anything else I can help with right now?"

"Not unless you are a qualified economics instructor." She chuckled, amazed that she could still find humor in this morning's activities.

"Sorry, can't help you with that. Why? What's the problem?"

"No major problem. I'm sure I can handle it internally. Professor Dawes' wife just called in to notify us that Harmon has pneumonia." A kernel of frustration crept into her voice. "Just what I needed today."

"Sorry to hear that. Pneumonia. Well, these days, it's usually curable."

"But in the meantime, someone else has to cover his classes and administrative duties." The campus campanile began to toll the hour. "Albert, I have to go. See you here at six."

Kane didn't even hang up; he just depressed the button and dialed Ginny's number. Dawes out with pneumonia? Yesterday it was a sprained ankle. This whole charade was really getting to him, and he decided to go after the weakest link, Ginny.

It rang four times before the answering machine came on. He hung up without leaving a message. As he tried Portofino's Baton Rouge number for the umpteenth time, Kane tapped a pencil against his desk in frustration. This time he answered.

"Damn it, Johnny, where have you been?"

"Who the hell is this?"

"It's Albert Kane, that's who."

"Albert, it's eight in the A.M. Monday morning, my time. I left Charlotte less than 24 hours ago. What the fuck's wrong with you?"

"Did you do the job?"

"Are you nuts? Of course I did. I told you that."

"Yesterday at the Petrini Health Center fundraising kick-off, his wife said he wasn't there because he hurt his ankle playing golf on Saturday."

"She's a whack job then, Albert. The only course he played on Saturday was in heaven."

"Johnny, I just spoke with the president of the university. This morning, Ginny Dawes reported him sick with pneumonia."

"Listen to me, Albert, and listen good. The only thing in his lungs right now is concrete. I did him about 1:30 on Saturday afternoon and put him in the project at 3:30 Sunday morning. Trust me, he ain't breathing anymore."

"What the hell's going on then?"

"Either someone is trying to get you rattled or they're on to you. Either way, I think we ought to hang up right now. I'm going on a little trip till this clears up."

The line went dead.

Jesus, Kane thought, if Johnny did the job, then maybe Ginny and that Gallagher broad knew more than they should. Ginny wasn't smart enough to come up with this fairy tale on her own. But Erin. . . she'd had him for lunch in their first encounter. He'd learned early on not to underestimate her. Could she know things she wasn't supposed to know? Could she have stumbled onto Tristar? Maybe Ginny, that bitch, confided in her, let something slip.

Perhaps it was time to extend the house tour invitation he made to Erin at the dinner dance. If he went to the university early, maybe he'd be able to arrange for his path to cross that of Associate Professor Erin Gallagher. A coincidence, of course.

Inside the white chevy van parked at the rear gate of Kane's mansion, two men smiled at each other. They removed their headsets and one rewound the tape and hit "play." After listening, he nodded. "Better call the boss and tell him we came up with something good."

"Yeah, I don't think they expected to get lucky so soon."

"They musta figured something would pop . . . that's why we were called out in the middle of the night."

GEORGE BALDWIN WAS in his office early this Monday. At three minutes past 9:00, when his secretary rang telling him the Raleigh office had priority information, he was genuinely pleased. He had left his daughter and her new friend less than twelve hours before. Thank goodness I ordered the wire tap from the plane, he thought.

"Mr. Deputy, it's Flanagan in North Carolina."

"Good morning, Paul. What do you have?"

"Not sure where you got this tip, but it paid off. We have a John Portofino from Baton Rouge, Louisiana, and your man Kane discussing what appears to be a contract killing in Charlotte. The transcription should be coming in as we speak."

"Thanks, Paul. Anything else I should be aware of?"

"Yes. Portifino plans to run and soon. Do you want him under surveillance?"

"Affirmative, but find someone outside the agency to do it for now. As I told you yesterday, there's no approval from the director yet."

"I understand. For now, I'll pull the Kane tape and forward it to you under security clearance FYEO."

"Good job, Paul, I owe you one. Keep the wire on Kane till further notice."

Baldwin replaced the phone and thought about his old college chum. Where had it all gone wrong with him? he wondered. It was becoming clear that he'd have to seek the director's approval eventually, but he needed more time to review the tale he'd been told last night. Perhaps Danielle and Erin were right about being the best informants for the time being. He'd have to get over the uneasy feeling that one of his operatives was his daughter.

He reached for the phone and, as he'd promised Danielle and Erin, ordered comprehensive background checks on Kane, Wiggams and David St..James. Next, the agency's financial division for a dig into the operations of Tristar Investments Inc. and First National of Boston. He knew he had about a week until the director would get wind of these activities and call him in. Until then, he'd do everything he could to verify the young women's suspicions.

IT WAS LATE afternoon when Gayle St..James heard the intercom for what seemed like the hundredth time.

"Professor Gallagher on two."

She put a smile in her voice. "Erin, how have you been?"

"Since all the excitement on campus yesterday? Much better than you, I presume. It must be hectic, dealing with the aftermath of the fire."

"Oh my, yes. On top of that, I've learned that Professor Dawes will be out sick for several weeks."

"Ah. Ergo the call to me this morning. Sorry I couldn't get back to you until now."

"Quite all right. Yes, we need to cover his classes. Might you be able to take Tuesday and Thursday from 1:00 to 3:00 and mornings at 8:00?"

"How long will he be out?"

"About two weeks, his wife said."

"As long as it's only for two weeks, I can help you with the afternoon classes."

The president sighed. "Thank you, Erin. That's a relief."

"My teaching load is already crammed full, but as a favor to you I'm willing to stretch the envelope a bit. As long as you assure me it will be only a couple of weeks. I can live without sleep that long."

The president chuckled. "I trust it won't be quite that bad. Two sections of the same course, so only one prep. And I'll assign you an extra assistant. I appreciate your help and believe me, it won't go unrewarded." She didn't wait for an answer. "Stop by my office today. My A.A. will have the necessary paperwork. Don't forget, you'll be eligible for additional pay, too."

"Thanks. That will come in handy. To cover the expense of my nervous breakdown."

"Maybe we'll have adjoining rooms. Good luck, Erin, and let me know if you need anything."

ALONE IN HER office cubicle, Erin groaned. She did *not* need this right now. It was all she could do to keep up with her current teaching schedule and still try to manage Danielle and Ginny. But her sense of duty was strong and a promise was a promise.

It was now a little after 4:00 p.m. and she was finished for the day. Might as well head for the president's office and get home early. She was still exhausted from yesterday—the early morning fire and Ginny's reaction to it, the Petrini Health Center ceremony, her tail of Kane to the storage facility and finally, the meeting with Danielle's father.

She locked her office, left the building and headed across university square. She loved this part of campus, with its beautifully mature oaks, maples and weeping cherry trees. It was crisscrossed by cobblestone walking paths and ornate concrete benches. It was an ivitation to sit and take in the beauty. As she made her way toward the large fountain in the middle of the square, she spotted C. Albert Kane sitting on the brick ledge that surrounded it. She turned on her heel, but it was too late; he'd seen her.

"Associate Professor Gallagher, Good afternoon."

Caught, she might as well be civil, she thought. She'd have to be careful not to tip her hand. He had no reason to think she knew anything about Tristar, or Dawes' mysterious disappearance. As far as he knew, nothing had changed since the dinner dance. "Hello C. Albert. What brings you to the world of academics?"

"Just enjoying the scenery before an emergency meeting called by the president."

"I'm headed to the president's office myself."

"Mind if I walk along?"

"Be my guest. On one condition."

"Oh? What could that be?"

"That you come clean."

His eyebrows shot up. "About what, my dear?"

"About what the 'C' in your name stands for."

His head reared back and he laughed till his eyes watered.

"I didn't think my request was that funny," Erin said, digging a tissue out of her handbag and handing it to him.

"I'm laughing like this because I was just wondering to myself how long it would take you to ask that question. You see, I don't give out that information to just anyone. But then, you aren't just anyone, are you?"

"Enough diversion, C. Albert. Are you going to tell me, or do I walk to the president's office alone?"

He fell in beside her and stretched his arm around her waist. She cocked her hip away from his hand.

"Okay, you win. It's Cedric. My mother thought it sounded distinguished. In case I ever ran for President of the United States."

"With your political ambitions, that's not entirely out of the question. So, Cedric, I'll be able to say I knew you when."

"Tell me, do you recall my invitation to see the mansion?"

"Sure do."

"Would you care to join me for dinner some night this week and collect on that tour I promised you?"

"Dream on. I'm on my way right now to pick up material to teach two additional classes for Professor Dawes. Until he's able to return, I won't have time to sleep, never mind eating dinner. . . with you or anyone."

"Really! What's wrong with him?"

"Pneumonia, I was told."

"Poor Ginny must have her hands full."

"Yeah, she does. I spoke with her yesterday."

"I wonder how he golfed on Saturday if he was so sick."

Erin shrugged. "Apparently he'd been sick all week but decided to play anyway. I suppose he pushed it too far. She said he had a weak spell coming off #10 tee."

"I'm truly sorry to hear that. I'll have to phone the professor with my good wishes for his recovery. But regardless of your protests about having no time, you will have to eat. If I promise not to keep you over long, will you reconsider my invitation?"

Erin knew she was being set up. The bastard knew very well where Harmon was. But maybe, if she played along and accepted the invitation, he would make a slip. "My extra classes are Tuesdays and Thursdays. So I suppose I could make it on Wednesday—my least loaded day."

"It's settled, then. Dinner with me at The Mansion, Wednesday night. Say seven-thirty?"

"Make it six-thirty and it's a deal."

"I'll send a car for you at six."

A moment of panic boiled up in her throat. "No need. I'll just drive myself there."

"Just wanted to demonstrate that chivalry is not dead. But I understand." He smiled and tipped an imaginary hat. "Well, here's the president's office."

"Her A.A. has what I need, so I'll just grab it and be on my way. See you Wednesday."

Erin left him as he was asking the secretary to announce his arrival. She walked to the parking lot, cranked up her old Honda and headed for Ginny's.

"You were right, Erin," Ginny said the second she opened the door. "Kane phoned this morning, before you dropped me off. He didn't leave a message in my voicemail box, but Caller ID picked up his number."

"He's bound to call again. In fact, I ran into him just now and he said he'd be phoning to offer your husband his get well wishes. That bastard. He knows good and well Professor Dawes doesn't have pneumonia. Maybe later this week, I'll find out what else he knows.

Ginny led her into the living room and motioned her to an easy chair. "Wiggams came by too. But I got rid of him fast. He seemed, I don't know, worried about something other than Harmon's illness." What Erin had said finally dawned on her. "What do you mean, you'll find out from Kane later this week?"

"He invited me to his home for dinner."

"And you're going? For God's sake, Erin, that's suicide!"

"I think we got to him. I'm sure he's going to pump me to find out what we know."

"Why you and not me?"

"'Cause he's already pumped you for two years." Erin smiled.

"And he thinks you're that stupid?"

"No, he knows I'm anything but. I'm counting on his ego. The kind of man he is. . .he'll believe he's smarter and can manipulate me."

"Jesus, Erin, please promise me you'll be careful. Please."

"Don't worry. I will be. I'll be sure to tell him that lots of people know I'm there. He wouldn't dare harm me and get away with it. I need your help. I got an idea as I drove here."

"What?"

"Call Kane's Wednesday night about 8:30 and tell him you saw his number on caller ID and finally worked up the courage to call him. Play along with him and keep him occupied long enough for me to search the study."

"What will you look for?"

"I don't really know yet."

"Erin, this is too dangerous."

"Do you want to find out what's happened to your husband?"

"Yes, of course."

'Then please do what I asked. Also, check my house at 11.00 p.m. If I'm not there, call Danielle at this number." She scribbled on a piece of paper and handed it to Ginny.

"Why?"

"Just call. She'll know what to do."

"All right. It's obvious your mind's made up."

"Sure is." Erin took a deep breath. "There's something else you can do for me. . . that'll help me with Kane."

"Anything."

"I'll be trying to pry information out of him, so it would help if I knew his Achilles heel."

"Honestly, Erin, I don't think he has one. For the two years of our affair, all he ever wanted was sex. But if you give him what he wants, he usually would talk afterward."

"Does he do drugs?"

"He used to do a line of coke before we had sex, early on. But not for over a year. I think once he decided he had a promising future in politics, he decided to clean up his vices."

"Anything else?"

"Yes. The place is loaded with security devices. They're all over, so be careful." Ginny stood up and came to Erin's chair. "I still wish you wouldn't do this. If Harmon really is. . . gone forever. . . you're the only friend I have left. I don't want to lose you too."

Erin stood up and put her arms around Ginny. "Ever read Shakespeare?" she whispered into Ginny's ear.

Ginny shook her head.

"I have. He's quite the student of human nature. Did you know that in his tragedies, the hero's best quality always leads to his downfall?"

"I did not know that. But what's it have to do with. . ."

"What's Albert Kane's best talent?"

"I'd have to say it's his legal mind, his ability to manipulate situations any way he wants. . . always to his own good."

"Right. And I can play on that. . . to bring about his downfall." Erin let that sink in as she broke the embrace. "I have to go Gin, it's been a long day."

At home, Erin got ready for bed. Before she turned out the light, she called Danielle and filled her in on the day's events. She wasn't surprised at Dani's reaction to the news she planned to have dinner at Kane's home.

"Have you lost your mind? If you're set on doing this, at least wait until Daddy gets back to us. Please, Erin, I'm afraid of what that bastard might do."

"Kane initiated this. I think he's running scared. Frightened people make mistakes. Don't you see? I have to take advantage of the opportunity."

"Considering what we suspect about him, you are flirting with danger."

"I know it's not for the faint of heart. I'll take precautions."

"Promise?"

"Promise. Talk to you tomorrow."

AT HOME FOR lunch the next day, Danielle bustled about the kitchen, her mind on everything but the sandwich she was cutting in two. "Ow," she said as the serrated blade nicked her finger. She stuck it in her mouth and sucked. When the phone rang, she wrapped a tissue around her finger and held it tight with her thumb while she picked up the receiver with her other hand.

"I figured I'd find you at home. Glad you're a creature of habit."

"Daddy. Hey. What's up?"

"Some new developments. But first, what's up with you? I hear worry in your voice."

"You don't miss a thing, do you. Ever consider becoming a spy?"

"Out with it, daughter. What's the problem?"

"Well, the minor issue is I just cut my finger with a paring knife. But more importantly I'm worried about Erin. She plans to have dinner at Kane's house tomorrow night and I can't talk her out of it."

"You have good reason to worry. Her suspicions about him are well founded. We tapped his phone Sunday night as you had requested. Early yesterday he made a call to a known hit man in Louisiana. Our interpretation of the dialogue is that Kane was confirming that indeed the hit was made. Erin's idea to spook him worked, but now we have to be extremely careful. I believe Harmon Dawes has been murdered."

Danielle staggered to a chair and slumped into it. "Oh my god, Daddy."

"Yes, I know, that's why I called. You need to be aware of what we're dealing with."

"Are you sure?"

"As sure as I can be without the body."

Danielle broke down in tears. Her father waited for the hysteria to run its course.

Finally, she composed herself. "Is Erin in any danger? Please be honest. I need to know."

"If Kane finds out that you have Tristar files, the exposure for both of you is. . . very serious."

"I guess if he took out his own partner, he wouldn't think twice about us."

"That's right, Danielle. Has Erin taken the files to an airport yet?"

"No."

"I suggest you do that immediately, young lady. This is not a game any more."

"She's been very busy. I'll take them to Greensboro today."

"Good. Both of you need to be totally alert right now. There's a part of me that wants to turn this over to the proper authorities. I'm very concerned about you two."

"Who would you give it to?"

"The FBI."

"Could Kane get to them?"

"I doubt it very much."

"Then why don't we do it?"

"Several reasons; one, they would bring Kane and Portofino in immediately and I think that's too soon; two, it would take them months to place operatives where you two already are and three, if they do use you and Erin as informants, they would remove your safety from my control."

"So what do you recommend?"

"I'm taking quite a risk with my job, but I think we have a week—give or take—until the director finds out what I've done. During that time, I want either of you to check in with me daily while I review the scam and attempt to find the body."

"We can do that; I'll tell Erin."

Baldwin gave his daughter a secure phone number where he could be reached at any time. "Dani, promise me you'll get those files out of Erin's home today. I mean immediately."

"Sure thing, Daddy. Thanks for everything."

Danielle sat there deep in thought about her father's call. She was playing it over and over in her mind. It was very frightening. She headed back to campus but with the accounting department still in limbo there was little anyone could do. Screw the job she thought, this new information was vital and needed to be shared with Erin ASAP. She headed for her office.

Erin, briefcase in hand, locked the door to her office and turned down the hall toward the first of her two extra classes. As she rounded the corner, Danielle rushed in from the outside. Erin spied her and waved. "Hey, Dani, here I am."

"Am I glad I caught you." She filled her in on George Baldwin's latest news and handed her the secure phone number for emergency use. "He's adamant that those files have to be out of your house N-O-W. So give me your key and I'll get them up to Greensboro."

Erin lowered her voice. "So Professor Dawes was murdered."

"Yeah. 'Fraid so."

"Shit. I was beginning to like the guy, even if he was a man. My gut instinct told me Kane had him killed, but a part of me always hoped I was wrong."

"This is getting to be really scary. What started out as a game to see if we could uncover some fraud or embezzlement has gotten way out of hand. "

Erin saw a janitorial supply closet and opened the door, motioning Danielle inside. "Damn it, Dani, we can't. They'll contact the local authorities, who will alert Kane. . and we're dead."

"My father figures it that way too."

"So what's his plan?"

"He wants you to wear a wire for your dinner date with Kane tomorrow."

"What?" Erin leaned the back of her head against a shelf of paint cans. "No way. It's too soon. He's still very suspicious of me. Let me ease his suspicions. I'll set him up on this first visit and spring a trap later."

A bell jangled just outside the closet door. "Jesus, Dani, I have to get to class. Can't deal with this stuff any more. Go ahead and clear out the files. I'll talk to you tonight."

AS THE AFTERNOON wore on, the background checks piled up on George Baldwin's desk. The man he'd admired at Harvard had taken a left turn somewhere. For close to 15 years, the report showed, Kane had developed close ties to the Las Vegas Mafia. Early in his career, Kane had represented two "family" members in criminal indictments. They'd walked away with acquittals. He also had a close brush with jury tampering in a Virginia rape case where the accused was one John P. Wiggams. Okay, that verified the information Danielle picked up from David St. James in Las Vegas.

Baldwin put down the first report and picked up the second. Wiggams, it appeared, had amassed an impressive laundry list of criminal complaints. Charges included fraud, embezzlement, theft, numerous sexual deviate arrests and statutory rape. For some, charges had been dropped or he'd been acquitted. For others, he'd served time.

How in hell had a convicted felon managed to become comptroller of Madison University? He could see Kane—a high profile attorney—slipping through the net but not Wiggams. There could be only one answer: Kane was responsible for Wiggams' job placement.

He thought he had sent his daughter to a well respected southern university, one that provided safety while she could receive an excellent education. Until the internship problem surfaced at the end of the spring semester, he had no reason to think otherwise. She sure was making up for those uneventful undergraduate years he thought.

He reached for the phone to call Paul Flanagan in Raleigh.

"Flanagan here."

"George Baldwin. I reviewed your information and supplemented it with more background checks of my own. I'm concerned about my daughter's welfare."

"Danielle? What does she have to do with all this?"

"She and a university friend are the ones who gave me the lead on this."

"No wonder you're worried."

"Paul, do you have a retired operative we can call upon to shadow her?"

"Yeah, I think I can get Tommy Logan to do it."

"He's a good man. I've worked with him in the past."

"I'll get back to you."

Baldwin knew his daughter well. Trying to keep her corralled was like harnessing a wild boar. He needed the satisfaction of knowing that someone was on her. He hung up feeling much better about the path he had chosen.

WIGGAMS STAYED IN his apartment all day Tuesday. There was nothing he could do at the university without an office in which to work. Instead, he compiled a comprehensive list of everything missing from his ransacked home. Crystal, sterling, some loose diamonds, major pieces of art, the entire home entertainment center, what little money he hadn't needed to pay off his debt at the MGM. And all the Tristar back-ups. Those, he didn't put on the list he would eventually turn in to his insurance agent. When would Kane permit that call? he wondered.

He phoned Kane's office, discovered he was in court all day and had meetings through the evening. He made an appointment for the next morning. It was high time he got some answers.

Next, he put in a call to David. It was several minutes before he came on the line.

"Yes, John, what can I do for you?"

"Have you talked to Kane or Dawes since you got back from Vegas?"

"No, but it's only Tuesday. We just got back Sunday. What's the problem?"

"I don't know. Has anything strange been going on at your end?"

"Not really. The only thing a bit odd was that someone hacked into Tristar files. After I checked things thoroughly, however, everything was fine."

"You don't know who gained access?"

"No, and that's what's so odd. We have excellent computer security. Whoever did it had better technology than ours."

Wiggams couldn't keep his suspicions to himself any longer. "David, I'm a little concerned about some happenings that seem to be less than coincidental."

"Such as?"

"You already know the Tristar files burned in the university fire. What you don't know is that my apartment was burglarized while I was in Vegas and for some reason they took Tristar back-up disks and files. Now Harmon Dawes is missing or sick, depending on who you talk with. That conveniently leaves Kane with the only ledgers and journals in existence."

"I have records of all transactions, John."

"But no company books, right?"

"That's right, why?"

"I'm just getting bad vibes, that's all."

"I think you're getting a bit paranoid. I wouldn't worry; everything is fine."

"We'll see. I plan to meet with Kane tomorrow and find out what the hell is going on. I'll let you know."

David hung up and let out a long breath. He didn't like Wiggams, never had. Considered him a loose cannon. After the incident in Vegas, he liked him even less. He decided to call his sister, inquire about how she was dealing with the fire aftermath.

He could seize the opportunity to discreetly inquire as to Wiggams' state of mind. His sister's A.A. recognized his voice and put him right through.

"David, how nice to hear from you."

"Just thought I'd lend a little moral support as you deal with the fire problems."

"It is pretty hectic right now, but I think everything is under control. Fact is, I'm here with our counsel going over our insurance claim, deciding on whether to demolish and rebuild the whole place or see if the structure can be saved."

"I'm sorry, I'll let you go."

"No, no, I have a few minutes."

"I understand it was the business office that was most affected."

"That's correct."

"I hope that nut Wiggams has been of some help to you."

"How do you know him?"

"Met him at your annual dinner dance just 10 days ago, remember?"

"That's right, of course."

"Seemed to me he is an odd duck, as comptrollers go."

"Wiggams may not come from the typical mold of accountants and bankers, but he's been doing a wonderful job on behalf of the university. His management of our investment portfolio has been outstanding. He's made us tremendous profits."

She put her hand over the mouthpiece and wiggled her fingers at Kane, sitting on the other side of the desk. He lifted his eyes to her face as she mouthed the words "thanks to you."

"I'm glad he's been of help. I may have misjudged him."

"David, let me get back to work. I'll call you later in the week when I have more time."

WEDNESDAY MORNING, WIGGAMS steeled his nerve and drove downtown to the plush offices of Hoover, Kane and Simpson. He parked in the adjacent garage and took the elevator to the 10th floor.

When he gave his name, Kane's secretary acknowledged his appointment but argued that Mr. Kane was in an important meeting and couldn't be disturbed.

"Send in my name and inform him I am here on an urgent matter and have no intentions of leaving until I've seen him."

She put down the intercom and nodded. "He'll see you in fifteen minutes."

"Damn lucky for you."

Kane kept him waiting twice the announced time. Wiggams' short legs propelled him down the corridor behind the secretary, through the door and to a stop as Kane came around his desk to meet him. "Hello, John. What brings you here?"

"We need to talk." He stood erect and waited for the secretary who had escorted him to retreat and shut the door.

"About what?"

"All these coincidences surrounding Tristar."

Kane made his way slowly back to his chair and lowered himself into its depths. He tented his fingers in front of him and stared at the little man. "Like what?"

Wiggams knew Kane was toying with him. He let his exasperation show.

"Damn it, the fire, my apartment burglary and Harmon, that's what. I went to see him on Monday, after I heard he was ill, and Ginny said he was sleeping. As I was leaving, I looked in the garage and his car wasn't even there. Where is he?"

"I think you are in no position to put such questions to me, John. Need I remind you that if it wasn't for me you would be in Fairfax County, Virginia, doing 10 to 15 without parole?"

Wiggams paced the ten foot width in front of Kane's desk. "I know, and I'm grateful, but I still want to know what's going on with Harmon?"

Kane leaned back in his chair, his fingers laced behind his head. "Let's just say he is on a very long sabbatical and will not return any time soon."

Wiggams halted in mid-stride and whirled. "You had him offed, didn't you?"

"Care to join him?" His voice was smooth, unruffled.

"I was just worried, Al, that's all."

"Seven years ago, I told you to just keep your nose clean, maintain a low profile and follow my orders. Remember?"

Wiggams hung his head. "I have, Al, I have."

"No, John, you have *not*. I know you have been gambling in Vegas, screwing young post-grad interns and hiring P.I.'s to gather information on me. You're out of bullets. Screw up one more time and you, like Harmon, will become another university pillar cast in stone. Now get the hell out of here and just do your job. And one more thing. Do not ever think you can win in a confrontation with me. I am way out of your league."

Wiggams left the office with sweat coming from every pore in his body. He hadn't felt this way since Kane had called him to the mansion several weeks ago.

He headed back home. While threading his way through traffic he became aware of this obnoxious odor. He leaned his body to the side and sniffed his underarms; it was him. He could sure use a shower. Damn, what a mistake to question Kane like that. The man was too well connected, too powerful. Wiggams had no desire to join Harmon, wherever he was. Besides, with Harmon gone, if Tristar continued, his share of the pot just got sweeter.

KNOWING THAT TONIGHT she would make every effort to expose the truth from someone capable of hiring a hit man to kill a business partner, Erin found it hard to concentrate on her Wednesday classes. The only other matter she had time to think about today was the delivery of the Tristar files to the Greensboro airport. Danielle had left a message on her office machine saying she'd done it, and mailed a spare key to her father. Thank God they were out of her home.

With her duties at the university finally over for the day, she trudged out of the building and headed home to prepare for tonight's dinner at The Mansion. By the time she unlocked her apartment door, her stomach was doing gymnastics. She opened the fridge, found some yogurt and downed a couple of spoonfuls to settle it.

As she showered, she reviewed her situation. She knew Kane would stop at nothing to find out what she and Ginny were up to. If she was ever to get any information out of him, Erin had to give him something. But what? Could she dare reveal her awareness of his business relationship with Harmon and Wiggams? No details, just that Ginny had shared comments with her about an investment business the three have? Then there was the sex issue—she'd have to play that one by ear. What happened—or didn't happen—in the bedroom would depend on how much information he would part with. Since he was suspicious of her already, she doubted that much would be divulged willingly.

She rubbed herself dry with the soft bath sheet then wrapped it around her torso. Time to select her attire. It had to be alluring but not too seductive. She wasn't advertising herself as a whore: will sell body for information. Even though, if it came right down to it, that's what she was prepared to do. She pulled out a sleeveless navy blue dress featuring a v-neck top with a hemline that crested just above the knee. Simple, elegant, sensual. She accessorized with a pearl necklace her mom had given her and some gold bangle bracelets.

She never wore much make-up, just a little mascara, blush and lipstick. Good skin didn't need to be covered, she always felt, just highlighted. She brushed her hair back from her face and swept it up into a French twist. Appraising herself in the mirror, Erin felt if any woman could get Kane to open up, she would be the one.

As she sat on the bed to pull on her panty hose, the phone rang at her elbow. Without preamble, Ginny screamed at her. "I can't do it. I can't bring myself to call that bastard tonight. You'll have to come up with something else. Sorry." And hung up.

Erin wasn't totally surprised. Ginny was at the end of her rope.

Okay, she was on her own. She'd either come home with something she could give the authorities to solidify this case, or she'd die trying.

Erin hoped that was only a saying.

CHAPTER THIRTEEN

Kane had ordered the cook to prepare Salmon Stravinsky as the entree with Dublin Cheesecake for dessert. He dressed casually in charcoal gray slacks and a silk, white-on-white shirt, with two buttons opened at the neckline. He wore penny loafers with no socks. Associate Professor Erin Gallagher would see a casual, laid back C. Albert Kane, something she might not have expected.

Erin arrived right on time and the butler ushered her to the great room sitting area. When offered a cocktail, she asked for a Presbyterian. She needed to remain on her toes tonight, so alcohol was out.

Her eyes, wide in awe, scanned the room. The ceiling had to be thirty feet high. The marble fireplace—black with spider veins of white and red running through it—rose the entire height of the great room. Displaying a custom-crafted white mantel, the fireplace presented a magnificent focal point. The great room, she realized, was designed as an extension of the foyer; the floors of both glimmered with polished teak parquet. Clear span balcony walkways stretched across what she surmised was the mezzanine or second floor level.

The butler slipped quietly into the room, slid a coaster onto the end table—a not very subtle hint to be careful with the highly polished and outrageously expensive furniture—and handed Erin her drink. As she sat on the edge of the sofa and jiggled the ice in her drink, Kane made his grand entrance from behind two huge double doors.

"Forgive my tardiness, Erin. I'd hoped to be on hand to greet you." His eyes swept over her from top to bottom. "How simply radiant you look."

Erin knew he had no intentions of being in the room when she arrived. Making a royal entrance was more his style. "Thank you, Cedric Albert."

He laughed. "Something tells me I'm going to regret telling you my first name."

Erin smiled at him and sipped her drink.

"Did you have any problem finding the house?"

"Not at all. Of course from its size, Stevie Wonder could have found it."

"It is rather large." Kane smiled. "Would you care to embark upon the tour I promised? That is your reason for being here—to hold me to my promise."

Erin stood and placed her glass on the coaster. "I'd be delighted."

He began the walking tour on the first floor. They entered the study/library, from which he'd made his grand entrance. "Wow" escaped Erin's lips, unbidden. Cherry bookcases lined the walls from floor to ceiling. "I'm amazed, Cedric Albert. I had no idea 18th century furniture. . . which I usually find cold and unappealing. . . could look so comfortable. Why, the camel back sofa and even the high back wing chairs are inviting." She sat on one of the chairs and bounced to test its stuffing. "Softer than it looks."

Kane merely smiled.

They continued through an awesome sized living room, a theater/ entertainment room and a kitchen large enough to serve the White House. They passed into what he referred to as the west wing, which housed the recreation facilities: An Olympic sized indoor pool, racquetball court, work-out area, and a sauna that easily accommodated twelve people. "What's this?" Erin asked as they strolled on, past the sauna.

"Massage room."

"Jesus, it's so Tibetan, I can almost hear the monastery bells. Where does the monk stay?"

"Monk?"

"The one that meditates in this amazing room."

Kane merely grinned.

He turned the sound system on. Erin listened for a moment, mesmerized by the exotic melodies. "Please assure me those braided baskets do not hold undulating cobras."

"No snakes here, my dear. I find the decor quite relaxing. It helps me practice mind control. Meditation is good for the soul, you know."

Erin shot him a gaze then relaxed. "I hadn't figured you for the contemplative type, but I can see how these surroundings could motivate you to take up Eastern cultures."

Kane placed his hand on the small of her back and gently nudged her. "Shall we continue?"

As they departed to an adjacent west wing foyer, he pressed a button next to what appeared to be large wooden doors. They slid open to reveal an elevator. The two stepped inside and the door closed. In moments, it opened onto a second floor hallway.

"This corridor serves four bedrooms; two of them overlook the pool area."

"So your guests can swan dive into the pool?"

"Something like that. There's nothing quite so nice as skinny dipping in the middle of the night as falling snow is observed by the light of the moon."

She allowed herself to lean into the arm that caressed her back. "I'll remember that the next time I have insomnia."

At the end of the hall was another foyer. It received a spiral staircase from the main floor and led to a walkway crossing over the great room. The north side of it had two gigantic six-paneled double doors. Kane opened them and ushered her into the master bedroom suite.

"My god, C.A., how big is this suite?"

"Three thousand square feet."

"In a house that is. . ."

"Nearly 20,000, if you don't count the 12-car garage."

"And you live here alone?"

"Most of the time." He smiled and squeezed her waist.

The ceiling soared to twenty feet—high enough to make the oversized Queen Anne canopy bed seem small. Cozied in a semi-circle before a large fireplace was a sitting area of oversized easy chairs and sofas. One wall contained an entertainment center with a full complement of video and audio equipment. Kane walked to a cabinet and slid open a door to reveal a wet bar including built-in refrigerator, microwave and dumbwaiter.

"The dumbwaiter's a nice touch."

"Glad you like it." With his gently guiding hand, he moved her toward the walk-in closets.

"Damn it, C.A., it's not fair."

"What's not fair, my dear?"

"One of your closets is larger than my entire bedroom."

"Keep walking. The master bath is just down this mirrored hallway."

"The size of a Roman bath house, I suspect."

"See for yourself." Kane opened a door that revealed fountains of running water cascading into a large bathing area, twin high-low showers in an area large enough not to require glass enclosures, three sinks nestled within marble cabinet tops, a sauna, bidet, telephone and even a built-in television opposite the commode.

Erin let her amazement show. "Breath-taking. No wonder Ginny liked it here."

"How do you know that?" Kane's eyes fixed hers.

"She told me."

"You know about our affair?"

"I know more than you think, Mr. Kane."

He leaned against one of the three sinks and folded his arms across his chest. "About what?"

"You and Ginny."

"What did she tell you?"

"That you had a two-year affair with her."

"I'm surprised."

"So was I."

"Shall we proceed to the south wing?"

"What's there? A bowling alley, a chapel and a skating rink?"

Kane laughed. "No. I don't bowl and I have no religion. But a skating rink. . . that's something I'll have to look into."

It was Erin's time to laugh. The tension of her revelation was broken.

They walked down the hall and he gestured to his left. "Just some more guest rooms down there in the south wing. Here, let's take the back stairs to the kitchen."

"For when your south-wing guests get the munchies at midnight."

"Exactly."

In the kitchen, she said hello to several cooks then turned to her host. "I'm surprised you didn't show me any servants' quarters."

"Oh, the cook and maids have a wonderful apartment over the garage. We also have an adjacent dwelling shared by the butler, chauffeur and gardener. Would you care to see them?"

"No, I'm afraid they would be nicer than where I live, and I'm not sure I could handle that."

"I'm sure your apartment is beautiful." Kane ushered Erin into the dining room and seated her at one end of a table large enough to accommodate one third the U.S. Senate.

She gazed at the full place setting in front of her: little did she know it was sterling, Baccarat crystal and Spode china. She looked up at Kane, now seated to her left at the table's head. "How did you know I live in an apartment?"

"I didn't, but I know that associate professors aren't paid very well."

"Tell me! I had to teach summer school just to make ends meet." Was it time to start digging for information? She wondered. Start slowly now, build up over dinner? "Professor Dawes seems to do very well. I'm not sure how, on his salary."

"Yes, he does live high."

"Has Ginny ever told you where the money comes from? It's certainly not from his university salary, and I don't think he publishes best sellers."

"Why would she tell me?"

"Pillow talk often reveals a lot, and I figure you two shared a few pillows."

"The only thing she mentioned to me is that he makes a handsome amount in the investment community."

"I wonder who his broker is?"

Kane shrugged. "I have no idea."

"Maybe I'll ask Gin."

He slid off the sterling silver ring securing his napkin, opened it and spread it on his lap. "You two are becoming quite chummy, aren't you?"

"Frankly, when Professor Dawes found out about the affair, she needed someone to talk to."

"Why you?"

"From vibes she got from me at the dinner dance, she says."

"I guess she's angry with me?"

"That would be an understatement."

"Yeah, I thought so."

"What did you expect?"

Kane leaned toward Erin and picked up his spoon. "Erin, this affair was her idea, not mine."

"Takes two to tango, counselor."

"Did she say how Harmon found out?"

"From John Wiggams."

"How the hell would he know?"

"Ask him."

"I will."

"I suspect you already did."

Kane's eyes widened. "Why do you say that?"

"I'm sure you remember my friend, Danielle?"

"The cute blonde who was with you at the president's party? Who could forget her?"

"She just spent a weekend in Vegas with him and he told her about some sexually revealing photos he has of Harmon and Ginny. He also told her about photos of her visiting here quite regularly."

"That stupid bastard! I told him to keep his mouth shut."

Erin grinned. This was going well. "Thought you didn't talk to him yet."

"You think you're very clever, don't you."

"I try."

"How much more do you know?"

Oh, no, not yet. She wanted to get him really keyed up. "Don't you think we should have dinner? I'm starved."

"Yes, of course. This fascinating conversation has made me forget my duties as your host." Kane put down the spoon and picked up a 24k dinner bell. In minutes the food began to appear.

Inwardly, Erin was grinning. She loved watching his wheels turn. And she'd really got them turning. She was on red alert now and expected just about anything from him.

They finished their appetizers and the staff started to clear. "You know, Erin, I'm always looking for good people to add to my organization."

"In your law practice?"

"No, no. I'm sure you know I'm running for office in November."

"Yes, I've heard that—at the dinner dance. Remember?"

"Right. Would it surprise you to know that my administrative assistant could make herself $75,000 a year plus perks?"

Under the table, Erin fiddled with her napkin. "Are you making me an offer?"

"Yes."

"What if you lose the election?"

"I won't."

"How can you be so sure?"

"There won't be an opponent. Trust me."

"Sounds interesting, but I have to ask: do the perks include being Ginny's replacement?"

He laughed. "Ah, my dear, that sense of humor of yours makes you sexy as hell."

Erin said nothing. Let him stew. She felt he was laying the groundwork for a trap of some kind. He had made a quick decision that she probably knew more than she had disclosed. Was he planning to bring her into the scam? Or keep her close enough that if he needed to dispose of her he could do it expeditiously?

"Well, what do you think?" Kane leaned toward her again.

"I'll sleep on it. There's no hurry, is there?"

"No, but I would like to know within two weeks so I can make other arrangements if you're not interested."

"That's fair."

The staff pushed through the swinging door and made a grand presentation of the main course, lifting the domed lids off the two plates at precisely the same moment. For the next half hour, few words were said except gracious compliments to the chef.

Over dessert and coffee, conversation turned to recent events at the university. "How's President St. James handling all the aftermath of the fire, C.A.?"

"I think quite well. I'm more than a little impressed with her administrative skills. She's kept five balls in the air for the last four days and hasn't dropped a one."

"Must run in the family. Her brother seems pretty good at juggling problematic issues too."

"Her brother?" Kane set his cup back in its saucer, tipping it a little. "How do you know him?"

"I met him briefly at the dinner dance, but Danielle spent some time with him last weekend in Las Vegas. She said he was a very astute gentleman banker."

Kane dribbled coffee onto the table cloth. "What else did she say?"

Erin knew that she was slowly getting to him. Each little tidbit of information she released regarding what he thought were private affairs caused increased agitation. This was fun. She'd tweak him a little more.

"Just that he was very knowledgeable and obviously involved with Wiggams in some sort of business venture."

"Where did she get that idea from?"

"From several business meetings they had."

"Probably university business."

"No, I don't think so."

"Why?"

"I'm sure you know the university comptroller has a yen for young post-grad students. Danielle slept with Wiggams."

Behind his napkin Kane coughed.

How far should she go? Maybe a little bit more. "Wiggams told her that Professor Dawes makes him and David a lot of money. That doesn't sound like university business to me."

"Erin, the man was probably drunk."

"No, she said Wiggams doesn't drink much at all. He told her it impairs his sexual performance and from what she described, he couldn't have been drinking." She let a sly smile play with the edge of her mouth.

"He's a sexual pervert, one might almost say a predator."

"That may be true, but don't you find it strange that the president's brother has a business relationship with the university comptroller?"

"Not at all."

"Wouldn't that be a conflict of interest or something? You're a lawyer, C.A. Don't you think it's at least suspicious?"

"As long as they're not using funds or other resources belonging to the university, it would be perfectly legal."

Erin rubbed her finger around the rim of her coffee cup. "I see. It just seems contrary to my understanding of ethics and morality. Perhaps I should mention it to Gayle St. James. Maybe she doesn't know. "

She figured Kane's blood pressure rose a few points as his face reddened. The man who, with his sockless penny loafers, was "Mr. Cool" when he entered through the double doors three hours before was now a fidgety, perplexed cauldron of bubbling emotion.

Kane drained his coffee cup and poured more from the carafe at his elbow. "I think you're blowing this entirely out of proportion, my dear. If you reveal this unsubstantiated claim to the president, you could jeopardize her position."

"Really? In what way?"

"She will have to expose this business relationship to the Board of Trustees."

"Didn't you say there was nothing illegal about what they were doing?"

"Yes. . . . No. There will still have to be an investigation and that won't bode well for her."

"I certainly don't wish to cause any problems for President St. James."

"Then, if I were you, I would forget about it. Why don't you let me take care of it. After all, I do represent the university's interests."

"That sounds like a good way to handle it, C.A. I'll leave it in your hands."

He forked the last bite of cheesecake into his mouth. "Is there anything else I should know?"

"About what?"

"The men we've been talking about. John Wiggams or David St. James."

"Anything else I should know about Ginny?"

"Touche, professor."

"You must have discussed many things over a two-year period."

"Yes we did, but very little of any substance."

"Come now, the lawyer in you certainly would have elicited information on Professor Dawes' investment business."

"Only that he did rather well in it."

"I'm not naïve, C.A. If Professor Dawes was making money for St. James and Wiggams, and you were sleeping with his wife for two years, you had to know something."

"We didn't waste time talking, Erin."

"Perhaps you were too busy 'doing a line' to remember?"

"Now, you're guessing. I don't use drugs."

"Perhaps not now. But that wasn't always the case, was it?" She nailed him with her stare.

"Son-of-a-bitch! Where did you get that from?"

"Ginny."

"You are just a wealth of information tonight, my dear."

"Too bad I can't say the same about you."

"All right, I'll level with you. I used to enjoy a little white powder on occasion and yes, I am aware of Harmon's business with St. James and Wiggams. Happy now?"

"Okay, we're getting somewhere. Seems odd to me that a man of your ego and intellect wouldn't have figured a way to cut himself in on that."

"You do have balls, Erin."

"Not yet, but soon I'm going to have yours."

Kane rose and came to Erin's chair, pulling it back for her. "You would like that, wouldn't you?"

"You have no idea how much."

"Perhaps we should adjourn to the bedroom. . . test the validity of your remarks."

Erin turned to face him, placing her hand on his arm. "I guess I deserved that. Sorry, not tonight. Remember, you promised to let me go early. I have a heavy schedule tomorrow. Besides, I'd rather wait until your memory improves."

She strode quickly toward the front door. "Your home is every bit as impressive as I'd imagined. The food, the ambience—well," she held out her hand—"I hope we'll do it again soon."

Kane lifted her hand to his lips. "It cannot be soon enough for me. I'll call you."

"Yeah, that's what they all say." She opened the door and let herself out.

She sat in her car for a few moments, her heart pounding. She'd pulled it off. . . gotten him riled up and eager for more. The double entendre about wanting his balls. . . that definitely tickled his fancy.

Yes, she'd be invited to The Mansion again. And the next time, she would be wearing George Baldwin's wire.

GAYLE ST. JAMES pressed her intercom button. "Gretchen, get John Wiggams on the line. It's Thursday, so he's still working at his home."

While she waited for the comptroller to come on the line, she studied the architect's proposal. After what they would collect from insurance, the university would still need close to ten million to rebuild the fire devastated portion of the administration building and renovate the part that didn't burn.

Her speaker phone squawked. "Yes, Madam President, what can I do for you?"

"John, we need to go over our investment portfolio to optimize timing of liquidation from our holdings to finance new construction. The earliest I have on my calendar is ten o'clock tomorrow. Can you be here?"

"Since my office isn't ready yet and I'm mostly just twiddling my thumbs, I think I can make it."

Wiggams hung up wondering when it was going to stop. Since his return from Las Vegas, it seemed one problem had piled atop another.

He sat at his desk and pulled out a pad of paper and pen, missing his 24k gold desk accessories. He jabbed some figures into a palm-sized calculator and came up with a low end of six and a high of eight million dollars. A figure that could cause Tristar some immediate problems. For nearly two months, the stock market had experienced corrections. The DOW and NASDAQ were down 27% and 23% respectively during this time, and it appeared as if a bear market had begun.

With Harmon gone and Kane in possession of the only Tristar books, he felt exposed and powerless. If it was true, as he suspected, that Kane had not only got rid of Harmon, but also was responsible for the university fire and his apartment burglary, he could be next on the list for elimination. It was apparent that Kane would stop at nothing to cover the Tristar scam and ensure his election to the Mecklenburg County bench.

He was in a vulnerable position. He couldn't threaten Kane with exposure or he would end up like Harmon. If things didn't settle down soon, he would have to flee Charlotte and go underground. If something went wrong, he would be the one to take the fall. C. Albert Kane would make damn sure of that.

His stash of money that the burglars didn't get was more than ample; however, he'd be damned if he'd leave town without his one-third share of the corporation's three million net value. But how could he take that money without sending up a red flag to Kane? If Kane had murdered once, a second hit wouldn't faze him.

Or he could just sit tight and see how the next several weeks played out. Maybe he would contact his old pal at Diskrete Investigations and have Kane tailed. Something might surface that could give him more leverage than he currently possessed.

THURSDAY MEANT A full class load for Erin, but she needed to meet with Danielle. For one thing, she knew Dani'd be crazy curious about last night's dinner at The Mansion. For another, she needed to know what George Baldwin was doing on his end. So she called Danielle early to tell her she could squeeze out an hour, from 11:45 to 12:45. Dani would pick up sandwiches at the cafeteria and bring them to her office. They'd have privacy there to go over their "classified material."

It was 11:45 when Danielle walked in with the food and drinks. Erin jumped up to help her set their lunch on the desk. "I could set my watch by you. Punctuality is a virtue, and you are a virtuous person."

"Ha, ha." Danielle unwrapped the sandwich and snapped the tab on her Diet Coke. "I'll go first," she said through a bite of ham and cheese on rye with mustard.

Her father's operatives had investigated the contents of storage bin #18 and found it contained Dawes' records on Tristar, the contents of all his desk drawers, a computer and other office equipment. The unit was also stacked high with elaborate and expensive household items. "So Dad questioned the ability of a university professor to accumulate such wealth. When I asked him to describe the items, it turns out they came from John Wiggams' apartment. Of course, then he put me on the hot seat as to how I would know this."

Danielle munched some more sandwich. "I said it was a long story that I'd explain at another time. He said they also found a second set of Tristar files, very expensive art works, some sterling silver and Waterford crystal."

Erin sipped her diet root beer. "And you're sure the expensive stuff belongs to Wiggams?"

"Yes, I distinctly remember the Waterford vase from the living room, and the Picasso and Dali art were in his bedroom."

"What does your dad make of this?"

"I'm not sure yet, but we know a carpet cleaning company was at his apartment on Saturday morning."

"Your dad's following up on this?"

"Sure. He asked me if I knew what carpet company drove bright red trucks with yellow lettering. Apparently the maintenance man at Wiggams' apartment building remembered the colors."

"That's Karpet Kleen. They do work for the university."

"I'll tell him."

"What I wonder is how stuff from both Wiggams and Professor Dawes got in the same storage bin."

"I don't know, good buddy, but I bet I know who does."

"Yeah, Kane. It looks like whoever killed Dawes may also have ripped off Wiggams."

"That makes sense."

"I wonder if Karpet Kleen also paid a visit to the Dawes' household on Saturday."

"This is getting more complicated by the minute."

"Not really, Dani. My guess is that Kane choreographed the whole thing to cover his ass in the Tristar scam."

"You really think he'd go this far?"

"Sure." She nodded. "Put the pieces together. The fire took out the files at the university, the burglary removed the ones at Wiggams' apartment and Professor Dawes and his files have disappeared."

"Then Kane thinks the storage facility holds the only information about Tristar."

"Exactly. He thinks he's safe."

"If he ever knew about our copies, he'd shit."

"Worse than that, I'm afraid. Far worse."

"Dad must have figured it that way—so he insisted we remove them from your house."

"Your father's an intelligent, experienced man, Danielle. And in his business, it pays to be suspicious, cover all the bases. Erin popped the last of her lunch into her mouth and tossed the wrappings into her trash basket. "I'm going to check with Ginny to see whether her carpets were cleaned on Saturday."

Danielle looked at her watch. "All right, girl, enough of that. It's time for you to spill your guts about last night."

"Not what you think."

"Damn it, I thought I was going to hear some goodies."

"I didn't have to bed him to get his attention."

Erin described the house, its staff, the cuisine. And how she carefully disclosed tidbits of information she possessed regarding his affair with Ginny, his business relationship with Harmon and Wiggams and the sexually explicit photos of the Dawes.

"Jesus, Erin, you're crazy!"

"Relax Danielle, I played it cool. I didn't go into detail, just generalities. I wondered aloud how someone as smart as he is wouldn't find a way to cut himself in on the investment deals that were making Dawes and Wiggams a nice piece of change. But he never tumbled to how much I actually know. In fact, would you believe he offered me a job as his judicial assistant for $75,000 a year plus perks?"

"Wow, you really did get his attention."

"You could say that again. Whether he wants me nearby because he thinks I'm cute and clever or because I'll be easier to bump me off—that remains to be seen." Erin finished her drink. "So let's kick this investigation into high gear. Tell your dad I'm ready to be wired."

"When?"

"Nothing's definite, but I suspect he'll want to see me Saturday night. I think he's intrigued enough that he won't waste any time getting back to me."

"Christ, Erin, we need to speak to my dad ASAP."

"Right. Set up a conference call for tonight."

"I'll try."

"I'll be home all night. Now get out of here; I have classes to teach."

Danielle acted immediately on Erin's request, phoned her father on the secure line and got right to the point.

"Erin has herself in deep with Kane. Last night's dinner went much further than expected and she's ready to wear a wire at their next meeting. But I'm truly worried about how safe she'll be. It's becoming clearer by the minute that the bastard is a murderer."

"Our people will be right outside in a van listening to everything. If she gets into trouble, our team stationed at the rear entrance of the estate will move in."

"Dad, how's she going to wear a wire if he wants to get in bed with her?"

"It won't go that far."

"You don't know Kane."

"I know more than you think. We got lucky. . . picked up a woman from Chicago who went to Baton Rouge looking for her missing husband, a Benny Caputto. Turns out he was on a trip with Johnny Portofino and never returned. She's singing like a bird right now."

"Anything good?"

"Portofino is a top Mafia hit man. She was sure her husband told her Kane had used him before. We think Kane is heavily involved with the mob."

"Oh God, this gets worse every day."

"No, honey, it gets better. Thanks to you, we may be able to penetrate much more than university fraud."

"Well, whoop dee do for us. But I'm still worried about Erin's exposure to this murderer."

"I'll fly into Charlotte on Friday. Don't let Erin make any further rendezvous with Kane until we talk."

WIGGAMS PACED HIS living room, from the fireplace at one end to the empty entertainment center at the other. He had to figure a way to provide the university with money to rebuild the administration building without jeopardy to Tristar. Much as he hated it, he needed Kane's advice.

Might as well get it over with, he thought as he phoned Kane. When he finally came onto the line, Wiggams explained the situation. "So how can we wiggle out of this now?"

"Simple, John. Point out that, thanks to you, their investments are tied into CDs earning nine or ten percent. Suggest that the university finance the reconstruction with 20 percent down at a seven percent rate. Long-term financing at that rate is a much more prudent use of funds rather than liquidating a portfolio earning higher rates. The executive committee will buy it. I'll see to that."

"Good advice. I'll propose it to the president."

Kane leaned back in his office chair. "There's something else we need to talk about, John."

"Oh?"

"I understand you had a very nice time in Las Vegas with that cute little blond intern. Exactly what did you tell her?"

"I really don't think what I do on my time is anyone's business, Albert."

"Remember what I told you yesterday about using up the last of your nine lives?"

Wiggams, pacing again, stopped in mid stride. "All right, then, I took her with me, but there really was a legitimate conference."

"Did you attend it?"

"Certainly did."

"Did you lay her, John?"

Wiggams did not answer.

"Of course you did. I take your silence as proof of that." Kane swiveled toward the window, watching clouds moving westward toward the city. "What did you tell her?"

"About what?"

"Me, you, Harmon, Tristar, anything."

Wiggams hated Kane when he spoke in a smooth, quiet voice. It seemed far more menacing than if he'd yelled. "She also spent time with David, you know."

"But I am not talking with David at the moment. I am asking you. What did you tell her?"

"Just some sex stuff about Harmon and Ginny."

"Anything about me?"

"Hell no, nothing, Albert. Believe me."

"You'd better be leveling with me."

"I am, honest."

Kane laughed. "That's a good one, John. You. . . honest. You forget how well I know you. The penalty for lying to me on this matter is. . . serious."

"You have my word, Albert. That's all."

Finished with Wiggams for the time being, Kane allowed his mind to return to his evening with Erin Gallagher. He was intrigued, no doubt about it. She was a woman with a personality, intelligence and obvious sexuality to match his own. He knew what he wanted from her. But what did she want from him? He needed to be certain of the answer to that question.

Could she be prying information out of him then setting him up for blackmail? If it turned out she knew too much. . . that would be unfortunate. He'd hate to have to dispose of a young woman he admired so much.

He sighed deeply. Something about her fascinated him. Both at the dinner dance and last night, she dared to match wits with him. She would make a formidable intellectual sparing partner. What a waste if she had to go. But if he did ultimately need to get rid of her, he would first make sure to experience sexual pleasure with her. What a lay she would be!

He'd told her he'd phone. Time to set up another date. Kane hit speed dial for the university's main switchboard and asked to be connected with Professor Gallagher in the economics department. When her voicemail clicked on, he left a message, feeling a letdown when he couldn't talk with her—both in his mind and in his groin.

Erin finished her last class and headed back to her office to make notes and check the weekly planner. Exhausted from this week's extra teaching load, she wanted nothing more than to go home and take a long, hot shower. She hit the button to retrieve her voicemail messages and was glad she did. First, Danielle confirmed her dad's arrival on Friday to meet with them for dinner. Next, Gayle St..James' voice told her she had found someone to teach all of Professor Dawes' classes and he could start on Monday.

"Yesssssss!" Erin whooped, grateful the president had worked so quickly and so well.

The next voice she heard was Albert Kane asking her to call him. She smiled to herself, knowing she was right about his not wasting time. She decided to return the call from home. It would give her time to anticipate and plan.

Excitement was climbing up her spine. Kane was obviously intrigued with her, but she'd still have to be cautious. He had no problem contracting for one murder, she reminded herself. She definitely didn't want to be the next one.

FRIDAY AFTERNOON, DANIELLE'S Porsche rolled to a stop outside Erin's home right on time. "Any new developments?" Danielle asked the minute Erin was seated in her car.

"I talked to Kane last night. I'm seeing him tomorrow at seven."

"Christ, Erin, you weren't supposed to see him until we spoke to Dad."

"I won't be. Look, he called and I felt the time was right."

"What if Dad hadn't come in to brief you tonight?"

"But he did, so there's no problem."

Danielle down shifted and pulled in the open lane. "Jesus, Erin." She stared at her friend. "Don't go off half-cocked." She pressed the accelerator, listened to the roar of the powerful engine.

"I already had it figured out, Dani. If you hadn't called me yesterday to say your dad was coming, I'd have phoned him. I knew he'd respond immediately."

"You sure you don't have balls?"

"You should know; you've had some close-up views."

My father is going to shit a brick."

A few minutes later, they were seated in a quiet alcove of the Hyatt dining room with the Deputy Director of the CIA.

Over cocktails, Danielle brought her father up to speed regarding Erin's scheduled date with Kane. "So it's critical that we have a plan in place to protect Erin."

He winced. "This is a little quicker than expected."

"I know, Mr. Baldwin, but right now Kane thinks he's running the show and I didn't want to give him any reason to think otherwise. So I said yes when he asked me for Saturday." Erin smiled up at Danielle's father and batted her eyelashes.

"Ok, Ok. There's not much we can do about it now. I'll put our teams in place within the hour."

Erin pointed at her friend, waving a tiny umbrella from her drink. "See, Danielle, I told you your father would be on top of things."

"You're just lucky he's so damn smart."

"Erin. . . Danielle's just a bit edgy about your safety. You're not an experienced operative. Believe me, I'll pull you off this case in a nanosecond if I think your safety will be compromised. But I want to assure both of you that everything will be okay."

"Where do we go from here, Mr. Baldwin?"

"At five o'clock tomorrow I want you to meet me in Suite 1100 upstairs to review our plans and wire you up."

"Dad, remember what I told you about Kane wanting to bed her."

Baldwin nodded. "We have a special transponder for these kinds of situations."

"God, where do you hide a microphone on a naked person?"

"In a locket around her neck. That's where." He smiled at Erin. "I presume you can somehow manage to keep that on."

"Frankly, Mr. Baldwin, I intend to keep everything on. Your daughter's prodigious power to create mental pictures has conjured up wild ideas of a sexual escapade involving Mr. Kane and myself."

"I am well aware of her active fantasy life. More than once I've been called upon to extract her from. . . situations. . . she wouldn't have been in without that vivid imagination of hers."

"You must have had your hands full when she was an adolescent."

"What do you mean 'had'?"

Danielle placed one hand atop the other and perpendicular in a "time out" gesture. "All right, you two, that's enough."

Baldwin stopped speaking while the waiter placed their entrees in front of them. Finally, he leaned toward Erin. "We also will provide you with a watch that has an electronic bezel back. You will feel a slight vibration against your wrist when the transmitter is working. In addition, the stem of the watch acts as an alert. If you get into trouble, just pull it out and the SWAT team will move immediately."

"Sounds simple enough to me."

"It is, Erin. Just make sure you feel the pulsations on your wrist. That way you will know we are recording."

"What if I don't feel it?"

"Then rotate the stem counter clockwise, to activate a backup transponder. We'll show you how to do all this tomorrow. We'll also brief you on some of the questions you need to get answered. Five o'clock, Suite 1100."

"I can't wait to get started." Erin winked at Danielle. "Yeah, it's the old cop in me. Can't help it. After three generations, I guess it's in my blood."

Between bites of tournedos of beef and Alaskan king crab legs, the three went over other recent events. George Baldwin reported John Portofino was under surveillance in the Bahamas; they'd uncovered no leads on Harmon Dawes' whereabouts; Ginny had not ordered her carpets to be cleaned on the day her husband disappeared, yet the next door neighbor confirmed he'd seen Karpet Kleen's truck parked in the Dawes circular drive for a couple of hours. . . and watched two coveralled men carry a carpet from the house to the van. Even though that company never opened for business on Saturdays.

On the way home, Danielle wasted no time. "I noticed you didn't eat much tonight."

"I could say the same about you, Dani. Too nervous. Maybe your father is used to all this stuff about lockets with micro chips, wrist watch transponder and SWAT teams ready to pounce, but I'm not."

"I'm so worried about you. I feel like I just want to cry."

"Believe it or not, I'm a little scared myself."

"I just want to hold you and know you'll be all right."

"When it's over, we'll have plenty of time to hold each other. And we'll do just that. Okay?"

"Promise me you won't take any risks with that bastard."

"Hey, give me a little credit. Don't worry, I'll be careful. I know what we're dealing with. And I want to continue living."

CHAPTER FOURTEEN

On Saturday, Erin figured that tonight's attire need not be as carefully planned as it was for her first time at The Mansion. She'd already yanked his chain. Now, she'd add some more links to that chain before she yanked it again. . . this time, wearing a wire. The tight skirt, sheer blouse and lacy lingerie she'd chosen should do the trick. Plus a very special locket and wrist watch, which she was on her way to pick up.

Erin breathed in and out a few times then knocked on the door of the Hyatt's Suite 1100. A good looking young man about her age answered. After she identified herself, he ushered her inside. Danielle, her father and several other men sat at a round table in front of a large window. She could see, in the distance, the spires of Madison University and thought how much simpler life was as an associate professor there. Prepare for and teach courses, mark exams, counsel students. Way simpler than getting Cedric Albert Kane to confess to fraud and murder.

Danielle spotted her and walked over to give her a hug. "I'm glad to see you."

"Likewise, but who are all these people?"

"Friends of dad's, mostly retired CIA or FBI agents."

"Not the guy who answered the door."

"No, Mike's the electronics genius from Spyglass Corporation. Dad's friend is the president. He's the president's son; I've known him since we were kids."

George Baldwin stood up from his papers, swiped a lock of sandy hair away from his eyes and walked up to her. "Ready to go?"

Erin stared into his eyes, as blue and penetrating as his daughter's. "As ready as I'll ever be."

"Good. Mike and Jeremy, one of my recording experts, are going to take you to the adjoining room to review the things we went over last night."

Erin nodded. "They'll brief me on using the locket and watch?"

"Exactly. First, I want to advise you of new overnight information."

"Oh?" Her eyebrows lifted. "What?"

"Johnny Portofino's body washed ashore this morning in Eleuthera, Bahamas. Shot twice in the forehead, typical Mafia style. We think Kane ordered the hit. One less witness. It's obvious we're dealing with a ruthless man. I'm not at all happy about my daughter's involvement. Or yours."

"We're too deep in it to climb out now."

"With the actual murderer dead and without Dawes' body, the only way we can get Kane on the hit is through a confession. Your attempt to expose him tonight is. . . more crucial than ever."

Erin took another deep breath. "Why do I feel there's a 'but' coming?"

"You're right. *But* if you want to, it's not too late to back out."

"I don't give up easily, Mr. Baldwin. I'm in this to the end. . . even if it's *my* end."

Baldwin nodded. "I had a feeling you'd say that. So, then, your mission is to concentrate on Dawes' murder as opposed to the fraud at the university."

"Why?"

"Because between Wiggams and St..James, we expect one of them will roll over on the Tristar thing plus we have all the evidence locked safely at the airport."

"Makes sense."

"Kane's going to be measuring you tonight."

"For a cement overcoat?"

Baldwin flashed another of his rare smiles. "I like that. . . you keep your sense of humor. No, I think you have fascinated him. You're strong, beautiful and not afraid of him. He's actually smitten with you."

"I think another 'but' is coming."

"*But* if Kane determines you know too much, you could follow in Harmon's and Portofino's footsteps. If, however, he feels you're not a threat, he'll want you around to play with or become a member of his team."

"Sounds like a no-win situation for me. Either way, I lose."

"Say the word, and we turn over this whole case to someone else and you're out of it."

Erin thought fast. She knew damn well George Baldwin was sending a message as to the importance of her timing and the danger associated with it. He wanted to be able to tell Danielle that if anything happened, he had given Erin every opportunity to withdraw. It was clear he'd picked up on how close the two had become and wasn't about to jeopardize his relationship with his daughter.

Erin had thought all day about the consequences of her actions tonight. She'd tried to come up with a plan but nothing seemed to work. She truly was in a "catch 22" situation. How was she supposed to elicit information about Harmon Dawes' disappearance unless she divulged her knowledge of the storage bin? Conversely, when she did, Kane would definitely consider her a risk. She could be signing her own death warrant.

"Mr. Baldwin, I understand where this is going. Remember, I have some experience as a cop. As I said before, I'm in it to the end. Now let me get going with the technology that could save my life."

Baldwin stood up and beckoned to Mike. "Sure. We'll speak again before you leave." He turned and headed back to the table.

Erin followed the other two and for the next hour listened to them repeatedly instruct her on the use of the locket and watch. They tested and re-tested them while recommending the type of questions to use on Kane.

"What if none of these work?"

"Then, professor, you are on your own."

"Thanks a lot."

"Remember, if a weapon becomes visible or you feel in imminent danger without the ability to pull the watch stem, use the code word and we'll take him down."

"HIBISCUS."

"That's it."

Mike led the way back to the main room and told Mr. Baldwin that she was wired and ready to go.

"Erin, good luck and remember we'll be monitoring everything."

"That's a relief. I think."

Danielle wrapped her arms around Erin. "Please, please be careful."

"I will." Erin bent her lips to Danielle's ear. "The next time a strange young woman wants to get acquainted with me on the beach, I'm going to run like hell."

With a nervous chuckle, Erin exited the room for her drive to The Mansion.

As the car approached the front gate, Erin touched her locket and asked God to grant her safe passage on this expedition for justice. A disembodied voice squawked from the speaker in the brick column supporting the gate. "Who may I ask is calling?" She laughed and hoped this was an omen that God had heard her prayer. She gave her name and the gate swung open.

Erin drove up the cypress lined winding road and parked in front of the eight white pillars beneath an expansive porte-cochere. The waiting butler escorted her through the magnificent foyer and into the great room. Although she had been here before, she admired her surroundings as if seeing them for the first time.

Kane entered almost immediately from the kitchen area with a drink in each hand. He gave her one of the drinks, sat down and leaned close to kiss her cheek.

"It's so good to see you again. It's been only since Wednesday, but to me it seems longer."

"Thank you, C.A."

He blinked and grinned. "I think I liked it better when you called me 'Albert'."

"But I enjoy giving my friends pet names. Danielle is 'Dani,' for instance. I rather like calling you 'C.A.' I think I'll keep using it."

"As you wish, then. It's only a minor annoyance. And what might I call you? Is there a nickname for 'Erin'?"

"Long ago—in what seems like a past life—my father called me Er Bear."

Kane tried it. "Somehow, it suits you. Makes me think of a teddy bear—a comforting toy to cuddle with."

Erin sipped her drink. "So tell me, C. A., what did you want to see me about?"

"I simply wanted to see you again. I don't mind confessing that you, my dear, have lit the embers of a very passionate man."

"Gee, and I'm thinking you don't even like me."

"Where would you ever get that idea?"

"Our last two meetings weren't exactly cordial. Other 'c' words come to mind: competitive, confrontational."

"Perhaps I can make amends for that."

"How, may I ask?"

Kane nuzzled his lips into her throat. "To be perfectly frank, I'd like to make love to you."

Erin sat up straight and nudged him aside. "You think that would make amends? Exactly what do you take me for? I'm not some empty-headed southern belle who married an economics professor."

"No, you are certainly more than that, Er Bear." Kane wasn't used to being rebuffed. He'd have to try another tack. "I'd like to start all over with you. . . without the competition or the confrontation. Okay?"

"Okay, then, let's see how you do answering a few questions that have bothered me."

"Of course. Shoot."

"To start, how about leveling with me about Professor Dawes' disappearance."

"So he doesn't have a sprained ankle as Ginny informed me on Sunday, and he isn't recovering from pneumonia, as Ginny has taken great pains to convince everybody since then?"

"You know that as well as I do. It was a story concocted for a specific purpose. . . and the purpose no longer exists. Harmon Dawes has not been home since Saturday. Tell me where he is."

"What makes you think I know anything about it?"

"Because he vanished less than a week after he confronted Ginny about your affair."

"Yes? So? What does that have to do with me?"

"Ginny told me he paid you a visit several days before his disappearance and threatened to expose information about your side business that would cripple your political aspirations."

"Ginny is an absolute gold mine of information, isn't she. Yes, he did. However, I simply dismissed it as the wrath of a husband scorned."

"And you never did anything about it?"

"That's right."

"And I suppose you also know nothing about storage bin #18 on Old Dowd Road?"

Kane leapt to his feet. "How the hell would you know about that?"

"I followed you from the Petrini kick-off."

Kane headed quickly for the bar. After fixing himself another drink, he turned to face Erin, his voice like ice. "I don't understand. Why would you do such a thing, Erin?"

"I watched you throughout the proceedings. You appeared anxious about something. Then when Ginny told President St. James that her husband had hurt his ankle, you almost fell apart. It wasn't like you. I became suspicious."

"Considering how Ginny aroused my curiosity with her comment about Harmon, what did you expect?"

"Only a guilty man would have taken the bait."

"Touche, my dear. Guilty as charged. Guilty of needing to check the storage unit where I keep old furniture and files. You know, IRS stuff, closed cases with former clients."

"And information from the business you are in with Wiggams and Dawes?"

He took a long drink from the glass in his hand. "Yes."

"And carpets? Do you store them there too?"

"Sometimes, yes."

Kane set his empty cocktail glass on the bar and returned to the couch. He took Erin's hands in his own and lifted her up. "Erin, this conversation has taken quite an unexpected turn. It seems the only reason you're here is to get me to talk, to unravel some sort of mystery you've dreamt up. You're not wearing a wire, setting me up for blackmail, are you?"

"Blackmail? Never gave it a thought, C.A." A smile curled her lip.

"This Q and A shit is not exactly what I had planned for tonight."

"What did you plan for us?"

"Certainly not taking half the night to dissuade you from some silly presumption that I'd have something to hide. . . or that I'd have anything to do with whatever's happened to Harmon." He slipped his arm around her waist. "I figured our talking would take place in the bedroom." He brushed her ear with his mouth. "Who knows, our pillow talk. . . afterward. . . could be quite interesting."

Erin hesitated for a moment then realized it was now or never. "So it's time for me to fan those embers into a raging fire?" She smiled, took his hand and they strolled silently to the elevator. Seconds later, they found themselves in the massive master bedroom.

As Kane closed the door behind them, he swung her around and into his arms. Erin returned his passionate kiss, darting her tongue along the inside of his lips. "How's the blaze doing, hmmmm?" He answered with another long, deep kiss.

As they came up for air, he began to unbutton her blouse. She felt his erection pressing strongly into her pelvis. "Now, C.A., it's my turn to say 'touche'." She backed away from him and slowly picked up where he left off, continuing to unbutton her blouse.

Kane rushed to the bed, yanked off the down comforter and lay down. He positioned the pillows to prop himself up. He didn't want to miss a second of this show.

Erin watched his eyes get bigger as she let her blouse fall to the floor. Reaching both hands behind her, she unhooked her bra and let it hang. She slowly slid the straps off her shoulders and released the bra to follow her blouse to the floor. With both hands, she caressed her breasts and gently pinched her nipples.

"Well counselor, are you convinced I didn't come here just to pry information out of you?"

"Ohhhhhhhh yeah." He crooked a finger toward her, beckoning her to the bed.

She smiled, shook her head and went back to her tease. She unzipped her skirt and let it join her blouse and bra. Once her long legs were fully exposed, Kane leered with obvious delight. Standing in nothing but her panties, she gently ran her fingertips across her breasts.

Kane patted the sheet beside him. "Now, come over to this bed and convince me some more." He pulled off his silk boxers and drew Erin's attention to admire his soldier standing proud.

Saying nothing, Erin slid out of her panties and approached the canopy bed. She mounted the steps and lay back on a stack of pillows, curling onto her side with one hip in the air. "See? No wire."

The locket lay between her breasts, just inches from her mouth and his.

He grabbed for her.

Erin rolled away from him. "Not yet."

"More questions, for God's sake? Can't we get to the main event? My fire is really lit!"

"Just one more." As she spoke, she caressed his erection. "You planning to replace Dawes in your investment company?"

"When he doesn't come back, I'll have to. The business is too lucrative to abandon." He caressed her hip. "Mmmmm, Er Bear, let's get it on."

"One more question." She rushed ahead, before his frustration level peeked. "Would you consider putting me in his place?"

Without answering he grabbed her beautiful body and began mounting her. The time for foreplay was long gone for him and as he began violently thrusting Erin knew there was no way to stop this now.

Afterward, Erin sighed. She'd gone further than she wanted to. Now, she'd have to make sure her sacrifice would reap rewards. "Not bad, C.A., not bad at all."

"I am more than happy, my dear. You were incredible. Made Ginny Dawes seem like unskilled labor."

"Don't compare me with other women you've bedded. That's tacky. If we're going to be partners. . ."

"Partners?"

"Don't tell me you've forgotten already. . . . My suggestion?"

"You're serious, then. You want me to put you in Dawes' place."

"Assuming your other partner will approve."

"Wiggams? He's history. Between his sex and gambling addictions, and his big mouth, he's too big a risk. He has to go."

"But that will leave you without a point man at the university."

"I got him his job in the first place, so I can get rid of him too. His destiny has always been in my hands."

"Why not replace him with David St..James? We can tighten the circle and reduce the exposure."

"That's not a bad idea. He's already in it to an extent, so he knows the potential for big money." Kane eyed his bed partner. "I always figured you for a straight arrow. How do I know I can trust you?"

"I *am* a straight arrow, and that's why you can trust me. Besides, I want the money. You know I don't make much as a professor. Like Ginny Dawes, I never had any. Now that I see my chance to make it big, I'm going to take it."

"What about your friend Danielle and her father? Can you keep from blabbing to them about your involvement with me?"

"I'm tired of her looking down her nose at me. All she does is buy expensive clothes and tell me about her rich, influential daddy. When I need to, I can make someone believe anything."

"It certainly is a tempting proposition."

"Look, it's a two-for-one deal; you also get me as a bed partner."

"Now, that, my dear, will be the best part of it." He spread his arms in an invitation.

She leaned over to kiss his nipples. While running her tongue around them, she reached down to stroke his second erection. He moaned sounds of obvious delight. She swung her leg over and mounted him this time.

THE OCCUPANTS OF the white van listened to the locket-transmitted conversations with mounting apprehension. When Danielle heard Erin propose a partnership with Kane, she jumped up, forgetting where she was, and banged her head on the top of the van. "Holy shit, Erin. You didn't have to go that far. Daddy, you have to stop this."

Her father shrugged. "What can I do at this point?" He leaned forward to listen. During a lull, he turned to Danielle. "This is actually going quite well. Erin's infiltration of Kane's business may turn up the only credible evidence we'll ever have against him. I doubt very much if we could ever get him on the Dawes murder anyway."

"Why? You know he did it."

"We have no body, no weapon, no witnesses and the probable murderer is now shark bait."

"So now what?"

"If he carries through with his threat to eliminate Wiggams, thanks to Erin, we may be able to catch him in the act."

"Yeah, and risk her life in the process. I don't like this one bit."

"It wasn't your choice, remember? She knew the risks and wanted to do it."

"You put her in a position where she had no alternative. If Kane didn't confess, you knew she'd do this, didn't you?"

"No, Danielle, I didn't. All I knew was that Erin has the courage of her convictions. What she would do was known only by her."

"Bull shit, Dad. You've been around Washington too long; you're starting to sound like the rest of them."

Jeremy removed his headset and turned to Baldwin. "Sounds like she's getting ready to leave now. Perhaps you want to pick it up from here." Jeremy returned to his station and slowly increased the volume so everyone assembled in the van could hear.

"Are you sure you won't stay over?"

"Positive, C.A. I told you I have exams to correct tomorrow."

"When will I see you again?"

"You tell me; you're the senior partner in this new corporation."

"I take that to mean you'll be joining me before the job opens up to be my judicial assistant?"

"That's up to you. I don't know what your plans are regarding Wiggams and St. James."

"Neither do I just yet, but I'll be in touch."

"Please do."

"Erin, I do hope you're not playing games. That would be a real waste of my time and your body."

"After what we just shared, I find it hard to believe you could say that."

"You think I would risk everything I've worked for in exchange for two hours of sex?"

"Albert, I'm sure you intimidated and threatened Dawes and Wiggams, but that won't work with me."

"Oh, really? Why not?"

"Because I understand something they don't. . . . No good partnership can function that way. So shove your offer where the sun doesn't shine."

"My, my, we have a temper, don't we?"

"That's right, Mr. Bullshit Bigshot, I do."

The slamming of Kane's immense mahogany door made enough noise to send Jeremy's gauges into the red zone.

The listeners heard Erin as she walked down the hallway, was escorted out by the butler, and opened her car door. She took a very deep breath and started her car. "If you're listening, and I'm sure you all are, I'm safely in the car and heading for home. I would appreciate it if we could pick this up tomorrow. Right now I need some time to myself."

Danielle began to cry. As her father moved to comfort her, she pounded her fists into his chest. "What have you gotten my friend into? You son of a bitch!"

George Baldwin held his daughter's hands and pulled her close, letting her tirade subside.

Kane sat on the edge of the bed, still smiling from his exchange with Erin. He liked her spunk. Tonight's exchange reinforced his opinion that she was quite a match for him. But could he trust her? That was the big question.

More than he could trust that asshole Wiggams, he reminded himself. He definitely had to go.

Could he persuade David St. James to move to Charlotte and become the university's comptroller? He had a cushy job in Boston, a house, a social life. Would he want to leave all that? Erin had hinted that St. James took a liking to Danielle. Maybe that would be enough to weight the offer.

Wiggams was another matter altogether.

When Kane had requested that Portofino be eliminated, he'd used up the last of his favors with the mob. He was savvy enough to know that any more requests would place his own life in jeopardy. This Wiggams situation. . . he may have to resolve on his own.

He headed for the shower, worn out. Whether by the sex or the contemplation of an interesting future with Erin, he didn't know.

THE SECOND ERIN answered the phone, she heard, "Care for a little company this afternoon?"

She opened one eye and peered sleepily at the clock radio. "Yeah, Dani, I would. Just don't make it too early."

"How's three o'clock?"

"Fine. Now let me go back to sleep."

It was the shortest conversation they had ever had, but Erin hoped Danielle had recognized the stress she was under and would give her some time to decompress.

Erin lay back and thought about last night. What might she expect of Kane now? Had she been convincing enough? Would he buy her change of loyalty from her job at the university to him and his investment company?

She didn't have long to wait. The phone rang again; this time it was Kane.

"Good morning," he purred. "How are you feeling?"

"Sleepy and I have a long day of paper work ahead. So make it quick."

"I thought I had better apologize for my comment last night."

"Which one does the apology cover?" She put icicles in her voice.

"I have that coming. Erin, I am sorry. I'm not used to trusting people. Comes from being a defense attorney, I guess."

"Words are cheap. Actions mean much more to me."

"I agree, that's why I called. I'm going to need some help with Wiggams. Can I count on you?"

"The question is, can we count on each other? I know where I stand. I thought I made that quite clear last night."

"You did. Forgive me for doubting you."

"Apology accepted. Now what can I do to help?"

"I have an idea about how to get rid of Wiggams and would like to discuss it with you."

"When?"

"My calendar is full all day Monday. I thought maybe Tuesday we could get together."

"That sounds fine. President St. James found someone to take Professor Dawes' classes, so I have a fairly easy schedule that day. But we need to settle some business matters first."

"Like what?"

"My one-third cut of the pie. We need to clarify the details before we go one step further."

"Can't that wait until Tuesday?"

"I suppose, but be forewarned: my cut better be equal to or better than Harmon's. I am taking his place."

"I assure you the parity between you, David and me will be equal."

"I assume you mean that with reference not only to money but also controlling interest in Tristar?"

As soon as the word crossed her lips, she knew she had made a mistake. She waited for his reaction, her stomach churning.

""Where did you get that name from?"

"Danielle. Where else?"

"The Las Vegas trip, right?"

"Yep, she played Wiggams like a fiddle."

"Well, his strings are about to break."

"How?"

"We'll talk more when we meet."

As she hung up, her hands were wet with perspiration. She had to be more careful now. Kane would surely have her watched and maybe even tap her phone. Being seen with Danielle or her father could be disastrous. She needed to find a form of secured communication.

Erin looked at the locket George Baldwin had given her, lying on the night stand, and reminded herself to find out its range. And quickly.

She spent the rest of the morning and early afternoon correcting papers. The time passed so quickly that when the doorbell rang, she could not believe it was already three. She answered the door and embraced Danielle. For a long moment, they held each other then Danielle headed to the fridge for a Coke. "Bring me one, too," Erin called to her.

When she returned to the living room, Erin filled her in on Kane's call that morning.

"We need to avoid each other now, Dani. He has to know that I put the business first, ahead of anything else. Including you."

"I suppose you're right. Erin, I'm so scared for you. When you get in bed with a snake, you're likely to get bitten."

"You need to ask your dad how we can communicate and whether or not I should be using the locket all the time. I don't know how far this thing will transmit."

"Anything else?"

"Ask him if he has any sophisticated pepper spray or something for my protection in an emergency."

"I'll talk to him about these things, but I know he's going to want a meeting."

"I want one too, but it has to be tomorrow and someplace we won't be seen together."

"How about my place?"

"Christ, Danielle, we might as well mount a flashing light on our cars. Our places are out; this is probably the last time we'll be here for a while."

"Dad will know how to set up a safe place for meeting."

"Don't call me with the information. From now on, I'm going to assume my phones are tapped."

"How about if I stop by your office tomorrow?"

"That's good; the university will offer us safe haven for a while anyway."

Danielle got up and walked to the window. She continued to stare outside as she spoke. "You know I heard everything last night."

"Everything?"

"Enough. Jesus, you 'fanned his embers of passion into a roaring fire'."

"Did I say that? Dani, you remember how you felt with Wiggams in Vegas?"

"Creepy. If it hadn't been so critical to get our questions answered, I would never have slept with him."

"That's how I feel about Kane. On my end, the embers of passion were stone cold."

"With Wiggams, I knew I was dealing with a sex maniac. But C. Albert Kane is a cold-blooded murderer." She turned from the window. "How will you handle the Wiggams issue?"

"At the moment, I have absolutely no idea. C.A.'s comment about 'getting rid of him' could mean anything. If he plans to kill him or have him killed, I suppose I'll do everything in my power to save the little pervert."

"Dad says if he attempts to murder Wiggams, we'll have to nail him on that since we'll never get him on Dawes."

"Really?"

"He says there is no evidence. You don't suppose we could convince Wiggams to come over to our side, do you?"

"To save his ass, he just might consider it."

"The risk is, if he turns on us and tells Kane, then, my dear sweet Erin, you're history."

"Run it by your dad and see what he has to say."

"Will do. I had better get out of here if I'm going to discuss all of this with him and have some answers for you tomorrow."

"Yes. Thanks. And, since you were listening last night. . . I'm not really jealous of your expensive clothes and your rich, influential father. I had to come up with a reason and that popped into my head."

Danielle put her arm around Erin and drew her close. "I know, dear friend, I know." She kissed her cheek.

Erin released her and nodded. "I'll see you at my office. My last class is over at 3:00, so come over about then."

After Danielle left, Erin couldn't get her mind back into her paper grading. She kept returning to Danielle's idea to approach Wiggams. Trusting her life to a consummate liar made her very uneasy. Wiggams had already demonstrated he would sell out for nothing more than a night of sex. Getting him to roll over on Kane could backfire. . . a risk she didn't want to take.

But David St. James. . . now, that made some sense.

Not only would the proper Bostonian be a much more reliable witness against Kane, his sister's position at the university might make him more apt to cooperate.

Was it time to ask for Gayle St. James' help? She'd have a lot to lose when all of this—the Tristar scam, her university comptroller being a convicted felon, the university's attorney's role in a hit, maybe two—came to light. The more she thought about it, the better she liked the idea. It offered a more attractive alternative than dealing with Wiggams.

Erin smiled to herself and, for the first time in a week, felt some relief. She had a plan. Tomorrow, she'd make an appointment to see President St. James.

On Monday morning, after the first full night's sleep in days, Erin was in her office by 7:00. Before her Economics class started at 8:00, she'd just have time to phone the president.

Erin closed her office door and pressed the buttons for the president's office. She wasted no time when she came on the line. "President St. James, please forgive me for rushing past the usual pleasantries, but I have some information about a potential university scandal that I think you should know about."

"Really, Erin? A university scandal? Is it of a serious nature?"

"I'm afraid so. But it's nothing I care to discuss on the phone. How soon can we meet?" She paused while the president checked her calendar.

"Not today. Meetings scheduled back to back. Can it wait until tomorrow?"

"It's not likely to become breaking news that soon."

"Fine, let's meet for lunch at the Uptown Club. Say noon?"

"Good. Since you were so efficient in getting me out of teaching Professor Dawes' classes so soon, I have a fairly light day tomorrow."

"You were quick to come to my aid, so I'm glad I was able to reward your diligence so promptly. I'm quite intrigued—and a little mystified—at the idea of a scandal. Is there anything you would care to share with me now?"

"No, but I will ask you not to discuss this with anyone, and I do mean anyone."

"I see. In my short exposure to you, Erin, I have never heard you sound so intense. This must indeed be serious."

"It most certainly is or I wouldn't be walking the plank I am."

"I will respect your wishes."

Gayle St.James hung up with a quiver in her stomach. She thought about the choice of words Erin had used. She knew her to be bright, conscientious and to the point. The word "scandal" was not something she would use in a conversation with the university president. Unless there was, indeed, a scandal.

Could it have something to do with someone in the St. James family? Surely not. Their credentials were impeccable. A father who enjoyed the respect of everyone in his hometown, where he'd been a family physician for 40 years. Couldn't be her mother, the consummate academician, who still conducted research at Stanford on the evolution of familial genetic depression. The ethics and morality of her parents were above reproach.

Did it relate to her brother? His problem with the bottle had been a well-kept family secret, known only to her parents and herself. His life in Boston seemed to be going along fine. No skeletons there. David had recently assured her that his alcoholism had been under control for years. And she knew her brother did not lie to her—never could, not even as a child. Every time he'd tried even the tiniest fib, his eyes would roll back to show their whites. It was a dead give-away.

Oh my God. The only thing left was her lesbian relationship with Joanne. Throughout the last three years, they had been so careful to protect not only her career but the reputations of her family. Joanne was aware of these conditions from the very beginning. She had just spoken to her last week, when the fire put the university in the media spotlight.

Had Joanne changed her mind? Was she trying to capitalize on the fire-generated publicity? Was she reneging on the vows they had made to one another?

Gayle's thoughts ran wild. Momentarily, she caught herself and laughed at her lapse into mindless anxiety. She took a deep breath. Tomorrow would be soon enough to find out about the scandal. Whatever it was, surely it wouldn't have anything to do with Joanne or any members of the St. James family.

AT 8:00 A.M. Monday, Danielle met her father at the General Aviation terminal. "Glad you could meet me before you had to leave," she said as they hugged. "Erin had a bunch of questions for me to ask you."

"Make it fast, honey. My pilot's getting the plane refueled. He'll want to leave in". . . he looked at his watch. . . "15 minutes."

"I can't be away from campus very long either. Now that we're moving into our temporary office this morning, we have a lot of work to catch up." Danielle took a deep breath and hurried on. "To begin with, Erin and I need a safe way to communicate with each other. She also wants to know how far the locket transmits and whether she is supposed to wear it all the time or just when she's with Kane."

"Tell her to wear it all the time; it will transmit as far as it needs to. The van will never be very far away."

"Next, she wants to know if you have some mace or pepper spray for her to carry."

"Of course. I'll have some sent to her office tomorrow. Plain brown wrapper." He grinned. "That's supposed to be funny, Danielle."

"I'll laugh later. Can we finish this, please?"

"Sorry, go on."

"Erin figures Kane, with all his connections, will get her phone tapped. To make sure she's being honest with him. How can we communicate without making Kane suspicious?"

"Use the white van. Tell her to instruct us via the locket as to the pick-up point and time. Tell her to vary the locations so there is no pattern."

"Got it."

"I want to meet with her tomorrow night. Can you get a message to her?"

Danielle nodded. "I'm seeing her in her university office at three."

"Tell her to go to the Silk'n Flower Shoppe at the mall. Be there at 5:30."

"What's there?"

"It's just a way to lose a tail. Tell her to walk through the store and out the 'employee only' exit at the rear. The van will be waiting."

"What about me?"

"You, young lady, are to just go about your business. Please stay away from Erin right now."

"You'll keep me informed, I hope?"

"You can count on it, my dear." He lifted his arm to peer at his watch. "Time's up. I'll do some work in D.C.—set up surveillance on Wiggams, since I think, if we're right, Kane will make a move on him soon—and be back here Tuesday to meet with Erin in the white van at . . . 5:30."

"Got it; Tuesday, 5:30," Danielle called over her shoulder.

On her way back to campus, Danielle let her mind skip back through the last couple of weeks.. She could hardly believe everything that had happened in just 10 days. She'd gone to Las Vegas with Wiggams, slept with him, had a sexual encounter with David St. James, then had a phone call from Erin telling her Dawes was gone and the university business office was on fire. Since then, her dad had discovered Portofino's death and possibly another one if Benny Caputto never shows up—probably Kane's doing—as was Dawes' mysterious disappearance. Her dear friend Erin was setting Kane up to expose the university scam and, if everything worked right, get him on an attempted murder charge or—if she got really lucky—pry out of him a confession of what he'd done with Dawes.

Erin needed some help. She couldn't do all this alone. Danielle wouldn't tell her father or Erin, but she was planning her own agenda. Wiggams' desire for sex was an addiction. He'd enjoyed her in Vegas, so it wouldn't be hard to get him hot and bothered again. When he did, she was poised to take advantage of this weakness and use it to persuade him that Kane might do to him what he'd done to Harmon Dawes.

Danielle parked behind Chase Hall and found her way to the temporary business office. Throughout the day, she put everything else out of her mind and concentrated on her accounting duties. Each time Wiggams walked by her desk, she smiled and winked then went back to work re-entering files into her desktop computer.

At ten minutes to three, Danielle found her supervisor. "I'm taking my break now. Be back in half an hour."

She nearly ran three buildings away to meet Erin as scheduled. Quickly, she relayed everything her dad had instructed her to say. "Like you said, he thinks we shouldn't be seen together until all this is over. Don't want to raise suspicions."

"Your father's right. The stakes are high, Dani. I sure don't want anything to happen to you."

"Or you." Tears started down Danielle's cheeks. "I wish I'd never gotten you into this mess."

"I know, but it'll all work out. I promise."

Erin said nothing about her plans to talk to President St..James, and Danielle likewise was mum about her plans with Wiggams.

George Baldwin had two loose cannons on his hands and didn't know it.

CHAPTER 15

In spite of a hectic Monday, C. Albert Kane had completed his morning workout and was in his office before 8:00 a.m. Tuesday. He had much to accomplish before his meeting with Erin this evening. He let his mind return to their recent dates. Young, beautiful, intelligent, sexy. . . Erin was a prize. She seemed to be as eager to spend time with him as he was with her. What a future they could have together. . . if she was sincere about coming on board.

He'd trusted her enough to divulge his intentions to get rid of Wiggams. Now, he had to be dead certain of Erin's loyalty.

He picked up the phone and called his reliable gumshoe. "Bubba, it's Albert Kane."

"It's been a while, counselor. What can I do for you?"

"There's a professor at the university that needs watching."

"Sure thing, bossman. What's his name?"

"It's a woman. Erin Gallagher, Economics Department."

"Got a picture?"

"No, but you won't need one. She's about 5'-8" with long auburn hair. And she is very, very attractive."

"You want weekends, 24/7 or what?"

"Pick her up as she leaves the university during the week and 24 hours on weekends."

"That's gonna trip the meter pretty fast, counselor."

"Just do it, Bubba."

"Sure thing. I'll report the usual way. Catch y'all later."

"Wait." Kane wasn't finished. "I also need a tap on her home phone ASAP." He gave the address.

"Consider it done, C. Albert. I'll get my man on that right away."

Kane smiled as he hung up; the first part of his plan was initiated. Erin had answered his question concerning her loyalty to Danielle but never addressed her allegiance to the university or Harmon Dawes. As genuine as her interest appeared, he had built a career on being suspicious of people's motives. Sure, Erin needed money. Who didn't? But would she sell out her values for it? Not unless he'd gravely misjudged her. And he never misjudged someone, especially on a matter as important as this. He wasn't about to simply accept her re-alignment of devotion. Bubba's tail would provide insurance. The supreme test of Erin's dedication to the investment scheme—and to him and his way of life—would come when she had to set up Wiggams' demise.

He once again reached for the phone. Step two in his plan. "Dr. Zachary, please. . . . I don't care if he's with a patient. Tell him it's C. Albert. He'll take the call."

After a short wait, a gruff voice greeted him "Yes, Albert. Make it quick. What can I do for you?"

"I need some of that drug that causes heart attacks and is undetectable at autopsy."

"Albert, I can't give you that."

Kane let contempt tinge his voice. "Yes, you can, assuming, of course, that you want to stay in practice."

"That sounds like blackmail."

"Not at all. I just have a long memory for the right kind of facts. Need I remind you of the two patients you killed?"

"You know as well as I do. . . that was years ago. I've more than paid my debt to society."

"Look, you escaped a double murder charge because the coroner couldn't detect the drug. Now you can pay your debt to me as well."

"You know damn well those deaths were accidental."

"Do I? The prosecutor didn't see it that way."

"I can't do it, Albert."

"Philip, either send me the drug or say good-bye to medicine. The choice is yours."

"You really are a bastard."

"Now, now, Cynthia wouldn't like that talk. By the way, is she still living the high life?"

Silence. Then, "All right, you win."

"I knew you'd see it my way. Ingestion of the drug will be 'accidental,' so I assume it will have to be in a liquid or powder form. Be sure to include instructions. Wouldn't want to overdose." Kane allowed himself a chuckle.

Dr. Zachary let out a long breath.

"I also need a placebo in an identical form," Kane added.

"When do you need the meds?"

"This weekend."

"I'll send them to your office."

"Of course not, you idiot. Mail to PO Box 1169, Charlotte, 28078.

"I hope I never hear from you again. This surely evens the score."

As he hung up the phone, Kane reminded himself how important it was to keep records of potential IOU clients.

DURING HER TUESDAY morning class, Erin was busy accepting compliments on her outfit. It was true, she had dressed up a bit more than usual in preparation for her luncheon meeting with President St. James. It was probably more noticeable because of her propensity to dress down every day. In her first year of teaching, she had learned that it didn't take much to elicit comments from both male and female students regarding her choice of clothes. Her physical beauty was hard to disguise.

She left the university around 11:30 and headed her Honda toward the Uptown Club. Traffic was light so she let her mind wander to what Ginny Dawes had told her about the exclusive club. For nearly a century, it had been the private domain of the local high and mighty—strictly men only. It had taken a court order to remove the restrictions of gender and race. Ginny was one of the first women to become a member. The club membership was still, despite the court order, entirely monochromatic.

Erin arrived fifteen minutes early. After depositing the old Honda with a wincing looking valet, she walked up the wide granite steps and into the magnificent vaulted foyer. An edifice as pompous as its members, she thought.

The maitre d' informed her that Dr. St. James had already arrived, so she followed him through the massive dining area. Holding her head high, she watched the male clientele nearly stop eating as their eyes followed her to the president's table.

She extended her hand. "Do you get the stares too?"

"Yes, my dear, but not the kind you just did." Gayle smiled. "Please sit down. Would you care for something cold?"

Erin eased into the chair and draped a starched white napkin across her lap. "Yes, that would be nice."

Dr. St. James simply raised her eyebrows and bobbed her head at the waiter. He responded in seconds to take their order.

"I'm impressed. . . a female gaining the immediate attention of a male waiter with a 'look and a bob'. It certainly speaks of your title and respect within the community."

"And all the time I've been thinking it's my charm and wit."

As they shared a genuine laugh, Erin recalled how often she'd heard around campus that the president's humor was one of her many respected attributes.

While waiting for their food to be served, the two talked about how nice it felt to garner the respect of the community, especially in a setting that only a few years before would have been closed to them. Both had come from meager beginnings and worked hard to prevail in a man's world. Once the waiter brought their lunch and deferentially departed, the president got down to business.

"But we're not here to chat about how we've clawed our way up against ego-laden men. You wanted to see me about something important."

Erin wasn't ready to launch into the subject. "I think it would be better to discuss that after lunch."

"Erin, I squeezed you into a very busy schedule. I'm still dealing with consequences of the fire as well as the usual university issues. I really have no time for the proverbial two-hour lunch."

"I realize that, and I'm grateful. But this is not something that can be fully understood in a short period of time."

"Try me. I digest things rather rapidly."

Erin could see that Gayle was not here to make small talk but was eager to hear the "scandalous news" she'd promised. She looked around the room and realized how close their table was to accidental eavesdroppers. She leaned toward the president. "Perhaps a more intimate setting with unlimited time would be more appropriate."

"Just a minute, my dear; you get an emergency meeting with the university president and now want to recant the time and place? Perhaps I have over-estimated your intelligence."

"All right, then. Please don't say I didn't warn you." Erin took a deep breath and plunged ahead. "There are major financial scams involving fraud and embezzlement being run on the university by your own people."

"You can't be serious."

"Afraid I am, Dr. St. James."

"This is absurd. Our finance committee meets once a month, and, frankly, the bottom line has never looked so good."

"I know. It's supposed to. The truth is: you are receiving one third of what you should from your investment portfolio."

"How in the world would you know that?"

"It's a very long story, which I will be glad to tell at another time." She looked around and lowered her voice. "Please trust me. I do know what I'm talking about."

"And who, might I ask, is involved with this purported scandal?"

"John Wiggams, Albert Kane and Harmon Dawes."

"This is crazy!" Gayle noticed the entire room had fallen still. She pierced Erin with her eyes. And lowered her voice to a whisper. "You're telling me my comptroller, our chief counsel and the chair of the Economics department are defrauding the university of funds?"

"Yes, that's exactl.y what I'm telling you."

Gayle pushed her chair back and stood. She leveled her gaze at Erin. "I used to have great respect for you, but I have just heard enough to change that opinion. I shall not tolerate baseless allegations concerning these men. . . or any other university employees." She darted her eyes around the room. "I want to see you in my office at eight tomorrow morning. . . and bring your lawyer. We will be discussing the severance of your contract."

"You'd better pull your chair back to the table, Dr. St. James. I really don't think you want to read your family's name in the newspapers when this scandal breaks."

Gayle St.James' face looked as if someone had just pulled the drain plug on her blood bank. "What do you mean, 'my family'?"

"Please sit down; you're attracting attention."

She sat. "Erin, you had better be right or you will never work in academics again."

"Look, I realize I'm risking a lot and what I've said is hard to swallow. Please believe me. I'm here because I care about you and the university. This is not for personal gain, I assure you."

"It's all just been such a shock." The president's voice softened. She reached her hand toward Erin. "I'm sorry."

Erin took her hand then slowly released it. "I'd like to tell you it gets better, but it doesn't."

"Oh, God."

"Your brother is their banker."

She sighed. "I guess that explains why he keeps asking me about John Wiggams."

"Unfortunately, this stretches far beyond fraudulent conversion. I'm hoping your brother is not involved with the murder of Professor Dawes."

Gayle gently placed her fork and knife on the plate. "Now you're going too far. I spoke with Mrs. Dawes just this morning. Professor Dawes, she told me, is feeling somewhat better, but the doctor wants him to take a leave of absence for the rest of the semester. And you want me to believe he was murdered? Erin, are you on some form of medication?"

"Sometimes I wish I was."

Gayle stared at Erin, daring her to lower her eyes. "Are you telling me Dawes is not sick with pneumonia?"

"Never was. He disappeared the night before the Petrini ceremony. Along with all his files on the fraudulent business. For reasons I'll explain later, his wife and I decided to keep his absence quiet for awhile. And Danielle agreed."

"Danielle? The intern?"

"Yes."

"Am I the only one out of the loop?"

"Far from it. Now that you know however, I'm trusting you'll not only keep this information entirely confidential but help us bring the mess to an end before anyone else gets hurt."

"I'll do what I can." She stared at her untouched food. "Do you know who allegedly murdered Harmon?"

"Kane hired a Mafia hit man. Who turned up dead, so the only witness has been eliminated."

Her head bounced up as if she'd been shot. "This is just too much to take in."

"I know. It all started when I went on summer break and accidentally ran into Danielle. She shared information about almost being released from her internship because of facts she had uncovered in the business office. Intrigued, I looked into it. . . and I almost wish I hadn't."

"You mean the kid discovered all this?"

Erin didn't want to tell about the break in at Wiggams' office, or Danielle's part in that. Not just yet, anyway. "Yes, more or less. She didn't know what she had until after we returned home. I did some research and finally pieced it all together."

"Are the police involved?"

"No, we're using Danielle's father. With Kane's contacts, we were afraid to use the locals. We're pretty sure they would alert him to an investigation."

Erin went into fast forward and explained how she had gone to Kane's mansion for dinner in an attempt to elicit information from him. She told Gayle about the wire and how Danielle's father recorded everything. She left out the bedroom seduction scene.

She described how, in two meetings with Kane, she convinced him that her need for money combined with her disillusionment with the university and Danielle had made his way of life so attractive to her. . . . She wanted to drive new cars, live in mansions, travel freely and shop at will.

"He bought into it and offered me an opportunity to replace Harmon. He also shared with me that Wiggams, because of his sexual and gambling addictions, had to be disposed of."

"Oh my god!"

"That's when I thought of you and decided to take a chance you might be willing to help."

"Certainly I'll help, but I have so many questions right now, my head is literally spinning."

"I told you it was a lot to digest at one meeting."

"Erin, let me apologize again. You were right in coming to me."

"Do you think there may be a chance to change your brother's allegiance?"

"I think so, but then again, I never would have believed he'd be a part of this."

"If he helps us, I'm sure the authorities will cut him a deal on the charges. Probably give him immunity of prosecution in exchange for his testimony against Kane and Wiggams."

"Obviously, I will do my very best. No matter what he's done, he's still my brother."

"Why don't you sit on this for a day or two and we'll talk again later in the week."

"Yes, I need some time to calm down and put this all in perspective."

"Please remember, not a word to anyone, especially David. Kane has eliminated Dawes and plans to get rid of Wiggams. Your brother could be next."

Gayle picked up her fork and pushed food around on her plate as if she might find answers under the vegetables. When she looked up, tears welled in her eyes. "Erin, I want to thank you for the opportunity to save our university. And my brother. Not to mention my career. You took a big risk in trusting me. . . and. . . I . . . thank you." Without a word more, Gayle motioned for the check and signed her name.

WHAT A DAY this had been. . . and it was far from over. By the time she'd returned from lunch with the president and finished Tuesday classes, Erin was feeling the awful fatigue that accompanies anxiety and stress. The meeting with Gayle had taken a lot out of her. She wasn't exactly looking forward to the meetings with George Baldwin and, following that, dinner on the town with Albert Kane.

She did as instructed, however, and at 5:30 arrived at the flower shop, walked through it to the employee exit and out to the white van parked behind..

George Baldwin greeted her warmly. "How's our newest undercover operative doing today?"

Erin groaned. "Don't ask." She took what Baldwin held out to her. "What's this? Looks like a ball point pen."

"Yes, it does, but don't try to write with it. Keep it in your purse."

"What is it?"

"The clip activates an emergency transponder while the plunger releases a paralyzing nerve gas from the barrel."

"All right!" Erin got into the spirit of things and gave him a high-five. "I feel like a James Bond associate." She dropped it into her purse.

"Glad to see you're wearing the locket."

"All the time, just as Dani told me."

"We'll use it again tonight when you're with Kane. I don't have to tell you to be careful."

"Then why did you?" She fingered the locket at her throat and lifted her arm to show him the wrist watch transponder. "I'm all set." She stood up to leave the van. "I'll be fine. We're not dining at his house tonight. I didn't want any more bedroom scenes for your men to . . . hear. They can get their jollies on their own time."

"Of course, I didn't mention that reason to Kane. I told C.A. to confirm my commitment to him, I wanted to show up in a public place, arm in arm, to be seen by all the important people of Charlotte. He chose Peabody's for cocktails, but we're dining afterward at the Capitol Grille."

Baldwin looked perplexed. "Is that significant?"

"Only because it is frequented by the power people of politics, industry and finance. C.A.'s once and future clients."

Armed with her new protective and security hardware she listened to Baldwins final instructions and exited the van. A nap could not come to soon as she headed for home.

It was the first time in her life she was happy about thunder and lighting. The noise of the storm woke her. She looked at the clock, hurried into the shower, dressed and left the house. Never seeing McBride or his car parked across the street. Her timing was good. She arrived at Peabody's valet parking right behind the black four-door Mercedes with the NC-1 plate. As she exited her ancient Honda, Kane approached with his arm extended. She took it gracefully and he escorted her up the stairs, through the lobby and into the cocktail lounge.

"I saw your license plate," Erin said as they waited to be seated. "How'd you get NC-1? I thought that was always reserved for the governor."

"In most states, perhaps. But in North Carolina, it belongs to me. Play your cards right, and you could have NC-2."

"Yeah, that would go nicely with my decrepit Honda."

"I see you in something far more elegant than that, my dear. An automobile as exquisite as you look tonight, I might add." He swept his eyes from the top of her shining auburn hair, worn loose to her shoulders, to the bottom of her mini skirt. "Very. . . sensuous."

She said nothing but only smiled and seated herself on a low swivel chair on one side of a tiny glass table. For the first time with him, she had worn something a little sexier than usual. From his repeated visual appraisals, she guessed he liked the way she looked. . . very much.

She stretched out her long legs to one side of the table, close enough for him to admire her well-muscled calves.

Over cocktails, conversation veered from politics, to his career and finally to the stock market. Although his emphasis on his own interests bored her, she pretended keen excitement. Had to keep up the facade, she thought, and act as if every word he uttered was golden. Finally, she'd had enough.

"Have you decided yet what to do with Wiggams?"

"As a matter of fact, I have."

"You said the other night that you needed my help. Is that still the case?"

"Absolutely."

"And what might that be?"

"Are you sure you don't want to wait until later to discuss this?"

"Anything wrong with now? Here, we can only ruin a drink. Why risk ruining a gourmet meal?"

Kane threw back his head in uncharacteristic appreciation of her retort. His laughter was short lived. He got down to business. "You are obviously aware of his fondness for pretty young women?"

"You're right. That does not come as a surprise."

"I'd like you to find a reason to visit him on campus. Can you do that?"

"Sure, any number of ways."

"Good. Then entice him into asking you out. That shouldn't require much." He eyed her again, letting his them linger on her legs as she brought them up and crossed one knee over the other.

"And. . ."

"Use whatever tactic you choose but lure him to the Sugarside Motel on the south side of town."

"What's that, a hot pillow operation?" She didn't wait for his reply. "And he'll presume our rendezvous will include sex?"

"Naturally. Once you have him inside the room and comfortable, tell him to open the blind a little then close it again."

"Why?"

"That'll be the signal for a local prostitute to knock on the door. Let her in and tell him you took the liberty to set up a threesome."

"Christ, from what Danielle tells me, he'll be ecstatic."

"She'll take over while you make an excuse about needing to get some ice."

"Sounds as if you have done this before."

He leaned over the glass table and caressed her hand. "Someday you'll find out."

"Then what?"

"That's all. Just get in your car and go home."

"The prostitute will dispose of Wiggams?"

"She has her instructions. Let's just say Wiggams is going to be the victim of his own addiction."

"She's going to screw him to death?" Erin let a wry smile play with her lips and just as quickly disappear. "How ironic."

"You might say that. Well, are you in or not?"

"Yes, of course. When do we do it?"

"As soon as you feel he's ready to go."

"If it's up to him, that could be tomorrow."

"A bit soon, perhaps. I need 24 hours to line everything up."

"Okay. I'll get started with the flirtation and be in touch with you."

Erin held up her empty cocktail glass and patted her stomach. Kane got the message and signaled for the check.

"C.A., why don't I leave my car here and ride with you to the restaurant," Erin suggested as they waited for the valet. "More time for us to talk privately." She dazzled a smile in his direction and nestled against his arm.

When they pulled into the street, Erin flipped the sun visor down so she could use the mirror to freshen her lipstick. Three vehicles back, a nondescript white van rolled along behind them. Erin prayed the locket had transmitted all the cocktail conversation to George Baldwin's people. Kane wasn't about to reveal the manner or method of death, but it was evident he had devised a plan to dispose of John Wiggams.

The Capitol Grille turned out to be the perfect venue to display Kane and Erin to the cognoscenti. Throughout the meal—which was, so far, the best she'd ever eaten in Charlotte—a steady stream of people stopped by their table to "meet the lovely lady," or "to shake the hand of our next Superior Court judge," or just to shoot the breeze. Erin couldn't get over how nice Kane could act in public. When he turned on the charm to the well-educated, well-heeled men and women in this room, it was easy to see how he won cases for his legal clients. And how he was assured of the judicial seat. She had to remind herself of the real Cedric Albert Kane—the man who almost certainly ordered the murder of Harmon Dawes. And the man planning the death of John Wiggams.

After an evening of forcing herself to smile at strangers and act the part of Kane's enamored companion, Erin was exhausted. Still, she played her role to the end, as Kane drove her back to Peabody's to pick up her car. "I must say, C.A., that you cut quite a swath in the local high society. My jaw hurts from all that smiling."

"I have managed to align myself with the right kind of people, my dear. You are known by the company you keep, and I intend always to be in the right company." He reached across the center console and squeezed her hand.

Erin returned the squeeze. "I think I'm going to like the lifestyle you can elevate me to. I've never seen so many beautiful people assembled in one place. . . except in the movies."

"People without power are always attracted to those who have it. They think they're sharing my spotlight." He turned toward Erin. "Can you imagine anything more ludicrous? I share my spotlight with no one."

"Really? I thought you wanted me at your side.. . . to share your life and your spotlight."

"Forgive me, my dear. I would like nothing better than to have you at my side. I was referring to all those so-called beautiful people you met tonight. Hangers-on, every damn one of them. They'll kiss the ass of anyone they perceive to be in a position to do favors for them And the minute the power's gone, so are the beautiful people."

"I take it, then, that they're not really your friends?"

"My dear Er Bear, I have no friends. I need no friends. What I do enjoy, in case you haven't noticed, is to have what other people want. All those ass kissers you met at the Grille tonight were quite impressed with you. I must say I took pride in receiving stares from men actively coveting you."

The thought of being considered Kane's private possession made Erin's stomach turn. It was obvious that her plan was working: just as she'd done at the dinner dance, she was turning his own ego to work for her. As long as she continued to play her part, she could make that arrogance bring him to the downfall he so richly deserved.

THE FOLLOWING MORNING, Kane took the next step in his plan. He called Bubba McBride "Hunt up a hooker by the name of Mandi and deliver her to the River Commons for a private meeting."

"Who's her pimp?"

Kane told him and added the location where she plied her trade.

"What day and time, bossman?"

"Tonight at dusk."

"What if I can't find her?"

"You're wasting time, Bubba."

The line went dead.

The gumshoe got the message. Bring a hooker to meet Kane at the river? McBride had known the bossman for a long time and this just wasn't his style. He began a series of calls to locate the pimp. After several hours and having no luck, he slammed out of his office to have lunch at his favorite Irish pub.

Just inside the door—once his eyes got used to the dark—he spotted Mac Finnerety, a detective he knew from the Charlotte police. He sidled up to him at the counter and motioned to the bartender. "Draw me one. And I'll have the Wednesday blue plate special."

Between bites of the ham and cabbage special, Bubba asked Mac what was hot at the station these days.

"Damn whores are driving us nuts. They get themselves drugged up then turn up dead or in the hospital. The last two weeks we had three hookers delivered DOA to Presbyterian, alone."

"I'll bet you could help me with a case I'm on, Mac." McBride polished off the last of his cabbage and lit a cigarette. "Would you know a hooker who goes by Mandi? I'm trying to find her pimp. A guy by the name of Candyman. Looked all morning. He's nowhere to be found."

"Yeah, and I know why. He's at the station right now for questioning. One of those DOA's was from his stable."

"Can I talk to him?"

"Sure, come on back with me and I'll set it up. Make it quick though or I'm gonna get my ass kicked."

"Will do. Thanks, Mac."

McBride jumped into Mac's cruiser and, five minutes later, followed him inside the station house. "Hang around in the office and I'll get him for you," Mac said.

Shortly McBride was shown into an interview room. Waiting for him was a sullen, street-wise Mr. "T" wanabe. The gold flashing from around his neck and his teeth was enough open up a jewelry store. McBride picked up a straight back chair and turned it around then sat, folding his arms on the chair back. He wasted no time. "Understand you could put me in touch with a girl named Mandi.

"Yeah, what's it to ya?"

"I need to find her. She has a problem.."

"You don't say. With who?"

"Look, I'm a P.I. and her father hired me to find her. Her mother is dying of cancer and wants to see her before she croaks."

"You're breaking my heart, Columbo. Now get me out of here."

"Not so fast." McBride scooted his chair closer. "Unless you give me Mandi, I'm going to tell the cops I witnessed you beating the crap out of that DOA of yours last week."

"You shit, my man. She OD'd. I didn't touch her."

"So what? Who are the cops going to believe, you or me?"

The pimp considered for a moment, playing with one of the gold chains around his neck. "I might know where you could find her. What's in it for me?"

"A good-lookin' dude like you? You'll save your ass from becoming a depository for the boys on Meadow Oak Drive."

Sweat trickled along his cheeks, flowing as if in canals beside his Fu Manchu "Mandi's rooming with another of my fillies." He gave the address. "Down by the railroad yards."

McBride winced. Not only was this the seediest section of town, but it was filled with drug addicts and other criminals he had helped put away when he was on the force. His reception there would be a cold one. He'd have to be on his guard.

Still digesting his lunch as he walked back towards his office, he glanced around to see if anyone he passed had got a whiff of the trail he left behind. He smiled at the passers-by, thinking they were either stone deaf or suffering from sinusitis.

When he reached the office, he popped a GasX into his mouth, crunched down then waited for it to dissolve before he called Kane. He rattled off the address Candyman gave him. "I'm goin' there now just to be sure she don't get busy and disappear on me."

"That's a wonderful idea, Bubba, but don't submit this time on your invoice as surveillance."

"But boss, I'm just keeping her under wraps until your meeting tonight."

"Save the crap, McBride. The Irish never could keep it in their pants and I'm not paying for your sticky mattress time with her."

"Does anybody ever get one by you?"

"No, they don't, Bubba. That's how I stay squeaky clean."

Bubba hung up, took his piece out of his desk drawer and holstered it. He went to the bathroom for a piss and splashed some cologne all over his body. While his zipper was open, he spritzed his genitals. The damn ham and cabbage was still hanging around.

He set out to find his client's prey.

ERIN WAS FINISHING her Wednesday afternoon office hours when Danielle walked in. She plunked herself down on the other side of Erin's desk, in the place usually reserved for students who needed counseling about how to improve their econ. grades.

Erin looked up and tilted her head to one side. "What brings you here, my dear?"

"It's a small university town and news travels fast."

"Now what?"

"How did your lunch with our les-pres go?"

"A little frightening, but otherwise all right."

"How come you didn't tell me?"

"About what?"

"You and Gayle having lunch, that's what."

"Ooooh, do I sense some jealousy here?" She gave Danielle her most benign smile.

"I've never been dropped for an older woman before."

They shared a good laugh. Erin explained the intent of her mission and how Gayle reacted to the news.

"Christ, Erin, sometimes I think you're a little nuts. You take a lot of chances. What if she tells her brother?"

"She won't. Right now, she's not ready to let him know what she knows."

"Do you think she will be able to get David to help us?"

"I hope so, because, for the time being, it may be the only avenue we have open."

"I see." Danielle squirmed on her chair. "I wasn't going to tell you, but I was thinking that Wiggams is probably getting nervous these days and when he does, he usually calms himself with sex."

"Yeah?"

"I was going to stop by his office and kind of entice him into a bedroom discussion that might help him come over to us."

Erin came off her chair. "Dani, you stay the hell away from Wiggams. Other things are in motion right now and I don't want you going near him."

Danielle motioned for Erin to sit down. "Whoa, I think I just stepped on a land mine."

"You sure did, sweetie."

"What's going on?"

"I was just about to call your father's safe number and set up a meeting. You might as well hear it then, as I have no intention of relating it all twice."

Danielle lowered her voice and crossed her legs. "From your tone, it sounds like something pretty heavy is going down."

"That, my dear Dani, is an understatement. Now let's see if we can make contact with your dad."

Erin reached for the phone and dialed the emergency number George Baldwin had given her. He answered quickly. Erin set up a pickup by the white van near the maintenance building on campus—close enough for her and Danielle to walk without being conspicuous. "Make it quick. . .half an hour will be fine."

Erin cleared her desk and locked it. They exited her office, left the building and began the stroll through the promenade to meet the van. As they approached Big Jake's territory, they spotted the white van parked in the shade of a monstrous oak tree. It seemed nearly invisible. Erin marveled at how well these people did their jobs, as she opened the door and climbed in behind Danielle.

Erin sat on the bench seat and leaned her head against the side of the van. "I guess you heard the recording from last night regarding what I'm supposed to do with Wiggams?"

George Baldwin motioned to the tape recorder and Jeremy at its controls. "I did and I also heard my daughter's half assed idea about Wiggams. You have two choices Danielle, behave yourself and stay out of this or I will have you locked down till it's over. Do you understand?"

Danielle knew her father all to well and this was not the time to be oppositional.

Sensing a family crises, before Dani could answer Erin interrupted with "Mr. Baldwin, I can deliver Wiggams to the motel, but I don't understand what will happen after I leave him with Kane's prostitute."

Baldwin tapped Erin on the knee. "My guess is that she will appear with a bottle of booze, get him all tanked up, wait till he passes out then inject some heroin into him. We would find him overdosed and the community would chalk it up to a suicide."

"And Kane walks away free?"

"That's my guess. Your involvement in getting Wiggams there would provide Kane the clout he needs to keep you in line."

"That stinks," Danielle mumbled.

"Sure does, but it's even worse than that."

"Why?"

"If we move in and pinch her in the act, Kane'll know you tipped us off. I'm sure that's what he's waiting for. . . a true test of your loyalty."

Erin shifted weight to her left side and slid her right leg over her left knee. "So what are we supposed to do, let the prostitute kill Wiggams? I don't see how that implicates Kane at all."

"That's the 'worse than that' I was referring to. He's a very clever man, Erin."

"So what can we do?"

"Suppose you accidentally leave your purse and return to the room in about 15 minutes to retrieve it."

"Then what?"

"I don't think the whore will do anything with you present, so if I'm right they will be feeling a little loose by then."

"And?"

"You'll bring ice—just as you and Kane discussed—yes, I listened to the tape of your cocktail conversation. Returning for your purse is a cover—a legitimate reason you can use with Kane to explain why you went back."

Danielle shook her head. "I don't see where this is going, Daddy."

"The only way to beat Kane at his game—and keep Wiggams alive—is to keep Erin there."

"Are you suggesting that Erin should proceed with a *menage-a-trois* to keep Wiggams from being killed? Holy shit."

Baldwin sighed. "Afraid so. Yes. Later we can pick up the prostitute for possession and still keep Erin's cover intact."

"Mr. Baldwin, I have a question." Erin uncrossed her legs and straightened her back.

"Yes Erin, shoot."

"What if she decides to use the stuff in my presence?"

"I don't think she'll be that bold, but if she does, use our code word 'hibiscus' and we will take the whole scene down immediately."

"Then I'm done, my cover is gone and we'll never get Kane."

"More than likely you're right, but we can't be a party to Wiggams' murder."

"May I ask another question?"

"Sure."

"I have been suspicious right along—same as you—that he's using this to check my loyalty. If I'm involved in a murder, he holds my life in his hands. But what if you're wrong? What if it's not heroin? Or they try something else? We will have blown everything. . . for nothing."

"You think this entire scenario may be a red herring, just to test your allegiance to him?"

"I'm not sure, but it would certainly fit his personality."

"Erin's right, Daddy. He goes to great lengths to ensure his people are true to him."

"How do you know?"

"John Wiggams told me."

"How the . . ."

"Now is not the time. I'll tell you later."

"I'm not sure I want to know." Baldwin remained silent for several moments. "We could provide you with a vial of VDRL to make a test. Suppose you told the prostitute you would like to shoot up before she did Wiggams and convinced her to give you the bottle and syringe to do it in the bathroom."

"Then I could quickly test the stuff to see if it's real?"

"That's right."

"And if it's not?"

"Then let her inject him and you play it by ear from there. If you're right, all of you could walk out of there alive and you would have passed Kane's test."

"And if I'm wrong?"

"You say the magic word and we're in there."

"You know, Dad, even if it ends up blowing Erin's cover, it might just be enough of a scare to turn Wiggams our way."

"Good point, Danielle. Maybe we could end up double-binding Kane. It sure would be a nice turn of events."

Baldwin turned back to his newest undercover operative. "Erin, I hate to put your life at risk. Do you still want to try your theory?"

"I don't see any other way, Mr. Baldwin. Do you?"

George Baldwin squinted, clenched his teeth, looked at Danielle for just a moment and shook his head. "Frankly, I don't."

"We've come this far," Erin said, "and I've had to do some pretty distasteful things already. Let's play it out."

"When do you plan to see Wiggams?"

"After I leave here. I'm going to try to set it up for tomorrow night at the Sugarside Motel."

"All right, there will be an envelope in your university mail box tomorrow morning. It will contain the testing fluid. You just need a drop in the vial. If it's heroin or any other narcotic, it will turn purple."

"If not, can I assume it's okay to give it to him?"

"I sure hope so."

The two women said their good-byes and began the walk back across campus. Danielle looked around to see if anyone was near enough to overhear them. The white van had already driven away, and they were alone. "If you sense things are blowing up, remember, we still have all the Tristar files tucked away. We can nail what's left of the terrific trio with fraudulent conversion. That'll end Kane's political career and, possibly, put him away for a few years."

"And let Kane walk away from Professor Dawes' murder? Never, Danielle, never."

"I understand your desire to nail his ass, but it's not worth another life. Especially yours."

"Not to worry. I promise to be careful." They walked along in silence as Erin considered her position. "And besides, we still have a chance of getting David St. James to cooperate. I haven't forgotten that, you know."

"Why don't we try that first?"

"Because I don't think he can provide any information on Harmon's murder. He would be helpful only for the fraud and conspiracy charges."

They nearly walked past the makeshift Business Administration Building. Danielle stopped, grabbed Erin and held her close. "Please be careful. I. . . love you dearly." Just as quickly, she turned and ran towards the parking lot.

FOR TWO HOURS, Bubba McBride sat in his car across from Mandi's apartment and watched for someone—anyone—to go in or out. Thinking about baby-sitting the hooker till time to deliver her to meet Kane brought a bulge to his trousers. His erection became insistent. He smoothed it down and opened the car door. . . time to see if she was in there.

He edged out of the car, rapidly crossed the street and walked the two flights to apartment 212. Somebody was making a lot of money, he thought, but it certainly wasn't Mandi. The damn place smelled worse than the aftermath of his pub special.

He knocked on the door and waited. He was about to knock again when he heard a voice.

"Go away, it's too early."

"Candyman sent me," Bubba called through the door. He heard three locks being unbolted, and a chain slid into place. A crack appeared. He peered inside and could see a blond who had at least one blue eye. It appeared she was wearing a short terry cloth robe with no slippers.

"What do you want?" came in a sleepy mumble.

"Your pimp will tell you later. Let me in."

"He's in jail."

"Yeah, and he's going to stay there if you don't let me in."

"You a cop?"

"Let's just say we met at the station house. Okay?"

"All right, all right, come on in." She shut the door, disengaged the chain then reopened it. The apartment reeked of cheap perfume and looked as if it hadn't been cleaned in months. Clothing, pizza boxes and miscellaneous junk littered the floor and every available surface.

McBride walked to the lone window overlooking the street and assured himself he had a good view of anyone approaching the front of the building. He then checked the other rooms.

"What the hell are you looking for? Did you come here to get the 'bunny' or conduct an egg hunt?"

Bubba moved back to the front window and turned to face the woman. "I came because a friend of yours needs a favor."

"Who?"

"Albert Kane."

"Ahhhhhhh, my man, Prince Albert."

"Glad to see you remember him." McBride smirked.

"Are you kidding? He gets me out of jail more than my pimp." Mandi brushed hair out of her eyes. She shook the last cigarette out of a pack and crumpled it. When she leaned over to hunt for a pack of matches under all the mess on the table, she exposed nearly all of one breast.

McBride stroked his groin. "Sure sure. He's known all over town as a good Samaritan." Another smirk. "And you pay him with. . . favors?"

"That's right. I deliver 'in kind' services in lieu of cash contributions."

McBride roared. "That's a good one. Where the hell did you learn that?"

"From him, of course. He's the lawyer."

"Your favorite lawyer wants to see you tonight, and I'm supposed to deliver you at 7:00 p.m."

"Damn it, man, I got a client then."

"You want me to tell Kane that?"

"No, no, I'll cancel out."

McBride sat on the window sill and checked the street again. "I'll be sure to tell the bossman of your priority treatment. I'm sure he will compensate you well."

She blew a stream of smoke toward Bubba. "He always does. Are you going to come by later to pick me up?"

"No." He checked his watch. "I've got another surveillance job in a few minutes. You're goin' with me. The bossman sounded like this was very important. No way you're gettin' lost."

"How soon we have to leave?" Mandi stubbed out her cigarette and crossed the room to the bath. She left the door open, and he could see her squeeze paste onto a toothbrush. "It'll only take a coupla minutes for me to dress. I'm pretty used to quick changes," Mandi said through a mouthful of toothpaste.

McBride grinned and moved over to the edge of the bed. He sat down and patted the mattress beside him. "Undress first, honey. Plenty of time to get dressed after." He shrugged out of his sport coat and unbuttoned his shirt to expose an almost hairless beer belly.

Mandi sauntered over to help him with his trousers. As she knelt in front of him, she looked up. "This is for Prince Albert. Make sure to tell him how nice I treated you."

He took her head in his hands and pulled her toward him. "I'll most certainly do that, Miss Mandi." McBride closed his eyes and let Kane's whore get in a little practice.

ERIN WATCHED UNTIL Danielle disappeared from view. She touched her fingers to her lips, blew a kiss in her direction and smiled. Then she headed up the walk to Chase Hall and Wiggams.

The clock just inside the entrance read 4:15, so Erin wasn't surprised to find nearly all offices empty. It was typical for most of the staff to bolt for the door at their scheduled four o'clock quitting time. However, she found Wiggams' private secretary still there. Erin stood in front of her desk and asked her to tell Mr. Wiggams he had a visitor.

"He usually doesn't see people at this time, but I'll try."

"Please say Professor Gallagher would like to see him."

"I'm sorry, Professor, I didn't know you were a faculty member."

"That's quite all right. I don't come by very often, so I wouldn't expect you to remember me."

The secretary buzzed Wiggams, announced Erin and immediately motioned her toward the private office. "He'll see you right away, Professor Gallagher."

"Thank you." She opened the door and closed it behind her. Even for a temporary office, it was decorated better than most other faculty members' permanent offices.

John Wiggams stood up and greeted her with a big smile. "What have I done to deserve such a wonderful surprise?"

Erin sat in the plush chair in front of his desk. "I'm sure by now you're aware that I am both terse and candid."

"Yes, the administration dinner dance taught me that. I never saw anyone take on Kane the way you did."

"At the time, I felt he deserved it."

"He always deserves a comeuppance but almost never gets it." Wiggams tapped a No 2 on his desk. "What brings you here, Professor Gallagher?"

"I suspect you are aware that Danielle and I were more than just close friends."

"Were?"

"Yes." Erin batted her eyelashes. "We severed our. . . relationship. . . in a less than amicable fashion."

"I see. But that's not the reason you're here. Am I right?"

"You are. She can be vindictive, and I suspect she'll come after me. I need to be prepared. You know. . . the best defense is a good offense?" She crossed her legs and revealed a flash of thigh. "I came to prevail upon you for any information she may have shared that I could use against her."

"Use against her? I'm not sure what you mean, Professor."

"Look, I know all about your bedroom scenes in Las Vegas, including your red ribbon expose, so let's dispense with the Little Boy Blue routine, okay?"

"I should have realized she would relate our. . . uh. . . escapades to her lover."

"Actually, I'm glad she did. I found them quite interesting. In many ways I was envious of her."

"Really? I never would have guessed."

"I am bisexual, Mr. Wiggams, not purely a lesbian."

He got up and came around the desk, sitting on the edge closest to her. "Call me John. Perhaps I can help you in both ways."

"Both ways?"

He squeezed her knee then ran his hand down her shin. "Yes, if you would be kind enough to visit my apartment. . . perhaps I could satisfy your envy while relating some interesting tidbits pertaining to Danielle."

"I couldn't do that."

"Why, because it's not as fancy as Kane's mansion?"

"What makes you think I know anything about Kane's mansion?"

"I have my ways, Professor."

Erin lowered her eyes then looked up at him. "It's not about your apartment. I have a concern that rumors may circulate around the university. . . and I wouldn't want Albert to find out."

"He's got enough other things to worry about. You are not even in his memory bank right now."

John Wiggams leaned back and folded his arms across his chest. This conversation was so unexpected, he wasn't sure what to make of it. On the one hand, the beautiful professor's sudden interest in him aroused suspicions as to her true motives. Try as he might, however, he couldn't think of any reason she would be anything other than genuine. So maybe Danielle had told her how well endowed he was and the energy he brought to his sexual encounters. The very thought of fucking this arrogant, passionate professor of economics was getting him aroused.

"If you're concerned about rumors, Professor, might you consider a more discreet place to meet?"

"Where?"

"One of the motels on the outskirts of town?"

"That might work, but now that I think about it, the whole thing may be a bad idea." Erin could see he was nearly salivating. She let him dangle. "Let's just forget it."

"Why?"

"Frankly, because your mouth is just too damn big."

"Christ, now you sound like Kane."

"Perhaps I do. Come to think of it, right now he's not too pleased with your mouth."

"He told you that? When? Where. . . .?"

"How do you say it, John? I have my ways."

Wiggams let his imagination run wild, dreaming of the ways Erin might use to gain information. He leered at her. "You are a very clever woman."

"I'll take that as a compliment." Erin gazed around the room then brought her eyes back to Wiggams. "Maybe we should get together. I can tell you a few things that Albert has passed along. . . concerning your future."

That was it for Wiggams. The thought of learning what Kane had said—along with screwing the sexiest bi-sexual on campus—simply took his breath away.

"Professor, you name the place, I'll be there. I promise I will never tell a soul."

"I know you won't, John. Because if you do, I promise that Gayle St..James will be told about your little scrape with the law in Virginia. . . the one Kane got you out of."

"Jesus, Professor, what don't you know?"

She gave him her sly smile and winked. "Considering the potential consequences, do you still want to meet me?" She waited, knowing there was no way in the world he would reject this offer.

"You bet I do. Where?"

"A quiet, out-of-the-way motel on the south side called The Sugarside. Tomorrow at seven o'clock." She stood and leaned toward him until her breast brushed his arm.

"I'll be there."

"And John. . ."

"Yes?"

"Leave the red ribbon at home."

Erin smiled, spun around and exited the office, not even waiting to see the look on his face. As she walked briskly to her car, she replayed the scene in her mind. Good thing she was quick-witted; she'd needed to change tactics a couple of times. But she got what she came for. She had counted on Wiggams' sexual addiction to overpower his better judgment. And she'd been right. She was amazed at how effortless this whole thing went down.

Please God, let tomorrow night be just as easy.

CHAPTER SIXTEEN

A lbert Kane was at the River Commons early to take up his position by the big oak tree just north of the covered bench. It was 6:50 as he watched McBride's old Ford Thunderbird park about fifty yards away on River Road. It brought back thoughts of his last meeting with Portofino. He'd truly liked Johnny and felt a bit sorry that he had to have his ticket pulled in the Bahamas.

McBride exited the car and escorted Mandi across the commons and up to the walking path along the top of the dike. He said something then motioned for her to approach the bench. Without looking around, he retreated down the embankment and back to his car.

As the P.I. pulled away, Kane came out from behind the tree and methodically walked toward the meeting place he had used for many of his clandestine meetings.

Mandi looked as if she'd had a hard day. Her blond hair, dark at the roots, hung in limp strands around her face. She was wearing make-up, but not enough to hide the red rims around her eyes. Or the deepening creases under them. He often wondered what kind of life she could have made for herself without drugs and alcohol. This beautiful woman was beginning to show the wear and tear of her profession.

She sat smoking, with legs crossed, displaying her impressive charms. Her breasts seemed to be searching for a way out as they stretched the limits of her plunging neckline. Ah, sweet youth of twenty-two, Kane thought as he reflected on the last time she'd lain beside him, only a month ago.

"It's good to see you again, Mandi. Glad you could make it."

"Albert, you know I always come when you call."

292 WILLIAM SCHUTTER & CAROLE J. GREENE

"Please assure me that your escort was a gentleman. I'd be unhappy if he forced you to do anything against your will."

Mandi blew smoke away from Kane and fanned the air. "He was fine. He took me with him to the university. We followed some redhead home and came here." She tossed her butt onto the sidewalk, stood up and tried to crush it with her stiletto heel. And missed. "When he showed up at my place, I was a good hostess to him." She grinned at Kane and sat down again.

"You shall be well rewarded, my dear. Let's get down to business."

"Yours or mine?" She laughed.

"Mine. I think you've probably had enough for today."

"The big Irishman was very fulfilling, to say the least."

Kane explained that a certain business associate had become a problem and must now be removed from his life. "He's about to sing to the cops. . . something that cannot happen. You understand, my dear. If my tit gets caught in the wringer, I won't be around to help you when you need it."

"Yeah, I get it. Whatever you want me to do is in my best interests. Right?"

"I knew you'd be quick to catch on."

Kane explained the signal she should watch for as she waited in the parking lot at the Sugarside Motel. He gave her directions to the rural area several miles south of town, and what she was to do when she saw it. "Got that?"

She repeated it back to him. "Before we have sex, we'll get high. Instead of heroin, I'll give the chump the drug that will make it look like he had a heart attack. But when I shoot up, it'll be with fake stuff. . . the vial with a 'P' etched on it."

"Can you pull it off?"

"Piece of cake, Albert. My colleagues and me in the profession do the switch routine all the time. We keep the good stuff for ourselves and give the fake 'H' to our johns."

"Make sure you wait to do this until the other woman leaves."

"What other woman?"

"The one who will entice him there. He thinks he's going to get laid."

"He is." Mandi lit another cigarette, dragged deeply and exhaled. "For a long, long time."

"When you've completed the injection, have sex with him for about half an hour. He should just doze off."

"It takes that long?"

"Yes, it's a slow-acting drug."

"Then what?"

"Leave. The Irishman will hang around outside waiting to drive you home."

"And what's in it for me, Albert?"

"A new life, Mandi. You'll move, take on a new I.D. and I'll give you $50,000 to start fresh."

"Sounds good. How about a new car too?"

"Of course. I should have thought of it myself."

"Okay, counselor. When does it go down?"

"Sometime in the next few days. The other woman is in charge of setting that up. The Irishman will let you know."

"You sure this stuff can't be detected?"

"They never have caught my doctor friend, Mandi, and he's used it several times before." Kane stood. "That's all for now." He handed her a wad of hundred dollar bills. "A token of my appreciation, my dear. Now, I want you to walk to the first intersection south of us. The gentleman who brought you will give you a ride home."

He watched her descend the dike and walk towards McBride's waiting car. Albert Kane smiled. Mandi would not let him down. Soon all loopholes would be closed; no Harmon, no Wiggams, no evidence. Nothing to threaten him with exposure.

He walked to his car feeling a great sense of accomplishment.

ERIN SPENT WEDNESDAY evening trying to get some supper down, but her queasy stomach wouldn't allow it. With every thought of what could go wrong Thursday night at the motel, her stomach did another somersault. After cleaning up the kitchen, she lay down on her bed and closed her eyes but the thoughts kept coming.

She knew Kane well enough to expect him to be careful to the extreme and ever so devious. She began to doubt her ability to be one step ahead of him. He had already disposed of Harmon and Portofino, and no one, including George Baldwin, could pin those murders on him.

This was ceasing to be fun. Even though she despised John Wiggams, if there was a mistake tomorrow, she could find herself acting as an accomplice to his murder. How could she do such a thing? She kept thinking of the hypocrisy of it: murdering one man in an effort to apprehend the killer of another.

Her thoughts shifted back and forth. At one moment she was elated at the thought of pulling this off and gaining Kane's trust enough to wangle his confession. At the next, she feared she'd wind up getting Wiggams killed. And perhaps herself.

GEORGE BALDWIN SAT in his Charlotte hotel room-cum-office gazing at the sun setting across the city. He was wrestling with how to manage the damn case from this point forward. How had he allowed his daughter and her friend's welfare to overrule his professional judgment? Here he was permitting a perfectly innocent young professor to place herself in imminent danger. If their plan didn't work, Wiggams could die. And Erin's life would be ruined by complicity to murder.

He reached for his wallet, pulled out a plastic card with all kinds of coded hieroglyphics on it and picked up the phone. "Mr. Director, G.B. here."

There was a long pause. "Obviously this is important."

"Yes, sir. Has the green light come on yet?"

"We're clear; the line has been swept."

"I would like to see you. Tonight, if possible."

Another long pause. "I can't say I'm all that surprised. We've noticed some strange behavior of late."

"Yes, sir. That's why I need to meet with you ASAP."

"Where are you?"

"North Carolina. I have the plane and can be in your office in an hour."

"This better be good, George."

"That I guarantee sir."

"See you in an hour."

He hung up the phone, turned off the lights and headed for the door. He had a deep intuition he would be back before midnight.

He landed at Dulles forty-five minutes later, took the limo that was waiting and in twenty minutes was asking the director's secretary to announce his presence. Obviously, the director had asked her to stay on. He thanked her for being there.

"That's quite all right, sir. Go right in; he's waiting for you."

George entered the magnificent twin cherry doors to find the director peering out his window with his back to the door.

"Thought you said an hour, George."

George looked at his watch. Since he spoke with him from Charlotte, an hour and ten minutes had elapsed.

"Sir, I just. . ."

Dan Billings turned from the window with a smile on his face. "Relax, George, I'm only kidding. I don't know how you made it this quick."

Baldwin relaxed a little. "It wasn't easy."

Billings motioned toward a chair. "Sit. Tell me what's been going on."

Baldwin took the chair. "It's a long story, Dan. I'll try to keep it as tight as I can."

George brought him up to date on what Danielle had been up to uncovering the scam at the university.

"God, George, what's she wasting her time for there? She could have served the internship here."

Baldwin laughed. "Now that I think about it, I suppose she could have." He finished the story with the Wiggams' predicament. "I'm afraid I may have gone too far in an effort to protect my daughter. . . and her friend."

"Whew, if that's the short version, I'm almost afraid to hear the detailed one."

"To be very candid, I'm not sure I've heard it all."

The CIA director meshed his fingers, turned them palms away and stretched them in front of him, cracking his knuckles. "I'm sure you know the FBI and the local authorities should have been called in long before this."

"Yes, I do, but I made a decision that Erin was better than any mole we could have planted in such a short period of time. I knew I could not get the agency's approval from you and I wasn't about to hang my daughter or Erin out there alone with people who play for real."

"Who the hell is Erin?"

"She's my daughter's friend and a professor in the economics department at Madison."

"Christ George, have you lost your mind? This whole process is not only illegal but now you've involved civilians, and family."

"I know, and you may have my resignation any time you want."

Billings shook his head. "First, we need to get the FBI involved immediately. You say this professor is meeting with the comptroller tomorrow night?"

"That's right."

He reached for the phone and asked his secretary to get Richard Springfield, the director of the FBI.

"It's a Code 4, Elizabeth, so find him."

"Thanks, Dan."

"Don't thank me yet. I'm not sure where we're going with this."

"We're on the verge of breaking this whole thing wide open. . . ."

The secured line rang. The director picked it up and waited the customary two seconds for the clearance light to go on.

"Hello, Richard, thanks for getting right back. . . . Deputy Director George Baldwin is in my office at the moment. . . . Yes, he is a good man. Glad you think so. He's put together a great case against fraudulent conversion of millions of dollars. However, it has escalated faster than he thought and now involves one murder and an imminent second one to eliminate witnesses." Billings punched the speaker button so Baldwin could be included in the conversation.

"Where's all this going down?" Springfield asked.

"In North Carolina. He and a couple other operatives have been undercover there for a while. He just flew in to brief me on the urgency of the matter."

"Does this involve inter-state, Dan?

"Very much so. It stretches from Charlotte to Boston and several points in between. In fact, it may even involve the boys in Las Vegas."

"Why don't we get together on it Monday morning, say nine o'clock?"

Baldwin inched his chair forward. "Mr. Director, Baldwin here. My daughter's in on this thing, and we need your guys way before Monday. The suspected second murder is scheduled to take place tomorrow night. Thursday. We have a plan to avert it."

"Why the hell is your daughter involved? And why the hell did you wait so long to bring us in?"

"It just happened," Baldwin said. "The perp decided to move unexpectedly. We have someone in deep and she picked it up on a wire."

"All right, Dan, what do you want?"

"This is a big package, Richard. I'm willing to hand you an early Christmas present, but I need your director of operations, an attractive female agent in her mid twenties and two field agents immediately if not sooner"

"As in tonight?"

"As in about an hour. I want them to fly back tonight with George. I'll catch you up tomorrow."

The speaker was silent for some time. "Are you that confident about this, Dan?"

"When this all goes down, our agency will step aside. You're going to look like a genius."

"The four you requested will be at the G.A. terminal in an hour."

Baldwin raised his voice. "Thank you, Mr. Director."

"I'll be in touch," said Billings and disconnected the line.

Baldwin breathed a deep sigh. "Thanks for covering me, Dan. I appreciate it."

"As I said, it ain't over yet."

"Obviously, you have something in mind. Why did you order a female agent?"

"If I have this thing right, your daughter's friend Erin is going to be in a room where a murder may take place with only a prostitute as a cover."

"Yes, but she will be wired."

Billings shook his head and tapped a pencil against his desk top. "That's not good enough. The comptroller doesn't know the prostitute, does he?"

"Don't think so. She's being supplied by an attorney who's in business with the comptroller, so it's possible, I suppose."

"We'll have to take that chance. I want the female FBI agent to switch places with the prostitute between her place and the motel. We'll keep the hooker on ice at a safe house and send in the agent with this professor."

"Then what?"

"We'll take them down at the motel, transport the hooker and comptroller to a safe house. We'll have the two FBI guys stand on both of them for a few days."

"I see where you're going with this. We'll plant a story in the local newspaper about Wiggams being found dead from a heart attack in the motel?"

"Bingo."

"Keeping Erin's cover intact. And no one gets hurt."

"Exactly, George. The key player will be Erin. She's going to have to get your boy Kane to confess fast. He may become suspicious if he tries to contact the prostitute to corroborate the death."

Baldwin thought fast. "It's up to us to lean hard on the newspaper and coroner's office. If nobody blows it, I believe she can do it."

The director stood. "You know what to do. Brief the FBI people on the way back." He came around his desk and slapped Baldwin on the shoulder. "And George, do a good job out there. I'd hate to have to ask for your resignation."

Baldwin crossed to the door then turned back "Thank you, Dan. For my sake. . . and my family's."

ERIN WOKE FROM her nap and raised up to check the clock. It read 9:08; she'd slept for two hours. Feeling much better, she lay back down and reviewed the plan for tomorrow night. She sat up and slapped her forehead. "Oh shit, I promised to let C.A. know a day in advance," Erin announced to the wall. She leaned over and picked up the phone

"C.A., it's Erin."

"I know, my dear; by now I recognize your voice in my dreams."

"How sweet of you."

"To what do I owe this pleasure?"

"You wanted a day's notice of my rendezvous with Wiggams."

"You talked to him already?"

"Yes, late this afternoon. I'm sorry about not calling you sooner. I fell asleep after dinner."

"That's quite all right. So when is it going down?"

"Tomorrow night, seven, at the Sugarside Motel."

"Great job, Erin, I'll take it from here. You know what you have to do now?"

"Yep. Take him there, tell him the signal to summon the hooker, make him think I've arranged a threesome, go for ice and never come back."

"Perfect. You're going to be a great partner. I like people who catch on quickly."

"You should know I respond quickly in everything I do."

"You sure do, baby. You take care now, because I probably won't see you until Wiggams' wake."

"That's right."

"Goodnight, my love."

She hung up with chills tingling her spine. Kane's last comment about the wake really got to her. She sat shaking on the edge of her bed when the phone rang again. What the hell does he want now? she thought.

"We need to talk about things as early as possible tomorrow."

"That would be after my 10.00 a.m. class."

"About the garden show."

Good thing she recognized George Baldwin's voice. He couldn't use his name, she realized, for fear of a tap or a trace. But to even risk the call at all. . . . She assumed it must be something very important. Garden show? That was surely code for the flower shop where they'd met before.

BALDWIN HUNG UP, looked out the jet's window at the lights of Alexandria, Virginia, then went back to explaining to the FBI agents the history of the case. He concluded with the new plan of action for tomorrow evening, as he and Billings had worked it out.

"Why should we pass up an opportunity to get Wiggams to sing?" the female agent said.

Nicole Griffith raised a good question. "What did you have in mind?" Baldwin asked.

"With Erin's help, we might extract something helpful in building the case against Kane."

"Why would he reveal anything to you two?"

"Suppose we let him shoot up first then tell him the heroin was contaminated."

"He'll never buy that."

"He might. . . if. . . Erin convinces him that Kane concocted this whole scene for the express purpose to take him out."

"You think he'll confess if he thinks he's dying?"

"It's a possibility sir."

Baldwin sat back in silence. Erin had told him Wiggams knew she was sleeping with Kane and was his new confidant. It wouldn't be hard for her to convince Wiggams that Kane would want to dispose of him. "It could work. But what's in it for him?"

"A way to get even with Kane."

"It's worth a try," said Darrell Kendis, the operations director. "If it doesn't work, we're going to take him down anyway, so there's nothing to lose."

The discussion continued regarding the acquisition of a safe house. Kendis knew of a place already. Making sure the editor of the local newspaper and the coroner would maintain confidentiality was critical to the operation's success. Baldwin explained how tight Kane was with the local police and suggested that during the next several days they be kept out of the loop.

"Make the editor and coroner aware of the consequences of a leak. Don't be afraid to lean on them a little."

Fred Cook bristled. "We do this sort of thing all the time. I think we can handle it."

Baldwin sat up. "Sorry if I ruffled feathers, I've been dealing with non professionals. Guess I forgot."

"We'll set things up with the paper and the medical examiner," Len Meltzer assured him. "But if Kane is so tight with the local cops, wouldn't he call them—and probably the coroner too—to verify this guy's death?"

Baldwin shrugged. "That's a possibility, but we can't cover the whole damn department. Anyone have any suggestions?"

"I do." Nicole leaned forward. "If we bypass 911, the cops don't get in on it. No cops. No ambulance. We can take Wiggams to the safe house. Erin and I can then leave the premises the same way we arrived . This way we need the cooperation of only the hospital administrator and the ER director."

"If Kane does call the police to verify the newspaper story, they will have to check with hospitals," said Kendis.

"Right." Baldwin

"What about cause of death and potential need for an investigation?" Nicole.

Baldwin looked up from the notes he had jotted. "Good catch. Fred, make sure the hospital staff covers that with a 'natural causes' statement."

"Will do," said Fred.

"Cops put onto this by Kane will ask who ID'd the body." Meltzer.

"That's going to have to be Erin. She does work with him, you know." Nicole.

Baldwin nodded. "It will strengthen her allegiance to Kane. Okay. We're making progress here."

As the plane landed in Charlotte, the four agents agreed to meet at Baldwin's suite at 8:00 a.m. to complete all arrangements and initiate contact with the newspaper, coroner's office and hospital personnel. If this was going to work, they had to be assured of complete cooperation by all the local authorities, except the cops, who would be kept out of it as much as possible. One weak link in the chain could jeopardize the entire plan.

THURSDAY MORNING, ALBERT Kane was in his office by 7:00 a.m. His meeting with Mandi had gone well the night before, and he was happy the elimination of Wiggams was finally going to happen. The thought of Tristar being run by Erin, St..James and himself brought a smile to his face. The last of the loose cannons would soon be lashed down again. He would take care of Mandi himself later. She wouldn't be the first prostitute found dead from an overdose.

He completed some office business and at nine reached for the phone to make sure McBride was still baby-sitting her. There was no answer at his office. He laughed to himself. Why the hell would he be there? His next call was to the P.I.'s cell number.

McBride answered in a raspy voice. "Yeah, who is it?"

"It's the boss, Sleeping Beauty."

"Oh, sorry, but this job doesn't provide for much shut eye. What with the pretty professor to and from the university and now, one very active whore. . ."

"I can well imagine." Albert chuckled.

"No, really, after she left you last night, I had to go on two appointments with her. We didn't get home until after two."

"I'll bet you just hated that."

"Well, I did get to watch some things I never seen before."

"And no participating on your part?"

"Absolutely not, Albert."

"I don't believe you."

"Well, yeah, by the second one it was just too much for me."

"I knew the Irish in you couldn't handle it." Kane laughed at how the vices of weak men always kept them from achieving their potentials.

"Irish, hell, I don't think anyone could have stayed out of it. Man, she sure is a hot one."

"That I know, me lad, that I know. Look, I called to tell you she needs to be delivered to the Sugarside Motel at seven tonight. It's off Highway 16, just over the Union County line. A bit out of the way, so be sure you find it. And on time. Stick around to take Mandi home when she's done."

"Thank god. I don't think I could've gone another night with her."

"You're breaking my heart. Listen up now. Stop by the airport today. You'll find a package in locker 423. Make sure Mandi has it before you drop her off."

"How do I get in the locker?"

"It's a combo. . . 14 left, 9 right, 21 left."

"Got it."

"There's also an envelope for you in there. Take it and get lost for a week. The ticket to Acapulco is a bonus from me; the cash is payment for a job well done."

"Thanks, bossman. By the way, the beautiful professor I've been tailing the last coupla days?"

"I have kept you busy, haven't I, Bubba. What about her?"

"She's boring. Home, university, home, university. No visitors, no social engagements. My phone tap guy rang my cell late last night to say the same thing. Routine shit. Occasional call from a student, some friends. . . oh, and a garden club event."

"Thanks for reminding me about that surveillance. I'll bump up the amount of cash in the envelope."

Kane hung up knowing no one could tie him to McBride. He'd been careful never to use his name when referring to him with the hooker. And if Mandi did her job as expected, this unfortunate situation that had started with Ginny and Harmon Dawes would soon be over.

AFTER DISMISSING HER ten o'clock class, Erin left campus and drove to the flower shop. She walked through the store, picking out several lovely silk carnations, and exited the rear door to the waiting white van. The side door slid open and she entered. . . and was overwhelmed by the number of people in there. Half of them she had never seen before.

She sat down as George Baldwin introduced the new members of the team. Having met everyone, she stared at Mr. Baldwin, eyes wide. She knew last night's call must have been important, but she never imagined that the next morning, she'd be meeting four agents of the Federal Bureau of Investigation. Holy shit!

"Erin, there's been a change in plans. After I talked with you last evening, I flew to Washington and met with my director."

"Yes?"

"We both think the previous plan exposes you to excessive danger. We put together another one which accomplishes the same thing but keeps you out of harm's way."

"Which is?"

"The FBI team will intercept the prostitute before she gets to the motel. Agent Nicole Griffith here will take her place." He motioned to the comely female agent. "So when you're in the room with Wiggams, you will have cover at all times."

"I like it so far. Do I just leave then as previously planned?"

"Not quite. You will stay. You and Nicole can use his weakness for sex to bring him to the point of shooting up some heroin."

"I presume it will not be the real thing?"

"Yes, you assume correctly, but the key is you need to get him to inject first."

"Why?"

"Because after he does, you will disclose that the heroin was contaminated and will cause his death within a half hour."

"And the purpose is?"

"We expect you can convince him that Kane orchestrated this to get him out of the way," Nicole said. "Tell him this is his last chance to get even by divulging information on the professor's murder."

"A dying man's confession?"

"That's what we're hoping for, but if it doesn't work we'll just take him in anyway."

"Where?"

"To a safe house we've acquired," said Cook, "where we can sit on him and the prostitute for several days while the papers report **College Administrator Found Dead From Natural Causes at Local Motel.**

"So Kane will think everything went as planned, and I still have my cover."

"That's it, Professor."

"He's going to check it out. You know how thorough he is."

"We've prepared a plan to cover that contingency." Kendis.

"Oh? Who's in on your plan?"

"The newspaper and the hospital."

"What about the police?"

"They will be forced to call the hospital for information. The administrator and ER director will be briefed on what to say. The coroner, too."

"Okay, it's a done deal." Baldwin caught the eye of the other four agents. He filled Erin in on how they could keep Wiggams and the prostitute on ice for several days, but no more. "After that, the story at the hospital or newspaper could develop leaks. We can't afford that."

"We shouldn't need much time after the staged murder to wrap this up, should we?" Erin said.

"No. But unless you can wrangle some kind of confession from Kane in the next few days, all your and Danielle's efforts over the past months will go unrewarded. Time is of the essence, and the clock starts ticking at the Sugarside Motel tomorrow night We will grill Wiggams, but I do not expect he knows where Dawes' body is."

"What about the storage facility?" Erin pressed. "Nothing there revealed any clues as to Professor Dawes' whereabouts?"

"So far, we've come up empty handed."

"So what do I do with Kane after tomorrow?"

"We have several options, but let's make that decision after Thursday night."

"Okay, I guess we'll be in touch then."

"Yes, and be sure to wear your locket. If Wiggams does cough up some information, we certainly want it on tape."

As she exited the van she turned back, smiled at Nicole and said, "Will you be wearing a garter belt?"

"Sure will. That's where I carry my piece."

"Funny, I carry mine right here." Erin tapped her derriere.

As Erin walked back into the flower shop, the van shook with the laughter of its occupants. Nicole Griffith wiped tears from her eyes. "For a non professional, that is one cool customer."

George Baldwin nodded. "Erin's the good friend of my daughter, who discovered this whole mess in the first place. Both of them are strong-willed and smart. And Erin's proving to us that she's brave enough to follow this case through to the end."

"You don't often find civilians like that. . . willing to jeopardize themselves in the public interest," said Cook.

Baldwin took a deep breath. "No, Fred, they should be examples to us all." He motioned to Jeremy to drive away. "We better damn well not let them down."

CHAPTER 17

John Wiggams sat at his desk staring up at the crumbling, water-stained ceiling tiles. He'd have to get Jake to replace the worst of them. The comptroller's office, even a temporary one, should reflect the importance of the work done within its walls. His thoughts segued to what he anticipated would occur tonight, within the walls of the Sugarside Motel. He would lay C. Albert Kane's girlfriend. The fact that she was bi-sexual turned him on even more. Once his fantasies began bouncing around in his brain, it was impossible for him to work. He finally decided to call it a day and at 3:00 p.m. left the office to prepare for this evening's frolic.

Wiggams made one stop—at the drugstore—to pick up some personal items. He knew she would demand protection, so he bought expensive lambskin condoms, a bottle of personal lubricant and Yohimbe for him. Only the best for this fabulous woman who, no doubt, had heard about his sexual prowess and wanted to test it for herself. And what a test it would be. He'd show her a thing or two this young woman had never imagined.

Professor Erin Gallagher was the most gorgeous woman on the entire Madison University campus. She'd come on to him, setting up this tryst. Unbelievable! Tonight, she would be all his. And there wasn't a goddamn thing Kane could do about it!

ERIN FIDGETED HER way through her final Thursday class, Advanced Micro Economics, her mind on other matters. While walking from the classroom to her office, she saw Gayle St. James approaching from the opposite direction. They met about halfway through the park.

"Erin, I'm so glad to run into you. I've been thinking about everything you said at the club."

"I realize it was a lot to digest."

"It certainly was, but I've finally come to grips with it."

Erin waited until a strolling couple passed them, nodding deferentially to the president. "Glad to hear that."

"Where do we go from here, Erin?"

"I'm a little busy right now, but I'd like to update you as soon as possible."

"Fine. Come over to my place late Friday afternoon. Four o'clock works for me."

"Your home? Great. What's the address?" Erin chuckled at the thought of being a guest in the president's private residence.

Gayle St. James gave her the address and they each went on their way.

Erin continued to her office. After disposing of an armful of instructional material, she sat back in the chair and pondered how to approach the issue of getting David St. James to cooperate. She knew his sister would apply pressure to convince him it may be his only chance to escape indictment. And serious jail time. She needed to speak with Mr. Baldwin about a plea bargain. With everything else going on, she had neglected to mention this and made a mental note to speak with him before she met the president tomorrow afternoon.

As she was getting ready to leave her office, the phone rang. She hesitated, but decided to answer because it might have something to do with tonight's scheduled meeting.

"Hi, I just talked to Dad. Everything with Wiggams is going down tonight?"

"Glad he's keeping you up-to-date. I've been a little busy. Thanks to your dad and the plans he's arranged, I feel a little safer."

"Yeah, he told me about the FBI agents."

"There's one named Nicole you'd really like." Erin laughed, and Danielle joined in.

"I'm glad to see you still have a sense of humor," Danielle said.

"These days, it's the only thing keeping me going."

"I just called to wish you luck. You probably want to get home now."

"Yeah, I do, but thanks for calling."

She hung up feeling the same special closeness they shared in the Cayman Islands. For a second, she'd toyed with asking Dani over to spend the night. It would be so nice to have someone to come home to after this evening's chilling encounter with Wiggams.

Erin threaded her way through the city's peak rush hour traffic and arrived home at 5:30. She undressed immediately and, in her terry cloth robe, flopped down to rest for just 15 minutes. She arose feeling more relaxed and began the search for tonight's outfit. She really didn't have much in the way of sexy clothing any more. She'd become so used to concealing her figure that she had let her seductive wardrobe diminish. Finally she selected a very short, pleated navy blue skirt that would show plenty of leg and the sheer white blouse she had used to tantalize Jake Gathers. If it worked for Gathers, it sure as hell would work for Wiggam's she thought.

She applied her make up and spritzed some cheap perfume that had been a gift. As she checked herself in the mirror for the last time, she knew her selection was perfect for this evening. She wondered aloud what agent Griffith would be wearing. Probably an outfit so hot Wiggams would lose it the second he laid eyes on the big brunette.

It was 6:15 as she locked the door behind her and headed for the motel. She'd never been there and wanted to give herself plenty of time. In the fading light of dusk, and in a rural area, the rendezvous spot might not be easy to find. She didn't want to be late. Too much was riding on this to risk his getting cold feet.

THE FBI AGENTS had stationed themselves along the only road that provided access to the motel. At 6:30 Fred Cook climbed up a large oak tree about 100 feet back from the main road. After positioning himself in a crotch of the trunk, nearly invisible in the heavy foliage, he waited with his hand-held VHF. He trained his binoculars on every vehicle heading their way, looking for the expected hooker.

He had to be right. It was his job to advise the other agents when to pull onto the main road. They had to intercept at the precise moment that would cause the hooker's car to come to a complete stop or veer off the road. Then they'd snatch her and make the switch with Nicole.

A long, black luxury car was boiling up dust as it approached. Cook focused the binoculars. "Wiggams," he mumbled into the VHF, having recognized him from photos Baldwin provided to all the agents. "Hell bent for leather. Thinks he's in for the night of his life." Cook punched the radio again. "He may be right."

At 6:45, Cook leveled his binoculars at another car, an aging Thunderbird in need of a paint job. "What the hell?" He thumbed the VHF. "A woman who is most assuredly our mark is coming, but there's a glitch. She's not alone. Some guy's driving her. Shit. We'll have to take him out too."

Kendis and Meltzer scrambled into the trunk while Nicole stayed behind the wheel of the rental car as planned. She started the engine and waited. Within moments she heard NOW! The tires spun and threw up dirt as the car quickly moved from the cover of roadside trees and brush into the intersection.

The Thunderbird braked hard, and the sound of rubber being laid on pavement screeched through the countryside. The car abruptly swerved to the left into a farmer's freshly plowed field. There had been no collision, thanks to the driver's prowess. Nicole remained in the car, which now sat across the entire southbound lane.

The Thunderbird's driver threw open his door and charged across the field with a red face, arms flailing, his mouth spluttering foul words. As he reached the pavement and approached the car, Nicole got out. The other two agents remained silent in the trunk.

She was dressed in an extremely short skirt that barely covered her ass and a bikini top that revealed more than it concealed. If the spiked heels were any higher, she may as well have worn stilts.

"Jesus Christ, honey, don't you look where you're going? You damn near killed us all."

"I'm so sorry, darling, but I couldn't see you coming."

"Yeah, it is a bad spot," the irate man muttered as his eyes scanned her entire body.

Nicole leaned against the side of her car. "I seem to have stalled it. "Do you think you could help me get it started?"

"Sure. Open the hood." He rubbed his hands together and sauntered over to Nicole's Bonneville.

As she reached into the car to trip the hood release, she purposefully kept her ass high for him to see. His eyes rolled in his head as he saw she was not wearing panties. The hood popped open, but he hardly noticed, his eyes glued to the unexpected sight.

"Is that the right one?" she called.

"Oh, yeah, it's the right one." He rubbed his groin and let his hand linger, enjoying his tumescence.

She backed out of the car, turned around and saw the stranger staring at her

"Everything okay, Mister. . . ?"

"McBride. The name's Bubba McBride, at your service. And everything's just perfect."

As they moved to the front of the car, Mandi came walking through the field. "Hey, Irish, we gotta go. Remember?" He and agent Griffith ignored her, never looking up from their inspection of the engine. Mandi joined them and peered in. "What're we looking for?"

Cook, in the tree, spoke quietly into his VHF. "They're all three in front of the car with their heads in the engine compartment. Take them now."

Kendis and Meltzer, using the remote control, softly popped the trunk open and unkinked their limbs to climb out of the cramped space. Crouching down, they each took a side of the car and moved swiftly to the front, where Mandi and McBride soon found themselves looking down the barrels of .40 caliber Glocks. "FBI," Kendis announced. "Hands on the car. Spread 'em."

They passively separated their legs and placed their hands on the front fenders, one on each side of the still open hood. McBride was stripped of his shouldered .38 caliber Smith and Wesson. Mandi wasn't carrying.

Nicole Griffith and Darrell Kendis stood vigil with guns drawn while Len Meltzer brought the old Thunderbird back to the road. He jumped out and held up a package.

Without thinking, McBride blurted, "Hey, that's hers," jerking his head toward Mandi. "All I did was pick it up at the airport."

Kendis took the package from Meltzer. "Very interesting. Wonder what we'll find in this." He watched Mandi's face blanch. "Cuff 'em and get 'em outta here."

Mandi and McBride were cuffed with arms behind them and placed in the back seat. Cook climbed down from the tree and slid into the T-bird's passenger seat. Meltzer drove the car away, taking the hooker and her escort to the safe house, to await the outcome of tonight's ruse.

Agents Griffith and Kendis closed the hood of the rental car. Nicole took the wheel, started the engine, gunned it and fishtailed across the gravel road, heading for the motel. Even with the surprise addition of an extra person, the entire interception had taken less than seven minutes.

They pulled into the parking lot and passed Wiggams walking out the door beneath a dingy sign hanging from one hinge: MAIN OFFICE. Nicole looked at her operations director. "Where you suppose the other offices are?" They shared a laugh then parked in an empty slot about half way down the lot.

Wiggams hunched along the concrete walkway shielded by a badly damaged aluminum overhang. After jousting with the key and lock, he shoved open the sticking door and entered unit #15 at the end of the building.

The agents quickly repositioned the car closer to the room and backed into a slot between two vans, one of them white—a slot that provided some cover while still offering a clear line of sight to the unit's door.

They were not there long when Erin drove up in her Honda clunker. She parked near the office and walked toward it with a stride that both agents admired. Within minutes, she exited and slowly walked past all the other doors until she got to #15. Kendis leaned toward the driver and whispered, "Wish she'd parked closer to that room."

Nicole nodded. "Yeah, but if everything goes okay, it really won't matter."

Erin tapped her knuckles lightly on the door and waited. Wiggams yanked it open and stood back, waving a bottle of wine. He grinned like an idiot as Erin stepped past him into the room and disappeared behind him. He leaned against the door, which stuck and wouldn't shut without a heavily-applied shoulder. He put down the champagne and leaned hard against the door. It rubbed the jamb but finally bumped into place.

Once inside, Erin felt out of her element. And totally alone. It wasn't like being with Kane in his mansion, where, somehow, the very elegance of it acted as her ally to bring down the arrogant bastard. Yes, this seedy little place offered the perfect setting to accomplish their goals. But it also scared her to death.

Wiggams welcomed her with a clumsy hug and a sloppy kiss. He stepped away and picked up a bottle. "How about we start with a little champagne?"

"Sounds good to me."

"I brought a magnum of Dom Perignon. I hope you like it." He put his hands on her shoulders and slowly twirled her around. "Professor, you look absolutely gorgeous." He didn't wait for a reply to his compliment. "Here, sit on the bed while I pour us some."

He went to the bathroom and returned with two paper cups. She watched this lecherous old man licking his chops as if he couldn't wait to get to her. My god, what must poor Danielle have gone through to secure the information on Tristar? She now had a new sense of appreciation for Danielle's perseverance and sacrifices.

"Here, honey, this ought to warm you up a little."

"I don't really need much warming, John."

"My god, this is wonderful. Tell me, are you really bi-sexual?"

"Does that matter?" She knew she was reeling him in. "Yes, I am. As a matter of fact, I prefer sex with women more than men."

"Why?"

"They're much more sensitive and creative. They have a light touch, are not rough and are not in any hurry to reach orgasm."

The cork popped out of the champagne and he quickly tipped the bottle toward a paper cup. He handed her the bubbly. "What I wouldn't give to watch you and another woman."

"Interesting you would say that."

"Why?"

"Just what would you be willing to give?"

"Anything, Professor, anything."

"Well, with the right information on Kane you could be part of a threesome."

"A threesome. My god. When?"

"Right now."

"Yeah, like you brought another woman with you."

Erin sipped from her cup. "Danielle told me about your little fantasy of being with two women."

"She did?"

"Go over to the window. Raise then lower the blinds."

"And what?"

"You'll see."

"Are you making a fool out of me?"

"I told you, I want something. And I usually get what I want."

He walked over to the window and pulled the curtain back but saw nothing. He proceeded to raise the blinds as instructed. By the time he was lowering them, a knock came on the door. He looked at Erin as if she was some sort of conjurer. He pulled hard to open the door and there stood Nicole—tiny skirt, bikini top, stiletto heels and willing smile.

Wiggams backed up until his legs touched the bed. "Holy shit!"

Erin went over to Agent Griffith and pulled her close. "John, I would like you to meet my friend Nicole."

"Hu hu hu hi," he stuttered.

"Hi, Johnny," Nicole purred. "Erin's told me of your wish. I'm here to help her fulfill it for you."

He jumped up and headed for another paper cup. "I don't believe this!!. Here, sit, let me pour you some champagne."

"Not too much now, alcohol dulls the senses and we don't want that do we honey?"

"Oh my god."

Nicole leaned over and kissed him heavily. She then walked over to Erin, sat alongside her on the bed and kissed her also. Wiggams watched with his mouth hanging open, ready to pop his own cork. When he handed Nicole her drink, she reached out, gently grabbed his crotch and turned to Erin. "My, my, you never told me he was Clintonesque."

"My information was hearsay." Erin laughed. "But we'll find out for ourselves soon enough."

"It feels like you're anxious to join us, John."

He was slobbering all over himself. "I most certainly am."

"*Maybe* he is, Nicole, but maybe not quite yet."

"What the hell do you mean?" Wiggams snorted.

"Nothing until I get information."

"Bullshit, Professor." His voice was husky with lust and eagerness. "We're gonna get it on, then I'll tell you whatever you want to know."

"Nope, not going to happen, John. I want the info first."

"Now, now, you two." Nicole got between them. "I have a suggestion to calm us all down."

"What?"

"I brought along some high quality 'H'. Let's all shoot some to take the edge off; it's better than booze," she held up her paper cup, "even this obscenely expensive stuff."

Erin did a 'clink' gesture with her paper cup. "That's a great idea. What do you say, John?"

"Man, this is great. I think I died and went to heaven."

Nicole reached inside her purse and withdrew a bottle and syringe.

Wiggams eyed the paraphernalia. "I hope you brought more than one syringe."

"No, I didn't. Why?"

"How the hell do I know what you two have? I got a great life and I'm certainly not risking HIV."

"Okay, how about if we let you go first," Nicole offered.

"You would do that?"

"Sure, anyone that worried must be clean."

Nicole handed the vial and syringe to Wiggams. They watched him nervously examine the bottle and walk over to look out the window. Thinking quickly about a diversion, Nicole began removing her bikini top. Erin caught on and abruptly opened the front of her blouse. As Wiggams closed the shades and turned to come back, he observed Nicole now reaching to fondle Erin's breasts.

Any misgivings he may have had were whisked away by the sight before him. Wiggams couldn't find a vein fast enough. He shot a full syringe into his left forearm. As he finished, he sat back almost mesmerized watching Nicole and Erin play with each other.

"Are you sure this is good heroin?"

"Why? You climbing high?" Erin asked.

"I'm not feeling the rush I normally do."

"There's a reason for that." Nicole looked at Erin then back at Wiggams. "As a matter of fact, it's not good."

"What? What's not good. The horse?"

"It's contaminated, baby, and you're headed for heaven very shortly," Nicole said with a smile.

Wiggams leapt off the bed. "Professor, is she nuts?"

"Nope, she's right on."

"What the hell's going on here?"

"You're going to die, John."

His little legs pumping, he bounced around the room as if searching for a way out. "Why, what did I do?"

"It's Kane's decision, John." Erin coolly crossed her legs. "Remember, I promised to tell you what Kane had in store for your future? This is it: you are a threat to him and he wants you dead."

"He used you to set me up, didn't he?"

"He sure did. He wants you out of the way so he can continue his nice life, become a judge, escalate his power. He's afraid you know too much. . . can take him down."

"That bastard! He wins again!"

Erin stood up and eased him back to the bed. "You're sweating profusely; it won't be long now."

"Screw you two, I'm calling 911."

"I don't think so," Nicole said, pulling a Derringer from her garter and pointing it at Wiggams' head.

Erin was startled to see this but at the same time grateful the agent was here to help her handle this situation.

Wiggams sat back down and began to sob. "First Harmon, now me."

"That's what I came here to find out, John." Erin fingered the locket at her throat. "Tell me everything you know about Harmon Dawes. Did Kane have him murdered?"

"Of course he did."

"How?"

"He called the mob to help him."

"Who?"

"I don't know who he called in Vegas, but the guy who did Harmon was Johnny Portofino."

"How do you know?"

"I was at Kane's house once when he talked to him."

"Do you know where the murder was committed?" Nicole asked.

"No."

Erin moved in closer. "Do you know what the murderer did with the body?"

"Not for certain; however, Kane once threatened that I too may become a permanent fixture at the university, just like Harmon. I never understood what that meant."

"That's all?"

"That's it." Wiggams took a deep breath and swiped his arm across his forehead. "Hey, you know what, it's been almost a half hour now and I'm feeling better."

Erin put a solicitous look on her face. "That's because you cleared your conscience."

"No, no, really, I'm not feeling anything."

"That's wonderful, John. That's how death should be."

Erin and Nicole got up and put their tops back on as Wiggams lay back against the pillows, watching and waiting to die. "The least you could do for a dying man is to grant him a last wish, like watching you two make love."

Erin rebuttoned her blouse. "You're not going to die, John. I have news for you. You didn't shoot up heroin; it was just a placebo. And it wasn't tainted."

His body came to life, bolted upright, and his eyes opened wide. "You two cunts did all this to pry information out of me?"

"Yes, but we weren't kidding about Kane's desire to eliminate you." Erin moved away from the raging bull sitting across from her. "He planned a slightly different scene, but the end result would have been your death."

Hearing this, Wiggams sprung forward as if shot from a cannon and knocked Nicole backwards. As she tumbled across the bed, her gun flew into the air and landed on the bedspread. Both Erin and Wiggams dove for it simultaneously. Erin wasn't swift enough and John Wiggams had Nicole and her now looking at the wrong end of the Derringer.

"Now," he snickered, "we'll see who's going to heaven."

"John, don't do something stupid. So far, you're clean. Kill us, and you'll rot in prison."

"Yeah? Well don't worry, I'm not going to kill you yet."

"John, listen. . ."

Wiggams waved the gun from Erin to Nicole and back again. "Shut up and start taking your clothes off, both of you, right now."

As Nicole began to remove her bikini top again, Erin unbuttoned her navy blue skirt and let it fall to the floor. She slowly stroked herself over lacy black panties. "Why, so you can see my hibiscus?"

"Your what?"

"My hibiscus," she repeated as she continued to stroke.

"That, baby, is a pussy. I have seen plenty of . . . ."

He never finished the sentence. Glass flew in every direction as an object crashed through the motel window. Erin and Nicole shielded their eyes. Wiggams turned to the window to see what was happening just as two agents came flying through the front door. They tackled Wiggams, pinned him to the floor, face down and quickly disarmed him.

As they cuffed Wiggams and stood him up, Nicole turned to Erin and a smile lit her heavily made-up face. "Thank God for your hibiscus."

After the second agent withdrew from the room, Erin motioned to Kendis. "Sit Wiggams down in that chair. We have some explaining to do."

John Wiggams sat and stared at Erin. "What now?"

"John, right about now, you're supposed to be dead. These agents and a few others—by the way, meet Nicole Griffith and Darrell Kendis, FBI—have worked out a tight plan to fool Kane into thinking he's safe, with all witnesses out of his way."

"Witnesses to what?"

"You tell us, Mr. Wiggams," Nicole said. "What do you know that could cause Kane major problems?"

"Plenty."

"That's what we thought. And, for the next few days, you'll have lots of time to tell us the whole story. We intend to put Kane away for a very long time."

"Do I get immunity?"

"Possibly. Depends on the quality of your information," Kendis said. "But right now, we need you to cooperate with the rest of tonight's plan."

"Oh? First you get me all sexed up, entice me to shoot some H that turns out to be bogus, then tell me I'm going to die to get me to make a deathbed confession. Now you want me to cooperate with some cockamamie scheme? Kane may be an arrogant son-of-a-bitch, but he's been a big help in my life."

"Yes, sir, we know," Kendis said. "If it weren't for Kane, you'd be doing hard time instead of living it up in Vegas and collecting fine art. No, you'll cooperate with us. . . or get sent up for so long the only way out will be in a pine box."

Wiggams exhaled a long breath but said nothing.

"The hospital and coroner's office are in on it, sir," Nicole assured him. "And the newspaper will carry the story of your demise here, in this motel. And a very flattering obit, I might add."

"You people are fucking out of your mind. Kane's in tight with all the local authorities. He'll smell a rat for sure."

The FBI is doing everything in there power to keep that from happening," Erin said. "But timing is critical. The longer we wait to spring the next part of the plan, the greater the chance he'll discover the deception. So, are you ready?"

Wiggams lifted his cuffed hands and slammed them down in his lap. "What choice do I have?"

Kendis stood up and threw a suit jacket over Wiggams' head. "Come on." Kendis held his arm and whisked him outside and into the rental Pontiac. Not wanting to risk accidental recognition of Wiggams by anyone who happened to be out and about, Kendis instantly drove off with him face down across the back seat.

NICOLE ACCOMPANIED ERIN out of the motel. "You're shaking, Erin. You were great in there. A real pro. I'd work with you any time."

"Thanks." Out of the corner of her eye, Erin watched the motel manager stuff a garbage bag into the dumpster. He turned toward her and gave a little wave. Creepy man! She edged closer to Nicole and watched the manager shuffle back inside.

Nicole responded to Erin's movement by slipping an arm around her waist. "Go home now and let us take over at the safe house. We have the prostitute that was supposed to kill Wiggams, the delivery man and Wiggams himself."

Erin hugged her and headed for the Honda. Then she stopped, looked at the white van and yelled. "Baldwin? You in there?"

The side door slid open revealing George Baldwin and two of his men.

"Thank God you were monitoring the locket."

"We had you all the time, Erin. You did a great job."

"What happens now?"

"We'll sit on Wiggams at the safe house for a few days. I'm going to send Agent Griffith home with you tonight."

"Oh, I'm okay. Doesn't she have to make a report?"

"Don't worry about that. We have everything on tape and tomorrow will be soon enough. I want you to feel safe. The next several days are going to be critical."

He motioned to Griffith to get her out of there. She took Erin by the arm and proceeded toward the little white Honda. Baldwin and the others quickly closed the door and abruptly left the parking area headed for the safe house.

Nicole offered to drive but Erin insisted she needed something to occupy her mind. Acquiescing to her request, Nicole took the passenger seat as they bumped down the two lane gravel road. They drove in silence for several miles. Then they simultaneously broke out in laughter.

"Are you thinking what I'm thinking?" Erin said.

"You mean that we look like a couple of boozed up, drugged out hookers as opposed to a college professor and an FBI agent?"

They both howled as humor became the prescribed medicine to reduce the left over tension from a very exciting night.

"Do you have a change of clothes, you painted hussy?" Erin asked in a wry tone.

"Back at the hotel I do."

"Where are you staying?"

"Right down the hall from Mr. Baldwin. He arranged for the rooms."

"That's all the way across town, a good hour away."

"I'm sorry, but I had no idea I was going to baby-sit you tonight."

"I understand. What size are you?"

"An eight. Why?"

"I don't know about you, but I'm exhausted. Rather than drive all the way over and back, I'll loan you some more appropriate clothes so you don't have to wear those tomorrow."

"Sounds good to me."

"Besides, if we were seen like this in the hotel, we might get a proposition too good to refuse. Professors don't make a lot of money you know."

They laughed some more and continued now toward Erin's apartment.

"Tell me something, Nicole. What if my locket wasn't being monitored? What would we have done?"

"We'd have showed him enough action that he would have had to join us."

"You would have had sex with me?"

"He had the gun, honey, and until we got him to drop the little Derringer and pick up his big gun and join us, we had no choice in the matter."

Erin said nothing for several miles. "Have you ever been with a woman before?"

Nicole reached over and pointed to the locket and motioned she couldn't respond to that because of the recorder. Erin nodded her head in understanding but saw the smile on Nicole's face. She didn't have to say a word. Erin already knew the answer.

They no sooner got in the front door and kicked off their high heels when the phone rang. Erin winced at Nicole as she debated whether to pick it up. "Gallagher here."

"How did everything go?"

"Like clock work, just as planned."

"Was there any struggle?"

"Not at all."

"Where's my little hooker friend? I've been trying to call her."

"I have no idea. I waited till she showed up then got out of there in a hurry. As planned."

"Yeah, who wants to be around a dead body, right?"

"Albert, I'd love to chat but this really took a lot out of me and I'm very tired."

"Of course, my dear. You've told me all I wanted to know anyway. The rest I can read in the obituary column."

His laugh sent chills down Erin's spine. She placed the phone back in the cradle with a look that Agent Nicole Griffith had seen worn only by people too furious to mess with.

"He's such a fucking bastard!"

"Kane, I presume?"

"Yes, that arrogant asshole thinks he has got away with murder again ."

"I knew you didn't like him, but I guess I never knew how much."

"I hate him for what he did to Professor Dawes and the university."

"He doesn't waste much time before checking on things, does he?"

"He's very thorough; that's why he's hard to nail."

It was only nine o'clock but Erin's body felt as if it was long past midnight. The night had been a grueling one, both emotionally and physically. She thanked Nicole for her help at the motel and suggested they both turn in. "My body is circling the drain."

"You'll get no argument from me. I've been on the job for forty-eight hours now without much sleep."

"I think a nice shower will do us both good and perhaps we can pick it up in the morning."

"You go first, Erin. I need to write up some notes."

Erin showed her to the bedroom. "I'll sleep on the sofa." She saw her guest's look. "I've done it lots. . . used to it. You take the bedroom, please." She laid out extra towels, a cotton nightgown and some clean underwear. "I'm sorry, how presumptuous of me. I should have asked what you usually sleep in."

"Not that." Nicole held up the nightgown and laughed.

"Little too feminine?"

"Just a big 'T' will be fine."

"I'll get you one."

Erin found the 'T' and handed it to Nicole. They said goodnight and Erin headed for the shower. As she stood in the steaming water and let it pound against her shoulders, she couldn't help thinking about the short-haired brunette in the next room. She compared her to Danielle; how different they were. As she toweled down and prepared for bed, she thought how comfortable it was to have somebody watch over her as she slept.

Mr. Baldwin was right again.

ALBERT KANE HUNG up the phone feeling very smug about the evening's accomplishments. He had, in one brilliant maneuver, eliminated John Wiggams and put Professor Erin Gallagher in a box she now could not get out of. She'd passed his test and would now be his forever. And what a team they would make!

He couldn't wait to see the headlines tomorrow about the university comptroller being found dead at a sleazy motel. He went to bed feeling a sense of comfort. Now it was just Erin, St. James and himself. What had appeared to be a catastrophe was finally resolved without any major fallout to him.

CHAPTER EIGHTEEN

At the safe house, McBride and Wiggams were being questioned in upstairs bedrooms while Mandi was being quizzed downstairs by George Baldwin himself. McBride, the hardened veteran, was screaming his bloody head off about being detained without probable cause. Wiggams, on the other hand, was scared to death but glad to be in the hands of someone who wasn't trying to kill him.

Mandi as yet had no idea whom she was with and was flirting with Baldwin over a ginger ale in the kitchen. In her profession she had been picked up many times by men she never knew; this was nothing earth shattering for her. She kept asking George Baldwin if he was a new pimp in town. "You must have a high class stable, George, 'cuz you sure wear nice clothes."

"Thank you, Mandi."

"With that there three-piece suit, I'd say you run the uptown district?"

"I work in a very prestigious district, all right. In fact you can barely tell the prostitutes from the politicians." Baldwin smiled at his own joke.

"At least you know when you're getting screwed by the prostitutes, right, George?"

"That's very astute, Mandi. You're an intelligent young lady."

Mandi sat up straight and fluffed her hair. "That's what Albert Kane always says too."

"You know him well, do you?"

"Pretty well." She giggled like a school girl then lit a cigarette.

"Is he a customer of yours?"

"Yeah, but. . ." she leaned close to whisper. . . "nobody knows it."

"Was it he who sent you to the motel tonight?"

"Yeah, some guy was giving him a hard time, he said."

"What were you going to do to the man?"

"Not what you think." She laughed.

"Something very special, I suppose?"

"Hey," Mandi said as if just becoming aware of how much she had spilled, "if I'm going to give up information, what's in it for me?"

"To be perfectly honest, Mandi, talking will save you about twenty years."

"What? Who the hell are you anyway?"

"My name is George Baldwin and I'm the Deputy Director of the CIA."

Mandi inhaled deeply and blew smoke toward the ceiling. "Yeah, right."

George Baldwin slowly reached for his wallet, flipped it open and held it out to her. "I'm sure you've seen many local badges, Mandi, but if you'll just take the time to read this one, I think you'll see the light."

She took the open wallet with the gold shield displayed and immediately ran her finger all around it. She turned it in a counterclockwise direction as she read the upraised letters: United States of America Central Intelligence Agency.

"Holy Shit! What the hell am I into now?"

Baldwin repocketed his wallet. "At the moment; aiding and abetting, attempted murder, possession of an illegal substance, conspiracy to commit murder and. . ."

The hooker sighed. "Okay, I get the point. It's serious stuff."

"Very much so, and although I can't promise anything right now, I'm sure the prosecutor will consider reduced charges in exchange for your cooperation."

"Christ, Albert promised to relocate me, give me a new car and $50,000; now I'm down to a half-assed promise."

"Would you like to come out to the van? We have taping equipment on board."

"What choice do I have?"

"None, really." Baldwin stood and motioned Mandi in the direction of the door.

Agent Cook came trundling down the stairs with a smile from ear to ear. Something had set him off and he didn't hesitate to interrupt. "Mr. Baldwin, may I see you for a moment?"

"Just a minute, Fred, our little bird here wants to sing."

"Then it will be a duet."

"Which one?"

"Wiggams."

"Great job, Fred. Go to the van and ask Jeremy if he can create two devices for us to bring in here."

"Knowing him, he could probably rig the entire house."

Baldwin returned to Mandi and began explaining details of what she was about to undertake. He told her she was under no obligation to do this and explained her rights.

She laughed heartily. "This is hardly the first time I've been read my rights. The only call I ever make is to my pimp, and I don't think he's going to be much help in this situation."

Baldwin smiled and explained their suspicions about Albert Kane and the direction he expected her deposition to take.

Cook returned. "Jeremy suggested taping one in the van and one in here."

"Tell him that's fine. When will everything be ready?"

"Give him fifteen minutes."

"Okay, you take Wiggams to the van and I'll use the portable machine here."

Cook disappeared with his instructions and Baldwin continued prepping Mandi for the deposition. He could still hear the Irishman bellowing upstairs and summoned to Meltzer to baby-sit Mandi while he resolved McBride's issues.

"What's going on up here?" Baldwin said as soon as he got upstairs.

"Mr. McBride thinks he is being held illegally," agent Kendis reported.

"Really? Maybe we should explain our concerns about his threat to national security and how we can put him on a plane for D.C. immediately."

McBride came up off his chair. "What the hell are you talking about?"

"Of course, that will require detaining you for some time in a holding tank while we scour your entire history from the time you left your mother's birth canal. It won't be hard to unearth an association with some bad guys in Northern Ireland."

"I'm no security risk; you're blowing smoke." McBride was sweating.

George Baldwin reached into his inside jacket pocket, removed a cell phone and began dialing.

McBride started to fidget. "What are you doing?"

"Ever hear of the Attorney General of the United States? I'm requesting an immediate court order to move you to Washington until we can clear you as a security risk."

"Okay, okay, I know you've got the clout to do it. What do you want from me?"

"For the moment, just to be quiet. We are going to take statements from Wiggams and Mandi shortly and I would appreciate your silence. You know the alternative and, believe me, I won't hesitate."

He stopped next door on his way out and told Wiggams it would be only a few minutes more. "You can go over in your mind all the workings of your university investment scheme. I wouldn't want you to miss any details from lack of preparation. That is, if you hope to ever see the light of day again."

He descended the stairs to the kitchen, where Mandi was smoking a cigarette and being wired with a microphone. Baldwin looked at the agent attempting the mic process. "Not much to attach it to, is there, Meltzer?"

"No, sir. I'm open to suggestions."

Mandi had one of her own. "Oh darling, y'all can just rest it between these two lovely mounds. They've had more than that little thing in there."

Meltzer flushed. "Yes, ma'am."

"I do declare, honey, your hands are cold."

"Sorry, ma'am." His fingers trembled.

"Just stick them down there and you'll be warm in a second."

"I'm sure you're right, ma'am, but I would appreciate it if you would do the honor."

Mandi reached for the little microphone and placed it in her cleavage. "There. We all set now?"

"Yes, ma'am."

"Then let's get started before I change my mind."

Baldwin moved into position on the kitchen chair. He listened to the agent explain the operating controls and shortly thereafter began his questions.

Mandi related that she'd met Kane five years ago when she came to town from her native Tennessee. Getting work wasn't easy for her and after much dissatisfaction with several waitress jobs, she was approached by the man who was now her pimp.

"Candyman explained how I could make $2000 a week instead of $200. I threw my apron on the table and told him we were wasting valuable time standing there."

"Did you have any idea what the work consisted of?"

"No, sir, I didn't, but this little girl from the Great Smoky Mountains never saw that much money in six months let alone a week."

"When did you find out?"

"Actually, that night I made my first hundred dollars."

"Did it bother you when you realized what you were expected to do?"

"Hell no, George. I been doing that stuff for free since I was 14. Gettin' paid for it was a pleasant surprise."

"Go on. How did you meet Kane?"

"Once when I got busted for hookin', Candyman didn't show up at the police station to bail me out. Mr. Kane happened to be there and heard me arguin' with the desk sergeant."

"What did he do?"

"He just talked to him, but I think he slipped him a coupla bucks."

"That's it?"

"No, he asked if I had a ride home, which of course I didn't."

"I suppose he offered to give you one."

"Of course. He's always been a gentleman to me."

"And how did you thank him?"

"He got kind of suggestive on the ride home and Mama always told me to thank people for good deeds."

"How did you do that?"

"George, you want the details?"

"No, but for the record we need to know if money for services changed hands."

"I was thanking him. I would NEVER accept his money."

"But you did perform sexual acts with him, is that correct?"

"Of course I did. Hell, my bail was $1000. He got a 'trip around the world'."

"Did you ever see him after that?"

"Yes."

"Weren't you scared your pimp would find out?"

"Yes, but I trusted Mr. Kane and he's never let me down yet. Besides, I made a lot of money on the side that I was able to send home to Mama."

"Have you ever done anything illegal for Mr. Kane?"

"Never."

"Do you know anything about the disappearance of Professor Harmon Dawes?"

"No, but Albert told me he loved having sex with his wife."

"Did Kane ever mention anything about getting rid of the husband?"

"Nope."

"Do you know a John Wiggams?"

"Never heard of him."

"Do you know a Professor Erin Gallagher?"

"Just that she was a better lay than Mrs. Dawes."

"Did he ever mention the name Tristar?"

"No."

"Did he ever mention the mob or Mafia or Mafioso?"

"Yeah, he bragged about his connections in Las Vegas."

"Did he mention any names to you?"

Mandi examined a water spot on the ceiling. "Sure. He was always telling me how clever he was and how tight he was with the big boys. During these stories he would get so full of himself that he'd let a few names slip."

"Do you remember any of them?"

"Figured it'd be in my best interests to remember 'em. Carlo DeCinti. He runs the MGM Grand. And Vincent DePaulo, who operates the Desert Inn."

"Anyone else?"

"Just a guy by the name of Johnny. Supposed to be a mob hit man."

"Did he ever do any work for Kane?"

"I don't know, but he implied they were close friends and he did good work."

"But did he ever do any jobs for Kane?"

"I don't know, but one night he did tell me that Johnny was due in town the next morning."

"Would you remember that date?"

"No way. But my little black book would." She giggled.

"You keep a journal?" Baldwin didn't try to hide his surprise.

"Not of everything, just of my times with Kane. It's kind of my accounting system of what I sent home to Mama."

"Do you still have it?"

"Sure."

"Would you make it available to us?"

"Sure."

"If I sent one of my men to your apartment, would you tell him where to find it?"

"Can't do that."

"Why?"

" 'Cause it ain't in the apartment." Mandi crossed her legs and leaned toward Baldwin. "I keep it in a safe place. . .at the Pak 'N' Ship where I rent a box."

She opened her purse and dangled a set of keys in front of Baldwin. The store was closed at this hour, but tomorrow morning she would be glad to direct one of his men to the location.

Baldwin thanked her and continued his line of questioning regarding Kane, Tristar and Professor Dawes. It didn't take an M.I.T. engineer to figure out that either Mandi was privy to very little information or she wasn't being totally candid. Her disclosure of the date of Portofino's trip to Charlotte, however, could prove to be a vital piece of evidence in the time frame of Dawes' disappearance.

"When am I gonna get out of here, George?"

"Not for several days, Mandi."

"What about my clients? I need the money. Besides, Albert is going to want a report."

"Do you really think he's going to get upset over a few days?"

"Are you kidding? He's probably huntin' me down right now."

"What do you think he will do?"

"Frankly, he'll turn the town upside down. He'll have every cop in Charlotte lookin' for me by tomorrow mornin'."

Baldwin rubbed his chin. The last thing he needed right now was Kane causing a ruckus with the locals. The likelihood of someone leaking under this pressure was very high. The staging of Wiggams' murder along with Erin's cover would be quickly exposed.

"Mandi, I'm going to need about an hour, then I want you to call Kane. Okay?"

"At this hour?"

"Yes."

"He's goin' to want to know where I am."

"I know. Just sit tight. I'll be back in a moment." He got up and left. In seconds, he was upstairs, bearing down on the room where McBride was being detained. Looking menacingly at him lounging on the bed, he boomed: "Where does Kane expect you to be now?"

"At this very moment?"

"Yes."

McBride checked his watch. "Getting ready to board a flight to Acapulco."

"Do you have the ticket with you?"

"Yeah, why?"

"I ask, you answer, fat boy. Hand it over."

McBride reluctantly rolled over and pulled his wallet from his rear pants pocket. He withdrew the ticket and handed it to Baldwin.

"Looks legit. Why do you have this?"

"He gave it to me along with some cash. He told me to get lost for a few days."

"Does he know where you would stay?"

"No."

Baldwin turned and bounded downstairs to the kitchen. Mandi was having another cigarette as he pulled up his chair. "I would like you to make the call to Kane. Tell him that everything went just fine and the guy won't be a bother to him anymore. Tell him you're at the airport, on your way to Acapulco with McBride."

"I'm not so sure he'll buy into that."

"Oh yes, he will." Baldwin smiled as he waved the ticket.

"What's that?"

"Kane gave McBride a ticket to Acapulco and told him to get lost for a while. Here, take this in case he asks about the flight."

"Okay, Georgie, you're the boss."

Baldwin motioned to an agent. "Bring McBride to the kitchen." When the burly Irishman appeared, he explained the set up to both of them and asked if they were ready to make the call. McBride laughed so hard his stomach bounced. With each sarcastic bellow, Baldwin's face flushed with anger.

"You don't know Kane very well, do you, Mr. CIA?"

"Why would you say that?"

" 'Cause he'll call the airlines and confirm that we boarded. He also will know from his caller ID that we're not at the airport. You government people are so stupid."

Baldwin snapped his fingers. "Thanks. We'd have thought of those. . . eventually." He turned toward Meltzer. "Get a Continental Airlines supervisor at Charlotte-Douglas International Airport on a line and send Jeremy in here ASAP."

In less than two minutes Baldwin was explaining to Jeremy how he wanted a call they were about to place to Kane appear on his caller ID as the Continental Airlines number at the airport. "Can this be done?"

"Yes, sir."

"I've got the supervisor on the line now, sir," Meltzer yelled from across the kitchen

Baldwin took the phone in front of him and explained what he wanted done if anyone called to verify that Mandi and McBride had boarded Flight 303 for Acapulco. He informed her that he didn't have time to explain but if she called a number he gave her, CIA Director Dan Billings would verify his authenticity. He hung up and looked smugly at McBride. "Anything else, genius?"

"Nope, you're on your own now, bossman."

"I appreciate your input, McBride and I'll see it's not overlooked at sentencing."

"At sentencing? What'm I gonna be charged with? I didn't do nothing,"

Jeremy poked his head in the door and indicated that everything was a go whenever he was ready.

"Let's do it."

"I'm nervous, George," Mandi cried, her face puckered in a pout.

"Mandi, I'm sure you have played many roles in the execution of your profession. Pretend it's just another portrayal and demonstrate the great actress I know you really are."

She took a deep breath which swelled her breasts to a point where no one was sure which would burst first, McBride's eyeballs or Mandi's top. She reached for the phone and slowly dialed Kane's number. She exhaled and waited

"Hi, Albert, it's Mandi."

"Where the hell have you been? I've been calling all over for you."

"I'm at the airport. I'm going to Acapulco with Bubba."

"Why?"

"He offered me a free trip."

"How long are you going to be?"

"I don't really know; he said for a few days."

"How did it go tonight?"

"Just as planned. The guy won't bother you no more."

"How was the other girl?"

"She was great, a real pro."

"Did Wiggams put up a fight at all?"

"Who?"

"The guy you took out."

George Baldwin smiled and nodded his head with approval. Kane had just made a fatal mistake. Perhaps the lateness of the call had caused him to forget that he had never identified Wiggams by name to Mandi. After all, it was after midnight, and Kane had been asleep when Mandi phoned. He had dropped his guard. Kane's obsessive need for checking and double checking had just cost him.

Baldwin motioned with a rotating finger to keep him talking.

"I'm sorry about not gettin' to you sooner, Albert, but I had to stop for some clothes."

"Is McBride there?"

"Yes."

"Put him on the phone."

She handed McBride the phone and with a look of disgust he reluctantly accepted it. Baldwin sat looking over his cutaway glasses with cold, steely eyes of warning. He pointed a finger at him.

"Yeah, boss, what's up?" Bubba spoke into the phone.

"Is she leveling with me?"

"Yeah, I'm taking a little treat with me."

"Why?"

"I figured I'd kill two birds with one stone."

"How?"

"She really is hot, as I'm sure you know, so I figured why look for a stranger when I can take a sure thing with me."

"And the other reason?"

"To get her out of town until the dust settles on this thing."

"Good idea, Bubba. In fact, you can triple the money I gave you if she happens to have a swimming accident and doesn't return at all."

Mandi listened to this with a look of astonishment. It faded quickly to one of fury. She opened her mouth to shout something at Kane, but Baldwin slapped a hand across her mouth and shook his head violently.

Seeing this, McBride had to make a quick decision. "I can handle that, Albert, but it will cost you more than triple."

"How much more?"

"I want $50,000 wired to me in Acapulco."

"Get me a wire number and it's done."

"Will do. Look, we have to run or we're going to miss the plane."

"I'll wait to hear from you."

As McBride hung up, Mandi stood and slammed her fist on the table. "That fuckin', two-timin' double-crossin son-of-a-bitch! He wants me dead!"

Baldwin seized the opportunity. "No doubt about it. We all heard it. Mandi, he thinks you're the only person left to finger him."

She stormed up and down from stove to fridge and back again. "Oh, I'm going to finger him, all right. I'm going to stick it so far up his ass he'll taste it."

"What did you have in mind?" Baldwin pressed.

"After all I've done for him, I just don't understand it."

"Don't try. He's a man literally out of control."

"You want to know about that prick, I'll tell you about the infamous Mr. C. Albert Kane."

Baldwin deftly reached across the table and pushed the Record button on the machine. He watched the tape begin to roll and calmly said to Mandi: "What would you like to tell us, my dear?"

"About how he controls the cops, about how he bribes judges, about how he killed a professor at the university. One thing about being a whore and playing roles is that the johns tell you everything. Yeah, I'll tell you about that bastard."

Baldwin didn't bat a lash. "Return to the issue of killing a university professor." They already knew of the cops and judges so while she was hysterical, he wanted to zero in on the Harmon Dawes disappearance. "Did Kane actually kill the professor himself?"

"No, he had that Johnny guy do it for him."

"Did he tell you that?"

"Yeah, several times. He loves to puff himself up with how brilliant he is to plan perfect crimes. And get away with them. How no one else is as smart as he is and won't be able to figure it out."

Baldwin looked her in the eye. "Do you know where the murder took place?"

"At the professor's house."

"Do you know why he had the professor murdered?"

"Yeah, because he was going to expose Kane's role in some embezzlement scheme to steal money from the university. That and he was screwing the professor's wife."

"Do you know what the murderer did with his body?"

"Only that he was buried where he worked."

"When did he confide all of this to you?"

"After we had sex, he would lie back and tell me how powerful he was and what would happen to me if I ever disclosed our little affair. He is truly a sex addict, you know. He can't get enough. Once I even joked with him and asked if he thought he was the president and he told me that in time he would be."

"Mandi, these other men are going to continue the questions regarding some details. I hope you will fill them in." He stood and backed toward the door. "I need to make a call, so please excuse me."

"At two in the morning?"

"Yes, Mandi. You've provided us with information that requires our immediate attention."

Baldwin thanked her and turned the interrogation over to his subordinates. He walked out of the room, down the steps and over to the van. He swung open the door and crooked his finger to Fred. As soon as Cook stepped out of the van, Baldwin whispered close to his ear. "How you doing with Wiggams?"

"Very good, sir. He's laying out the details of the Tristar operation."

"Okay, keep on him."

Baldwin headed back to the house, avoiding the kitchen where Mandi was still ranting in full voice, and proceeded directly to an upstairs phone. He placed a call to his director.

"We're getting close to wrapping this up now, Dan. Wanted to keep you in the loop." He gave the condensed version of what had transpired so far that night. "Shall we proceed with trying to locate Dawes' body or arrest Kane now and rely on depositions, testimony from Wiggams and Mandi and Tristar documents?"

"As long as you're certain Kane is oblivious to the investigation and Erin's true role, it makes sense to keep going," the director advised.

"Agreed. I'm sure we've covered all the tracks. Besides, his own arrogance won't allow him to think he'll be found out. We've got the bastard."

CHAPTER 19

Friday morning Erin sat at her kitchen table, her head in her hands. Nicole came to the door and leaned against the molding. "You have classes today?"

"No. I called my department assistant and asked her to post a notice that I've been called out of town on a family emergency. After last night, I couldn't think straight enough to recite the multiplication tables, let alone conduct a Macro class."

Nicole poured herself a cup of coffee and sat across from Erin. "Tell you what, I'll check in with Baldwin on my cell phone, then you can take me to the hotel when you're ready. Okay?"

Erin waved her hand in the air.

When Baldwin came to the phone, Nicole identified herself.

"Nicole, good morning. How's Erin doing?"

"She's fine, sir."

"We caught a break last night. Mandi and Wiggams rolled over on Kane. I need to see Erin ASAP. Get her to bring you here."

"We've already planned to do that. I'll check to see how soon we can get there. Hold on."

Nicole turned to the kitchen table but it was empty. Apparently, Erin had decided to get ready while she talked to Baldwin. She raised her eyebrows and headed for Erin's bedroom. She knocked on the door. No answer. She knocked again. . . several times. Nothing. "Erin? Mr. Baldwin wants to know how soon we can get there." She put her ear to the door and heard water running. Must be washing her hair or something, she thought.

Nicole picked up the phone. "Sir, she's not answering my knock. Must be in the shower."

"We have a game plan to put together," Baldwin barked, "and can't very well do it without her."

"Understood. I'll try again."

Griffith went back to the bedroom door and eased it open. She could hear the shower still running. As she walked towards the bathroom, it stopped. "Erin, it's Nicole," she yelled.

"Yes, what is it?"

"I'm talking to Mr. Baldwin and he wants to. . ."

The sentence swung in mid air like an empty trapeze. Standing in the bathroom door, Erin wrapped a towel around her torso, but not before Nicole caught an eye full. "Quite a figure you're sporting there professor."

"Thank you, Agent Griffith, for that professional assessment." Erin rubbed herself with the soft towel then let it slip to the floor as she lotioned her legs. "Is Mr. Baldwin still waiting for an answer?"

Nicole couldn't take her eyes off Erin's long, slender legs. "What? Oh! Oh my god, yes. He needs to meet with you right away. How soon can you get me there?"

Erin looked at her alarm clock next to the bed. "It's ten now. Let's see. . . lunch with Danielle at noon, meeting with Gayle St. James at four. Tell him six o'clock."

Nicole shook her head. What the hell was the matter with this woman? No one, but no one talks like that to George Baldwin. "No way. He said there was a break in the case last night. Mandi and Wiggams provided valuable information and he needs you to review a plan they have apparently devised."

"He'll just have to wait. I had a difficult night and these meetings are important to me. I need a break."

"I understand, Erin, but he won't."

"He doesn't have a choice," Erin snapped. "I'll drop you off on my way to meet Dani, but I have no time to see him. . . until six."

Nicole grinned and returned to the kitchen. She related Erin's earliest availability and got the expected response. "Sir, she was quite firm. You'll have to live with six o'clock."

"Okay, okay, so be it."

Nicole waited for Erin in the kitchen. When she finally appeared, Nicole relayed Baldwin's acceptance of the time. Erin smiled but said nothing. "I laid out some of my clothes. You can't walk into the hotel in the get-up you wore last night. Get dressed and we'll be on our way."

"Listen, Erin. . . about last night. . . you seemed on the verge of being interested in a. . ."

". . . little sex to ease the tension? Yeah, it crossed my mind. How about yours?"

"Crossed it so much I could hardly sleep. Kept thinking of you on the sofa when there was an empty space right beside me in the bed."

"Nicole, my mind is a muddle. Too much going on right now. If it had happened last night, I'd have. . . put up no resistance. . . but in the cold light of day. . . I'd rather wait till my life is less tumultuous."

Heading for the bedroom, Nicole called over her shoulder, "If it's supposed to happen, it will. I'm a patient woman."

ALBERT KANE COMPLETED his usual morning workout, showered, dressed and sat down to breakfast. The maid served it to him in his study so he could make a few phone calls. While having coffee, he dialed up the hospital morgue, thinking how wise he'd been over the past several years to become chummy with the coroner's office.

"Asad, it's Albert Kane. Glad I found you in."

"Yes, Mr. Kane. News travels fast, doesn't it?"

"Meaning?"

"You are counsel for Madison University, as I recall. . . we have the comptroller, DOA last night."

"What! John Wiggams?"

"Yeah, looks like an MI, but we're checking to be sure."

Kane acted distraught. "My god. Are you sure it's Wiggams? Who identified the body?"

"His wallet carried plenty of ID. To verify, however, we ran the usual thumb print and what a surprise we got."

"Like what?"

"This guy had a rap sheet longer than your arm."

"The university comptroller? That is a surprise."

"Doesn't that university screen its employees, Albert?"

"I don't really know, Asad, I'm just the counsel there."

"Isn't going to look too good in the paper."

"You say it looks like natural causes, not suicide?"

"Right. The manager of the no-tell motel where he was found said he was with a hooker."

"My god. This just gets worse by the second. Have they located her?"

"Couldn't tell you. By the way, what were you calling me for?"

"I just wanted to tie up some loose ends on the Kerrigan case."

"I see. Let me check for you." He was back on the phone in seconds. "Report's not done yet. Waiting for DNA to come back from the lab."

Having assured himself of Wiggams' death, Kane called the Sugarside Motel to verify the prostitute story. Passing himself off as a homicide detective, he asked for the hooker's description. The manager, really getting into his fifteen minutes of fame, described the woman who had asked for the deceased man's unit number: about 27, long, auburn hair, height approximately 5'-8" and weight about 125 lbs.; wearing a short, navy blue pleated skirt, a see-through blouse and high heels.

"Thanks, give us a call if she shows up again." Kane started to hang up.

"Don't you want a description of the other woman that came out of that unit?"

Other woman? Mandi wasn't supposed to show herself. She had her instructions: wait for the signal, go in, do the deed, leave with the waiting McBride. "Sure," Kane answered. "What did she look like?"

"A big gal. Dark brown hair cut short, legs that went up to her armpits. Bikini top, short-short skirt and stiletto heels."

What the hell was going on? That wasn't petite, blond Mandi. Something was wrong.

Kane didn't like what he was hearing. In discovery mode, he immediately called Erin, who didn't answer. He left a terse command to call him as soon as she arrived home.

ERIN MET DANIELLE at noon for lunch, to acquaint her with every sordid detail. For nearly three hours, she meticulously plodded through the events the way they occurred, even telling her what Nicole related about grabbing the real hooker and her escort. When she reached the point where Wiggams lunged at Nicole and took the gun from her, Danielle screamed, "Oh my god!"

"Dani, please, the entire restaurant is looking at us."

Danielle dipped her head and plastered her face with mock chagrin. "I'm sorry."

She went on to explain how the FBI spirited Wiggams out of there and off to a safe house where he and Mandi were now being grilled. "Mandi and Wiggams have both turned on Kane. What they've said, I don't know yet. I have a meeting with your dad at six tonight, I'll find out then."

"What's going to happen now?"

"I don't really know."

The waiter delivered the check on a little tray and Danielle scanned it, tossed her credit card on top and signaled it was ready for pick up. " Why are you seeing Gayle St. James?"

"Because she wants to discuss her brother. In fact, I had better be going; it's already 3:30 and I'm due there in half an hour. I can hardly wait to see the president's residence."

She blew her a kiss and darted away.

Following Gayle's directions, Erin had little trouble finding the house. It was situated in a quaint little residential section of town she had never seen. The neighborhood was well maintained and dotted with two-story brick homes fronted by white pillars. The landscaping of every home was well manicured, shaded by mature oak and sycamore trees that testified to the age of this Charlotte suburb.

The president saw the car pull into the driveway and waited for Erin at the door. "Have any trouble finding the place?"

"None at all. What a lovely neighborhood."

Gayle held the door open for Erin to enter. Once inside the foyer, she took in the elegant 18th century furniture. She recognized a vase on the table as Baccarat crystal. The living room was equally impressive. Although not a large house, the president's residence was decorated with excellent taste.

"The decor is just splendor to the eyes, Gayle. Did you have a decorator do it?"

"No, this project was totally mine."

Erin strolled around the room, stopping to admire silk flower arrangements, plump toss pillows along the back of a traditional sofa upholstered in striped damask, a striking collection of graceful Lladro porcelains. "You're to be complimented; it's truly a work of art."

Gayle smiled. "Thank you, Erin. You and I must share the same tastes in furnishings." She motioned Erin to a comfortable chair and sat on the sofa across from her. Bending forward, she picked up a porcelain tea pot. "Care for some?"

Erin waved it away. "No thanks, I just came from lunch."

"Perhaps some dessert later then?"

"Perhaps."

The president poured herself a cup of tea, inadvertently letting it overflow. "Oops." She dabbed at the spilled liquid with a napkin. Adding two cubes of sugar, she stirred with a tiny spoon for a good minute. "Is there anything new in the case, Erin?"

"Quite a bit, actually, but nothing I can share with you right now."

"Does it pertain to Professor Dawes?"

"Indirectly, yes."

"Why are you being so elusive with your answers?"

"As I told you at the club, this is a major criminal investigation involving embezzlement, fraud, arson and murder."

Gayle sipped her tea and nodded then placed her cup and saucer on the tray. "Yes, I've given great thought to our earlier conversation."

"Have you discussed it with anyone?"

"No, you were emphatic about that. But I haven't slept very well since then, either."

"How about David?"

"He called last evening and asked some questions about Wiggams, but I played it very straight." She leaned back against the sofa pillows then sat upright. "Will he go to jail?"

"Probably, but I will tell you this: Wiggams turned state's evidence last night to the FBI. If I were you, I'd advise David to turn himself in immediately."

"Oh my god."

Erin found herself easily slipping into her old police interrogation tactics, pointing out how a suspect could best help the investigation and also himself. "If he comes forward now, he can still be a corroborating witness to Wiggams and receive favorable sentencing from the prosecutor."

"I see. You're sure that's the only way?" She didn't wait for a reply. "How should I approach him?"

"Pick up the phone and tell him what information is already in the hands of the FBI. He'll see that he really has no choice but to come forward. That is, if he believes you."

"My brother won't question my word."

"Will he run to Kane?"

"Not likely, especially if I tell him not to."

"Gayle, if he does, I'm dead within 24 hours."

"As bizarre as that sounds, I do believe you. Tell me, do you think there's any way I can save the university from embarrassment?"

"That would take heroic measures, I'm afraid."

"Like what?"

"The biggest problem right now is that we can get Kane on the fraud and embezzlement but not the murder."

"Yes. Go on."

"The only way I can see you assisting the university is by collaborating with us to locate the body, find the murder weapon or secure a confession from Kane."

"How do I do that?"

"I have no idea. Do you?"

"Perhaps."

"You do?"

WILLIAM SCHUTTER & CAROLE J. GREENE

"Although I am indeed the president of a prestigious university, I have people around this campus who are loyal 'snitches,' I suppose you would say."

"And?"

"Since you revealed this information to me, I have discreetly called in some IOU's, and facts have been made available that may be very helpful."

Erin leapt to her feet. "Gayle, I told you not to say anything!"

"Do not fret, my dear; I was careful to reveal almost nothing."

"Let's hear it, and I'll tell you whether or not it was worth the risk."

"In a minute. First, Erin, I want to get in touch with David and bring that issue to a close, if you don't mind."

"You're absolutely sure he won't run to Kane?"

"I'm sure."

As the president reached for the French cradle phone on the end table, Erin was impressed by her coolness. If she was nervous, she sure didn't show it. The only sign of edginess the entire day was the tea spill. And the protracted stirring of the sugar. Could Gayle be as anxious as she was about David's ability to keep his mouth closed? If he bolted and informed Kane, the attorney would stop at nothing to get her.

"David, it's Sis."

"What's up? You okay?"

"Well, I've been better."

"I thought your voice sounded stressed. Anything I can help with?"

"Indubitably." She told him the entire story as it was unveiled to her by Erin. "How could you, David? For God's sake, think of my position here at the university. Think of our family's good name. How could you wreck it all by getting into bed with Kane, Dawes and Wiggams? What started with fraud and embezzlement of university funds has now escalated to arson and murder. Murder, David!"

Gayle fell silent while, on the other end, her brother said something. She paced the room, trailing the long cord of the French phone. "David. . . David. . . you're an accomplice to murder. A professor on my own campus. It's. . . despicable. It's that alcoholism of yours. You are obviously still a very sick man."

David's voice was loud enough for Erin to hear. "I had no idea Kane was going to do any of that. He's the sickie·in this, not me."

"I want you to call a number I'll give you and turn yourself in to George Baldwin," Gayle said.

"Who's he?"

"He, my stupid brother, is the Deputy Director of the CIA. Everything I have told you is known to him and the FBI. Erin has come forward at great risk to help you and the university, so I strongly suggest you cooperate."

"I see. Will you hold on for a minute?"

Gayle fell silent again and stepped lively around the living room. She stopped in front of Erin and assured her that David would come forward and not expose her to Kane.

In mid conversation they both heard an explosion, muffled but unmistakable. It resonated loudly out of the telephone in Gayle St. James' hand. She banged the receiver to her mouth. "David. . . David. . . David. . . please answer me," she screamed.

The phone bounced off the table. Gayle's knees buckled, but Erin grabbed her, saving her head from hitting the coffee table. Erin pulled Gayle onto the couch and laid her head back on one of the overstuffed pillows. She headed for the kitchen, returning with a wet towel. She began to swab Gayle's neck and forehead. She reached down and quietly placed the handset back in it's cradle.

After a few minutes, Gayle began to come around. Her skin was pasty white and clammy to the touch. Erin worried she might faint again. Gayle lifted her hands and clung to Erin's shoulders, buried her head in Erin's chest and sobbed hysterically.

Erin stroked her hand. Finally, the intensity of the sobs decreased. "Let me make a call. I'll be right back. Promise."

"Please don't do anything yet; I need a moment to think."

"It's okay, Gayle, I won't disclose anything." Erin reached for the phone and dialed the hotel suite's number. "I need Mr. Baldwin. Tell him Erin Gallagher."

"He's a little busy right now."

"Listen, you get him now or your next assignment will be in East Timor."

In seconds, Baldwin was there. "Yes, Erin, what's so urgent? I thought you had a meeting."

"I need you right now, this instant, in fact."

"What's wrong?"

"Please, Mr. Baldwin just get over here NOW."

"Okay, okay. Where?"

She gave him the address. "I want you here alone. No agents, no nothing, understand?"

"All right, Erin, I get the message."

"You better or you'll blow this whole fucking investigation."

She slammed down the phone and returned to consoling Gayle. "Don't worry. I've just called George Baldwin, Danielle's father. You know who he is."

"Yes, of course. He'll know what to do."

In fifteen minutes, Baldwin rang the bell. Erin answered it and brought him into the living room, explaining as they went.

"I'm so sorry, Madam President." Baldwin sat in the chair Erin had occupied before.

Gayle did not look up. "I don't know whether he's alive or dead."

"If you'll please give me his number, I'll take it from here."

She gave him her brother's phone number and address in Boston.

Baldwin stood. "Erin, are you and the president going to be all right? You both look a little pale."

"I'm going to call her doctor now."

"Good. If you'll handle that, I'll get some people in Boston to check things out."

Baldwin disappeared to the kitchen. Using his cell phone, he spoke with the regional director in Boston and explained what needed to be done. "As soon as you know, call me at this number. It's a Code 2. . . . That's right—no release of information without my approval. For now, David St. James' home and business office at the bank are to be sealed off, even from the Boston police."

Back in the living room, Baldwin beckoned to Erin, pointing to the kitchen. She hurried to meet him there. "Her doctor's on his way. I told him to just come on in when he gets here. I'm sure he'll give her a sedative."

"Good. Maybe you should have some too."

"No, I hate medicines. I'll be fine. What did you find out?"

"Nothing yet—just set an investigation in motion. You mentioned that prior to this. . . terrible. . . incident, Dr. St. James said she had a suggestion that might help us bring down Kane on the murder charge."

"Yes."

"Has she revealed anything at all regarding how?"

"No, she wanted to talk to her brother first."

Baldwin's cellular rang. He reached into his inside coat pocket and pulled out the tiny phone. He listened, mumbled his thanks and flipped the phone closed. "He swallowed the barrel of a .357 magnum. There's really not much left of his head."

Erin sagged against the counter. "Shit."

They took their time walking back to the living room where they'd left Gayle lying on the couch. The doctor sat at her side. He looked at them and glanced toward the door. Baldwin caught his eye and signaled that he should stay a minute.

Baldwin approached the sofa where the president lay. He leaned down. "How are you doing, Dr. St.James?"

"I'm much better now, Mr. Baldwin. Have you heard any news about my brother?"

"Yes, I have. I'm sorry to report that my people in Boston have confirmed his death."

"Noooooooo!"

"It was instantaneous. He did not suffer." Baldwin motioned for the doctor and Erin to come to the door. "Doctor, could you stay a while?"

"I suppose so, for a few minutes more."

"After he leaves, Mr. Baldwin, I'll stay a bit longer," Erin said.

"Under the circumstances, Erin, we won't meet tonight. Stay here as long as you want. Notify the university that President St. James will be out for several days."

AFTER THE DOCTOR left, Erin put Gayle to bed and stayed beside her until the sedatives kicked in. With her adrenaline level so high, that took longer than usual. To calm her down, Erin did everything possible to convince her she was not responsible for her brother's death. "If you want to blame someone, it should be C. Albert Kane. He took advantage of your brother's weakness and coerced him to break the law."

"I made the phone call, Erin. I told him he was stupid, an embarrassment to the family. If only I could take back those words."

"Don't, Gayle. Please. You had no idea he'd. . . do what he did." Erin wrung out a cloth in a bowl of ice water at her bedside. "Here. Keep this on your forehead. It'll help."

Eventually, Gayle slipped into sleep. Erin jotted Gayle a note and let herself out.

It was after 10:00 when Erin finally arrived home. Her head was about to explode with memories of that hideous sound coming through the phone. She wondered if she'd been stupid to turn down the doctor's offer of a sleeping pill.

She passed through the kitchen and saw the light blinking on her answering machine—only one message. She'd had enough for this day but pressed the Play button anyway. Albert Kane's voice grumbled at her, wanting her to call. She groaned.

Tomorrow was Saturday, the end of a hellish week. Baldwin would most likely want her for a meeting to go over the next step in their plan. Maybe she should find out what was on Kane's mind.

"What's up, C.A.?"

"Where in the world have you been?"

"I met a friend for lunch, attended a university meeting"—only a little lie—"and went for a walk.

"It must have been some walk."

"Actually not. I sat for a long time thinking about last night."

"Speaking of which, my dear, when you met Wiggams at the motel, did you get out of the car?"

"Of course. I checked in the office, found out which unit was Wiggams' and went inside. I tantalized him and convinced him he might get lucky with a threesome. Then he raised and lowered the blind, your hooker friend arrived, and I left 'to get ice' so she could take it from there. All according to plan. Why?"

"Just wondering."

Erin knew better. "You don't wonder, C. A. Did something happen?"

"No."

"So Wiggams is dead then?"

"Sure is. I checked with the coroner's office this morning. He confirmed the cause as an MI. . . myocardial infarction. The drug worked its magic. . . simulating a heart attack. . . and it can't be detected on autopsy. We're home free."

"Glad to hear that. Why, then, are you calling and asking a stupid question about whether I got out of the car?"

"Now, now, don't lose your cool. I spoke with the manager of the motel and he gave a description of the prostitute that matches you perfectly."

"Yeah, so? I wasn't exactly dressed like an economics professor, C.A. A prostitute is what the manager thought I was."

"Tell me what you were wearing."

"Why are you so damned suspicious?" Questions of her own bounced around her brain like droplets on a griddle. Had he found a hole in their story? Was he checking her version against another one he'd learned? She had to choose her words carefully. The truth—or a close simulation—might be best.

"For the first time in my life and only because of the occasion, I wore a short navy skirt and a see-through blouse. What did you hear I was wearing?"

"What kind of shoes did you wear?"

"High heels. Really, C.A., this is getting to be too much. What's your problem?"

"Nothing now, Erin. Perhaps you're right, it may have been someone else." He took in his breath.

"Is this why you called me, to check whether I turned Wiggams over to your hooker friend as agreed? He's in the morgue, isn't he?"

"You're right."

"Then let's call it a night. I'm tired."

"Guess I got your Irish temper up. Sorry." Again, he breathed heavily. "Oh, one more thing, Erin. Describe the hooker I sent."

Erin's heart beat so hard she thought her ribs would break. She had no idea what *his* hooker looked like. And she sure couldn't describe Nicole to him. She'd have to wing it. "For God's sake, C.A., I've had enough of this. If you don't trust me after all I've done, you can go to hell."

She slammed down the receiver and sank to the floor.

WHEN HER PHONE rang for the umpteenth time early Saturday, Gayle St. James roused enough to stagger into the next room and pull the wire out of the wall. She returned to bed and didn't fully awake until nearly noon. She got up to use the bathroom then returned to her bed. As she lay cocooned between silk sheets, her mind kept going over last night. Had her brother really shot himself? Through the fog remaining from the heavy sedative, it all seemed like a bad dream. She knew she'd been too hard on him. She should have been more sisterly than presidential. She guessed that, in his mind, he was saving the family from the disgrace of a trial, perhaps a long prison term. She turned her head and sobbed into the pillow.

Finally, Gayle rationalized that Erin was right—it was Kane who had drawn David into this scheme. Now Harmon Dawes—and her brother—were dead. She silently made a commitment to herself that she would stop at nothing to prove Albert Kane's responsibility for these deaths.

Ginny Dawes must have felt like this, Gayle thought, when she realized Harmon must be dead. Her university informants had reported that prior to Harmon's disappearence, Ginny had been

Kane's mistress. It must have been difficult for her to accept the possibility that her own infidelity may have caused her husband's death. Ginny, Gayle decided, must hate Kane too. She leaned over, picked up the phone and cleared the heaviness from her voice.

"Ginny, good morning, it's Gayle St.James."

"How nice to hear from you. And what a surprise."

"It has been a while since we spoke, and I apologize. My mind has been on other things. I should have checked on you more frequently."

"Apology accepted. Are things smoothing out for you now?"

A wry laugh escaped Gayle. "Hardly. Let me get right to the point. Last night my brother committed suicide over this business Harmon and he were in with Wiggams and Kane."

Ginny gasped. "I didn't realize your brother was involved with the business. Gayle, I am so sorry."

"So am I, Ginny. I still can't believe it, but it's true. I've been thinking that you must have experienced the same terrible thoughts I'm having."

"Every day I wake up to an empty bed and wonder if it was my fault."

"That's how I'm feeling right now, Ginny. I called my brother to persuade him to turn himself in. I was hard on him. Too hard. He. . . shot himself while I was still on the line."

"Oh, Gayle, that's awful. If it's any consolation, I have reached the point where I understand my role in Harmon's tragedy, but I know I'm not responsible for his death."

"May I ask who you think is?"

"That bastard Albert Kane, that's who."

"I feel the same way. I just didn't know if I was being honest with myself."

"Oh, he's responsible, all right. We just can't prove it."

"Forgive me for asking this, but when you slept with Kane, didn't he reveal something that might help us convict him?"

"Believe me, I have been wracking my brain ever since Harmon. . . disappeared."

"Did Kane display any areas of weakness or habits we may be able to exploit?"

"You're starting to sound like Erin."

"If you think of anything, please let me know. We have to get this son-of-a-bitch."

Gayle hung up convinced that her need to convict Kane for murder was more than legitimate. The question now was how to do it. Perhaps a brainstorming session with Erin and Ginny might turn up something. She scribbled a note to set up a meeting.

LATE SATURDAY MORNING, Erin opened her front door just enough to grab the newspaper. She tucked it under her arm and shuffled into the kitchen. She spread out the front page and sucked in her breath.

The headline of *The Charlotte Observer* screamed "Double Tragedy Strikes University." The right-hand story reported that the comptroller, John P. Wiggams, was found dead from an apparent heart attack in a seedy motel on the outskirts of town. It described how he was purportedly in the company of an unidentified prostitute. Wiggams' background was detailed, including his prior scrapes with the law in other states. It alluded to a possible connection between Wiggams' death and the suspected arson that destroyed his office only a couple weeks earlier.

Baldwin's people had done an excellent job, Erin decided, to create the report. No one would doubt its veracity.

After last night's conversation with Kane, Erin read every word but found nothing in the article about the prostitute's role. Or her description. Obviously, Baldwin's people didn't want it in the story. She wondered if Kane would find that omission unusual.

The other half of the front page was devoted to the story of David St. James' suicide. Shit. So much for the security George Baldwin promised.

Her thoughts went to Gayle St. James and how she might be spared calls from the media. She dialed the university switchboard. It rang 20 times. Finally a harried voice answered and Erin dove right in. "Professor Erin Gallagher here. President St. James asked me to inform you she will be incommunicado for several days."

"The media's having a field day here, Professor. TV crews are stationed outside the admin. building, and reporters are everywhere."

"Get the university's public affairs official on them. The president will set up a press conference at a later time. That's it."

She placed her next call to Gayle and was not surprised when the machine answered.

"Gayle, if you're there, pick up. It's Erin."

Gayle's sleepy voice followed the click of a phone picked up. "I'm here."

"Have you seen the paper?"

"No. Those sedatives really wiped me out. I haven't got out of bed yet. Why? What's in it?"

"It's the *Observer*'s idea of a university edition. Not that I can blame them."

She explained to Gayle the Wiggams story as published but could not bring herself to divulge that it was a ruse. She'd have to ask Baldwin if it was okay to tell her the truth.

Gayle sighed. "A heart attack. Poor John. Wonder if the fire in his office put him under more stress than we realized."

"A lot of things are reported in the story that you may find interesting. But the worst part is the other half of the front page."

"Now what?"

"All I can say is Baldwin's security promise didn't work"

"Oh no! They picked up my brother's suicide, didn't they?"

"Yes. It's not that much coverage. Someone leaked just enough for a headline and a cursory report."

"No wonder my phone was ringing off the hook this morning. I've been in such a state of shock, I said the hell with it and disconnected the phone and answering machine in the other room. I even turned off the ringer on my bedroom extension. I just five minutes ago replugged and set the machine to monitor calls, or I wouldn't have answered yours."

"I figured you were in no condition to talk to people now. I told the switchboard to get the public affairs person on the job and you'd arrange a press conference later. So just continue to monitor your calls."

"Excellent idea, Erin. That'll buy me time to speak with my family. I'll call the public affairs guy and set up the conference for. . . say, six tonight."

Erin rang off and headed for the shower, running the story through her mind. Kane was expecting a funeral, and tomorrow's paper better say when or he'd get suspicious. She wondered what kind of plan Baldwin had in mind and when he was going to send for her.

AT THE SAFE house, the FBI and CIA people completed taking depositions from Mandi—whose intimate knowledge of Kane was most helpful—and Wiggams, who was only too glad to squeal on the man who so carefully planned his death. Once the lab report came in on the chemical they'd found in McBride's car—it turned out to be not heroin but a fatal drug that simulated a heart attack—the P.I. spilled his guts about past assignments from Kane, rather than be tried as an accessory to Wiggams' attempted murder.

George Baldwin, although pleased with the way things were going, was nonetheless at a loss to come up with a plan to force Kane into a confession. After several hours discussing options with his personnel, he found that none seemed feasible or immediately productive. They were at a standstill.

"Let's take a recess," Baldwin suggested. "After lunch, we'll pound away at our songbirds again. . . see if there's anything we've missed.

He ventured upstairs to the call center and dialed Danielle's number. "You doing all right?" he asked when she came on the line.

"Not bad, considering."

"Yeah, I know. Time is of the essence before Kane catches on to our deception. And we still haven't come up with an acceptable plan."

Danielle's voice was panicked. "Dad, if you don't, Erin's going to get hurt."

"I know, honey, that's why I'm calling. You need to get a message to her. . . you're my go-between in case Kane's tapping her phone."

"Sure."

"I want to see her at my hotel. Two o'clock. No excuses."

"Right. I'll leave now. Oh, Dad, by the way. . . thought you'd like to know Logan's doing a good job."

"If you know he's on you, it's not that good." The line went dead and Baldwin smiled.

Baldwin pressed his fingers against both temples, trying to rub away his apprehensions. If they couldn't produce a feasible plan by tomorrow, they would have to pull Kane in and run with what they had. The evidence on the fraud and embezzlement was overwhelming. Erin and Danielle's Tristar documents plus Wiggams' testimony left no doubt about a conviction on those two counts. With testimony from Erin, Mandi and McBride, they could surely get Kane on attempted murder of the comptroller.

It was the murder of Harmon Dawes that continued to haunt him. They still had no body, no weapon, no witness. He knew that Kane would probably get 15 to 20 years on all counts but with good behavior, be on the streets in five to seven. He desperately wanted him to be convicted on the murder rap. He wanted him sent up for life.

SHORTLY AFTER HANGING up with her father, Danielle tracked Erin down at her office. "What the hell you doing there on Saturday?"

"I couldn't stay home. I can always think here. Why were you hunting me?"

"Stay put. I'm coming over." She hung up and was out the door in seconds.

Danielle parked in Lot F, reserved for professors, but today it was nearly empty. She jogged her way into the econ. building and up the stairs to Erin's office. No secretary to get past, so she rounded the corner and plopped into the chair in front of Erin's desk. "Whew," she huffed, "guess I'm a little out of shape."

"What's the big hurry?"

"Dad wants to see you by 2:00 p.m. at the hotel and no later."

"Oh really? It's 1:15 now."

"Erin, you know better than to fight him on this."

"I won't, Danielle. I'm very much aware we're down to crunch time."

"Yeah and I'm getting a little scared for you. The next 24 hours are crucial. If we can't get Kane's confession. . ."

"I know. . . we might never obtain justice for Professor Dawes' murder." Erin opened her desk drawer and pulled out a small notebook. "I'll be there. . . with the few ideas I have."

Danielle stood, lifted a foot to the chair and retied her shoelace. "I'd better go. Dad said he'd call me back in an hour. Wherever he is, he obviously doesn't want me contacting him." She ducked out the door and was gone.

For the first time since they had known each other, she and Dani had conducted a simple meeting in less than. . . she checked her watch. . . three minutes. "Hmm," Erin said to the solitary air, "this must be getting serious." It was becoming harder and harder to keep her sense of humor.

She locked her office door and headed for the parking lot. Driving to the hotel, she wondered what, if any, plan was in store for her. FBI, CIA or not, in the end she knew it would come down to her and Kane. A former cop turned straight-arrow economics professor versus a shrewd, devious attorney turned murderer. The deck was stacked against her.

She parked the car and took the elevator to Baldwin's floor. Her knock was answered by one of the younger agents she recognized from the motel.

"Hello, Professor Gallagher, thanks for coming."

"Agent Cook."

Baldwin came into the living area from the bedroom. "The bewitching hour is here." He motioned her to sit at the table by the window.

Erin sat and gazed down at the passing traffic. "Not sure I like the sound of that. What's the plan?" She refocused her eyes directly at Baldwin's.

"I've spoken to the director and he agreed that as long as Kane is in the dark as to our involvement and your cover is still intact, we should try one last time to get him on the Dawes murder."

"I couldn't agree more." She pulled her notebook from her handbag and held it toward Baldwin. "I've made some notes."

Baldwin eyed her. "Oh? That's good, because the director and I, along with the others here, have discussed alternative plans. Frankly, all either have major safety flaws or would take too long to develop."

"How much time do you think we have?"

"Twenty-four hours. Kane's too smart to buy into this fiction we've concocted for more than that. Or somebody will leak all over the place."

"Yeah, he's already questioned me about what I wore at the motel. I think he quizzed the motel manager. He also wanted me to describe his prostitute, but I got out of that. He's plenty suspicious right now."

Baldwin's head jerked up so fast it almost popped. "Erin, that is not good. Perhaps we ought to call this whole thing off right now. We have him tight as a drum on many other counts."

"What will he get for them?"

"Depending on the judge, probably 15 to 20 years."

"Which puts him on the street when?"

"Probably no more than seven."

Erin slapped the notebook against her palm and shook her head. "Not nearly enough for what he's done."

"No, it isn't, but going forward will be very dangerous for you. I'm not willing to sacrifice you in return for a murder conviction."

"Neither am I, but he's not walking for murdering Professor Dawes if I have to go it alone. I want the bastard doing life in Leavenworth."

"Erin, be realistic. If you. . ."

"No! He's not walking. Professor Dawes was a good man and Kane's going to pay for killing him."

Baldwin got up and paced over to the service bar, opened a Coke, got a nod from Erin and opened a second for her. He brought them back to the table. "Erin, you've done enough. We can't ask you to do any. . ."

"Look, you're not asking, okay? He thinks Wiggams is gone and he knows Harmon and David St. James are dead. The only one left on the inside is me, and time is running out."

"What are you saying?"

"There's no one else that can do it. I go in alone."

"What do you mean alone?"

"No Nicole to cover, no cars, no nothing. Just my electronic supports—the locket and watch."

Baldwin gulped his Coke. "That's too dangerous. I can't let you. . ."

"You got a better idea?"

It was Baldwin's turn to stare out the window. "Erin, if we're going to do this, I think for safety reasons it should be tonight. I'm afraid of leaks. There are journalists all over the place now. The St.James suicide ramped up the media coverage. These investigators are good at digging. . ."

"Agreed. I want to get this over with. The sooner the better."

"Can you set something up that quick without him becoming suspicious?"

"I think so. Don't forget, his ego has him convinced I'm in love with him and ready to jump into the university scam as a partner."

"I don't suppose you know how you're going to do this?"

"Not entirely. But it has to be Kane and me alone, at The Mansion."

"Makes sense. That's his safe zone. He won't venture far from it right now." He downed the rest of his drink. "One problem. We can still monitor the locket and listen for your code word. . . in case. . . but we can't get inside very fast to help you in an emergency."

"Why not?"

"We've discovered he's recently installed two more cameras on a utility pole scanning the roadway approaching his entrance. He can now see for miles in any direction."

"I thought placing a personal object on a utility pole was illegal."

Baldwin winced. "Not for him, Erin."

"Yeah. What, have I lost my mind?"

"Just so you understand. . . if you need us, we can't get there for a good ten minutes."

"Ten minutes. Jesus. Okay, I'll keep that in mind." She checked her watch. "Gotta go. . . I've got work to do." She stood up and headed toward the door.

Baldwin followed her. "Keep the locket on at all times so we know when and where the meet is scheduled."

"Don't worry. I'll have it on even when I pee."

Baldwin moved to hug her but stuck out his hand instead. "Good luck and please be careful."

Erin shook it. "The luck of the Irish shall always prevail, me lad." She smiled and walked out the door.

CHAPTER 20

O n her way home from the hotel, Erin's thoughts fired at millisecond intervals. She envisioned flashbacks of the entire case. . . . how all this got started in the Grand Cayman Islands. "Where would this investigation have gone if Danielle and I hadn't coincidentally met?" she wondered aloud. Would anyone have pursued this, or would a young intern's discovery have been swept under the rug like many other academic scandals?

A horn beeped behind her, jolting her thoughts back to the present. Questions kept repeating in her head. How was she going to get Kane to confess? What ploy was available to her that she might be missing? Tonight's discoveries were obviously going to be the determining factors in whether Kane would be charged with first degree murder.

She arrived home to find the damn light on her answering machine flashing again. One of these days, she had to get caller ID. What the hell, she thought, and pushed the Play button.

"It's Gayle St. James. Ginny Dawes is here and we're looking out the window at several dozen reporters and their camera crews. Ginny's helping me prepare for my six o'clock press conference. Please give us a call."

Erin listened and wondered why Ginny was at the president's house. Even more mystifying was what they wanted with her. She picked up the phone and pressed Gayle's home number.

"It's Erin," she said when the president answered. "What's going on?"

"Ginny came over to keep me company. She told me how helpful it was when you consoled her about Harmon."

"Yes, I was glad I could help her through that time."

"We've been talking about Kane and how much all three of us want revenge for his actions. We're trying to find his Achilles heel. All we have come up with so far is sex, power and ego, but nothing more specific."

"I've thought of those too. I think we all want the same result . . . to put him away for life . . . or worse."

"We thought perhaps if the three of us got together, we could come up with something to help Mr. Baldwin."

"I have news for you two. It's down to me. I just came from Baldwin, and he wants me to meet with Kane tonight."

"Tonight?"

"Baldwin's come up as empty as we are, so the plan is to send me in to make one last attempt at securing a confession."

"My god, Erin. The bastard has already murdered several times. Killing one more—you—certainly won't bother him."

A nervous laugh escaped Erin's lips. "Thanks for bolstering my confidence level."

"I didn't mean it that way," Gayle said. "I'm sorry. You know we're behind you. Is there anything we can do?"

"Pray."

Erin hung up shaking her head. Kane was so slick that not even a woman who had slept with him for two years had any clue how to entrap him. She headed for the bedroom to lie down and collect her thoughts.

GAYLE TOLD GINNY about the conversation and how Erin was meeting with Kane this evening. Ginny was horrified. "She can't do that."

"Why?"

"Because she will never come back. I know him."

"What do you think he'll do?"

"If he's suspicious, he'll kill her."

"Oh, Ginny, he's not going to do that himself."

"When he's desperate, he'll do anything. I've seen him."

"But she's doing this with Mr. Baldwin's approval. Surely he wouldn't jeopardize her life."

"He may be in the CIA, but he's met his match with a conniving, unscrupulous bastard like Albert Kane."

ERIN NODDED OFF, the day's emotions catching up with her. The early morning conversation with the university president, her attempts to plan a trap for Kane, Danielle's surprise visit, the meeting with Mr. Baldwin and the phone call from Gayle and Ginny had fatigued her to a point where sleep wasn't hard to find. It seemed as if she was always tired anymore.

After about forty-five minutes, she awoke. Shit, she thought, if I'm going to meet C.A. tonight, I'd better get going on it. It was Saturday, so he would probably not be at the office. If Baldwin was correct, he'd be in his comfort zone. She tried him at home.

"Erin, what a surprise. After you told me to go to hell, I figured I'd give you some time to get over your snit."

"You were completely out of line Albert and you know it. I did what you asked with Wiggams and there was no reason for your doubting me"

"Your right, but it's all over; time to celebrate."

"Not just yet. I ran into the Baldwin girl today on campus."

"Yes? And?"

"Are you aware that her father is in town asking a lot of questions?"

There was a long pause. "No, I'm not."

"From what I can gather, this was caused by the nearly simultaneous demise of Wiggams and David St. James. Apparently she called him and said something was very suspicious."

"That little bitch has her nose in everything."

"She can be that way."

"I thought you two parted ways."

"We did. I was crossing campus and we literally bumped into each other."

"You teaching Saturday classes now?"

"No, but I had to do some work at my office. Don't know why she was on campus."

"What else did she tell you?"

"Some things I think we better discuss privately."

"I see. How about tonight at my place?"

Erin made her voice sound erotic, eager. "What time?"

"I'll pick you up at six."

"That's not necessary."

"I insist." His voice was cool.

She could be firm too. "I'm capable of driving, C.A. I'll be at The Mansion at six thirty."

"Okay, I'm not going to cause another argument over this"

Kane never let the handset hit the cradle; he immediately dialed his friend Paul Robinson, Chief of Police. "Do you know anything about a guy named Baldwin poking his nose around town?"

"No. Should I?"

"Don't know. Anything strange going on?"

"Just the hospital and coroner's office acting funny about this guy from the university that supposedly bought it with a heart attack when he was fucking a whore."

"What do you mean 'acting funny'?"

"We never got a call on it, and when I read the story in *The Observer* this morning, I had it brought up at roll call. Nobody knew anything there either, so I called the coroner and he's been vague as hell."

"Did the hospital know?"

"Yeah."

"What are they saying?"

"Not much. It's like pulling teeth. Pretty unusual for them. I'm not sure what's going on."

"If you hear anything, let me know, will you?"

"Sure, Albert."

Kane hung up and sat staring at the wall. First the motel manager's description of the prostitute didn't match Mandi; now the police were having problems getting information from the coroner and hospital. Something didn't seem right. He placed a call to his secretary at home. "I want you to call every hotel and motel in Acapulco. Find out if a McBride is registered anywhere."

"Sir, that would be a monumental job. This is Saturday. I'm on my own time."

"Margaret, if you want to continue on your own time, without a job, just stay with that attitude." He waited for her to get over her pique. "Get started right now and call me immediately on my cell when you find him."

"Yes, sir."

He quickly punched up the coroner's office. He had saved the ass of one of the technician's busted on a drug charge about six months ago. He was about to call in the IOU.

"Rodriguez, please."

"Yeah, Rodriguez here."

"It's Albert Kane. Remember me?"

"Yes, sir."

"I need a favor."

"Anything you say."

"Do you have a cold one in the ice box by the name of Wiggams?"

"Yes, sir; came in late Thursday night."

"Go down and take a look, then come back and describe him for me. I'll wait."

As Kane waited, he couldn't get over the feeling that something didn't add up. He was becoming fidgety, it was now 5:15 and he had to shower and dress before Erin's arrival. Where the hell was Rodriguez?

"Sir?"

"Yeah, go ahead, I'm here."

"Something very strange has happened. . . there's no body in the vault. And when I asked Judy, she said the paperwork was in order, but she never saw a body come in."

"Look, Rodriguez, don't you have more family you want to bring to the States?"

"Yes sir, my brother and sister."

"You keep looking for the body and let me know what you find out as soon as possible. If it's good, I'll have the rest of your family here in a week."

He gave Rodriguez his cell number and hung up. He was on full alert by now, his intuitions buzzing in his head like swarming bees. He intercomed Juanita, ordered a meal for Erin. As usual when he changed her plans late in the day, his cook rattled off a string of Spanish cuss words. He laughed and headed for the shower, his mind racing with all kinds of possibilities.

Could these discrepancies all just be coincidences? Was he becoming unduly alarmed over nothing? Perhaps, at the moment he phoned, an autopsy was being performed on Wiggams' body. But why didn't the police know anything?

Massaging shampoo into his scalp, he began to think about Erin. Of all nights to be seeing her. He had already contemplated that after dinner they would have magnificent sex. Now he had to deal with all this uncertainty. Because of it, their evening could be spoiled.

About the time Kane exited the shower, Erin's car made its way through his front gate. She proceeded slowly up the drive, hoping that some sort of last minute miraculous plan would crystallize in her brain. Unfortunately, it did not.

Before she knew it, Kane's butler was opening the car door for her. She smiled and followed him into the house. He informed her that Mr. Kane would join her shortly and invited her to have a drink while waiting. Moving out of her normal modus operandi, she accepted and ordered a gin and tonic with a twist of lime. He returned momentarily and held out a silver tray. She lifted her drink from it and he retired.

She laid her purse on the sofa and sipped the gin. Her eyes took in the fine art around the great room. He had a da Vinci, a Monet and a Van Gogh in this room alone. Obviously, the money he had fleeced from the university through the Tristar investment scheme was much more than she'd imagined.

"Erin, how wonderful to see you."

"Why C.A. I didn't hear you come in."

"You were so immersed in my art collection, I thought it best not to disturb you."

"It is quite an example of ambitious acquisitions."

He gazed at the Van Gogh with her. "I'm quite proud of it. Come let's have dinner and you can tell me more about the Baldwin girl."

They ventured to the dining room where he ordered his cocktail. Juanita had magically transformed one pheasant into two. As they ate, he again repeated his request for information on the Baldwin girl. She couldn't ignore the issue any longer.

"She told me her father was in town investigating the coincidence of David St.James' and John Wiggams' deaths." She could imagine that if Baldwin was in the van monitoring her locket transmission, he would damn near choke when he heard that. A smile played with the corners of her mouth.

"That's what you said earlier. I've thought about it ever since then. Can't figure out why the CIA would become involved."

"That's easy to answer. Danielle asked her father to look into it. She thinks there is a connection between the two deaths and the disappearance of Harmon Dawes."

"Why would she think that?"

"Don't forget, C.A., she spent time in Las Vegas with both Wiggams and St. James, and God knows what they told her."

"Do you really think two high placed professional men would confide in a university intern?"

"She did have sex with both of them."

"So what?"

"She's very good. With her sexual prowess, she could coerce anyone to engage in explicit pillow talk."

"That's right. I nearly forgot. You would know that, wouldn't you?"

"Yes, I would."

"She really is that good?"

"Better than you can imagine."

"Perhaps you can invite her here some evening."

Ah, Erin thought, sex might be used against him after all. "Perhaps."

Kane leaned toward her, brushing her cheeks with his fingertips. "Do you think she would come?"

"For me, I think she would. We're not on close terms any more, but memory of our hot times together might do the trick."

"Really? Is a threesome with another woman something you could accept and still maintain our relationship?"

"Of course. Do I appear that insecure to you?"

"No, my dear Erin, you have never appeared the least bit insecure."

Erin fell silent, again thinking of what Baldwin would be hearing. He knew his daughter was bi-sexual and most likely suspected she had a relationship with Erin, but hearing she'd slept with both Wiggams and St. James would just about blow his mind.

"Penny for your thoughts, my dear."

"Just thinking how excited you're getting about this *menage a trois.*"

"Ummm. How old is she?"

"Twenty-two. Old enough. And young enough."

"Christ, the two of you might just kill me." Kane put his head back and howled.

"I doubt that." Erin grinned. "But when we're done with you, you might want to die."

Although she certainly hadn't planned this, the conversation played right into one of his known weaknesses—sex. She saw his guard come down and decided to make a run in that direction. At the moment, it was the only avenue open to her.

He wiped his mouth with a large table napkin and said, "Care to have dessert served in the bedroom?"

She answered seductively, "Wouldn't have it anywhere else."

They walked arm in arm up the stairs to the master suite. Once inside, he kissed her passionately. As their lips parted, he asked if she wouldn't mind something a little different tonight. She hesitated briefly. "What, exactly, do you mean by 'different'?"

"I've always had this thing for handcuffs and blindfolds."

She backed away and put her hands up in front of her. "Whoa. I can't get myself excited about the prospect of being immobilized and rendered helpless, especially by a male."

"How well I know."

"But I might consider it if you were to grant me something in return."

He moved toward her, his voice velvet. "And what might that be?"

"You know my inquisitive nature. . .somewhat like yours"

"I certainly do. As I've told you before, it's your curiosity and attention to detail that first attracted me to you."

"I know about Wiggams, because I was in on that, but how in the hell did you kill Dawes and what did you do with his body?"

Kane had his shirt off and was working on Erin's blouse. "That's a mouthful of questions, my love."

"You're asking to sexually dominate a non-submissive feminist. That doesn't come cheap."

"Why do you want to know?"

"You were the one who raised the bar tonight with this blindfold and handcuff wrinkle, so I thought I may as well take advantage of the opportunity and raise it a little myself. Remember, I told you that as partners, we can't keep things from each other." She began to run her fingers along his groin. "Besides, knowing the answer might make the sex even more exciting."

He was now down to his silk boxers. "You truly are an exhilarating woman." He sucked in his breath through clenched teeth.

"Well?"

"It's a deal. . . but on one condition."

"And that is?"

"I tell you everything while you're handcuffed to the bed and blindfolded. It will heighten the pleasure I derive from my sexual fantasy."

"Hmmm. You know I always want you to be fully pleasured."

By now he was like a little boy. He nearly bounded out of the room to get his sex toys. Erin shivered, hoping this was the last time she would ever have to sell her body for information.

As Kane retrieved his play things, the cell phone rang. Jesus, Margaret's timing is lousy, he thought, as he listened to her information: McBride was not registered anywhere in Acapulco. She'd phoned every hotel and resort, even the sleaziest of the sleaze, but no McBride.

Kane rang off and wondered if she'd really tried them all. Margaret was typically as thorough as he demanded, so his money was on her diligence. McBride could have used a phony name, though. Well, his alarm bells weren't jangling about this, so maybe that was the answer.

As he went back to the bedroom, he found Erin parading around the room nude. "Did I hear a phone?"

"My secretary. . . with some important information on a case I'm preparing."

"Hope you can put your legal eagle attitude aside for a couple hours," she purred.

Kane stood there, holding his toys and admiring her as she climbed back in bed. "I never cease to be amazed by your beauty."

"Well, are you coming aboard, Captain?"

"Oh, I sure am."

She spread herself across the king-sized bed so that each of her long arms reached one side of the massive headboard. Her legs were still together, with her right leg slightly bent over her left, just barely exposing her pubic hair.

Kane approached her with glassy eyes and affixed the cuffs to her wrists. He clicked them around the posts of the headboard. With each movement, he became more sexually aroused. He moved to her legs and gently spread them apart and repeated the process with cuffs on her ankles. He took the black blindfold and walked to the side of the bed.

She heard it again, that same melodic sound she'd heard before. "Don't tell me that's your damn phone again."

"Yeah. I left it in the bathroom."

"Do you want to get it?"

"Not now, baby. Whatever it is will wait."

"Maybe it's about that case again. Why don't you take it and then shut it off?"

He remembered that he'd told Rodriguez to call if he found anything and decided to take Erin's advice.

She winced as his bare ass waltzed toward the bath. She hoped this would be over shortly. How much more could she take? The personal indignities, the lying, the hypocritical practices were taking their toll on her. She was beginning to wonder who she really was.

"Kane here."

It's Rodriguez, sir."

"What did you find out?"

"There never was a body."

"What do you mean, 'never was'? I don't get it."

"I talked to the admitting secretary. I used to date her. She told me there never was a body."

"Are you sure about her?"

"Oh yeah, she signed the body in as a favor to the boss."

"The coroner put her up to this?"

"Looks that way."

He thanked Rodriguez and immediately dialed up the coroner's number from his cell phone memory. That bastard better have something smart to say, Kane thought.

"Asad, it's Albert Kane."

"What can I do for you?"

"There's a scam going on with Wiggams' death. If you want to live to see the light of day, you better tell me what the fuck is happening."

"Albert, I'm between a rock and a hard place on this one."

"You and your family are going to be imbedded in rock permanently if you don't give me information."

"The FBI and CIA are all over town, and I think they're after you."

"For what?"

"I don't know, but I know who does."

"Spill it."

"Some professor at the university. Apparently she's working with them."

"*She*?"

"Yeah, I overheard some FBI agents talking about her."

"What did they say?"

"Something about her being the best mole they ever worked with. I don't know what that means, but that's what they said."

Kane swiveled his head in the direction of the bedroom. When he turned back, his voice was icy. "Anything else?"

'No, Albert, I swear that's all I know."

Kane hung up and sat on the side of the bathtub, his mind reeling in astonishment. That professor was in his bed right now. She was the only one who was smart enough and close enough to bring him down. She had used sex to con him into making her a partner. And he fell for it.

"C. A., are you coming?"

He looked around, as if searching for what to do next. His eyes narrowed. "I'll be right there, baby."

He picked up the intercom beside the toilet and instructed the butler to find his guests purse, take it and the little white Honda to Antonio's Scrap Yard and park it by the office.

"Before you go, give Juanita the night off . Take a cab home from the scrap yard home. I won't need either of you for the rest of the night"

With a smirk on his face, he returned to the bedroom. "I'm here, my love."

"Thank goodness; these things are beginning to hurt."

He leaned against the foot board post and folded his arms across his chest. "Really!"

"Yes, especially my ankles."

He picked up the black bandanna he'd left on the bed and climbed up to straddle her. He sat for a moment, just smiling at her.

As she was about to say something, he lurched forward and forcefully slapped the bandanna across her mouth.

Her eyes grew large with fear as she twisted her head from side to side. Kane grabbed a handful of hair and pulled her head forward. He attempted to tie a knot in the bandanna behind her head as she violently thrashed. When he finally succeeded, he withdrew his hands from behind her neck, throwing them into the air like a rodeo cowboy roping a calf.

During his macho maneuver, his fingers got caught in her necklace, and the locket went flying across the bed. It struck one of the canopy posts and sprung open, coming to rest on the carpet below, emitting a beeping sound. Kane turned his head and stared at the locket. Without saying a word he dismounted her, picked it up and went to the bathroom.

Erin heard the toilet flush and knew she was in very deep trouble.

BACK IN THE van, Jeremy told George Baldwin he thought they had lost transmission.

"What were the last sounds you picked up?"

"Just some groaning."

"Were they about to have sex?"

"That's what it sounded like. Yes."

"She didn't use the code word or push the watch stem, did she?"

"No, sir."

"We'll have to wait. Perhaps they were simply moans of passion."

WHEN KANE RETURNED, he said nothing but began a full-body search of Erin's immobilized figure, one orifice at a time. He made no effort to be gentle. He ripped off the only item left—her wrist watch—and returned to the bathroom to flush it away to join the locket.

He strode to the closet, opened a safe and began throwing packets of $100 bills into his carry-on bag. After virtually filling it, he walked over to his dresser, removed several passports and threw them on top of the money. He zipped it, put on some clothes and walked calmly back to Erin.

She lay motionless, gagged and cuffed to the bed, her eyes registering terror.

"Now that the bugs have been removed, we have but a short time to talk. Then I'm going to dispose of you." He slowly shook his head. "What a waste."

He reached around her head and pulled the bandanna off. As it fell free of her mouth, she gasped for air.

"Why, Erin? Why would you operate as a mole for the Feds? I gave you everything you wanted."

Erin knew she was dead. Nothing more to lose by being honest. "I told you. It's about Professor Dawes."

"What was he to you?"

"Just my mentor. . . an honorable man who thought women were far more than playthings."

"So that you won't die in vain, I will satisfy your curiosity by telling you that it was I who had him killed."

"Why?"

"He was going to expose Tristar and take away my judgeship to get even for me fucking his wife. I couldn't let him ruin my life."

"Who did it for you?"

"Johnny Portofino, a mob hit man."

"Where's the body?"

"It's buried deep under a concrete column at the Petrini Health Center." He laughed. "On campus, right under their noses. Now, tell me, since you are about to die, whose wire were you wearing?"

"Fuck you!"

"My, my, you're still a feisty little thing, aren't you."

As she was about to say something else, he slammed the gag in place again. This time her head bounced off the headboard. He walked over to the closet and yanked out several belts. He took the handcuff off and rolled her over to a point where he could hold both wrists together. He wrapped the flexible leather belt around her wrists, tightening till it cut into her flesh. She screamed in agony, but the sound was surreal, muffled by the bandanna. The second belt he placed around her neck like a noose.

"We're going for a walk now, and if you make any attempt to run, I'll strangle you instantly."

BALDWIN'S FACE WRINKLED in worry. "How long has it been, Jeremy?"

"Seven minutes, sir."

"Wait three more and then go in. Alert every one to the time frame."

KANE RELEASED ERIN'S ankle cuffs, grabbed the neck chain and picked up his carry bag. "Let's go, my love. I need to dispose of you. I have a plane to catch for Paris."

He led her down the mezzanine steps to the main floor, through some rooms she had never seen and finally to what appeared to be the basement, finished nicer than the interior of most homes she'd seen. He yanked her along to a door with a wooden sign above it painted with intertwining grape leaves. He pushed open the door to the wine cellar and shoved her inside the cave-like room. Every time he pulled on the belt, it took her breath away. Between this and the gag in her mouth, she could barely get her breath.

At the end of the long narrow wine cellar was another door. He stopped and pulled out his key chain. Once the door was unlocked and opened, Kane reached inside and switched on a light. He turned, smiled at her and gestured toward the end of a tunnel. "When I built this mansion, I always knew the day would come when I needed to escape. My life has gotten me involved with some. . . strange. . . people and, as you know, I try to cover every base."

She grunted an inaudible sound as he pulled her down this dimly lit passageway. They walked for what seemed like miles. She counted steps as she trudged to get some idea of how far they were traveling.

"It won't matter what you know, now," Kane said as he explained how he'd flown in Mafia contractors from New York to complete this project. "I sure never wanted the locals or anyone else to know about it." It was designed to clear the back gate and bypass all alarms. It exited at the bottom of the hillside below the house and 100 feet from Lake Norman, where he'd constructed a boathouse to keep his 50 foot Sunseeker Express Cruiser.

They exited the tunnel and made their way to the boathouse and dock. Kane led her aboard with the belt, throwing her to the aft deck. She lay naked with scraped knees and blood flowing freely from a busted lip. He fired up the engines, removed the bow and stern lines and eased her out. Soon they were skimming across the lake towards where she didn't know.

Erin's mind zipped into warp speed, trying desperately to figure a way out. She knew he would either strangle or drown her, or both. In either event, her body would end up at the bottom of the deepest part of the lake. Probably never to be found as she had seen him unshackle the anchor from the rode before they had left the dock.

While he was operating the boat, she raised herself up to where she could see above the gunwales. Off in the distance the lake narrowed slightly, and she could make out what appeared to be a man fishing from a smaller craft and the silhouette of a large dog. She made up her mind that if they got anywhere close to it, she would fling herself overboard.

She lowered her body and remained still, pretending to have passed out from the chill of the night. When they approached the smaller craft, Kane slowed his boat to keep from throwing a wake that would draw attention to them. When he did, Erin lurched upright and lunged backwards over the side. With hands bound, her body knifed into the water and went under within seconds. The force of impact with the water had ripped the bandanna from her mouth.

When she finally surfaced after what seemed like an eternity, she heard a dog barking. Her feet were going as fast as they could, treading water. Before she went under again, she looked around to figure her position. And her chances to survive.

Kane had seen her get up but surged aft too late to stop her from jumping. He swung the wheel to circle the boat back to her entry point and as he saw her struggling to keep her head above water. With full throttle, he bore down on her.

She surfaced again and knew from the speed of the boat he wasn't coming to pick her up. Her only chance was to dive deep enough to get under the boat's hull and propellers. She filled her lungs to aching and kicked her body downward. She felt the water swirling about her and the roar of the engines pass over her.

Thank God, she thought, as she furiously made her way to the surface for air again. Although she had felt nothing, she saw what could only be blood staining the water black. She could feel consciousness slipping away and, before blacking out, managed one last scream for help in the direction of the fishing boat.

Kane came around for another attempt to finish her off but saw the redneck with the dog, in his Boston Whaler, screaming and throwing things at him. The fisherman fired his flare gun, striking the 50-footer's starboard side. Kane reconsidered and decided to head for the tourist area across the lake, where he could pick up a cab to the airport. Whoever had monitored the now destroyed locket could not be far behind.

BALDWIN'S PEOPLE PENETRATED the mansion and searched the bedroom. "Nothing here," Jeremy called.

Baldwin met him on the mezzanine. "Open safe, open drawers. . . I'd say he's high-tailed it out of here. Probably took her with him."

"Probably plans to kill her outside the house," Jeremy offered.

No trace of either of them. Agent Griffith, searching the mansion's grounds from the vantage point of the verandah, looked over the treetops at the lake in the distance. In the light of the full moon, she could see nothing but a lone boat. It made a U-turn and disappeared from sight.

Baldwin's people were mystified. As they continued to search this huge palace, his phone rang.

"It's Martin Bishop, the hospital administrator. I was given this number to phone in case something came up."

"Yes. What's the problem?"

"I don't know if this is important, but we just got a '911' call from a boater on Lake Norman. He pulled onto his boat a bloodied, naked woman trying to get away from another boat. Her wrists were bound and her neck trussed up with leather belts. She was mumbling your name."

"Where is the boater?"

"He's bringing her to The Cove Marina on Lake Norman. We've dispatched an ambulance already."

"Is it anywhere near Albert Kane's mansion?"

"I believe the marina is a few miles north."

"I need directions."

After listening for a moment, Baldwin hung up and called to Nicole. "Someone found her." He was already running toward the front door.

Nicole and the others hot-footed to catch up. "Is she all right?" Nicole asked.

"Doesn't sound too good."

The agents raced down the stairs and out to the van. Jeremy took the wheel as Baldwin relayed directions. The van thundered over back roads until Nicole spotted a sign.

"There it is. . . Cove Marina. . . make a hard left." They turned in and careened down this lakeside dirt road. Less than a hundred yards away saw the ambulance backing up to a boat at dockside.

Baldwin jumped out before the van rolled to a stop. He raced towards the boat as paramedics pushed a gurney down an embankment to the dock. He ran up and verified the swathed figure lying there was Erin.

"Hey, how's my favorite mole?"

"That you, Baldwin?" came a weak voice. Her eyes were closed and she looked like hell.

He was pushed aside as the EMT's feverishly strapped her onto the gurney. Baldwin flashed his badge and asked to climb in the back with the patient. Seconds later, with full lights and sirens, the ambulance thundered off toward the hospital.

"How is she?" Baldwin asked

"Don't really know. I'm going to check her vitals now and hook her up to the monitors. I do know we need to get her some blood very very soon, she is already in shock"

Baldwin nodded and made a call. Then he turned back to the patient. "Erin, it's George Baldwin."

"She may not hear you."

"Erin, Erin, it's Baldwin. Can you tell me where Kane is?"

She tried to say something but he couldn't make it out. He leaned over and placed his ear to her mouth. "Airport," she croaked out.

"Where's he headed?"

"Paris." Her eyes flickered open then faded out again.

The EMT shouldered him aside. "Sir, I need to get in there. You'll have to move."

Baldwin slid to the end of the gurney. "It's okay; I got what I wanted." He reached for his cell phone again and called Jeremy in the van.

"Put out a Code 1 to all agents. Kane is headed to the airport. Check all flights with connections to Paris. Yes, Paris, France. Apprehend with caution, as he may be armed."

Jeremy acknowledged and Baldwin hung up. He turned his attention to the medical technician working on Erin. She was now hooked up to monitoring devices. An I.V. ran into her left hand. Oxygen flowed through a canula into her nostrils. The paramedic worked to stem the flow of blood from a severed artery in her right leg. She'd lost a lot of blood. . . in the lake before her rescue and since then. Perhaps too much.

Baldwin prayed she would be all right.

Erin began to murmur unintelligible sounds as she reached for consciousness. He motioned to the EMT to ask if he could talk to her.

"Erin, it's Baldwin. Did he tell you anything?"

A faint nod.

"We didn't get it; the transmitter stopped sending."

"She nodded and bent her head toward him. "While he was out of the room talking on the phone, I had time to activate his bedroom cameras and recorders." She managed a faint smile. "He confessed to his own equipment."

"You mean his own paranoia ended up providing the evidence we need?"

She smiled and nodded again.

He reached for his phone and looked out the rear window of the ambulance. "Nicole, tell Jeremy to turn around and go back to Kane's. Erin activated the security cameras in the master bedroom. Confiscate everything. Thanks to her, we have audio and video of his entire confession."

"Hot damn for Erin," Nicole whooped.. "We're on it, sir."

Before he had a chance to put the phone away, it rang. He listened, let out a whistle, flipped the phone closed and motioned to the medic. "She needs to hear this."

"Come on over, then, but make it quick" the EMT said, making room.

Baldwin leaned down to speak into Erin's ear. "Fred Cook got Kane at the airport. He offered no resistance. It's over. Thanks to you."

She smiled at him and stuck her thumb in the air. Her eyes rolled back in her head and she faded away.

"She okay?"

"She's lost a lot of blood and is very weak. But I think she'll come around. She is one strong lady."

"I can testify to that." Baldwin took his place at the end of the gurney and let the medic get back to Erin's side. "One of the best I've known."

The ambulance reached the hospital and backed into the emergency entrance. As hospital personnel opened the rear doors of the ambulance, Baldwin saw his daughter Danielle waiting. She mouthed a "thank you" for his phone call that got her there.

Danielle pressed forward to say something to Erin before she was wheeled inside. "Hey, good friend, glad to see ya."

Erin opened her eyes wide. "Nice to see you again."

"You doing all right?"

"Naw. I broke my rule of never swimming nude."

For a moment they just looked at each other with tear-filled eyes. Danielle leaned over to kiss her on the cheek. "They say you'll be okay."

"That's good."

"No man could do you in, right?"

"Nope."

"How about next week we head out to Grand Cayman?"

As the paramedics wheeled the gurney through the ER doors, Erin smiled. "Not on your life. That place could be hazardous to a girl's health."

Order Form

To order additional copies, fill out this form and send it along with your check or money order to: Stone Bridge Press, P.O. Box 110826, Naples, Fl 34108-0114

Cost per copy $14.00 US and $19.00 Canadian plus $3.95 P&H.

Ship _____ copies of *The Professor* to:

Name_____

Address:_____

City/State/Zip:_____

❏   **Check box for signed copy**

Please tell us how you found out about this book.

☐ Friend   ☐Internet
☐ Book Store   ☐Radio
☐ Newspaper   ☐ Magazine
☐ Brochure
☐ Other _____